fighting
MR. KNIGHT

ROSA LUCAS

PAGE
&
VINE

Page & Vine
An Imprint of Meredith Wild LLC

Paperback ISBN: 978-1-964264-25-7

1

Bonnie

You can tell a lot about a man by his nostrils. Pay attention and they're full of clues. If his nostrils flare and his lips part, he's picturing you naked.

The nostrils of the guy in the sharp blue suit at the top of the boardroom are fat with anger.

Max, my boss.

He checks his watch as the team piles in, taking the seats around me. Technically, they're on time, but they're on Big Ben's clock, which is five minutes slower than Max's.

Twenty of us—architects, interior designers, planners—make up Bradshaw Brown, one of London's smaller architecture firms.

As far as design firms go, we're not sexy. We don't design shiny pointy things in the London skyline shaped like shards of glass or walkie-talkies, and if I listed ten of our projects to the public, eyes would glaze over.

Restoration of old abandoned heritage buildings—that's our bag.

The two sales guys take seats at the front. The Antichrist to us creatives. Their strategy is to pimp us out for deadlines that we can't meet, then they ignore our calls because they're too busy on the phone, selling us to new clients.

Max hooks up his laptop, and the boardroom screen comes to life.

But this morning, it's not displaying the Bradshaw Brown

team agenda.

Twenty jaws drop to the floor as we stare at an attractive blonde posing seductively on sand while rocking a red bikini and Santa hat.

Then slowly, like dominoes, nineteen slack jaws swivel to stare at me.

Well, shit.

My body stiffens in defence, and I shoot them back death glares.

I force my horrified eyes back to the screen.

The photo is in a message from a *Danielle*. To summarise our boss's emailed response in big print: Danielle in a Mrs. Claus outfit makes his dick hard.

It's not even Christmas.

Danielle smiles playfully at us with wide eyes as she lives her best life on a beach somewhere.

Max is too busy checking something on his laptop to notice that he's broadcasting his digital masturbation bank to the design team. His inability to pick up on the tension in the room is astounding.

"Uh, Max," Nisha, Bradshaw Brown's contracts manager and my close friend, says sharply beside me. "That's not the agenda you have on-screen."

Confused, Max pivots and then flinches as if Danielle jumped out and slapped him in the face. "Shit!" Choking painfully on his own saliva, he frantically yanks the cable from his laptop.

We watch gobsmacked. Awkward sniggers sprinkle the room.

Max levies us a glare as if it's *our* fault. "Moving on."

Nisha cocks a brow at me in a "you okay?" as Max recovers, plugs his computer back in, and replaces sexy Mrs. Claus with the meeting agenda.

I plaster a bright smile on my face. Mortified is the understatement of the century.

So Max is dating again.

Max, the man I spent the past four years with. I was a fresh architecture graduate wet behind the ears when he was a qualified architect at Bradshaw Brown. He took me under his wing and became my mentor. Then he became my boyfriend, my fiancé, and eventually my boss. Then my ex-fiancé. But still my boss.

Not an ideal sequence of events.

My gaze trails up his body as he strokes his tie in agitation. I know every inch of this man, every freckle, birthmark, and vein on his dick. How he sneezes after sex. I could write his medical records from memory.

Does Danielle know his dick veins, too?

He wasn't supposed to start dating again. He was supposed to become a fat monk.

"Status updates," Max orders, turning his attention to the project managers sitting at the back, confidence fully restored. "Darren, the Mayfair project. Where are we with it?"

I can barely hear Max over the sound of my heartbeat in my ears, like a drum smashing against my brain.

Who the fuck is Danielle?

Darren shifts uncomfortably in his seat. "All going well, boss. We're preparing the preliminary cost estimates. I'll perform a requirement drill-down with the team to ensure we're singing from the same hymn sheet." He nods curtly in my direction. "Then we'll finalise figures, dot the i's, cross the t's, and present back."

Huh? I have no idea what the fuck Darren's saying. Scraping all his fingernails down the whiteboard would have achieved the same result.

"I've planned a workshop with Bonnie today," Darren adds.

Calling it a workshop is a stretch. Ten minutes ago, Darren popped a fifteen-minute meeting in my diary. A meeting to say he's in a meeting.

"Bonnie," Max says sharply, rapping his knuckles on the desk like a headmaster. "Treat it as urgent. Do you need me to help prioritise workload?"

I stare back at Max in disbelief. Is he really going to get on my grill after that little exposé?

"Bonnie and I can take this offline," Darren cuts in before Max can detect that this full-blown workshop is a chat on the way to get coffee and some of the walnut cake they have in the cafeteria.

Darren takes everything offline, which means nothing will happen. He'll give the same update phrased slightly differently next week.

He'd be a great politician.

Next up is Layla, the other project manager. Layla prefers to keep everything online, which means she'll monopolise the meeting talking about her project in irrelevant detail.

Everyone drifts to faraway places while Max reins in Layla. Eighty percent of people are thinking about sex during meetings, and many of the scenarios involve other people in the room. It's the same with conferences, weddings, and funerals. That's my theory.

I often wondered what co-workers thought of Max and me. I suspect it's less *fifty shades of office romance* and more *old married couple who schedule sex*.

I guess that was the red flag.

With Max, there was no steamy elevator sex or sneaky boardroom leg rubbing under the table. No uncontrollable bouts of horniness or unexpected semis. Not once did we have to rush out to the stairway to claw off each other's clothes.

On the clock, we talked shop. Off the clock, we talked about ... quite a bit of shop.

Our sex life at home was decent enough, though. After years together, I never expected to be swinging from chandeliers, letting loud guttural moans rip through me in an Oscar-worthy performance.

But what we did have was stability. Max was simply, always *there*. A constitutional force in my life not to be questioned.

Nisha breathes angrily beside me as Layla rambles about a Notting Hill church conversion into luxury flats.

"That's enough, Layla," Max cuts in sharply. "If there are no escalations, let's move on."

"Can we talk about the Lexington project?" Nisha asks.

Everyone's spine straightens. The Lexington East London project has been the buzz of the office for weeks. Wider than that, it's *the* hot topic across the UK construction industry.

Everyone from politician to pop star is wading in with their opinion.

The Lexington Group, Europe's largest property empire, conservatively valued at a humble seven billion, has bought huge swathes of land east of Canary Wharf, London's version of Wall Street.

Right now, it's old wharves and docks spread over thirty hectares, mostly brownfield land where youths skateboard and take drugs.

They plan to create a whole new urban village full of flats, bars, restaurants, and artsy buildings to house all the hipsters flooding in. It will be the new Thames South Bank of the east.

At its helm is local East Ender property tycoon, Jack Knight, propping up the "Top Forty Under Forty" UK rich list, not to mention national tabloid gossip with his rampant, outrageous sex life.

In his own words, he plans to "reshape the east of London." At this rate, he'll own more land than the Crown.

It's the largest regeneration project London has seen in years and every architect's wet dream.

One of the most exciting projects of my career if we win the bid.

The catch?

Jack Knight.

I'd rather work for Satan on designing hell after what he did.

"Yes, I wanted to spend a decent amount of time discussing this." Max looks pointedly at Nisha.

"I have news," he continues irritatingly slowly, looking around the room until he's confident he has everyone's undivided attention. He unsuccessfully tries not to grin. "We've nailed it. The project's ours."

A loud cheer breaks out. It's not often the office celebrates, but this is a huge deal for us.

As part of the wider regeneration, Knight's vision is to convert London's oldest factory, the London Motor Works, lying derelict for decades, into apartments and shops.

To work on a historic landmark like this?

CV gold dust.

"We beat Porter & Partners?" I ask incredulously. They're a global powerhouse and front-runner for the bid.

"They didn't feel it was a good fit."

"Porter & Partners backed out of the bid?" Nisha asks slowly, her chin tilting to the floor.

Max's nostrils flare to full capacity. "That's not what should be the focus here, but they turned it down."

We stare at him blankly.

"So, we didn't nail it," I murmur, exchanging glances with Nisha.

"Why on earth would they do that?" Darren pipes up from the back.

Max raises his palms. "It's not relevant. What's relevant is that we have won the work and will do our damnedest to show we are the best for the job. Now, as you may be aware, Jack Knight and I go back a long way, so I'll be overseeing this project."

I internally roll my eyes. Max isn't exactly on Jack's speed dial. Due to one common connection, they occasionally attend the same parties. Max learned most of his knowledge from Knight's biography, hidden in his sock drawer. I thought it would emasculate him if I told him I found it.

"Several of you will be reassigned to the project ASAP. Lexington expects to see condition surveys, treatment plans, and conceptual design drafts within twelve weeks."

Nisha gasps.

I inhale sharply. We haven't even visited the site yet. That's an unreasonable ask for a building of that size and complexity.

"Now we know why Porter turned it down," Nisha says.

"We'd never pull together credible designs within a few weeks even if we weren't dealing with listed buildings."

"Uh-huh." Max, irritated, raises a brow. "Are you going to be the one to tell Jack Knight that?"

"Won't he listen to you, Max?" She pouts. "Isn't it already in the bag if you guys"—she makes air quotes—"*go back a long way*?"

It's not even in the trolley, never mind the bag.

"It's not enough time," I say to Max with more bite than I intended. "Can we negotiate an extension?" *And who the hell is this Danielle woman?*

He inhales a lungful of air through his nostrils, meaning *shut the fuck up*.

The conversation is fruitless. If Lexington says jump, we get a long pole and launch ourselves into space.

My eyes fix on the Lexington Group HQ, a great big forty-something-floor glass brute dominating the London skyline and blocking our sunlight.

Jack Knight pretty much owns this skyline with his fancy hotels and luxury apartments. The guy thinks he's a bloody god and London is his monopoly board.

"The partners and I will be discussing resourcing this afternoon," Max says.

Nisha nudges me.

And *that's* why I'm sitting here, enduring the soul-sucking experience of working under my ex-fiancé.

Bradshaw Brown promotes once a year and that date is four months away.

I won't cut off my nose to spite my face. I've worked too hard to leave without the title of senior architect. *And* they're putting me through the training to get admitted to the elite architectural Conservation Register.

Bricks before dicks.

Otherwise, I have to claw my way up somewhere else.

"Another bleeding hipster village where the normal folk won't be able to afford housing," Steve, my fellow architect, grimaces.

"Jack Knight's a cockney, has he no shame?"

"Guys, focus." Max's lips press tightly together. "Now the deal's secure, Jack has called a meeting next week to talk to us *personally* about this. I'll send out the statement of work. You'll need to know it inside out. Everyone assigned to this project must live and breathe it until I say otherwise."

We exchange glances across the room.

"Why is *he* meeting us?" I ask Max suspiciously. "Surely his construction leads will handle this?"

"That shows how important this project is to him," Max snaps back. "Nisha, I'll need you to drop what you're doing and support the design team on the commercials. We may be buddies, but Jack is not a patient man." I do another eye roll in my head as Max looks at his watch. "Too many minutes wasted today—next time be early, folks."

Nisha grunts beside me. "More all-nighters to pull this out of my ass in time."

Everyone spills out of the boardroom while Max loiters at the front. "Bonnie, a minute please." He gives me a thin-lipped smile as a frenzied conversation erupts in the hallway about hot Danielle and Max's dick.

I grind my teeth into a smile to stop murderous threats from escaping. "Yes, Max?"

"Sorry about that little mishap earlier. I didn't mean for you to see that."

Guilt briefly flashes across his face. It's gone so quickly I might have imagined it.

"Me and the rest of the team." I titter defiantly. "Look, it's fine. Doesn't bother me. I'm dating too."

That's a big fat lie. These days I'm busying myself with a variety of fake dicks. I alternate between different shapes, sizes, and colours as I'm not racist. No need for men to be attached.

With the number of mechanical devices in my bedroom, I'm surprised I have any feeling left down there at all.

"Glad to hear it." He's not convinced. "Listen, if you play

your cards right, the partners will promote you. You can use this project to get noticed."

They better bloody promote me.

"But I need you to give it everything." He's adopted that tone he uses to dangle work carrots in front of me. "I'm putting my neck on the line offering this chance. Sometimes it seems like you're stuck in fourth gear, and you can't get to the next level. I don't want to give you too much to handle."

My eyes widen. "What? I'm not stuck in fourth gear!" What does that even mean? "I can handle this project. I'm in top gear. Driving like I stole her."

He exhales heavily. "This deadline is bad timing with the wedding, but we'll just have to manage."

That's the sucky thing about our break-up—so much of our lives still overlap. Our friends Kate and Sean are getting married on the weekend, and Max and I are part of the wedding party because we spent years together as a foursome. They were supposed to repay the favour, but that requirement is now null and void.

I nod vigorously. "I'll work every hour I can. You don't need to worry about that. You know that. You know *me*."

His frown says he's not fully appeased. I know what's coming.

"That's not all I'm worried about. Look, I understand you have some . . . issues with Jack Knight. And I'm not saying they aren't justified, but it was a long time ago, okay? You need to treat the wedding as a networking opportunity. Be professional. Be *civil* to the guy at the very least."

The icing on the wedding cake—Kate's marrying into the Knight family.

"I'll behave in front of the great and glorious Mr. Knight," I say through gritted teeth.

"See?" Max glares back at me. "That's what I'm talking about. The attitude."

"Max, I'm not going to mess up the chance of promotion. I'll follow the required bridesmaid etiquette. Last time I checked, it included being nice to the guests."

Even if the guest list includes an obnoxious, arrogant Knight who dumps pawns off his board when he's got no further use for them.

I swallow the lump in my throat. *Simple.*

2

Bonnie

"Just ask him who she is," Nisha grumbles beside me. "I can't handle this version of you."

She's right—I'm the worst version of myself today. Ever since Max's little faux pas, I'm completely on edge. Like a caged lab rat forced into caffeine testing.

I spent most of today cyber-sleuthing Max, checking if there are any new blonde females in the background of his photos.

So far, across all his social media accounts and even his LinkedIn, he has no blonde friends called Danielle.

My eyes narrow on Max across the office, where he's subtly applying aftershave at his desk. He looks good. He's got that Clark Kent thing going on—well-kept hair, great jawline but never with stubble—overall attractive but a bit stiff looking.

Is the aftershave for Danielle?

It doesn't escape me that Danielle and I could be sisters. Blonde. Blue eyes. Pale skin. Max has a type.

Last night my therapist asked, "Is your grief about losing Max or the loss of an old way of life?" *Who the fuck knows?* All I want to feel is numb. Sometimes, I wish I had the brain of a sociopath.

The internet says six months is a decent time frame to recover from the break-up of a long-term relationship, but my therapist won't give me a timeline because she's charging a hundred pounds a session. Time frames aren't in her best interest.

Spotting me gawking at him, Max stands up and strolls right

up to my desk.

"Bonnie." He nods curtly. "I'm going out with the partners this evening. Some of the seniors at Lexington will be there." He pauses. "It would be wise for you to be there rubbing shoulders with them."

I wanted a night out with Bradshaw and Brown as much as I wanted to suck a bag of flaccid dicks, but I need to land this promotion. Bradshaw is a tits person, and Brown is a bum person, meaning I'll get sleazed on from all angles.

Both knew about our relationship and were invited to the doomed wedding. You would think it would be awkward now, but Max project-managed the split perfectly.

According to Max, "our bond had naturally transitioned into a caring friendship, and we were starting afresh on different paths." I keep meaning to find out what website he stole that blurb from.

Before his side of the bed got cold, he had wrapped the whole thing up, sold our flat, notified HR, cancelled the wedding, and announced the *decoupling* to all of our friends, family, and colleagues.

I was a mere spectator in the meticulous execution.

I crack a strained smile. "Sure. That sounds great."

At least the aftershave is for the two little partner cretins rather than Danielle.

My phone buzzes, and I get it out.

Oh, God.

Three missed calls from The White Horse pub.

Dad.

My stomach heaves. I always fear the worst.

I hold a finger up. "Give me a minute, Max. The White Horse has been calling."

He makes a snorting sound. "I don't have all day, Bonnie— they're going now."

I eye him with a flicker of annoyance as I hit redial.

Max has always been snobby about Dad.

fighting MR. KNIGHT

No answer. Now my stomach really twists.

His brows slant in heavy disapproval. "He's an adult. Stop babysitting him."

Max is right. I have an entry into the big boys' club. I can't walk away from this opportunity but...he's my dad.

Cursing under my breath, I lock eyes with Max in an unspoken exchange.

"Priorities, Bonnie." He shakes his head and walks away, probably taking my chances of promotion with him.

∽

Call me overly cautious, but when a guy is being hauled out of a bar by two bartenders, barefoot and slurring absolute shit before dinner time, it's probably time to reassess your local boozer.

Especially if the guy ejected is your dad.

Dad's not leaving without a fight. One foot sticks stubbornly in the doorway in protest.

Now he has everyone's attention. It's exactly the time when every office worker across East London spills out of the office and into the pubs.

He has the red bulbous nose of an older man, and I wonder if all men's noses eventually go like this over time. That's why personality is so important.

I sigh audibly.

Fuck my life.

Had it been past the watershed hour, he would have attracted a smaller crowd, but when you're the only one completely annihilated in broad daylight, all eyes are on you.

My first instinct is to turn around, sprint back down the street, and spare myself a bucketload of cringe. There's still time.

But pangs of guilt keep me rooted to the spot.

Besides, Uncle Pat has already clocked me.

"Dad," I address him sharply as the doormen deposit him against a wall. "Dad," I repeat loudly when both his eyes refuse to focus on me.

The stench of whiskey sends me into a coughing fit.

"He's barred for tonight, Bonnie," Gerry, the doorman I've met a few times this year, tells me. Sometimes I wish they weren't nice enough to call me when Dad decides to have one of his sessions.

"Just tonight?" I mutter.

Gerry shrugs and walks away.

"There's my Bonnie," Dad mumbles as his head tilts down. I'm shocked he can even identify me. "My girl's an architect," he roars to a group of guys in the beer garden, who look like estate agents, and I die a little inside.

I turn to Uncle Pat, who thankfully doesn't seem to be on the same level of shit-faced. "What the hell? How did he get so smashed?"

Pat looks at me wearily. "Tonight's your parents' thirtieth wedding anniversary."

Except it's not.

I let out a heavy breath. "I'll help you get him home."

I never realised the date. I don't even think Mum did either, but then again, she's living her best life with my stepdad, Phil.

Dad never found anyone else after Mum. He seemed to get stuck in time.

Dad shuffles along beside me, mumbling something about the state of the country and the Conservative Party and other ramblings I have to listen to on a frequent basis.

My cheeks fill with shame as people avert their gaze.

Shame. I'm ashamed of my dad.

After all he's done for me and all he's been through.

Dad pats my shoulder softly. "I love my girl."

I hate how he gets emotional when he's had a drop. I should be back-slapping and ass-licking Bradshaw and Brown. Max will be deducting points from my promotion board for this.

I smile stiffly, feeling like the worst daughter in the world for hating my dad right now.

3

Bonnie

Winning the Lexington project couldn't have come at a worse time. After a frantic early morning site visit to the *Motor Works* factory and a three-hour drive in heavy traffic, I'm now late for bridesmaid duties. Sean and Kate get married in two days' time, and I'm now on the clock.

"Jesus." Nisha glances at me from the passenger seat. "What is this place, Britain's most haunted castle? It looks the perfect scene for a murder, not a wedding."

I shift gears and my dinky city car stalls on the gravel. A grey-stoned, eye-popping medieval castle where the royal family would feel right at home awaits us at the end of the driveway.

"They're trying to pull off a Downton Abbey vibe for the cousins coming in from the States. A Ye Olde English wedding," I explain as we inch deeper into the sprawling estate. "Wow." My nerves flutter. I've never stayed anywhere this fancy before.

"It's more Jack the Ripper than Downton Abbey," she mutters.

"I think a few were beheaded here back in the day. It used to be owned by a knight."

"A knight as in Jack Knight?"

"No." I grin. "Not that Knight. It's one of the few plots of land in England he doesn't own."

"How much did you say this place is costing us?"

I shake my head. "Oh, you can close your purse. It's not costing us a penny. Jack and the Lexington Group are footing the bill as a wedding present. Otherwise, we'd be camping on the lawn." A lot of the Knights seem to work for Jack. Kate's fiancé, Sean, is a senior construction project manager at Lexington. "You'd think it's *his* wedding the way he flashes his cash." I pause for effect. "Fifteen K."

Her mouth slackens. "Fifteen grand for three days? That's a year's rent in London!"

"Dream a little bigger, love." I snort-laugh. "Fifteen grand a *night.*"

"A night?" Spit flies from her mouth and lands on the dashboard. "Shut the front door! That's . . . forty-fucking-five grand. That's an actual house down payment. God, I can't wait to see the shampoo in the room."

"Yup. Some of the royals have even stayed here."

"Holy hell. He's generous to his employees, I'll give him that. I suppose it helps that Sean's his cousin."

"Generous to the underlings he likes," I hiss through my teeth.

"Bonnie, you need to be a better actor than that." She side-eyes me. "Why do you hate him so much anyway?"

I grip the steering wheel tighter.

Nisha doesn't know my beef with Knight.

How could I not hate him after I helped Dad pack up all his possessions and say goodbye to the house that had been my nan's and survived two world wars? After that, Dad was never the same. I'm all for men expressing their emotions, but seeing your father weep is pretty soul-destroying, even for a nineteen-year-old.

A month after Jack laid off fifty workers, he entered the UK rich list.

But the thing that pissed me off the most was that the night he fired my dad, Jack sauntered into The White Horse pub, dick swinging and cash flashing, with women hanging off him and he *winked* at me.

A slow, arrogant wink aimed at me.

I don't *hate* the guy. I don't hate anyone. He's a businessman, and I'm sure it wasn't personal. It's more of a festering dislike.

And the most annoying thing? How much I know about the man. It's hard not to. East End boy made good, and nobody in the area is allowed to forget that. The Knights were a rags-to-riches story, all because of Jack.

The White Horse pub even has a damn photo of him on its wall.

I sigh. "It's complicated."

She groans. "Well, this is bloody weird. How the hell are we supposed to relax with our biggest client here? I'm surprised he agreed to stay in the castle with us. Doesn't he have security? What if someone plans to kidnap him?"

"Kate said he has security, but you never see them. They'll be staying close enough if there is an emergency." I grin. "Maybe you can ask him."

"No chance," she scoffs. "I'm going to mind *everything* I say in front of this dude. What the hell do you say to a billionaire? How's work going? I have zero common ground with this guy."

I laugh. "Maybe you can ask him hypothetical questions like what yacht you should buy if you get a seven billion pound pay raise. Or 'Hey Jack, I'm thinking of getting my biography done because my life is too damn interesting. Who did you use?' Or 'Hey, jackass, how many men did you fire this week?'"

"Quit already." Her eyes gleam. "His bodyguards will be buff."

I think about the bodyguard smut I read last week.

Yes, please.

"He might have snipers on the roof."

"He's not the prime minister." I roll my eyes as we crawl into the parking bay of the castle grounds.

Mild panic rises in me as I see throngs of people decorating the lawn drinking in the late afternoon sun and am reminded that as a bridesmaid, mingling is mandated.

What started as an intimate affair turned into a guest list of nearly three hundred for the big day and a two-day pre-wedding celebration for fifty of Kate and Sean's closest family and friends.

Kate runs to the car, peering in wildly before I get a chance to turn off the ignition.

"Bonnie!" She flings her arms around me as I step out. "I'm so glad you guys are here. Sorry, I'm being extra needy today." She's slightly breathless. "The whole wedding is going to shit."

My eyes widen as I take in her fake mahogany complexion, but I recover quickly. Kate is too nice for her own good. Her cousin and aspiring beauty consultant begged for the job of fake tan artist and appears not to have understood the bridal brief for a natural glow.

No wonder Kate's distraught.

On the plus side, it makes her teeth and eyes look really bright.

"My flower girl peed when she tried on her dress, and now it has to go to the dry cleaner's. Apparently, there's only one in the area, in England, in bloody Europe that will do it in a day! We have to change the seating plan *again* because Sean's dicky cousin is turning up but never RSVP'd. Sean keeps telling me to relax while he gets drunk on the lawn, and honestly, I'm close to telling him to go fuck himself." She says it all in one breath.

No mention of the botched tan.

"Okay." I nod encouragingly. "We'll sort out any minor mishaps. These are all fixable." I'm talking out of my ass because I've got no clue. The furthest I progressed in the matrimony process was sending out invitations. "It'll be *fine*, Kate. It's just pre-wedding jitters."

"We're at your service," Nisha chips in, nodding vigorously. "That's what we're here for."

Neither Nisha nor I are qualified to advise.

Kate doesn't look convinced. She draws in a deep breath. "Sorry, I'll start over like a normal person. Come and say hi to everyone."

Heads turn as we stride towards the lawn. Not because Nisha and I are an exciting duo but because the conversation between families forced together has clearly dried up.

Glancing around the crowd, I feel self-conscious. I have that disorder where your brain empties names when you're nervous. Also, there appears to be a pre-wedding dress code I wasn't informed about, centred around trouser suits, tailored dresses, and professionally blow-dried hair.

I'm wearing black leggings that have been washed so many times they are grey and balding at the knees. My hair is scraped up into a donut, which adds about two feet to my height, and I'm wearing an oversized jumper with the *Friends* cast on it. I expected to go to our rooms to freshen up before the meet and greets.

My gaze flits across the crowd at familiar faces—Max, Sean, Kate's sister and maid of honour Becky, among others—and many strangers. Kate's creepy uncle Dom eyes Nisha and me like a man on hunger strike eyes steak.

Holding court at one table is Kate's mum, talking two octaves higher than necessary. Kate's tanning expert cousin has attacked some of the table's occupants who glow like they have bathed in mustard.

At the opposite table, marking her territory, Sean's mum is surrounded by Knights and other members of Sean's extended family.

Awkwardly, I wave at everyone.

"There's *Poppy*, the little monster who decided to wait until she was in her flower girl dress to piss her pants," Kate says through a tight smile as we approach them. "See how innocent she looks? She doesn't realise how close she is to getting sacked."

I follow Kate's gaze to the animated girl dressed as a princess as she acts out a scene with a collection of sparkly ponies. Large muscular arms wrap around her waist, preventing her from falling off the knee of the person she's seated on.

Kate mutters something about Poppy being clever enough not to piss in her princess dress yet conveniently pissed in the flower girl outfit she screamed she didn't want to wear.

My attention, however, is stolen by the savage creature

directing his signature grin at Poppy. The guy holding her. The hairs on the back of my neck stand to attention like a cat ready to attack.

"Where's the entourage?" Nisha asks in too loud a whisper.

Kate shushes her with an elbow.

"He doesn't look like a man that belongs in an office, does he?" Nisha murmurs.

No, he does not.

I wish he was grotesque.

With his masculine frame, Jack Knight looks like he lived up a mountain with wolves all his life instead of ruling from a glass box in the sky, trampling on the little people.

I guess he built his muscles on the construction sites. Maybe muscles built from old-fashioned manual labour rather than crafted in a gym are carved sexier.

Jack Knight's a grafter. I can't deny him that. He worked his way up from builder's apprentice at sixteen to property tycoon one brick at a time, or so Max's copy of the biography says.

And I also begrudgingly can't deny that no one could describe Jack Knight as anything other than handsome. Show-stoppingly, in fact.

But, boy, does he know it.

Dark eyes from his Italian mother match his thick, dark brown, overgrown hair, styled in a topknot. Strands fall messily over his forehead framing the scar that runs through one of his thick eyebrows.

He's dressed even more casually than me, in a black singlet T-shirt revealing his thick biceps and a glimpse of chest tattoos, declaring zero fucks given. It's an outfit only he could get away with.

Which came first? The swagger or the money? I saw him in pubs when I was younger. I'm pretty sure he had the swagger when he was poor.

A glance around the lawn confirms that every woman in the vicinity is jealous of flower girl Poppy, who must be a niece, judging by the similar facial features to Knight.

The fools.

His tongue traces his full top lip, and I am reminded of the rumours about what those lips could do to a woman.

Shuddering, I avert my eyes.

Damn. I need to get laid.

Or, at the very least, experience a tongue that's not my own in my mouth.

Disgust fills me.

I haven't had sex in a *very* long time. The cracks are showing. I never used to perve at Jack Knight, of all people.

I call up my best acting skills and pretend I'm not a lust-crazed horny woman who hasn't felt the touch of human lips in months.

"Hi, guys," I call awkwardly, as we walk over to the tables.

"Oh, it's the other bridesmaid," Sean's mum announces.

Sean frowns and gets up from the table to greet us. "*Bonnie*, Mum. You've met her many times."

"Hi, Mrs. Knight," I greet her politely. "Yes, I'm Bonnie, the other bridesmaid. You met me at Sean's birthday party last year."

"Oh, yes. Bonnie." She applies a fake, full-strength smile. "Remind me what it's short for, sweetie?"

"Nothing." I shrug. "It's just Bonnie." She asks me this question every time we meet.

"Sean's mum is being as pleasant as usual," Kate whispers as Sean and Max approach us.

Max makes a show of giving me a massive hug.

"She's the bridesmaid that was supposed to get married to the best man," Sean's mum says in a loud conspiratorial whisper.

I plaster a large smile on my face. It's not Max's fault he doesn't love me anymore.

Nisha and I stand on display shyly, being pelted with questions that no one needs the answer to. *How's traffic? I heard there was an accident on the motorway. What time did you leave London?* Yada yada yada.

"Jack, this is Nisha, our commercial manager at Bradshaw," Max says briskly. "She's been with us three years but has worked with major construction firms for a decade. Excellent industry knowledge."

I give him a sideward glance.

"Hi, uh, Mr. Knight," Nisha says stiffly, coming forward to shake his hand. "Lovely to meet you, sir."

"Jack," he corrects her cheerfully. With one arm wrapped around Poppy, he stands and pulls Nisha in for a hug. "No need to be formal. Great to meet you, Nisha."

"Of course, you already know Bonnie," Max adds, gesturing at me like a curator exhibiting a new piece.

My eyes meet Jack's. He treats me to an arrogant smirk like the big bad wolf that spotted a pig.

My lips curl upwards exposing teeth in what I hope is a pleasant smile. "Hi, Jack."

"It's been a while, Bonnie." Before I know what's happening, he has let go of Poppy and pulls me into a bear hug, crushing me to his chest. I lean into the embrace awkwardly.

God, that feels good. Smells good, too.

The injustice.

I free myself from the hard wall of muscle.

"Bonnie is paired with Jack for the wedding," Sean explains to the wider group who "ooh" and "ahh" with pleasantries.

I see some looks of recognition, and I awkwardly try to hide my *Friends* jumper with my arms.

That's poor dumped bridesmaid Bonnie, their faces say. *How hard must this be to watch her best friend get married? And the best man is the man who left her? It's like a Jerry Springer episode!*

My face heats.

"Which means I'm the second luckiest guy in the wedding, after Sean of course," a deep voice says beside me.

"Lucky guy, indeed," Kate's creepy uncle Dom says, staring freely at my breasts. "Be sure to save me a dance, Bunny."

Ugh.

"*I'm* paired with Uncle Jack," Poppy wails, stamping her feet. "I'm marrying Uncle Jack. Not her!"

"And you'll always be my favourite, sweetheart."

He's talking to Poppy.

Obviously.

But when I glance up, Jack's staring directly at me.

4

Bonnie

For two hours, I play the role of a dutiful bridesmaid. I laugh at Sean's mum's unfunny stories, and I pretend not to notice Uncle Dom staring at my tits.

Fortunately, Jack took a call before Max could go into any more details about our CVs. Jack's mum and sisters are nice, so I guess I can't tarnish them all with the same brush. His twin sisters are closer to my age, thirty at a guess, and pretty chatty. The flower girl, Poppy, one of the twins' daughters, seems to rule the roost.

Kate offers to show us our rooms so that we can finally freshen up.

"Holy shit." My voice echoes as we ascend the grand staircase. "It's the English equivalent of *The Shining*."

An explosion of paintings with people from centuries past stare down at us like an eerie dead audience.

"According to the website, these poor souls were murdered by the knight and still roam the castle. Legend has it if you look at them too long, you're beckoning them from the other side," I deadpan.

"What?" Nisha grabs my arm. "I don't believe this shit, but I can't unhear that now."

"People have reported that they woke up in the middle of the night to find the knight watching them sleep." I bite back laughter.

"Will you stop being an asshole?" Nisha hisses, stopping sharply. "I'll be standing in the shower feeling like dead people are watching me instead of enjoying the billionaire bar of soap. If I hear noises, I'm gonna jump out the window. Next time, we're going to Ibiza."

"Don't worry." Kate laughs. "Any loud moans or lights flickering will be the living Knight banging the bedposts. Did you know that *Michelle Allard* is coming to the wedding?"

"The supermodel?" My eyes widen. "I didn't realise he's seeing her."

"Uh-huh." Kate smiles conspiratorially. "I don't know how serious it is, but he must like her as he hand-picked her last year to be the Lexington hotel ambassador."

I nod, remembering I had seen her in an ad for the hotel chain, and then I gawk up at the crucifix greeting us on the wall at the top of the staircase. "He might burst into flames if he gets up to anything naughty here."

"You'll know, Bonnie." Kate smirks at me. "You're staying in the room next to him."

"Where the fuck am I staying?" Nisha asks. "I'm not sure I want to sleep by myself."

I roll my eyes. "You're being a tad dramatic, Nish."

Kate stops outside one of the doors as her phone buzzes. "Nisha, this is your bedroom." She glances down at her phone. "Oh, shit, it's the caterer. I need to let them in downstairs."

She waves an envelope at me.

"Call into Jack's room and give this to him, will you?"

"*Me?*" I grimace.

"No, *her*." She points to the woman in the black and white portrait staring down at us. "Yes, you, silly. What's the problem?"

"Maybe you could give it to him later," I suggest. "He might not like me interrupting him."

"Don't be ridiculous," she scoffs, shoving the envelope in my hand. "He won't mind. Go. He's in the last room at the end of the South wing called 'Knight's Tale.' You're in the one right next door."

Fitting.

Max's voice fills my head. *Be the best version of yourself. You're representing Bradshaw Brown.* What does Max expect me to do? Ask the priest to deliver subliminal messaging through prayer?

I nod and leave them, following on down the eerie hallway. My footsteps echo as I try to avoid eye contact with the ancestry of whatever knight beheaded everyone.

What's the best version of myself?

An intelligent, accomplished architect who keeps up with world affairs and can engage in witty and dynamic conversation with a brooding asshole billionaire.

I'm half expecting the girl twins from *The Shining* as I turn the corner to the South wing.

"Jack?" I say loudly as I knock on his door. No answer.

I knock louder.

A muffled voice responds to me, telling me to come in. I think. Turning the handle, I peer into the room. Room is an understatement. It's a studio with a separate lounge area the size of my rented London flat.

Scattered evidence confirms Jack's presence—expensive watch, wallet, beard oil, his trademark gold necklace, skipping rope. I divert my eyes quickly from his boxers on the sofa.

Where is he?

"Jack?" I call out tentatively. Maybe he's in the bedroom.

I take a few steps forward as the bathroom door swings slightly ajar and I glance through the door crack.

Fuck. Me.

Jack stands in the steam with nothing but a flimsy towel resting dangerously low around the most mouth-watering body I've ever seen. His tousled waves are slicked back and black from wetness, like a feral ovary-whispering Italian Tarzan.

I stare, slack-jawed, as he runs long strokes of the blade down the angular curve of his jaw.

I don't know how to breathe. Pheromones have blocked my nose.

Wearing wireless earphones, he talks, or more accurately,

growls, into thin air.

Pierced nipple.

I wasn't expecting that. Or the adrenaline pumping through me at the sight of it.

Lucky water droplets trickle down the grooves of carved, tight, ridiculous abs, culminating in the muscled V before disappearing into a treasure trail of dark hair . . . *oh fuck*.

So, this is *the Jack effect*.

Turns out I'm not as immune as I'd hoped.

I catch a few words as he growls at whoever is on the other end about compliance regulations and flood risks, oblivious to the perv party behind him.

Like a horny hedgehog, every hair on my peeping Tom body stands to attention. This is probably how Kate's creepy uncle, Dom, started out.

I haven't seen another dick but Max's in five years. This could send me to an early grave. The weekend is in danger of turning into one wedding and a funeral.

I'm thinking with my vagina and my vagina does not appear to discriminate against assholes. My therapist never warned me about this.

Drop the towel, Jack, my traitorous vagina begs. It should be a song. Or a prayer. If a god is up there or a friendly ghost in the house, help a woman out.

Let there be a freak-of-nature gale force wind in this room. *Please.*

As if he is telepathic, or a past tenant of the manor is answering my prayers, he casually tugs the towel off, like he has no further need for it, so I can see every inch of his long, thick deliciousness in the full-length mirror.

Jack Knight stands as naked as the day he was born.

You can send me to hell. I've lived a good life.

The Knight's jewels jut out between his legs, as arrogant and dangerous as the rest of him.

It's beautiful.

5

Bonnie

Jack Knight's big dick. I've heard the rumours, but they don't do it justice. That meat could keep a woman fed for a lifetime.

He spreads his large thighs wider, shifting his weight from one foot to the other, and every muscle in his sculpted tight butt flexes. My knees are one flex away from buckling.

I groan inwardly.

I hope inwardly.

The two hard mounds of ass look like they would break a hand if you slapped them. He must be permanently clenching to maintain that level of tautness. I make a mental note to follow suit, there are a lot of advantages to having an ass like that.

My eyes get dragged back to his dick. And what a dick it is. A masterpiece.

Thick suck-worthy girth, length that would reach your ribs, smooth skin, not too veiny, groomed with a few stray hairs but nothing that would choke you, and a great healthy glow.

Is he semi-hard or is that how it hangs? Shockingly, it's holding its stature with the air con blasting.

Circumcised, interesting. I only have experience with ones with helmets.

Kate said he hasn't had a proper girlfriend in ten years. Now I understand why. It would be too much pressure for one woman to have that all to herself. A single woman couldn't afford the gallons of lube required.

Like a simpleton, I stand pinned to the floor with my jaw hanging. I have to get out of here before he spots me.

But my brain is stuffed with cotton wool, and all organs are failing except my damn clitoris.

He grumbles to the poor person on the phone about missing cranes and delayed construction works.

Meanwhile, as the horniest woman on earth, I'm in danger of bursting into flames. He must be able to hear my heart hammering through his headphones.

What would it be like to be fucked by someone like Jack Knight?

One night of hate sex.

It's not an unreasonable ask.

Those muscles on top of you, that confidence, that experience, that voice growling at you . . . fucking you hard and deep because that's the only way he knows how?

I would grab that topknot like a rein and ride him like a thoroughbred racehorse.

Argh, I'm a weak woman.

Remember your focus: bricks, not dicks.

I step back as quietly as I can, and my foot crunches on something. The envelope. In my lust-haze, it must have slipped from my fingers.

If I leave it on the table, he'll know I was in here when he was in the bathroom.

I stoop into a squat, grab the paper and reverse backwards, cowering low until there is no chance of him seeing me. Then I stand up and skulk towards the front door.

Taking a few deep breaths, I yell his name loud enough for the entire wedding crew to hear and tramp into the room like an elephant.

The bathroom door swings open, releasing a gust of steam as he emerges, this time with the towel wrapped low around his waist. *Dangerously* low as if he's not bothered whether it's covering the massive shaft lurking underneath.

I won't survive a second slippage.

Eyes up, Bonnie, eyes up. Bradshaw Brown's most important client.

I stand three metres away, within safety of the door, and try to remain calm. That's what you do when you're cornered by a wild animal.

"Bonnie," he drawls, flashing me the infamous Jack Knight smirk. It does weird things to my stomach.

"Hi," I say stiffly. "Apparently, it's important I give this to you. Sorry, I caught you at a bad time."

"It's fine." His smirk deepens into something more dangerous. "It's not a bad time."

I swallow hard. *Okay.*

I glance around the room, which really is spectacular. *Shit*, are there cameras in here? Did his security witness my peep show?

"What are you looking for?"

"Uh, just checking out the room," I say, flustered.

"I'm not a fan of the mounted moose head." He nods towards the giant stuffed moose above the bed that I barely glanced at before. Please God, don't let there be a moose head in every room.

Maybe his security installed cameras in the eyes! That's where they go in the films.

"Ha, ha, yeah, I wouldn't want him watching me all night."

He laughs, deep and sexy, even though I'm not particularly funny. "How are you? It must be months since I saw you. I think Sean's birthday drinks, yeah?"

He scratches below his pec.

I rip my gaze away from the distracting small silver ring cutting through the nipple. "Yup, that would have been it," I add. "I'm great. How are you?" I'm not exactly grabbing the opportunity to sell Bradshaw Brown here.

"Never been better." He nods to the envelope. "What is it?"

"Something from Kate. I'm just the delivery girl."

He steps forward until I'm in eyeline with his tattooed chest. I'm close enough to smell his man musk, and he's close enough to hear my ragged breathing.

As he reaches out to take the envelope, his slightly damp arm brushes against mine. My skin tingles. "Thanks for being my delivery girl."

Oh, piss off, you panty-wetting cockney.

"I hear you're helping Max on my new East London patch." He makes it sound like a monopoly board square. Which London is for Jack. "I'm expecting great things since you and Max won the award for the Queen Mary Tower."

I feel the flush in my cheeks deepen.

Technically, Bradshaw Brown won the award for the Tower design. I was just part of the team, so he's being generous with his wording.

I didn't expect Jack Knight to even know I was involved.

I smile wonkily. Is the man seriously expecting me to have a conversation with him while he stands like a loinclothed caveman?

"The whole team feels so honoured to get this opportunity to work for Lexington on such a ground-breaking project," I gush. "We won't let you down." Maybe I'm laying it on too thick, considering the bitching over the deadlines.

His lips quirk. "I've no doubt you'll live up to my expectations. Will you be all right working under Max on this project, given your history together?"

My eyes widen. *Shit*. Does he think I can't handle it? I can't get taken off this project.

"Yes, of course," I say, taken aback. Why does he even care?

I raise my palms, and they end up dangerously close to his chest. I can almost feel the heat from his body. "You don't need to worry about the split impacting our work. Max and I keep things *very* professional. We always have. The project will absolutely *not* be affected," I say in a business-like tone.

I can't decipher his expression as his dark eyes watch me. "You seemed pretty amicable on the lawn. So, your relationship is purely platonic now, huh?"

"Platonic . . ." My voice trails off. "Yeah, I guess you could call it that." Whatever it is, I won't get into labels with Jack. "He's like a big brother now."

That sounds weird.

"It's been six months since your split."

I'm not sure if it's a statement or a question or where he's going with this. I run a hand over the back of my neck, flustered.

"So, it's definitely over between you and Max?"

I blink a few times. Do you lose your brain-to-mouth filter once you become a billionaire? What business is it of his?

I open my mouth and then close it.

"Sorry I asked," he says with gravel in his voice. "It's none of my business." He snaps his gaze from me and turns his back, telling me I'm dismissed. "See you downstairs."

Asshole.

I storm out, making a mental note to stay away from Jack Knight with his big dick and insensitive questions for the rest of the wedding.

6

Bonnie

I haven't shared the strange encounter in Jack's room because I'd rather not admit to myself I'm a weak, pathetic woman who falls to pieces at the sight of hot cock.

Besides, Kate has the subtlety of a rhinoceros, her sister Becky will skin me alive, and Nisha will demand granular details that I don't trust myself to disclose without soaking my underwear.

Again.

"Can't you put your foot on the gas," Kate says with an edge to her voice that I never hear.

We've spent the day in the chapel, practising our walk, faffing about with flowers—moving them then moving them back again—and generally trying to stop Kate from having a bridal breakdown.

All day, she has alternated between panic attacks and apologising to me for putting me in such a painful situation.

After my decoupled status went public, she'd asked if I still wanted to be her bridesmaid.

Blindsided is not a strong enough word to describe my reaction when Max informed me that his preference was "I don't" rather than "I do." To be honest, I don't want to attend a wedding for a good decade, but Kate has been with me longer than Max.

No way was I going to cancel.

The four of us are crammed into my car on the way to the castle, two miles from the chapel. A bridesmaid's life is not easy. I'm exhausted.

"Can you drive quieter, please? That noise is so loud," Nisha says, moaning. "Make it stop." She's slumped, eyes closed, mouth open, head pressed against the headrest. I'm the smug friend that is glad I went to bed early last night.

"It's the engine. Unless I fly through the air like Mary Poppins, you'll just have to tolerate it. Ten minutes and we'll be back."

"You better not be bloody hungover for my wedding tomorrow," Kate scolds from behind me.

I roll down the window. "Let's get some fresh air in. That'll help you, Nish. It's nice to be out of London for a change. This countryside is amazing."

Nisha grunts. "Take a picture of it. I'll look at it later."

"You shouldn't have inhaled all the tequila," I chide.

Her lips quiver, but her eyes remain closed. "Don't say that word."

Becky tuts from the backseat. "Good one, Nisha. I was planning to get Jack drunk and seduce him, but you cleaned us out."

"You didn't get lucky with him last night?" Kate asks.

Becky sighs. "No, but I'm slowly chipping away. The weekend is still young. If only we could swap groomsmen, Bonnie."

I shift uncomfortably in my seat. If only we could.

Nisha is now open-eyed and smirking at me. "Bonnie had a private trip to Jack's bedroom yesterday."

Damn you, Nisha.

The minute she saw me yesterday, she knew I was holding something back from her.

"You've been very quiet about it," she adds. "Too quiet, if you ask me."

"No. Bonnie, you can't." Becky leans forward in the backseat to peer in at me. "I'm having him at this wedding."

"You're safe," I tell her. "Believe me, I would never go there. He's all yours."

"Oh, please," she scoffs. "You have eyes."

I laugh loudly. Too loudly. "He knows Max and is one of our largest paying clients. I'm about to do a project that could advance my career." *And he turfed my dad out on his ass like a piece of shit.*

She nods feverishly. "I agree. Terrible idea. Career-destroying."

"I wouldn't worry. Bonnie has taken a vow of celibacy," Nisha says dryly.

Ouch. "It's not like I don't have my reasons."

"You don't have your reasons. Not anymore. Especially now we know Max is dating."

The car falls silent.

"Nisha's right," Kate says softly. "It's time you started having fun again."

Nodding, I sigh. "Fine. I'll join one of the dating apps." It's probably healthier than trying to be a cyber detective to find out who Danielle is.

"I'll need to train you up first," Nisha says beside me. "You're too green. It's like sending Bambi out into a field of wolves. As far as online dating goes, you might as well have been born yesterday."

Kate leans forward to give Nisha a look. "Oh, Nish, stop being so overdramatic. We'll go and watch rugby in a pub and talk to some nice men."

Nisha snorts. "For God's sake, Kate, you are in no position to give dating advice. Meeting IRL is an extinct concept."

"Meeting who?" I ask, putting my indicators on to turn into the manor's driveway.

"*In real life,*" Nisha explains. "There's a brutal dating world out there that you've not been privy to. I've been around the dating block for a few years. These days, you don't sit in a pub looking pretty and wait for *nice men* to approach you." She rolls her eyes in disgust. "People are disposable. Too many choices. When you go on a date, you might think it went great, but you need to remember that you are on a conveyor belt of vaginas and there's a good chance you'll get ghosted."

Kate replies, "I hardly think—"

"She's right," Becky cuts in. "Last year, I dated a guy for three months. I was gonna introduce him to you, Kate. Remember lanky dentist Tom? Then he ghosted me. Three months! The only decent explanation I would have accepted was if he had passed away. Then I saw him on another dating app! People today can't even be bothered to send a simple message saying, 'I'm not interested anymore.'"

Kate's quiet for a moment. "That was very rude of the dentist."

I frown. "You guys aren't exactly selling dating apps."

"It's fine." Nisha shrugs. "You'll develop thick skin after the first few dates."

"I don't want to develop thick skin. Is there any way I can stay away from the nasties? What do I need to look out for?"

She thinks for a moment. "Men who don't transition online to offline. They get their kicks chatting. Gaslighting. Love bombing. Catfishing. Those types of things."

Becky leans forward from the back seat. "Men who tell you you're amazing, then you never hear from them again. Amazing spicy banter one minute, then radio silence the next. Men who straight up tell you they don't find you attractive within the first few minutes of a date. That can hurt."

"One guy wanted me to lick his perineum on the third date," Nisha casually tells us.

My mouth hangs open. "That seems very intimate. It's so close to the ass. What's even down there?" I've never investigated that wasteland.

"I never checked. I ghosted him."

"Sounds like I'd be better off writing to a death row inmate," I mutter.

"Married men," Becky adds, "that's a bummer. Or just men with girlfriends."

"Men with multiple girlfriends," Nisha chimes in. "Guys shorter than their profile claims."

"Guys *older* than their profile claims," Becky counters in this weird ping-pong.

"Men who live with their mums," Nisha adds, groaning. "That's my showstopper."

I tilt my head to give her a double take. "What, but everything else you listed is fine?"

Kate and I exchange looks in the mirror. "Here I was thinking that the only ones to avoid were those posing in the gym. This all sounds very draining." I sigh. "I guess I was spoiled with Max. He always treated me well."

Nisha mutters something inaudible.

I blow out a breath. "Maybe I'll stick with my werewolf book-boyfriends."

"Werewolves!" Nisha tuts. "Reverse harem. Other technical things I can't remember. How is anyone supposed to live up to that?"

"That's like gang-bangs?" Becky asks excitedly. "Having sex with loads of men at the same time? Yeah, you need a specialised dating app for that. I never thought you had it in you, Bonnie."

"What? No," I snap. "Look, it's just fiction. If you read horror, do you spend Halloween in a crazed clown mask, living in gutters, and killing people in small towns? No. I only read about it. I don't do *any* of the things I read about."

God, I sound like a loser.

Nisha shakes her head. "It's time, though. If you're not careful, you'll end up seventy and surrounded by vibrators and cats. You need to get your head out of those books and deal with real men again. Farts and all."

I chew on my lips.

I think of my battery-operated gentle lovers who treat me so well and don't have the capacity to gaslight, love bomb or catfish me. Their only purpose in life is to serve me pleasure.

Then a visual of a naked Jack Knight flashes before me.

I bet even his perineum wasteland is hot.

"Okay." I grin at Nisha. "I'll do it. I'll set up a profile."

Satisfied, she rolls her head on the seat and massages her forehead. "That's good. We'll have you addicted in no time."

"In your new dating profile, are you going to tell them you want a group of men?" Kate pipes up from the back.

I ignore her.

We drive up to find a sausage fest on the lawn, everyone drinking beers and bantering loudly.

"Is that all he's going to fucking do?" Kate shrieks as Sean appears on the lawn with more beers. "Does he think this is some type of *holiday*?"

Probably. I made that mistake, too.

"Kate," Sean shouts as we get out of the car. "Love of my life, come join us."

She glares incredulously at him. "Are you drunk? You do realise that we're getting married tomorrow?"

He saunters over and wraps his arm around her, ignoring her scowl. "Don't worry, love. All the hard work will pay off and soon we'll be relaxing on our honeymoon, doing sweet FA."

That's the wrong answer for Kate. "You've been doing sweet FA since we got here."

Becky and I exchange glances.

"He's right, Kate. Relax," I say. "Everything's ready for tomorrow. It'll be a fabulous day, then you have your honeymoon in a few weeks."

"We'll likely sit beside the pool in the hotel drinking like he's doing now." She crosses her arms. "While Sean works on his beer belly."

He laughs. "That's the best kind of holiday. You can work on your tan, love, and I'll work on my beer belly."

"Uh, do not think we are turning into that married couple."

"There are plenty of mountains to hike in the Canary Islands. Make sure you keep Sean busy, Kate."

I turn to see Jack grinning at us.

"No fucking chance." Sean groans. "Jack's idea of a relaxing holiday is free climbing over a mountain with wild bears for company."

Jack chuckles. "I highly recommend it. Me, a tent, the

mountains—that's all I need for a successful holiday."

"Sounds amazing," I mutter. "My type of holiday."

Jack looks at me. "Do you climb, Bonnie?"

"Uh, no. I just meant I like the sound of getting away from people." I need more hobbies. "I went on a running holiday once." It's the most interesting thing I can conjure up.

"That's right, Sean told me you were a runner. You're doing the London Marathon this year? I'm doing it, too."

I nod, visualising those two hard mounds. My training tactic is to find a good ass and chase it.

"Maybe we should train together, go for a few runs around the old haunts in East London," he says casually. "I used to run past your house when I lived in the area."

My body goes rigid. Does he mean the house I grew up in that got repossessed? "Do you mean Brook Close?"

He looks at me funny. "Yeah, of course."

I relax a fraction. He isn't such a sicko to suggest running past the house ripped out from under us. Brook Close is where Mum and I moved in with Phil, my stepdad.

Kate and I grew up within a one-mile radius of the Knights, which in London is probably a million people, but in that area, it still feels like a small town.

"Sorry, I'm already part of a running club."

"Okay." He shrugs, unfazed. "The offer's always open."

Kate saves me. "Come help me, will you, Bonnie?"

"There she is," Kate says between gritted teeth as we enter the wedding reception marquee.

Kate's soon-to-be mother-in-law is deep in conversation with a pursed-lipped wedding planner, jabbing fingers at walls and tables. Mrs. Knight rules the wedding like a benevolent dictator. Kate is allowed some liberty on matters of lesser importance, such as underwear, but Mrs. Knight has absolute authority.

Thanks to her, my new name has stuck, and I am now referred to as "the other bridesmaid" by the entire wedding crew.

"What the fuck is she saying to my wedding planner? She's got her nose in everything. I need to separate them. Go put these on the top table, will you?"

I take the wreaths of greenery from her and head off.

The marquee could host a small rock concert. Kate and I didn't talk about finances, but I have a feeling that Jack is bankrolling the entire event.

I glance up at the tent wall, confused.

"Excuse me." I stop a girl affixing ribbons on seats. "Do you know where the mosaic went?"

"The what?"

"The large collage of the bride and groom? It was hung up there."

"Oh. Mrs. Knight had it taken down."

"Why?"

She shrugs, bored. "I dunno. She said something about it being out of place. Distasteful? Maybe ask her."

I go completely still. Sean's mum said it was distasteful?

I spent hours after work every night for weeks collecting pictures throughout every year that they were together to create that mosaic. I wanted to get them something unique and personal. Kate had wanted it mounted for the wedding reception.

The girl looks at me strangely, and I return a strained smile before chucking the rest of the wreaths onto the top table.

Was Kate lying when she said she loved it? Maybe she was just being nice. Like with the fake tan, she couldn't say no.

I won't push it. It's Kate and Sean's day, it's about what makes them happy, and Kate is too stressed right now to mention it.

I message Kate and tell her I'll be back in forty-five. I need to be alone.

A familiar voice right outside the tent stops me in my tracks.

"I'll get there on time," Max says. "I'll leave early and avoid the traffic."

My pulse quickens as I eavesdrop.
"No, stop worrying, my angel. I'll be there."
I can't breathe.
I used to be his angel. It seems heaven is pretty full.
Couldn't you have found a new nickname for Danielle?
Today is too bloody hard.

7

Bonnie

The Jacuzzi is in a hut tucked away at the back of the grounds, perfect for hiding. No one has used it since we got here because the lure of alcoholic bubbles is stronger.

I push open the hut's doors and stop short when I see the last person I want to see sprawled out in the Jacuzzi.

The damn nipple ring twinkles, teasing me.

"Do you think I have time to clean up your mess?" Mr. Big Dick snarls down the phone.

I draw in a sharp breath. Jesus Christ, the man has me on edge within seconds.

"I'll come back later," I mouth as he locks eyes with me.

I get a grunt in response. He shakes his head and beckons me with his hand like a king summoning a servant.

I start to leave.

"Bonnie, wait," he says in his deep gruff voice.

"It's fine. I'll come back when you're finished."

His dark eyes flare with annoyance. "One minute," he barks into the phone. "Do I have a contagious disease I'm not aware of? Get in the hot tub."

I glower at him.

Bossy bastard. Somebody needs to put this guy in his place.

"You don't need to leave because I'm here. You're making me feel like an ogre. Give me two minutes and I'll be off this call, okay?" His gaze falls to my breasts, then he abruptly returns to his phone call.

My face heats as I tug my bikini top self-consciously. Walking out now will look like a snub. Probably not the best networking strategy.

Awkwardly, I remove my shorts, fussing with my bikini triangles to not give him an eyeful. From snippets I catch, he's talking about his new hotel in Waterloo, central London. It'll be the tallest hotel in Europe when it's finished. At thirty-eight, he's only ten years older than me, but with how he talks, it seems like fifty.

Whoever's on the other end of the phone has fucked up or is in the process of fucking up. I'm nervous for them.

I've never seen Mr. Big Dick in work mode. Max and the other seniors have led discussions whenever we've worked for Lexington. Maybe it's a good thing.

My crotch is directly in his line of sight as I step into the tub, and I pray I have no stray hairs. My grooming regime slackened after the break-up. In the dark days of the split, I sported a full bush. Removing body hair seemed fruitless when there was no-one to admire the results. Yesterday was the first time I had a full bikini wax in six months.

A new beginning.

Water splashes up against his phone as I slosh into the Jacuzzi. "Sorry." I wince.

He ignores me and keeps talking.

My eyes widen as I grasp the gist of his conversation. *Jesus.* This person is actually getting fired.

This isn't the chakra-balancing calming haven I had envisioned. Leaning my head back, I wonder how long I could survive submerged.

Who's in the right here? Okay, so he was in the Jacuzzi first, but isn't this supposed to be a stress-free zone? Instead, the guy is taking up most of the space with his big bulky limbs while casually shitting all over some poor bugger's life. Exactly like he did to Dad.

"My lawyers have issued contract termination. Remove your people from the site with immediate effect."

Who are these poor people being terminated at five p.m. on a Friday? What a start to the weekend. To top it all off, they must hear the bubbles and realise Jack's having a fantastic time.

My eyes flicker down to find him already staring at me with such an intensity I feel like I'm the one being fired.

And the alarming thing is I kind of like it.

I look away, examining a chipped tile on the ceiling.

He snaps his phone shut, and his face immediately melts into a crooked grin. "Sorry."

Give me bloody strength. I've got whiplash.

"It must be such a pain sacking people. Doesn't it bother you?"

He shrugs, unaffected by the wrath that must be spitting from my eyes. "Not if they deserve it. Can't get the staff these days. I gave a small company a chance, only to find out they were stealing materials. I don't work with guys who think they can pull a fast one because Lexington's too big to care or notice."

Fine. Maybe this company is in the wrong, but it's not like I can empathise with Jack. I steal stationery from Bradshaw Brown, but those two cretins steal all my time. For all I know, the poor guys stole a few pens.

Regardless of what they did, I feel sorry for the company. If Jack gets pissed off enough, their mistake will be reputation-destroying. It's likely they'll go out of business.

"You're always working." But that's because he's got no qualms about doing business shaving or in a hot tub. "Don't you ever stop?"

He flashes a grin, displaying a beautiful set of white teeth. The kind you want latching on your nipple. "I've no time to stop. Three big projects on the go right now. The Waterloo hotel, the apartment complex in Liverpool, and the East London project."

"Can't you delegate?" I'm genuinely curious. "Surely owning the company means you get to relax and watch others do the work for you?"

He shrugs, running a hand through his thick, wet hair. "I like it. There'll always be a part of me that's still the sixteen-year-old brickie."

I nod. "You're very hands-on."

Too hands-on. His fingers circle his nipple ring, mindlessly, as if it's a habit he doesn't even know he's doing. Like hair-chewing.

How would he like it if I played with my nipples in here?

"Have to be. Particularly with the East London project. You know my nan lives in the patch we're building on?"

I didn't. "You'll be rehousing her?"

His grin widens. "Like every woman in my life, she busts my balls when I don't do exactly as I'm told."

"Maybe you deserve it," I mutter.

He lets out a deep throaty chuckle. "I probably do."

His arms splay over the sides of the hot tub, revealing thick underarm hair, and a flash of unwanted lust rages through me. I must have a caveman kink.

I force my eyes up. "It makes sense why it's a personal project for you."

"Very personal. The area means more to me than bricks and cash. Especially since I need to honour my dad's place of death."

Of course. How could I forget? That's why he's so involved.

Jack's dad was murdered by one of East London's deadliest gangs, the Wicks family, not far from the factory. It must have been nearly a decade ago.

I don't know what to say. Jack might be a bastard in business, but he didn't deserve that.

"I'm sorry," I say softly. "That must be hard. What are you planning . . . for the, uh, spot?"

He smiles sadly. "A boxing gym for young guys. It'll be named after him. Dad was a semi-pro boxer, you know? That's how I got into it. I almost went pro myself."

"That's really nice. I'm sure he would have loved that. Why didn't you go pro?"

He pauses. "After Dad died, I never wanted to box again. Not if it wasn't with him." There's a hint of pain. "I threw myself into work instead. By the time I started boxing again, I was too old to compete professionally."

What the hell do you say to a guy whose dad was murdered, with the story splashed over the papers in gory detail? Jack was pretty famous back then, so even though murders are a dime a dozen in London, it still made headlines.

"I'm sure your dad would have been happy to hear you're boxing again. That must have been such a difficult experience to go through. I can't imagine."

He shrugs roughly, and I sense he doesn't want to elaborate further.

Seems like we all have our demons, even billionaires. Maybe his tragedy is why he's so ruthless in business today. I wonder how things would have turned out if his father were still alive.

I don't want to feel sorry for the guy.

He looks at me for a long moment. "Are you okay? You seemed upset when you came in."

My cheeks heat. He's surprisingly astute for a guy who'd been in the middle of firing a company. "It's nothing. I'm fine."

"Tell me." His voice softens. "Please."

"It's stupid." I shrug, feigning indifference. "I just wasted time on something. Kate said she wanted something personal in the marquee for her wedding. We talked about displaying photos of her and Sean so I said I would make a mosaic. I got it printed to hang beside the top table."

He gives a nod of recognition. "I'm not surprised to hear you made that. It took me about thirty minutes to take it all in. So much detail."

"Oh." I look at him, surprised. "You've seen it?"

"As soon as I walked in. How many photos did you use?"

"Over two thousand," I admit.

He lets out a low whistle. "Where did you find over two thousand photos?"

"I've been secretly videoing them for years."

He stares at me.

I smirk. "I'm joking. Social media, photos from when we were growing up. It's frightening how many photos you can find on the internet. Friends and family. You even gave me some, Jack."

"I did?" He frowns, confused.

"Your PA did."

His frown deepens. "Did you contact me?"

I deliberated for hours over whether to include his email address. After all, he is a friend of Sean's, and I asked Sean's other friends.

In the end, I'd included him. And a lovely PA named Jess responded.

"I hope that's all right. Jess was really helpful. I think she got the pics from your sisters or mum."

"Of course, it's all right. I'm sorry—your email never made it past my PA."

I shrug. "You need thousands of pictures to make a good quality digital mosaic. I didn't quite have two thousand, so I added places they went on holidays together, houses they lived in, their favourite restaurants, other life moments like that." I laugh. "When I say it out loud, it sounds a little stalker-ish."

He smiles. "Kate and Sean are lucky to have you as a friend."

My blush deepens, and I sink lower under the bubbles. "What did you get for them?" I ask, changing the subject. "Oh, this place, of course. Duh! It's a present someone could only dream about."

"Sean's been a right-hand man to me since I started Lexington, it was the least I could do. You haven't explained why you were upset, though. Did something happen to the mosaic?"

I squirm in the water. "I feel like I might have overstepped the mark. Sean's mum had it taken down."

A scowl mars his face. "For fuck's sake. That's bullshit."

"It's fine. I'll put the massive picture of Kate and Sean as the centrepiece in my bedroom," I say, feigning cheeriness.

His scowl deepens. "It's not fine. I'm sorry my aunt upset you.

If someone made that for me, I'd be honoured. You're such a visual storyteller. No wonder you're an architect."

I eye him suspiciously.

Max's voice fills my head. "Speaking of architecture, we have some fantastic ideas for the factory," I say, launching into my pitch. "We're going to bring to life the fact that the factory was the industrial backbone of London. When people visit, they'll get an understanding of the history."

He breaks into a smile. "That's very important to me. And my nan, of course."

"If you like the mosaic, I'll talk to the designers and maybe we can add some to the factory interior showing the history of the neighbourhood. Like the amazing New York City mosaics and murals on the streets in Harlem," I say excitedly. "They tell the story of all the communities that emigrated into the area. But they'll be subtle in our work. We'll make sure that they blend in with the whole concept of loft-style living."

He nods. "I love it. Be sure to add it to your proposal."

I raise my brows in surprise. "Seriously?"

"Come on, look at me. I practically use my body as a canvas. Of course, I like the idea."

My eyes flicker down to his tattooed chest, and I can't help myself, I ask, "What do they mean?"

He lifts his muscular forearm. "The roman numerals here are the date Dad died." His hand moves up his arm and stops at a shield with an armoured soldier's head above it. "The Knight family coat of arms."

I could have guessed that one.

"Dad had the same one."

I grudgingly drool as he explains ten or more tattoos on his chest and arms. "I like them," I say hoarsely, concerned that I may have a deranged smile on my face.

"Glad to hear it." There's more gravel in his voice this time, and it triggers a shift in the air.

He studies me, eyes darkening. His throat works as he

swallows.

A quick glance down confirms I don't have a breast hanging out of my bikini top. When I glance back up again, he's still staring at me.

This is weird.

As I'm about to break the strange silence, his eyes drop to my mouth, then follow a heated trail down to my neck, lingering there. His lips part.

He leans forward in the tub. His nostrils tent. Did he just . . . *sniff* me?

Holy fuck, he's going to kiss me.

"What are you . . ." My throat dries up.

My breath hitches audibly as his hand brushes my collarbone. I swear I feel it in my clit. To my horror, my nipples too.

"Did you make this?" he asks in a rough voice. His fingers skim over the stone wrapped in silk threads resting above my breasts.

"Yes," I say thickly as his hand drops. "It's an amethyst crystal."

"It matches your eyes."

"It creates protection against negative energy and emotion." I swallow, hating myself for the fact that if his hands accidentally found their way into my bikini bottoms, I wouldn't have the willpower to stop them. "Well, it's supposed to."

"The wedding must be hard for you."

"A little," I reply tetchily. I let out an awkward laugh. "At least I know I won't be getting lucky with a groomsman."

His lips twitch. "I wouldn't rule it out."

A snort erupts from my throat. Not the sexy, husky type, more the type when you have a terrible cold.

Is Jack Knight flirting with me?

This tub is too hot.

Oh. Sean has three groomsmen—Max, Jack, and Sean's teenage brother. Maybe he's talking about me getting back with Max.

"There you are." The loud voice behind me makes me jump.

I turn to see Nisha, who stops dead when she sees Jack. "Oh! Eh, hi, Jack. Actually, you're both wanted. Kate and Sean need to go over the order of service or something."

"Ladies first, after you," Jack says, gazing at me.

No fucking chance. Getting out first means exposing my fat bum to him.

"No," I say firmly. "You go first, there's only one changing room, and I'd like to spend another minute or two in here."

He exhales harshly and climbs out of the Jacuzzi awkwardly like he has a cramp in his thigh.

And that's when I see the substantial tent in his swim shorts.

Oh my God.

He's hard.

Not half-assed lazy hard either, he's ready to buck. Either firing people gets Jack Knight off or . . . I did it.

A shiver snakes down my spine.

"Was that awkward?" Nisha says in a loud whisper the second Jack leaves the hut.

"A little. When I walked in, he was in the process of firing a squad of people over the phone."

"Seriously?" Nisha groans.

"Yup. The guy's a psycho."

A smile tugs at her lips. "It must have been absolutely *horrendous* sharing a hot tub with him."

"The worst," I say with an edge in my voice. "Absolute nightmare."

8

Bonnie

It's moments like this I'm glad I was dumped.

The aisle walk is procession by importance, in ascending order. I am the least important, Becky is maid of honour, and Kate and her father walk in last.

That means I'm the one walking in first after the priest, but no one looks at the priest, do they?

I'm so bloody nervous.

Yesterday we rehearsed this walk a million times, and I was even in my six-inch heels, but I was also wearing stretchy yoga pants, not packed into a bandage dress like a sausage casing. We look lovely but are highly dysfunctional.

"This is us!" Becky says breathlessly as we pull up to the chapel, downing the last of her Bucks Fizz.

Poor Becky got no chat out of me on the way over as I repeated my useless affirmations. *I release my worries with every breath.*

We are already thirty minutes late. One of the drivers slept in. It happens to the best of us.

The first limo stops outside the church, and I see Kate's dad and the limo driver helping Kate out of the car.

Kate looks beautiful and free in a long, flowy, hippy-chic white dress tapered at the waist. She could be pooping under that thing, and you couldn't tell. I'm jealous.

My lip quivers watching my fair-haired freckled best friend of two decades.

I blow Kate a kiss out of the window, and she waves back, her face a contortion of nerves and shock. It's finally happening. The first four hours of her wedding day were pretty slow as we rotated in and out of styling chairs. And poor Kate had the nervous poops.

After being watched and judged all day, she'll have to put on the bedroom performance of a lifetime.

It sounds exhausting.

The priest and an altar boy greet her at the steps of the church.

Our limo driver opens the door for us and Becky shuffles out of the car first. I step out quickly behind her. Too quickly.

I feel a sharp object punch my eye socket as Becky accidentally elbows me in the face.

Fuck. That hurts.

Really hurts.

The temporary blindness and confusion are quickly followed by a stinging pain in my socket.

"Fuck!" I hiss loudly, trying to flush out the eyeliner seeping into my eye with rapid blinking. "Fuck, fuck."

The priest is staring at me, snarling, and I remember I'm cursing loudly outside his father's house.

"Has she been drinking?" Father Donaghy snaps at the wedding planner.

Kate peers worriedly over the planner's shoulder.

Becky turns. "Are you okay?"

I can only see her out of one eye.

"Why do you have your eye closed?"

"It's fine." I grimace. "You nudged me with your elbow. Don't worry."

"Sorry." She appears more preoccupied than contrite, but I'll forgive her today. "We're fine," Becky calls, then turns to me sternly. "Let's go. Kate is already anxious that we're so late."

I force a strained smile and brush a stream of water off my cheek.

Father Donaghy opens the double wooden doors to the chapel. It's clear from the sound of shuffling and throat-clearing that the crowd has been waiting for a good show for a while and are restless to the point of being fed up. We are eating into their boozing time.

"Ready, ladies," the wedding planner prompts, guiding us like children into the right order, with me at the helm. "Bouquets up. Heads up," she commands in a tone fitting for army marches. "Big smiles. Wide eyes, Bonnie. Wide eyes!"

With a smile showing all my teeth, I force open my tingling right eye.

"Honey, you look like you have menstrual cramps. I need you to smile harder. Brighter."

I'm scared.

The music begins to play. That's my queue. *You proceed when Father Donaghy is three pews up from the back.*

Heads turn as I set foot into the chapel. The pews are full of hats, fancy hairdos, tuxedos, and very made-up faces.

With all eyes on me, the nerves fluttering in my belly threaten to launch into a tornado.

Father Donaghy makes good speed down the aisle. I suppose this is just another daily commute for him.

The slow dramatic walk I perfected yesterday has gone to shit. My swelling eye won't allow me to focus on synchronising my walk with the music.

I try not to fall over my feet, and blink away the water mixed with eyeliner and mascara from my weeping eye. Everything is clenched. Ass cheeks, stomach muscles, face cheeks. As a stress ball, I hold the bouquet in an iron grip.

Row upon row of people smile back at me, pushing cameras in my face.

Head up, bouquet up, try not to look like a massive tit.

My theory about sexy thoughts applies to weddings. Most people are in their own heads, dreaming about better sex than their reality permits.

I catch the eye of Kate's creepy Uncle Dom and blink.

He winks, breaking into a salacious grin.

My skin crawls.

Halfway up and I turn my head ninety degrees. Michelle Allard, the supermodel. She's friggin' hot. Legions above anyone else at the wedding.

Or on earth.

Sean's side all look like money.

As I approach the altar, Sean, Max, and Jack come into focus. All three smile at me.

My heart breaks a little as I take in Max's suit. It would have been similar to his groom's suit for *our* wedding.

Jack looks sensational in a black tuxedo. Inappropriately sexy for mass.

I shuffle into the second pew and sit down, relieved that Becky is now the focus of attention.

Before I know it, Becky is beside me in the seat, and finally, Kate reaches the top of the aisle to a lot of "oohs" and "ahhs" and incessant camera flashes. The whole thing must have taken a minute or two but felt like a feature-length film.

"You look amazing," Nisha whispers to me from the pew behind.

I turn subtly and mouth, "Thanks."

As Father Donaghy welcomes us, Nisha leans in and quietly wipes under my eye. I feel a few eyelashes fall.

"What happened?" she whispers as the choir launches into "Gloria."

That means it's obvious *something* happened.

I lean back in the pew, saying through gritted teeth, "I got knocked in the eye. Is it bad?"

"No. It looks a little . . . irritated. Like you have a sore stye on your eye."

For fuck's sake. I think I preferred when I was just *the other bridesmaid.*

"Can you give me my bag? I need to check the damage."

She hands over my satin bag made from the same material as my dress. The impracticality of being a bridesmaid: the only thing you can carry down the aisle are flowers.

As I join in a bad warble to "Gloria," I discreetly search my bag for my phone. If Father Donaghy sees me with my phone, I'm fast-tracking to hell.

Unable to find it, I fling the bag down.

Behind me, a guy chooses this moment to start a conversation. His voice mixes with the chorus.

Becky shoots me a look, and I shake my head in disapproval and agreement. It's damn rude.

Her brows lift pointedly like she wants me to do something. What does she expect me to do? I'm not the noise police. I glance lazily over my shoulder to silence the obnoxious chatterer who clearly doesn't understand the social mores of not talking through someone's wedding.

Father Donaghy glances down.

The chatterer has an American accent . . . it actually sounds familiar.

There's an audible groan over the music.

Holy fucking hell. My phone.

Is this seriously happening?

I fumble with my bag. Oh, my God, where's my phone, where's my phone, where's my goddamn phone?

Please, God, if you are here with us in the chapel as Father Donaghy claims, answer my prayers.

The longer I don't locate the phone, the more flustered I become. I'm going to have to hurry out of the chapel carrying my bag like it's a screaming baby.

My ears burn so hot they cremate themselves.

I know what happens next.

The singing peters out as the choir finishes the last few lines of "Gloria." The sounds of ruthless alpha wolf Caleb from the *Red Moon Canines* taking his virgin mate take over.

Nowhere in the order-of-service booklet does it mention howling horny wolves.

Finally locating the phone, I hold my finger on the power

button.

Shut down.

Shut down.

The damn thing dies, and I let out the breath I was holding.

"What the hell?" Becky mouths, giving me a sharp look.

This is worse than farting.

"Quiet." I shush her dismissively, deciding that going on the offensive is the best tactic to sweep this little audio mishap under the carpet.

The service picks up speed, first reading . . . second reading . . . gospel acclamation. I try to pay attention, but Father Donaghy could have performed a satanic ritual. For all I know, I'm now in a cult.

When we get to the good part—*I do*—I can't help but shed a tear. My best friend is married.

Will she still be my best friend after the werewolf fiasco?

Father Donaghy tells us to go in peace.

"Thanks be to God," I agree loudly as everyone claps and snaps pictures. Now I need alcohol. All the alcohol.

Every last drop.

Father Donaghy is the first to walk down the aisle, followed by the newlyweds. Max and Becky link arms and follow.

I step out into the aisle. As dark, smouldering brown eyes level on mine, I suddenly feel a hundred times more nervous about my second trip down the aisle.

"You look beautiful," Jack says gruffly as he extends his arm for me to loop mine through. His gaze brazenly rakes my curves. "A real head-turner."

"Stop lying," I say sullenly. "My eye is swollen. I look like Sloth from *The Goonies*."

"Nonsense." He laughs as we proceed slowly down the aisle. "You can hardly notice it."

My skin feels hot against his arm. I glance up and see the lie clear as day on his face.

"How bad does the other guy look?"

"It was Becky's elbow," I say between my teeth with a smile plastered on my face for the guests waving. "Just as we got out of the wedding car."

"Ouch. I'll find some ice for you when we get to the marquee."

I stiffen. "Don't worry." I don't need him doing me any favours. "But thank you. Sorry I can't walk any faster. I can't feel anything from the knees up in this dress."

His eyes flicker down my body. "It's worth it."

Okay.

"You don't scrub up too badly yourself," I grudgingly say.

Not too bad at all.

"Thank you." He chuckles. "Glad you approve. I think."

I glance at his hair in a topknot but more groomed than it has been these past few days. "They let you keep the hair."

His smile widens into a grin as we reach the doors, and he takes my hand as I shuffle like a penguin down the steps. "The hair was non-negotiable."

I trip on the last step and fall against the slab of unmovable muscle. "Sorry," I splutter. "I've been waiting for that to happen. At least I waited until after mass."

He wraps his arm around my lower back to steady me. "Good thing I'm close."

"Jack! Bonnie! Get in line. Chop, chop," Sergeant Wedding Planner shrills.

"Better do as we're told," Jack murmurs, his lips skimming my ear.

As the guests pile out of the chapel, congratulate Kate, and tell us what beautiful people we all are, I steal a glance at the square-jawed face, feeling his grip around my waist.

He catches me staring and responds with a wink.

In that instant, I know I need to stay away from Mr. Big Dick before I do something I'll severely regret.

ॐ

I make it through dinner and speeches in a dignified manner worthy of a bridesmaid, with a permanent regal smile and a very patient bladder.

The crowd has hit the after-dinner lull where cheeks are sore from obligatory laughter at Kate's dad's long, mumbled speech, followed by Max's best man speech—confident, precise, every pause premeditated and measured.

When Sean pays homage to Jack's dad, missing from the wedding, I can't help but dart a glance at Jack. His smile does nothing to hide the storm raging in those dark eyes. Maybe time doesn't heal everything.

I grab Nisha's arm as she walks past. "Hey, can you take a pic of me to send to Dad?"

"Sure." She takes my phone from me. "I thought he was invited?"

"Weddings and big gatherings aren't his thing." And secretly I'm glad. At things like these where he's out of his comfort zone, he ends up drinking too much. "Did you hear that in the middle of the ceremony?"

"Your wolves? Yup. Heard it."

Oh my God.

She holds the phone up and takes a picture. "I think it's the only part of the ceremony I listened to," she says cheerily. "Catholic masses are so damn long. Don't tell Kate."

I polish off the last of my champagne and grab a flute from a passing waiter. "This is not good. You could actually identify it as werewolves fucking?"

"Only because I've listened to your dirty audio books before. Don't worry, most people wouldn't have caught on that it was werewolves fucking. That's not the first thing that springs to mind. I mean, most people don't even know that's a thing." She smirks. "It could have been worse."

"How?" I ask, exasperated. "How on earth could it have been worse?"

"Could have been your vibrator."

"Why would I take a *vibrator* to the church?"

She shrugs. "Kate and I think you're addicted. At least you didn't go arse over tit down the aisle. That rates higher on the *bridesmaids from hell* scale."

"Are you saying I'm on that scale?" I hiss.

Father Donaghy walks past and gives me a curt nod as I curse under my breath. That priest is going to get me sent to hell in flames.

"How bad is my eye?"

She examines me. "It's a little swollen. It probably feels worse than it looks."

"It feels like I've been hit in the face by a heavyweight boxing world champion, so that's good. I guess."

She looks between both my eyes, frowning. "But there's something else not quite right. I can't put my finger on it." Leaning over, she breathes right in my face. "You have no false eyelashes left on your right eye. It's like you're making a weird fashion statement. Why don't we go into the toilets and see what we can do?"

I feel thoroughly depressed now.

"I can't." I groan. "The first dance is finishing soon. I have to join for the second. Then I think my duties are finished. Which is good because I've barely had time to pee today."

"Looks like your sexy dance partner is raring to go."

I follow Nisha's line of sight. I'd almost forgotten I'm dancing with Jack.

That's an unconvincing lie.

He licks his lips like a predator at the top of the food chain.

A predator who has spotted dessert.

9

Jack

My gaze turns to Bonnie as the DJ invites the bridesmaids and groomsmen to join the newlyweds on the dance floor.

With her blonde hair cascading down her shoulders, her striking blue eyes—one slightly bruised and bloodshot—and ridiculously high cheekbones, she looks like a seductive Viking.

A Viking that has been in a fist fight.

Now she's looking at me like . . . she's ready for another fight.

That look I can't quite decipher whether she wants to fuck me or fight me, and I don't know which I would prefer or in what order.

Walking across the dance floor, I scan her slowly from her feet upwards.

The dress accentuates the definition of her collarbone, an underrated part of a woman's body, in my opinion. Bonnie has an exceptional collarbone.

Her hand comes up to stroke her neck protectively.

I'm going to enjoy this forced proximity.

Unlike most other women, it always takes her a little longer to relax in my company. Whether it is stoicism or nerves, I can't gauge, but she always has a bit of a bite to her tongue. I suspect now it's related to the pressure of winning the *Motor Works* factory project since she and Nisha seem to freeze whenever they see me at the castle.

"Shall we?" I reach out my hand, and she nods, letting me

lead her onto the dance floor. "Can you dance?" I ask.

"Actually, yes," she says, as if I've offended her by even asking. "I took professional lessons with Kate. Can you?"

My hands slide down the smooth fabric on the contour of her back before resting on her waist. "I have a few moves. To play it safe, we can do a simple sway and I can spin you out a few times."

She eyes me critically. "We really should have agreed on a strategy in advance."

I smile and pull her flush to me as I relax us into a sway. My mouth comes close to her temple. "I'm sure we'll figure it out together." Her head just about reaches my shoulder.

"I hope this is a long song," I say with intent, not breaking eye contact.

Her teeth latch onto her bottom lip.

Oh, Viking, I'll have to make a conscious effort to keep this dance PG.

"See? We figured it out," I say huskily, tilting my head down until our foreheads are nearly touching.

Except we haven't figured this out at all.

My left foot moves forward, as does hers, and her stiletto lands squarely on my big toe. In fact, with every step I take, Bonnie pulls in the wrong direction, as if in defiance, making it impossible for me to maintain any rhythm.

I search her face, confused, and she seems to gain false confidence. The last thing I need.

It's like watching a new-born calf trying to walk for the first time. All sliding limbs that it doesn't know how to use, so it slips around the ground, struggling to gain any sort of balance.

Bonnie is bad.

The worst dance partner I've ever had.

As she freestyles all over my feet, we transition into a weird fusion between a botched foxtrot and a teenage disco sway. The height difference between us makes it even worse.

A quick glance around the dance floor tells me all eyes are watching us in amusement.

I study her face for any signs of self-awareness.

Holy hell, she actually thinks she's a good dancer.

"Bonnie," I say firmly as, undeterred, her foot comes down heavily on mine again.

"Whoops." She looks up at me with those eyes that make my heart rate spike, despite the eyelash inconsistency. I've never seen eyes so expressive. "Little mistake. It's because the dress is too tight."

The dress has nothing to do with it. In fact, it should be restricting her limbs from flailing all over the place. Now I understand how she walked into an elbow. I've done semi-pro boxing for years. Those guys, packing two hundred pounds of pure muscle, they're predictable. Bonnie, on the other hand, must weigh no more than one-twenty, tiny compared to me, but is doing serious damage to my feet.

"Let me lead, darlin'." I restrain her with an iron grip. "And get a refund for those dance lessons, will you?"

She scoffs. "What are you saying?"

Do I need to spell it out?

I grin down at her, relieved to have gained control. *It's okay, darlin', you still really fucking turn me on.* "Your feet are spending more time on top of mine than on the floor."

"Just because I'm willing to try something that requires a little more skill. Your feet are too big, that's the problem."

She scowls but thankfully relents as I force her to relax into a boring but safe sway.

"*Darlin',*" she hisses back at me.

But the boring sway isn't as safe as I expected, and I become extremely aware of those perky tits pressing against my lower chest.

That's all it takes for my cock to stir in my tuxedo trousers.

Her core grinds softly against my crotch whenever we shift weight. Maybe it's her version of revenge for me stifling her dance moves.

"Isn't this much better?" I ask gruffly, trying to stifle the raging erection threatening.

"I suppose," she says stiffly, her cheeks burning a sexy scarlet.

I stroke the dark red jewelled necklace decorating her neck as an excuse to touch her collarbone. "Did you make this one? What's this one for?"

"It's called a Fire Agate stone. I had to work with a colour that matches the dresses." She nods in Becky's direction. "See? Becky is wearing a matching one."

I don't look at Becky.

Bonnie's mouth twitches. "Apparently, it stimulates physical energy."

Apparently, it does.

She touches my own gold chain. "You always wear this. Does it have any special meaning?"

"It was my father's." I don't consider myself sentimental, but I wear that chain pretty much everywhere.

She flinches. "I feel like I keep putting my foot in it."

"Your feet are definitely a problem right now," I tease. "You have full permission to ask me anything."

"He was from Hackney, right?"

"Yup, just off the flower market."

"And your mum's Italian?"

"Yup."

"How did they meet?"

I know why she's asking. There are legends about Dad. He's famous from beyond the grave.

I keep my face stoic. "My mum's family is Mafia. Dad worked for the Kray brothers, and they wanted to broker a deal between the Italians and the East End mob."

Her eyes widen. "So, the stories are true."

I chuckle. She's fun to play with. "That's why you need to let me lead. I'm pretty dangerous."

She purses her lips. "You're bullshitting me."

"My mum came to England. Worked as a nurse and lived in a flat with other nurses in Hackney." I grin. "Met my dad in a pub. Back then he was a bit of a looker. Like myself so you can only imagine." My grin widens. "That was enough to keep her in England. That's the story. No mafia. No mob. Just a man who met a woman and knew she was the one."

"You almost sound like a romantic."

I laugh. "Why do you sound so suspicious?"

"Just . . . nothing." She shrugs. "Can you speak Italian?"

"*Sei la donna più accattivante della stanza.*"

"What does that mean?"

"You're the most captivating woman in the room."

She makes a face. "Sounds like a well-used line. I hope you know more than the chat-up lines."

"*Sono ferito.* I'm wounded. I don't use lines." Seven billion pounds usually does the trick. "No need. I'm telling it like I see it."

She's not convinced.

Her lips match the stone around her neck. Blood red. Lips perfect for kissing. She stares up at me, lips parted in a strange blend of malevolence and innocence that could freeze the balls off a man.

What I wouldn't do to have those big blue eyes staring at me as she wraps her pouty lips around my cock.

It's imagery I could do without right now.

Thankfully, she interrupts my filthy thoughts. "Did you have something to do with the mosaic being put back up?"

"Nope," I lie. "I think my aunt saw sense."

Her expression says she doesn't believe me, but she doesn't push it. She loosens her grip on my neck and slides her hands over my shoulders to settle on my chest.

Her thumb gently brushes over my nipple ring through my white shirt.

I stifle the groan in my throat. "Darlin', you shouldn't do that," I warn her gruffly.

"Do what?"

I cock a brow. Bonnie knows exactly what she's doing.

Her fingers brush my nipple ring then rest there for a moment making my nipple harden. Then she tugs on the ring. Almost like she's annoyed with me.

Fuck.

Any harder and that will hurt.

My breath jerks. "Easy, Viking."

Everyone is watching. My workers, my aunt, my sisters, *my mum*, for God's sake. This is neither the time nor the place.

"*Viking?*"

"You're fierce. I'm afraid if I get too close those cheekbones will slice me."

"I don't know whether to take that as a compliment."

"Believe me, it is."

Her smile comes out lopsided like the two sides of her face are in conflict.

As the song fades out, Bonnie drops her hands from my chest. "Thanks for the dance, Jack." She tries to move away but I pin her with my hands.

"Wait," I say hoarsely. "I need a minute."

And she knows damn well why.

We stare at each other in a loaded silence with her body tight against my raging erection as oblivious guests fill the dance floor.

I clear my throat. "Let's go outside for a while."

Her eyes slant. "Why?"

"I want to talk to you alone."

For a second I think she's going to leave me hanging, something that hasn't happened to me in well over two decades.

"Just for a minute. Please."

Despite her mutterings, she lets me guide her in front of me to keep my exit from the dance floor PG.

"Jack, where're you off to?" My mate Tristan slaps me on the back.

"Later." I ignore his smirk and keep walking until we're outside on the patio.

"Dance with me here?" I ask as a sexy jazz song starts. I couldn't give a fuck about the rest of the crowd, but I need to feel her against me without every female member of my family watching.

She steals a cursory glance at the tent in my trousers. "*Here?*" she asks in a high pitch, looking around.

In response, I widen my stance and grab her by the waist, crushing her body against mine. "Yes, right here. Now will you be a good girl and let me lead?"

"I haven't decided," she says thickly.

It's clear she wants me. She might not say it, but her body does—her flushed cheeks, parted lips, dilated eyes. Those sexy breasts heaving up and down.

Oh, darlin', your lips might lie but the rest of your body screams the truth.

But something's holding her back. Maybe she likes to be chased.

My right hand slides lower to the grey area between lower back and ass.

She wraps her hands around my neck, and we begin to rock slowly.

"See, this isn't so bad?"

"Could be worse." She's biting her tongue. Maybe it's a self-preservation thing. "I can't believe you implied I'm a bad dancer. Kate said I was really coming along in the last lesson."

I chuckle. "Kate's a primary school teacher. That sounds like a line she uses on her students."

Those eyes, *fuck.* They stop my breath short every time they focus on me. A shade I've never seen in anyone else.

"I know a lovely jazz bar in Soho where you can throw all the short-circuiting robot moves you want. Let's grab some dinner this week then head there."

"Dinner?" she repeats in a tone that suggests she's never heard of the concept.

"Yeah. Dinner. This week."

"Like a meet and greet with the design team? Shall I get our HR to arrange it?"

Either she's torturing me, or the woman has been out of the dating scene for so long she doesn't know an attempt to date her when it hits her in the face. "I think I'm capable of arranging it myself. No, I don't want your design team to be there."

"You and me? Us two?" She eyes me as if I've suggested we round everyone up to come outside and drink the Kool-Aid.

Not quite the reaction I'm used to. "My ego's taking a bit of a beating here."

"I'm sure your ego is fed just fine, Jack."

Touché. "You're not answering my question."

"Is this to talk about the project?"

Jesus. "No. We won't be talking construction over dinner."

"So, it would be a friendly dinner?"

"No." I pull her flush to me. "Does this feel like two friends dancing?"

Her upper thigh pushes against my erection at just the right point, and I can't help but let out a low tortured groan. If she keeps on writhing against me like that, I might actually come in my pants like a pathetic boy.

I stare down at her, desperate to touch her. I run one of my hands up her rib cage and under her breast, making her breath hitch.

Her hand leaves my neck and runs down my chest. She tugs on my nipple ring again triggering my hands to travel south to cup her sexy ass so possessively that her feet lift slightly off the ground.

I can tell she's wearing those large spandex pants. Probably best, a thong would have tipped me over the edge.

We are both really fucking horny, shifting from side to side pretending to dance when we're dry humping in our clothes.

"Bonnie," I prompt hoarsely. "Is that a yes?"

"I'm busy for the rest of the year," she deadpans, except it comes out breathy. She's fucking with me. I think. Little does she know her feistiness is my aphrodisiac. "Besides, haven't you forgotten you're already on a date? Lining up a date on a date isn't cool, you know."

"Who? Michelle? She's not my date. She asked if she could come with me. She wanted to see Sean get married."

Still, she eyes me sceptically. "I didn't think I'm your type. I'm surprised you're even interested."

I pull back slightly so I can properly look at her. "Does it feel like I'm not interested?"

"That's because I've had four hours of professional help getting ready today. I don't look like this every day."

"Really?" I grin. "You don't usually look as if you've been in a fight? It's not going to work in that case."

She slaps my chest, but I tighten my grip on her.

"I'm aware of what you look like when you're not playing bridesmaid," I say seriously. "If you want to turn up in those tight yoga pants, be my guest. Believe me, there is nothing you could wear that could make me any less attracted to you."

"*Oh*." She bites down on her lip. "You're very sure of yourself, Jack Knight."

I shrug. "I know you're attracted to me, too."

This does not go down well. Her scowl is so fierce she looks constipated.

"You made that obvious when you watched me in the bathroom."

The bright Viking eyes widen in horror. "You saw me."

I chuckle. "That's how mirrors work, Bonnie."

"But you acted like you didn't see me."

"Did I?"

She groans. "Oh, my God, I'm so embarrassed."

"Don't be. I'm happy to give you a repeat show any time." I wink. I just can't help myself. "Don't worry, it's not as intimidating as it looks."

Her jaw drops. "Were you always this arrogant or was it the biography that did it?"

My lips twitch. "So, you've read it?"

"I don't need to read it—your life is splashed over the tabloids." She rolls her eyes. "For my clarification . . . you're talking about an actual *date*?"

I've never been cross-questioned this much when asking a woman out. "Yes, Bonnie. A date. Me and you."

Excitement flashes across her face then it's gone.

Someone clears their throat from behind me.

Bonnie jumps away from me as if I'm contagious.

I turn to see Damon, a guy that Sean and I went to school with, watching us in amusement. Michelle Allard, the face of my hotels, appears behind him.

She stops short when she sees Bonnie with me. "I've been looking everywhere for you, Jack." Her eyes narrow. "What's going on here?"

Damon smiles condescendingly. "I think that's obvious."

"Nothing," I reply coldly. Damon Manning is the last person I need to know my business. "Bonnie and I were having a chat."

"You're needed inside," Michelle says coolly. "I said I would find you." She eyes Bonnie. "And now I have."

I sigh and turn back to Bonnie, leaning in so only she can hear. "Dinner. This week. I'll message you so you have my number."

As I turn, I swear she curses at me under her breath, which only makes me chuckle.

It's not often I have to play a game of cat and mouse, but if Bonnie wants to play . . .

Game on.

10

Jack

In the darkness, I stare at the silhouette of the giant mounted moose head above the bed. Say what you want about my high-end hotel chain, but no one ever adds "nice moose head" in reviews. Sean's mum railroaded them into getting married in the castle.

The goddamn grandfather clock in the hallway makes sure I know what time it is. The chime sequence sounds on the hour. There goes another hour of missed sleep: three a.m. Can Bonnie hear it? It's right outside her room.

This castle is fucking noisy. Everything is moving and creaking.

I'll never sleep. Not when my dick is painfully hard as I'm thinking of all the filthy things I'm going to do to Bonnie Casey when she finally stops resisting our insane chemistry.

A never-ending list.

It's taken every ounce of willpower not to stride into her room, climb on top of her, and spend all night with my face buried between her legs.

Instead, I said goodnight with a kiss on the cheek like a well-behaved boy.

All the best things come to those who wait.

I watched her all night, and she knew it. I barely got to talk to her, but my attention was always on her.

She liked it. Hell, she *craved* it.

An unspoken game between us.

She's so damn *feisty*. Everything she says has a bite to it. And that look she gives me could whither a man's cock off.

I watched her read my text message; blush viciously then ignore it. I'm not surprised. She can protest all she likes, but she started something when she watched me in the bathroom and there's no turning back.

Sighing, I pull back the covers and grab a pair of boxers.

I pad out into the hallway as my eyes adjust to the darkness. There are soft drinks in the central kitchen, and I need the sugar hit more than water. I'm at the age where my hangovers begin before I go to bed, not the morning after.

I need to leave early tomorrow to get to the Waterloo site. Tristan promised we'd be out of here by eight.

A sound stops me in my tracks.

Soft whimpering.

Bonnie's room.

Is she having a nightmare? Is she crying?

I stop outside her door, trying to focus.

Damn, she's definitely crying. What do I do in this situation? I can't leave her crying, but I'm not sure if Bonnie would consider me a friend.

Knocking softly, I push open the door by a few inches.

If I were a man who believed in ghosts, I might think she's been possessed by some demon haunting the manor. The blankets have been thrown off her. She lies in the middle of the four-poster bed like a sexy apparition, her back arched, her eyes scrunched up, and her beautiful heart-shaped face contorted like someone is pumping a funnel of vinegar down her throat.

I'm half expecting her to start levitating until my eyes travel downwards and I jump out of my skin.

The fuck?

A soft moan escapes her, and my heart nearly crashes out of my chest.

I need to get the hell out of here, but I'm frozen. The only thing capable of movement is the blood frantically rushing south.

I stare, transfixed, as her fingers hammer her beautiful pink cunt like her life depends on it while her other hand fists the sheets.

She bites down on her bottom lip, stifling another moan.

Oh, Christ.

She's drenched. Completely fucking drenched.

I suppress a groan raging in my throat coming directly from my cock.

Her top has bunnies, which doesn't really fit the scene, but she's naked from the waist down.

Just when I think my eyes can't take anymore, she widens her legs, showing me every fold of flesh. Her fingers spread open her wetness, rubbing at her clit. God, I need to know what that wetness tastes like.

My cock strains like a racehorse.

She might be the worst dancer I've ever witnessed, but she excels at the art of self-pleasure. It's a performance that could reach a global scale.

Except it's not a performance. This is a massive invasion of her privacy, making me a monster. I shouldn't be watching.

But I can't tear my eyes away from the sexy blonde Viking.

I suck in a sharp breath.

She's close. She's even fucking sweating.

Those whimpers.

I could come here in my boxers listening to her breathless little jerky moans even without the visuals.

She's got headphones on. What's she listening to?

What will she do if those pale blue eyes open? Hate me forever and never speak to me again?

Or invite me to join in?

My dick pulses, begging for an invitation to the party.

A low sound erupts from my throat. She doesn't hear me. What the hell is she listening to?

Every part of her body is shaking. Her toes, her legs, her belly. Her head jerks violently backwards and her toes scrunch up in the bed as she rubs herself towards climax.

Closing the door as gently as my shaking hands will let me, I stand in the darkness of the hallway, with more wood than the Amazon.

I'm breathing like I've run a marathon.

Is she thinking about me? Max? Maybe someone else entirely.

"Jack?"

I look up in the dim hallway to see Kate's sister, Becky.

She flicks the light on her phone, pointing it at me. "Where are you . . ." Her jaw drops as she focuses the light downwards.

I glance down, dazed. Fuck, my dick is so hard it's pushing through the slit in my boxers, giving her an eyeful. There's no point trying to pretend it's not there.

I rearrange myself and try to compose myself, which is pointless.

"Becky," I address her through clenched teeth.

A red satin night set accentuates her pert breasts.

The light flashes between my face and my dick as if she's unsure which to focus on.

"Do you want company?" She seems to be asking my dick. "I can't sleep either."

"I'm going to get a soft drink," I mutter. Now I need something much stronger.

Becky blinks a few times, chewing on her lips. "*Okaaay.*" The look on her face tells me she's not going to let me escape that easily. "You look . . . stressed . . . like you need help relaxing. We can go chill out in the living room for a while."

"I'm fine," I snap in a ragged voice. Change of plan, I need to get back to my room and have a freezing cold shower.

She sucks in a breath. "You don't look fine."

My cock rages in agreement with her.

I glance in the direction of Bonnie's room. I hope to God she doesn't hear us out here.

"Good night, Becky," I growl unnecessarily, and turn back in the direction of my room with one very angry, unsatisfied cock.

11

Bonnie

What the hell is wrong with me?

Jack Knight-triggered oxytocin has been pumping through my body *all night*, leaving me a hot mess. And that's with a stuffed moose head watching me.

The guy looks, smells, and dances like sex. I didn't stand a freakin' chance. After the dance, a million women fangirled him all night, Max being the ringleader.

That dance. Holy fucking shit.

He was *hard*.

The guy practically humped my silk bridesmaid dress on the lawn . . . and I let him.

I can't figure out if I'm happy that I had the chance to knock Mr. Big Dick down a peg or two, or because the possibility of angry sex might be on the cards—not that I would *ever* go there.

But it's a fantasy for the Bean Bag.

Besides, Max encouraged me to network. I'm only doing what I'm told.

The breakfast room is the stereotypical aftermath of a British wedding, everyone that looked fabulous last night looks slightly worse for wear today.

Tans are patchy, makeup is still half on, eyes are reduced to slits, rogue pins are sticking out of slept-in updos, and there is a general demeanour of dehydration.

Voices that were roaring last night dull to an idle murmur as they mull over the breakfast buffet, trying to decide whether it'll make them feel better or worse.

Nisha mumbles incoherently beside me. I banged down her door this morning to get her out of bed.

"Huh?" I ask, distracted, scanning the room for six-foot-something monsters with topknots and ten tons of muscle.

"I feel horrid." Nisha groans. "I can't look at that fry-up. Why did you let me drink so much last night?"

"Last time I checked the bridesmaid manual, it didn't mention keeping guests from overindulging."

He's not here. I don't know whether I'm relieved or disappointed.

"I'm not drinking ever again," she says firmly as we meander around the buffet. "Okay, at least until Christmas." She looks at me crossly. "I mean it this time."

"I'm not doubting you."

She lifts a lid, sees it's black pudding and makes a retching sound, closing it quickly. "Why are you so cheery this morning? Aren't you tired?"

"I'm exhausted," I mutter. "Go get us a seat, Nisha. I'm going to pop to the loo."

She sighs and moves towards empty seats.

"Not there," I hiss as Nisha veers towards Kate's creepy uncle, Dom.

I turn towards the main hallway where the bathrooms are, after giving the room a final once-over.

Maybe Jack's left already. He mentioned he's getting a lift in Tristan Kane's helicopter. Talk about upstaging the bride, who arrives in a friggin' chopper?

"The other bridesmaid is a bit of all right, isn't she? That Bunny."

What?

I freeze, trying to connect the bodiless voice to a face from last night.

Me?

"What's going on between you two?" the same male voice around the corner asks.

A knot of anxiety tightens in my belly.

The guy I can't identify must be talking to Max about me. Why does eavesdropping on Max talking about our relationship freak me out after all these months? Maybe I don't want to hear from the horse's mouth how well he's coping without me.

I lean against the wall and take out my phone to pretend to read.

"Absolutely nothing, mate."

My head jerks at the sound of the low gravelly cockney voice. Jack.

Someone is asking *Jack* about me?

There's a pause. "You two looked a little cosy."

"Nope." Jack's tone makes my stomach lurch. Cold as ice. All the warmth he had last night is gone. "Definitely nothing of interest going on there."

The other guy chuckles. "I guess Michelle Allard is more your type, lucky bastard."

Another pause, and my pulse quickens.

"Michelle Allard is everyone's type," Jack says dryly.

My cheeks flame with heat. Wanker.

Obviously, I agree, but hearing it from his mouth crushes me more than it should. I shouldn't even care.

"She hasn't got a set of pipes on her like Michelle, but Bunny polishes up good enough."

I tug at my bra strap, annoyed. Who is this guy?

"Careful," Jack says, his voice more strained. "Watch your manners. Bonnie is . . . a friend of Sean and Kate's."

Huh. I'm only mildly appeased. It's not exactly a knight-in-shining-armour response.

"Mind if I get her number?"

Another pause.

"Knock yourself out," Jack replies in a level tone. "No reason for me to mind."

"So? Do you have it?"

More silence.

"Thanks."

Thanks? THANKS?

He did *not* give some random guy my number.

My chest tightens as I back away from the corner. So, Michelle Allard is more his type?

Him and his big dick and his *darlins.*

Stupid, stupid, stupid, Bonnie, says the annoying voice of reason in my head. Billionaires get more attention than babies and bunnies. I witnessed that myself last night. *What did you expect?*

Father Donaghy would say this is karma for disrespecting his God's house yesterday.

I can't believe I even entertained for a tiny slither of a moment the notion of maybe, just maybe, sharing some food with Jack Knight for an hour. All for networking purposes, of course.

I've been a fool, but I've learned my lesson.

After a ten-minute pep talk in the bathroom to pull myself together, I make my way back to the breakfast area.

Kate waves me over.

I'm irrationally annoyed. It's probably the champagne after-effects and the low you get after hitting it too hard, that's all.

"Hi, *Mrs. Knight.*" I beam at Kate as she pulls me in for a massive hug.

"Mrs. Knight," she repeats, squealing. "Mrs. Knight! Jesus, I'll look around for Sean's mum every time someone calls me that. Thank you for yesterday, honey. You were on your feet all day. I think you must have taken me to the bathroom five times last night."

"Don't worry. I hope you enjoyed your day?"

She thinks about it. "You know, I really did in the end. I mean, I wouldn't rush out to do it again and I'm *really* glad it's over, but waking up beside my husband this morning..." Her grin fades and she squeezes my arm. "I'm sorry, Bonnie. Are *you* okay? I know you put on a brave face, but it's such a hard thing to go through given the circumstances."

Huh. This is the first time I'm upset about something other than my split in months.

All thanks to Mr. Big Dick. Maybe he did me and my not-as-good-as-Michelle-Allard pipes a favour.

"I had a brilliant time." I smile. "Kate, do you mind if we head off? Nisha's in a bad way. Also, Bradshaw is doing an important piece of work for Lexington, so I should get at it today, or the week will be a nightmare." *And I need to get the hell out of here before the Lexington CEO appears.*

"Speak of the devil." She grins over my shoulder. "Jack, you bad man. Is your company working Bonnie too hard?"

I turn, horror rising slowly, to see Jack and Michelle Allard behind me.

Jack is back in casual clothes but still looks as deadly as in the tux, if a little more tired in a grey tee and jeans.

Michelle grips his forearm possessively, looking bored. He stiffens but doesn't remove her arm.

Unlike the rest of us, her skin glows as if an invisible team of lighting technicians is following her around, illuminating her with soft white light.

"Morning." Jack turns his attention to me. His dark eyes burn a trail up my body. "What's this about?"

"Bonnie's gruelling deadline for Lexington," Kate pipes up, poking Jack's abs.

If only I had duct tape handy.

His brows rise.

"Kate's only joking," I hiss, telepathically telling her to shut the fuck up. Max will bloody well flip if he hears about this.

Michelle looks at me suspiciously as her arm tightens around Jack's. "I know you. The other bridesmaid. From the lawn."

I look between Jack and Michelle. He shifts his hand into his back pocket, forcing her arm to drop.

Not a date, my arse. Michelle is clinging to his side like a bodyguard.

"That's me. The other bridesmaid," I reply stiffly.

"This is Bonnie, Michelle," Jack corrects her.

Michelle and I never really spoke last night, so there's no need for awkward hugging. "Lovely to meet you, Michelle."

I give Kate a quick hug and then turn to Jack and Michelle.

"Jack." I pull my lips back from my teeth in an attempt to smile. "I look forward to working on the *Motor Works* factory for Lexington."

Before he can respond, I turn on my heels and grab Nisha.

"Aren't you going to have any breakfast?" she asks, as I march us out the door.

"Nope. Not hungry."

"I know I wanted us to leave quickly, but slow down a bit," she grumbles as I jog towards the car, dragging her along as if we've stolen half the castle's valuables. "Hey, when you were talking to Kate in the breakfast room, I saw the tech tycoon Danny Walker eying you up. I repeat *Danny Walker.*"

"What?" I scoff. "Isn't he with the hotshot lawyer Tristan Kane's sister? Wise up, Nisha."

"I mean it, he looked interested. He kept looking over." She pants, trying to meet my stride. "Hold up, woman. I'm not training for a marathon, and I had a skinful last night."

I slow down a fraction. "They have young kids."

"These rich guys have their baby mamas and women on the side. I didn't say you should *go* there."

The car beeps open as I point the key fob at it. Heavy footsteps churn the gravel behind us.

Oh, shit.

Just as I pull the car door open an inch, a hand covers mine and a deep voice says, "Wait."

I tilt my head over my shoulder, my pulse quickening. My back is against the chest of the guy I'm running from.

Jack leans forward, his breath hot on the nape of my neck. "Somebody's eager to get away. Where's the fire?"

His hand is still on mine, caging me between the car and him. I've never seen Nisha move so quickly as she leaps into the passenger's seat.

I turn to face Jack, backing towards the car. "I want to beat the traffic," I reply in a level tone.

"It feels like you're running away from something." He towers over me, cocky grin in place. "I'll see you for dinner this week. Does Tuesday work?"

Arrogant ass. I never actually said yes to the date. And apparently, I'm interesting enough to spend a Tuesday with, while the Michelle Allards of the world—everyone's type—get him on a weekend.

Be cool.

Big client. Most interesting project ever. Senior architect title. Get the fuck out of Bradshaw Brown.

Leave your emotions out of it.

"Sorry, busy Tuesday," I say more bluntly than I intended.

"Wednesday."

"Perhaps the team and I could arrange a working lunch?" I smile helpfully. "We can do it in Canary Wharf, near the office. I'll talk to your PA. I'm sure the partners and Max would love to attend."

His forehead creases. "We're back to playing this game? Okay, next Friday or Saturday night if you're busy during the week."

"I can't do next weekend," I reply flatly.

His eyes narrow a fraction. "What are you doing that's making you so busy?"

I'll be answering my phone to all the guys you pimped me out to.

"Running. I've got a really intense training schedule for the marathon over the next few weeks."

"Okay. No dinner. We can run together to not interrupt your schedule. I can come to your area."

"I can't focus when I'm running with other people. Perhaps best to leave it."

His dark eyes burn into mine in silence for a heated moment. "That must make your running club awkward."

Shit. I forgot I told him that.

"Fine," he says in a measured tone, a slight tic in his jaw. "I guess I misread everything."

He goes to walk away, then turns abruptly.

"What was last night? You were flirting with me. If you're not interested, why?"

Feeling cornered, I go on the defence. "I'm a bridesmaid— we're supposed to be nice to the guests. Maybe I wanted to make the other groomsmen jealous," I blurt out.

His eyes blaze. I get flashbacks from the hot tub of when he fired the poor guys.

"I see," he growls. "You did a fantastic job. Very realistic." He turns then stops again. "By the way, Danny is not remotely interested in you, so get that out of your damn head."

Mouth hanging open, I watch him storm off before letting me respond. Jerk!

"Bonnie," a small voice calls from inside the car. "Get in."

I pull open the door to the driver's side and slump into the seat. "Did you hear all that?"

"Yup, although I must have heard it wrong because it sounded like you were blowing Jack Knight off. What the hell?"

I'm too tired to give her blow-by-blow details. "He asked me out last night when we were dancing. This morning I overheard him talking to some other guy about how he wasn't interested in me, and then he gave the other guy my *number.*"

"He asked you out?" she shrieks. "Holy shitballs."

"So?" I scowl. "Didn't you hear the rest of the story?"

She waggles her brows. "He wants to share you with another guy. Maybe you could form your own harem."

I roll my eyes.

"Why on earth did you imply you were making Max jealous?"

"I got flustered." I exhale. "He thinks he's God's gift. I suppose I want to bring him down a peg or two. And . . ." I pause. "Maybe it's partially true."

"When he said the comment about Danny Walker, it looked like you could cook bacon off your face."

"Great," I mutter dryly.

"Did you flirt with him?"

I wince. "I may have *rubbed up* a little against him. It's not the best networking strategy I've ever had. But I'm only human and *look at him*, for Christ's sake."

"But you hate the guy."

"I don't *hate* the guy," I say sullenly. "I just think he's a ruthless bastard."

"And you're still attracted to him?"

"I'm sexually attracted to him. Some inmates are attractive too, you know. They get really buff in prison. Doesn't mean they're good people."

She nods. "I'd like to have sex with Darren, and he disgusts me. He's a real hottie to look at, but it's kind of unsexy when the guy is bad at his job."

I get it. In my first year at Bradshaw, watching Max work was sexy. Max is a great architect. But she's right, Darren is the laziest guy at Bradshaw Brown.

She smiles slyly. "But Jack, he seems pretty good at his job. He's not doing too bad for himself, is he? Must be doing something right for seven billion pounds."

"I suppose." I sniff, not accepting her bait. "Right, let's get the show on the road."

"Bonnie, by the way . . ." She pauses. "I heard Becky talking about getting Jack's number. So maybe you should forget it."

That gets a snort. "Come on, Nisha, as if I thought anything would actually happen."

She doesn't look convinced.

So, I really am just *the other bridesmaid*.

"He called me a Viking."

"A *Viking?* Like a big angry hairy ginger man?"

"Exactly." I tut. "The guy's a dick."

She hums in agreement.

"When did, uh, Becky tell you she got his number?" I ask casually.

"When you left me at breakfast this morning. She told the funniest story. She said she met him wandering the hall at three a.m. She thought he was sleepwalking or drunk because he looked dazed. Then she noticed he had a raging hard-on the size of a tree."

"What?" I turn my head to look at her. "They hooked up?"

"Apparently not. He said he was getting something to drink and went back to his room."

"The guy was just walking the halls of the castle, *hard*? How messed up is that?" I slump in my seat, secretly relieved. "But he asked for her number?"

"She got his number this morning. Sorry, I didn't ask for the details."

Sounds like Jack is giving out numbers left, right, and centre.

She studies me. "You know who Jack Knight is. And as much as I want you to get back in the dating game, it's probably not the most strategic move—shitting on your own construction site."

"Don't be silly." I scoff, starting up the engine. "I know the score. Now let's get the hell out of here."

Yes, I know who Jack "Big Dick" Knight is.

Men like him get pissed when their pawns don't move around the board as they order. What they forget is that if a pawn moves fast enough, she becomes a queen.

12

Jack

"Doesn't this thing go any bloody faster?" I snap through the headset. My mate Tristan is flying Danny and me back to London in his helicopter from the wedding venue. Like children, we called dibs on the front seat, and I won.

I'm too tired to enjoy the English countryside below us. I've had two hours of sleep max, staring up at the ceiling all night imagining all the sordid acts I want to carry out on the angry Viking. Fantasising about every inch of her body. Thighs, wrists, neck, stomach, cheekbones, lips, eyes, even her damn ears when she blushes.

It took every ounce of willpower to close her door last night before she lost control.

How's a man supposed to sleep after that?

The thirty-minute cold shower this morning did sweet FA.

Now my balls are so blue, I'm surprised the chopper can take the extra load.

"No, princess." Tristan chuckles through my headset. "A hundred and fifty miles per hour is the fastest I'm going to be able to deliver you into London. You want me to let you out and see if you can find a faster route?"

"What the hell is wrong with you?" my other mate Danny asks from the back. "You look rough as fuck. We were in bed at midnight last night. That's pretty tame."

Tame?

Tame is not a word I would use for last night.

Teasing. Torturous.

Cock draining. Those fit.

I grunt in response.

"Relax, man. What's the rush?" Tristan asks. "We're not playing golf until four."

Shit, I forgot.

"I can't today." I sigh. "I have to visit the site."

"Fuck off, mate," Danny growls through the headset. "I got a pass for us to play golf. You are not letting me down. Do you know how difficult it is to leave the house with three kids under three?"

Of course I don't.

"Sorry, I forgot, man." I turn to him sheepishly. "I've no time for anything right now. There aren't enough hours in the day."

"You used to be the fun one of the three of us," Tristan says dryly. "What the hell happened? You know you're basically the annoying boss that interferes with everything, right?"

I grunt. "Stop busting my balls. They've had enough this weekend. You know this project is personal. It's not just erecting nice digs for rich ex-pats."

Tristan glances over at me. "Are you sure you should be so close to this project? You've been around the block enough to know emotions and business don't mix well. Let Sean take care of it. He knows how important the area is to you."

"Not gonna happen." I clench my teeth. "This one stays with me."

"Sure," Tristan says, dropping it. "How's it going?"

"Good. Phase one block of apartments is nearly complete. We're ready to rehouse the existing residents."

Tristan darts a glance at me again. "And that includes some of the Wicks family, right?"

"Don't worry, I won't build a gas leak into their flats. Even if they are murdering bastards," I say with a calmness learned over the years. It would be nice to forget about my dad's killers for one day. "Phase two and Phase three are kicking off. I've given phase three, the *Motor Works* factory, to Max and Bonnie's company to design."

Danny chuckles. "Such a shame Bonnie and Max have split up, isn't it? He's got a bit of a stick up his ass. Good thing you've stepped up to console her. She seems nice."

"Don't fucking talk," I snap. "The woman gives me whiplash. One minute she's grinding against me, then the next minute she's acting like I'm the worst man alive."

They laugh. I'm too tired for it.

I turn to scowl at Danny in the backseat. "Bonnie thought *you* were interested in her. Well, her friend did."

"Everyone was watching you two dancing, if that's what she's thinking. Me included." He chuckles, sprawled out in the back. "It was quite entertaining."

"Sparks were definitely flying during that dance," Tristan says. "What did you do wrong?"

"Nothing. I was an angel. I asked her out on a date like a gentleman. She got me all warmed up like a professional fluffer then this morning turned me down, said she was trying to make her ex jealous. She played me."

Tristan smirks. "I'll notify Guinness World Records immediately. This is a big one for them."

"Perhaps we should drop you off at the hospital?" Danny adds. "Before you go into acute shock at being rejected for the first time in your life."

The pair of them are two smug ass-wipes now they're all loved-up. Both are older than me by a few years, as they like to remind me. Jealousy.

"Fine, let me off at the hospital," I mutter. "Maybe they can do something about my big blue balls."

"Mate, when you have twins under two and a newborn at home, you can complain. You and that dog of yours sit around answering to no one," Danny grumbles. "And I'm sorry, Tristan, I know she's your mother, but fuck me, I'm dying here. I don't get a minute's peace. I think she's moved in and not told me. The easiest solution is for me to move out."

Tristan laughs. "Rather you than me. Mum's posting pics from your house every day."

"Fuck's sake. I don't want my life splashed over social media. It's a bloody security risk. I'll need to rein that shit in and try to teach your mother about her digital footprint."

"This is why I'm not having kids until at least forty," I grumble. Danny is engaged to and has three baby daughters with Tristan's younger sister, Charlie. The couple started seeing each other when Danny's tech firm, now the largest in Europe, acquired the company Charlie worked for.

Tristan laughs again. "You do realise that's only two years away, right?"

"Better make it forty-five then."

"You'll change your mind when you meet the right lass," Tristan tells me. "Maybe you already have."

"Nah," Danny says. "She's not interested. Poor wee Jack will have to put his tail back between his legs."

The helicopter drops slightly. Tristan doesn't flinch but I do. "When have you ever seen me give up on a challenge? The woman wants me. There's just something holding her back. Maybe her ex, Max. Maybe she's terrified of my massive dick."

"Maybe she's more terrified of your massive ego," Danny scoffs.

"I have an ego for a reason, mate."

And Bonnie is going to realise that very soon.

Truth is, I haven't been rejected before, and I kind of like it.

She can keep playing this game of cat and mouse. I like the chase. It makes the catch all the sweeter.

It's only a matter of time, darlin'.

13

Bonnie

I throw my overnight bag onto the floor. "Alexa, turn on the telly."

I'm convinced couples stay together in London because it's too expensive to live alone.

Max and I had a lovely two-bedroom garden flat just off Clapham, South London. It had enough outdoor space for a potato patch and a small barbecue. I only have a handful of friends anyway.

I thought we would upsize to an actual house. Instead, I've downsized to a one-bedroom flat the size of a prison cell above a fried chicken shop.

When you first walk in, it's confusing whether you're in the living room or kitchen, then you realise it's both. Though with the kettle within spitting distance of the sofa, it's convenient for making tea.

Moving day was stressful. It wasn't just because I stuffed a moving van full of things I never use—tennis rackets, dumbbells, obscure kitchenware, unopened cookbooks—but also because after years of sleeping beside the same man, I was solo.

Kate called a state of emergency and stayed over for the first few nights. I can't remember too much about them. I sat round in a daze weeping and staring at my phone like I was hypnotised, whilst she made me food. Waiting for Max to realise the error of his ways, apologise for his rash words, and revoke his ridiculous decision.

But the phone never rang, and Kate couldn't stay forever.

For the first month, the loneliness was difficult. I was on autopilot, as unsettled inside the flat as outside.

Dad actually asked me to move in with him. I couldn't but it broke my heart to break his heart.

Breaking up with Max left a big hole in my schedule. Breakfasts eaten alone. Evenings alone. Weekends were the worst, Sunday mornings especially. I arranged lunches, dinners, drinks, and walks with friends but still couldn't fill all the hours.

Being with Max was all I knew for so long that I forgot how to just be with *me*.

Then after a few months, I began to appreciate the positives of solo living. No one to snuggle with but no snoring in my ear either, and I didn't have to listen to that constant clearing of Max's throat that made me want to choke him in his sleep. The toilet seat remains down permanently. I can do whatever the fuck I like within these walls without judgement.

I pee with the bathroom door open, listening to my reverse harem audiobooks. Volume hitched as high as it will go. I pig out on takeaways in large pants and watch *365 Days* on repeat getting unreasonably emotional. It's strangely liberating.

I need new hobbies.

My phone buzzes.

Nisha: Have you set it up yet?

Me: Give me a minute.

I only dropped her off thirty minutes ago, and she's already nagging me about my dating profile. We agreed in the car that I need to cast my net much wider, i.e. men I've never met before.

I should really go straight to sleep. I have to pack two days of work effort into one tomorrow.

Except Nisha said it would only take five minutes to set up a profile. I might as well have a quick look. See what the pool is like.

The belly flutters over Jack Knight might have been misplaced, but they gave me hope that I could put myself out there again. Finding out that Max is dating again came at me from out of left field. When we were both in a weird limbo, not with each other but not moving forward, I was okay. Now, Max has stirred everything up.

But I can't let a few bad cocks skewer my judgement of dating.

The first part of filling out the profile is easy. Almost feels like applying for a passport.

What do I say about myself?

Who am I?

Bonnie. 28. Architect. Runner.

Is that it? Is that the culmination of me? Do I have GSOH?

Oh! I make my own jewellery. Though, I'm not sure if that's going to be a good hook to reel in the blokes.

Bonnie. 28. Architect. Runner. I listen to smutty audio books while relaxing on the toilet. Sometimes I text from there too. Occasionally I eat dinner directly from the saucepan. My phone is full of hundreds of selfies of me sitting on the sofa, just because. I'm in desperate need of a sex life that involves warm living penis. Maybe plural.

Nope, nobody needs to know the truth.

All my photos are with Max or the girls. I find one photo of me on my own where I look half decent.

Easy. Now I'm into the catalogue.

How far should I cast the net? I'll stick to the London zones. That should be a few million single guys to work with.

What am I looking for?

Sensitive, emotionally mature, intelligent man to build new hobbies with. Good head on his shoulders.

Fuck that.

Arrogant, half-Italian, half-Cockney alpha who looks like dirty sex and thinks he rules the world.

Tattoos.

Nipple ring.

Dark hair in topknot.

Permanent grin that you want to wipe off his face.

Excessively overgrown penis.

Reminds me of alpha wolf Caleb from *the Red Moon Canines*.

Abort.

I'll just do some window shopping.

Oh, hello, Barry.

Jim's not bad on the eyes, either.

Nope.

Nope.

Nope.

Sam says he's the best catch in London. These claims should be validated with a blue tick as they do for celebrity profiles.

Hello, Officer Nigel!

Maybe.

Dear Lord, Jordan with the hot abs is a pilot. Some guys definitely get more sex because of their job.

So many options.

Jerome doesn't want to go out with any Labour Party supporters. I haven't decided how I'm going to vote this year.

God, this is fun. How many have I swiped?

NINETY MINUTES.

This is an addictive game.

Not a game. It's a sport. My eyeballs are hanging out of my head, and adrenaline is pumping through me like a current.

I'm never building new hobbies at this rate.

I bet there's a diagnosed addiction now for swiping.

In a year's time, I'll be standing in a room with a twitchy finger announcing, "Hello, my name's Bonnie, and I'm a serial swiper."

I must ask Nisha how many swipes per day are too many. Maybe I'll run out of swipes before I can become addicted.

Although, London's a big place, and if I run out, I can widen my catchment area to Kent and the home counties.

I transition from sofa to bed, still swiping on my walk.

Nope.

Maybe.

My finger stops abruptly.

Nice.

Christopher. Six-foot-four. Nice manly face. Gorgeous eyes. Recruitment manager, not a layabout. Pictures seem normal enough. No dick pics. Oh, he looks good in a suit. He looks like he could be Spanish or Italian. Annoyingly slightly like Jack Knight . . . I'll click for some of this.

I swipe right to connect.

And . . . we match immediately.

Oh my God, Christopher loves me. This is way better than my therapy, and it's free!

The instant gratification . . . oh my.

Our future flashes before my eyes. Our kids are going to be gorgeous. Christopher is originally from Wales, so he'll have a lovely accent. Not that gruff cockney tone.

I'm not sure if I'd want to settle down in Wales if it comes to it, but I would be willing to negotiate.

Maybe Christopher has a pierced nipple and a big dick.

Bonnie and Christopher. Bonnifer! It really is meant to be.

I'm a freak.

I'll wait to see if he messages first. I'm sure that's the rule. Nisha can help me with the responses.

Time to gain willpower and close the app. I need to cut this shit out. I'm going cross-eyed from the radiation emanating from my phone.

My fingers hover over the browser button.

Except . . . I'm a glutton for punishment.

I type in *Jack Knight* and click news.

What I'm expecting to do with the information I find, who the fuck knows? I appear to have branched out in my stalking.

Jack Knight made me feel like shit. *Definitely nothing of interest going on there.*

There's been no new news in the past few hours. Literally hours after the wedding, pictures of Jack and Michelle Allard at the wedding made their way into clickbait. Kate's gutted she's not in them.

I click on more images of him.

What the—

It takes me a second to realise the naked man with a massive boner is Jack's face juxtaposed onto someone else's body. I know better. That's not the same dick I saw a few days ago.

I *really* need to have my delayed rebound. Tomorrow I'll strike up a conversation with Christopher.

Then there are the women with him. So many women. In bars, nightclubs, theatres, beaches, water, strip clubs. East End. West End. Miami. Los Angeles. Berlin. Sydney. Even Vatican City.

I type one more thing into the search bar. *Archie Knight East End murder.*

I remember the night he died. We were used to hearing sirens around our way, but when three helicopters appeared above, we knew something big was up. When it came to the Wicks mob, the police brought out the big guns.

Word spread from house to house like wildfire.

Father of local big shot Jack Knight had bled out, his death caused by Donnie Wicks. Although it seemed they never managed to make it stick to Donnie.

The pictures of the funeral are hard to stomach. Jack's haunted dark eyes bore into me from the screen.

Grief dominates his handsome features. Raw, intense sorrow that I can't relate to because I've never lost anyone close to me.

I can't look at this anymore.

I click play on my audiobook, snuggling under the covers. It's time for Stella to play with the four brothers of the mountains.

14

Bonnie

It's official. I've been surfing the online dating wave for four nights, and it's already bleeding into my offline life.

I have fifty-two matches, all hot leads. At this rate, I'll need CRM software to manage all the conversations.

Today, his highness is going to meet us to discuss his vision for the *Motor Works* factory, and I'm absolutely exhausted with swiping fatigue. I'm also a bit anxious about the awkward way Jack and I left things after the wedding.

I sip my coffee, sifting through emails, when a meeting invite pops up from Max.

Catch-up 09:15 Happy Bean Cafe

Strange. His meetings are usually anally scripted. Even for a quick catch-up, he'll bullet point his agenda.

And we rarely do them outside the office.

"I'm away to give Darren a kicking," Nisha says, getting up from her desk. "I'll meet you back here to walk over to the Lexington office at ten, okay?"

I nod, getting my coat. The meeting with Jack Knight isn't until ten thirty, but since it's on one of the top floors of London's version of a skyscraper and we have to get through security, we need to go early. "See you at ten. I'm popping out to meet Max first."

"Wait up!" she calls from the opposite direction. "Why do you have your Facebook status set to Jack Knight?"

"Huh?" I wrinkle my nose. "What are you on about?"

She strides back and shows me her phone with Facebook open.

I do a double take, clamping my hand over my mouth.

No. Shit the bed.

"I haven't," I whisper.

"You have, you fool. Hurry up and remove it."

All the air leaves my windpipe. I must have set it last night.

"Were you creeping over Jack Knight, naughty girl? Bit strange for someone who claims to dislike him so much."

"Oh, God, it's been like that all freakin' night," I whimper, jabbing my phone code in.

I might cry.

"Calm your tits. I only just saw the notification that 'Bonnie is feeling Jack Knight.'"

"This is horrendous." I quiver as the damn status is finally wiped. "I've been feeling Jack Knight all night."

"I wouldn't worry. Your profile is boring. No one will look at it."

"Gee, thanks, even my fake life is boring."

"This is why I need to supervise your online dating."

I screw up my face again.

What a start to the day. This is a bad omen. I knew I should have worn my black obsidian crystals—the stone of protection.

***

Max is waiting in the back corner of the Happy Bean Cafe, a cafe full of stressed bankers and executives psyching themselves up to join the Canary Wharf rat race.

"Morning!" I take a seat opposite him. "It's dark here. You know there are seats out front beside the window?"

He shrugs and runs his hands through his hair. "It's quieter here. How are you?"

"Can't complain for a Thursday. You?"

"Yeah, not too bad. Not bad." He leans forward, putting his hands in the prayer position on the table. "Did you have a good time at the wedding?"

"Great time, you?" I respond, confused by the small talk.

"Fantastic. Really good day." He keeps smiling at me, and I smile back, unnerved.

Oh, shit.

Of course, it's obvious what Max wants.

"Max, the status has been cleared," I say in a rush. "I was doing investigative Facebooking for the project when I accidentally set Jack Knight's name as my status."

"Status?" He frowns. "What are you on about?"

Oh. "Never mind." I titter. Sounds like Nisha's right. "Just a thing on my Facebook profile."

"I don't look at your profile. Anyway, Bonnie, I, uh . . ." He clears his throat like he has something trapped in it. "I wanted to wait until after the wedding to talk to you."

"Okay." I swallow. "Go ahead."

"You know how important your happiness is to me." He pauses for a long beat. "We were together for four years. You were—still are—an extremely important part of my life. I still have a lot of affection for you."

My eyes widen.

Shit.

This is actually happening.

I shift in my seat, drawing in a sharp breath. As much as I had fantasised about Max asking me to get back together—the grovelling, the begging on his knees, the strangled wailing of a tormented man—I'm not prepared.

I didn't think he'd bloody well do it in a cafe beside the office.

"Go on," I say breathlessly.

"I want you to find someone who makes you happy, like I have."

Like he has.

Like he has what?

Three subtle words slipped in at the end.

The three simple words that grow legs and kick me hard in the belly.

"Come again?" I ask in a strangled voice.

"Recently, I've been spending time with someone."

"Danielle." I quiver. "I know this."

He blinks. "What? No. No, not Danielle. We were just messaging, I never met her. That was a mistake."

"Pretty intimate messaging if you are talking about your dick." I scowl.

His jaw ticks. "It was a private message you weren't supposed to see. I learned my lesson." He pauses to adjust his cufflinks. "It's Olivia."

"Olivia?" I repeat slowly as if I'm trying to learn the English language. "Okay. Who is she?"

His frown deepens. "*Olivia*. In our admin team."

"From the office?" I freeze. "The admin at Bradshaw?" I add because he must be talking about another admin in another office.

He looks at me wearily.

"Are you fucking joking?" I choke out. "You hooked up with someone from the *office*, Max?" This is a joke. Sometimes Max's humour is off. "You're joking." My voice cracks.

"No," he says firmly. "Bonnie, I—"

"Could you not have looked farther than across the boardroom to find happiness?" I cut him off in a high-pitched squeak.

I think of all the meetings I've sat through with Olivia and Max and feel sick. With her blonde hair and fair complexion, she could be Danielle's and my younger sister. "God, you're so predictable, Max."

Silence.

"As I said, we're spending time getting to know each other."

"Stop talking in riddles. Sex. You're having sex with her."

"Calm down, Bonnie," he says through gritted teeth. "People are listening."

"Calm down? This is bloody disrespectful, Max! You don't do this to someone you were engaged to. Could you not have picked one of the other millions of people in London? Not someone I see every day." I search his face for some sort of emotion. "Can you not see how insensitive this is? Giving me a front-row ticket to your new romance?"

"We both need to move on, Bonnie."

My arms flap like an agitated wasp. "This isn't moving on! This is rubbing it in my face."

"Well, that's not my intention."

Looking at him, I believe him. He hasn't given me a second thought. Bradshaw Brown is a convenient hunting ground, and he just replaced me in a matter-of-fact way.

I should quit. I should quit on the spot. But who would that harm?

Me. Not Max.

"These things aren't planned. Olivia and I want to do everything possible to make sure you feel comfortable."

How dare he.

I laugh. A demonic laugh. "What do you expect us to do? Should the three of us skip around the office holding hands like the *Teletubbies*?"

I avert my gaze out the window and bite together my trembling lips to hold back the flood of tears. I feel like the last four years meant . . . *nothing*. If he really loved me as much as he said he did, this would be much more difficult for him.

When I look back, I catch him checking his watch. He only gave himself thirty minutes for this meeting.

"How long? How long have you been shagging her?"

"Don't be abrasive." He draws in another deep breath. "We started *getting closer* a few months back."

"When?" I need precision. "A few is anything between two and eleven."

"Three, maybe four."

I make a noise like wind being sucked from a windpipe.

Four it is then. Maybe five. Only two months after our wedding was cancelled.

"You have to be fucking joking." Unless...I stare at him, horrified. The timing is so close to our break-up. "Did you start seeing her before we separated?"

"No. You're being ridiculous." He scowls at me. "Don't you know me at all?"

I breathe a little easier.

"I thought you were over me, Bonnie," he says in a tone that sounds like he's blaming me.

"I didn't expect you to move on with someone in the bloody office," I snap.

"That's why I couldn't tell you—in case it didn't work out. I didn't want to unnecessarily hurt you."

"Gee, thanks, you're so considerate." I stiffen. "Is she the reason that we broke up?"

His frown deepens. "No, of course not."

"And you choose work hours to tell me. Right beside the office."

He at least has the grace to look sheepish. "I apologise for that. I wanted to do it today before I'm out of the office tomorrow afternoon."

"You have the sensitivity of a cockroach."

He opens his mouth and then closes it, probably deciding arguing is fruitless.

I narrow my eyes. "Why is it suddenly urgent now?"

Now he looks *really* uncomfortable. "Olivia and I are taking a few days' break. It may become more obvious around the office. I've informed Bradshaw and Brown, so it's all out in the open. They're fine with it." He looks at me as if I should care what the partners think about my replacement.

Of course, they are. They're both old millionaires. So long as we're making them money, they wouldn't care if we all have a massive orgy together.

Notably, the partners are higher up on the list of people to be notified about the new happy couple than me.

I don't know if I want more details or not. "Where're you going?"

There's a long, loaded pause. "This hasn't been easy for me either, Bonnie."

"Answer the question."

"Since I had done so much research about it, we're heading to Svalbard."

No.

Pain funnels into my heart. I don't understand this version of Max. "Our *honeymoon destination*?" The trip we lost a hefty deposit from. The trip of a lifetime we were due to go on in a few weeks as a married couple.

He stays silent.

"Svalbard's mine," I snarl.

"I'm sure Norway would beg to differ."

It's the damn twitch of his lips that makes me see red. Before I understand what I'm doing, my hand has connected with the open bottle and is spraying water over his face like a victorious Formula One driver.

He reacts too slowly. Water runs down his face and shirt.

There's a collective gasp around me. I got him good.

He gawks at me open-mouthed, blinking water away from his eyes. "Are you out of your mind?"

"You're an asshole. I hope your dick falls off."

"Mature, Bonnie. Really mature." He stands up, wiping his shirt down. "I don't have time for this. I expected you to react like an adult. Do you realise we have to be at Lexington in thirty minutes? Lucky for you, I've got a clean shirt."

"Well, you shouldn't have time-boxed this." I can't even see him properly through my tears. I didn't think I had any tears left for Max. But he keeps on delivering.

"I'm willing to forget this but pull yourself together before the meeting. Do you want me to send Nisha down?"

He hovers over me.

I shake my head.

"Let's talk about this when you've calmed down."

"It was our honeymoon," I choke out as he walks away.

Eight weeks. Eight weeks was all it took to get over me. The first four weeks were spent cancelling the relationship. How did he have time?

And it's not even a shag. Or a fling. You don't go on holiday with a fling. No, a holiday is a promise of intent. An agreement in principle that this may be serious.

Svalbard. Out of the two hundred or whatever number of countries there are in the world, he had to go to the place we picked for a honeymoon destination? I hope he gets eaten by a bear. Or better, his dick gets gangrene and really does fall off.

When I track this on the mood spreadsheet my therapist is making me keep, the graph will go into a negative spike. I've been incrementally on the up. This will look worse than a crypto crash.

My phone vibrates in my bag. Nisha.

Max is probably back at the office already in work mode, rallying the troops. I cancel the call and message her saying I'll walk to Lexington by myself.

At least there's one thing I know for sure—this day can't get any worse.

15

Jack

With a knock on the door, my PA, Jess, pops her head in. "Jack, Bradshaw Brown are waiting for you in boardroom four." She looks at her notebook. "Then you have the board of directors at eleven. I'll have lunch ready for you at twelve thirty. I've booked dinner at The Ivy tonight for you and your mother. Your sisters cannot attend, unfortunately."

"Thanks, Jess." I nod. "On my way."

An army of them, suited and booted, are waiting for me when I enter the room. Not surprising considering the contract on the table for a company of their size.

Max jumps to his feet to shake my hand. "Jack."

I don't like Max as much as he thinks I do.

"Max." I shake hands and take a seat at the front of the room beside Sean and two of my other senior managers.

All the Bradshaw crew look nervous, but Max tries to hide it.

"Max, is this the full team?"

His brow furrows. Just as he is about to respond, one of my assistants opens the door and Bonnie rushes in.

I'm late, which means she is very fucking late. I check my watch. Twelve minutes to be precise.

"Sorry," she says without even looking at me, scanning the room for an empty seat.

I clench my teeth, my anger only slightly tempered by disbelief. "Did you have somewhere better you need to be?"

She gapes at me.

Maybe I wanted to make the other groomsmen jealous.

Her eyes are red and tired looking. What the absolute fuck? Is she hungover?

I take in her blue dress and laced-up boots, which look like flat biker boots. On her, they are sexier than stilettos.

"Personal issue," she mumbles, squeezing past everyone to take a seat at the back only to realise there isn't enough room. "Sorry, excuse me" she mutters as she reverses, finally taking a seat at the front.

I glare at her. She thinks she can swan in at any time she likes? "I have thirty minutes so it's in your own interest not to waste my time. You just wasted two."

The room collectively inhales a breath and holds it.

She nods, looking contrite enough that I decide to let her off the hook.

I turn my attention back to the room, pausing to roll my sleeves up. "I've built urban villages all over the UK, but this project is special to me. If you haven't already figured out by the accent, it's where I call home. We're not just building shiny apartment blocks. It takes a lot more to take an existing community entrenched in working-class culture, and sensitively build a whole new community for thousands—two thousand new jobs, twenty-five hundred people to rehouse. Community centres, schools, new parks, new health centres."

Everyone's eyes are glued to me, with one exception.

Bonnie stares down at the table. She's on a different fucking planet. Every so often, she glances over at Max like some lovesick puppy.

My nostrils flare. No one has disrespected me like this since . . . well . . . never.

Nobody.

"Businesses will look to the east for headquarters as they would Bond Street and Canary Wharf. The economic benefits are enormous for an area that has been neglected for too long. I need a brilliant team to create equilibrium that builds a new progressive community while keeping our heritage alive."

Bonnie looks at me briefly then it's back to staring at the table.

"You have a great responsibility," I continue, eyeing up the team. The rest look as eager as they damn well should be. "You will be transforming a London historical landmark. London doesn't have a car industry anymore, but that grey factory sitting idle was the backbone of the East End for years. It provided jobs for thousands."

As I launch into the details of my regeneration plan, Bonnie doesn't look up once. Not once.

Max asks a question as I glare at Bonnie. I answer him and move on. The more senior members of the team pepper me with questions, and I reply through my growing annoyance.

Sean steps in to answer the finer details.

"You'll be collaborating closely with the teams working on the other phases, so you'll move into our office until construction tenders are ready for the building contractors," I add. "We've allocated an open-plan space close to the Lexington team overseeing the project."

Bonnie looks down at her hands as if this is the last place she wants to be. Is she even fucking listening to a word I'm saying?

"Bonnie," I growl through my teeth, "do you have any questions?"

Her eyes hit mine like a cow caught in headlights. Her mouth opens and then closes.

"Are you incapable of hearing me?"

Her teeth latch onto her bottom lip as she crosses and uncrosses her toned legs. My adrenaline spikes.

"No, Jack," she says, her voice cracking. "I have no questions at this moment."

"Mr. Knight," I correct her as the room stiffens.

"Mr. Knight," she repeats, looking like she needs a hole to be burned in the floor so she can disappear through it.

"You have no questions at all about a project of this size?" I demand. "Of this importance to your company?"

I see the exact moment she stops breathing. She scans the room for help. "Not right now, Mr. Knight." Her throat wobbles as she swallows. "I'm sure I'll have questions when I digest all the information."

"Sounds like my work here is done," I say sarcastically, crossing my arms over my chest.

"Jack." Sean frowns at me. "You have ten minutes left."

"Uh . . . Mr . . . uh . . . Jack," Max pipes up, confused about what to call me. "Rest assured the entire team is giving this project our utmost attention. And thank you for extending the deadline."

I extended their deadline because that doe-eyed vixen hit my soft spot at the wedding.

I'm not having this. Regardless of how much I want to drop to my knees in front of her and demand she open her legs to let me kiss her.

"Get out."

The cow in headlights is back.

"Me?" The blood drains from her face.

"Jack," Sean says, "is this necess—"

"Bonnie," I cut him off, "get out. If you are incapable of listening, leave the room."

"I am listening, Mr. Knight," she protests softly.

"In that case, tell me what Sean said about the access statement stipulation from the planning authority. And what I said we need to do about it."

She swallows and stutters through a vague response.

I stand from my chair and walk over to open the door wide.

She gapes at me, blinking.

Max looks between Bonnie and me, his mouth opening and closing like a dying useless fish. "Bonnie," he prompts quietly, "it's best you leave now."

She nods and lifts her bag onto her shoulder, but the strap falls off. It's like she's lost motor skills. Some of the contents of her bag scatter and Nisha hurries to pick them up.

She walks past me, cheeks burning. Close enough for me to smell the perfume she wore at the wedding. And close enough for those bright blue eyes to make me feel a miniscule amount of guilt.

"Sorry, Mr. Knight," she whispers, a fire burning in her eyes. She is as angry as she is scared.

I grunt under my breath as she disappears out the door.

Bonnie

Son of a bitch.

"I have to call him Mr. Knight? No one calls him Mr. Knight. I heard a cleaner call him Jack. He's a bastard," I whisper angrily to Nisha. We are still in his offices and, as much as I hate the guy, I'm not setting a foot wrong to further antagonise him.

I press the power button on my laptop too hard.

Nisha swivels in her new shiny chair to look at me sympathetically. "I'm sorry, love. Maybe you should call in sick for the rest of the day? You could pretend you were feeling poorly during the meeting."

"No." I sigh, slumping back in my chair. "It'll probably start more gossip. I'll just stay here and ride it out."

The entire situation is ridiculous. That was the first time I've witnessed Jack Knight's wrath, and it was directed at *me*. I always listen in client meetings. Even if I'm tired, I can muster up enough professionalism.

So, I had an off day. The guy had no right to call me out publicly.

The ball of anxiety builds substance in my stomach. Maybe I have gallstones.

"It wasn't as bad as I thought, right? It probably seemed worse in my head and I'm blowing it up too much. Like the banged-up eye at the wedding." Which still looks bruised.

Maybe Jack kicks someone out of every meeting. It's his

thing. Barbarian boss persona.

Nisha looks like she's sucking lemons.

"Just lie, Nisha. So I can get through the rest of the day."

Her smile is brittle. "Since it's *mindful Wednesday*, how about we go to a yoga class after work? The guy even does face yoga. That'll relax you."

"That's not lying. That's changing the subject. And what the hell is face yoga?"

"Apparently it tightens your face muscles. I'm worried I'm getting jowls."

I roll my eyes. "At thirty, I think you're okay for another few years. Knight needs it more than us to get rid of that tic in his jaw."

This is a horrible, sucky day, and it's going from bad to worse. As the others continued the meeting, I loitered outside the room, festering and stewing, wondering what the hell to do. Did he mean for me to leave the office entirely or just the room?

I feel like a schoolgirl on the brink of expulsion. Max dropped the Olivia bomb on me, and Jack reprimanded me like a naughty student.

Under other circumstances, this would have been an awesome day.

After the meeting, we got a tour of the Lexington building and access passes. Sean talked to me briefly. Following his advice that Jack would likely calm down in a few hours, I tagged along with imposter syndrome.

Ten of us on the team have been upgraded to fortieth floor views overlooking Canary Wharf until we get the designs nailed. It's one of the C-Level floors but how or why we got this privilege is beyond me. Everyone is deliriously happy as we set up our IT in a corner of the office.

Except for me.

Canary Wharf isn't packed full of great historical buildings like London's centre, but the peninsula of chrome-and-glass skyscrapers is our version of New York or Hong Kong.

I don't know how they get any work done on the Lexington

top floors. As it houses the most senior members of the company, I suppose they have time to admire the view while the underlings work below.

There's a rooftop garden bar on the top floor and a lush gym on the bottom with a spa. An actual *spa* with wet rooms.

Wet rooms would never work at the Bradshaw Brown office. The fear of running into the two partner cretins would be too great.

In the Lexington office, we get "mindfulness day" every Wednesday when massage therapists offer back and head rubs and there's free yoga in the gym. Thursdays are designated social days for colleagues with free drinks in the rooftop bar. It's an illusion of being in a holiday resort, so you forget that you're stressed as fuck with draining deadlines.

I connect my laptop with the large monitor and then spin my chair around to face Nisha. "I can't believe that for a fleeting second, I considered saying yes to his dinner," I whisper. "He was all charm and banter at the wedding, and I thought maybe he's not that bad." What happened with my dad was a long time ago. People change, yada yada. "But it's obvious now. The guy's a fucking psycho. Kicking someone out of a meeting for being late once? Seriously?"

Nisha leans in. "Look, keep your head down and work your ass off. It'll be forgotten soon."

I'm not finished. "I've never been kicked out of anything in my life," I huff. "He humiliated me. Who does that? It's like primary school. He put me in the naughty corner. Do you think this is because I didn't fall at his feet at the wedding when he asked me to go for dinner?"

She shrugs. "Your guess is as good as mine."

"Ugh. I wanna grab his stupid nipple ring and pull it until he screams."

"Bonnie," Nisha warns, giving me a stern look. "Pipe down now. We can talk about it after work. Keep your emotions under control."

I nod, sighing. Everyone is already watching me after the showdown this morning, so I'm not helping myself.

I know what I need to do. Just say "yes sir, no sir, three bags full sir," whatever the hell he wants.

Knight, King, Billy big bollocks—whatever he wants you to call him, do it with a big smile.

"How was the rest of the meeting?" I ask.

"Tense. No one dared to blink. I literally did not take my eyeballs off the man for a second." She laughs quietly. "I don't know how he didn't balk from the attention."

I roll my eyes. "He thrives on power. All eyes have to be on him."

I get a flashback of how Jack looked at me when we were dancing, his brown eyes glazing with need. The possessiveness of his hands gripping my waist. How his hard body felt under my fingers.

I shake my head, shattering the image.

"Max is back."

I follow Nisha's line of sight to where Max is storming down the aisle with a grim look on his face.

Oh, *fuck*.

"Bonnie," he says in a low voice as he leans over my desk. "I tried to talk to Jack, but he wasn't having any of it. You're walking a tightrope here. He's got a short fuse, and you've managed to get yourself in his bad boo—."

"I know," I cut in before Max can decide something that won't be in my favour. I search his face. "It won't happen again. It was a temporary moment of insanity. I'm never late, Max, you know that."

He blows out a hard breath. "It wasn't only about being late. He's not happy with your overall attitude. If Jack requests it, you're off the project. I'll have no choice."

My stomach drops. "Has he?"

He shakes his head. "Not yet. But I've had to inform the partners about the unfortunate incident. In case they heard it elsewhere."

My eyes widen. He makes it sound like I rolled up a joint in the middle of the meeting and smoked it. All I did was arrive a few minutes late and avert my eyeballs at the wrong time.

Bradshaw will one hundred percent pull me from the project.

"Please, Max. What can I do to redeem this? You at least owe me that, considering you were the cause of the *incident*."

He glares at me. "Leave your personal issues at the door when you enter this building."

"I can't leave you behind at the door, can I?" I let out an annoyed huff.

His eyes narrow. "I'm not making any promises, but I'll do my best to keep you on this project."

"Thank you."

I watch him walk away. Why is it that my career is in the hands of two arrogant men? Four, counting Bradshaw and Brown.

"Bonnie, look who's coming," Nisha says through gritted teeth beside me. "Nine o'clock."

I don't need to look up to feel his presence. The vibe in the office shifts as if everyone has been given an adrenaline shot at the same time.

My gaze travels upwards to see Jack's dominant frame stalk down the aisle.

He walks more like a fighter than a CEO with that shoulder swag. He radiates too much masculine energy for an office, especially in those blue jeans and white T-shirt, making him the least formally dressed person here.

A walk that says *get the fuck out of my way.*

I swallow hard and bury the primal cavewoman instinct to jump up and bring the beast to his knees.

There are more important things at stake here. I need to make everything right.

He nods to some of the team as he passes, with the lucky ones getting the infamous Jack Knight grin.

I swallow the big lump in my throat and try to catch his eye.

"Mr. Knight," I call after him.

He hears me. He looks me right in the eyes. Something flares in them for a fleeting second, maybe regret, but it's gone so quickly it might be wishful thinking on my behalf.

His square jaw flexes and he keeps on walking.

I recoil in horror and look at Nisha, who seems equally shocked.

She shakes her head as he disappears into an office at the end of the aisle. "Just leave it."

I feel every eyeball in a ten-metre radius boring into me. When I turn, they all divert their gazes like I'm Medusa about to turn them into stone.

I resist the urge to flip him off. Behind his back, obviously.

It's a lose-lose situation. The worst-case scenario is I'm thrown off the project. The best-case scenario is I get to stay on, but I have to watch him swagger up and down past me every day, the two of us hating each other.

The only bittersweet win for me is that the humiliation of getting kicked out of a major meeting is that it will distract me until quitting time from thinking about Max's love life.

"Wine or yoga, which one will help more?" Nisha asks in a low voice. "Or both?"

"I can't. I have to run fifteen miles after work. Marathon training."

"Jesus. I haven't run fifteen miles this whole year. Each to their own. Endorphins are supposed to make you happy," she adds hopefully.

My eyes travel to the glass boardroom where Jack is seated, talking to about twenty people.

He swivels abruptly in his chair, and his gaze collides with mine. His lips move but his focus is solely on me.

Wincing, I look away first.

Believe me, fifteen miles worth of endorphins won't even make a dent after today.

16

Jack

The only thing that relieves tension when I'm wound up this tightly is to get the shit kicked out of me by my trainer. He's an Albanian hard nut who trained world heavyweight champions and now wants an easier life. I pay an extortionate amount to have him at my beck and call in the gym, and it's worth every penny.

"Jack." Sean knocks at my office door. "Give me a minute."

Grunting, I beckon him in.

He eyes the gym bag. "Something happened that you need to let off steam?"

"If you've got something to say, out with it, Sean."

He closes the door behind him.

"This better not take long."

"It won't." He smirks. "Shoot me down for overstepping, but don't you think you were a little hard on Bonnie?"

I fold my arms across my chest. "Then stop overstepping. No, I don't think I was too hard. Do you know how everyone else looks when they walk into that boardroom? Fucking appreciative. She looked like she was stuck in traffic on the motorway."

God, she pissed me off.

Sean chuckles. "Fair enough. She looked a bit distracted. Just don't be too hasty, okay? Max just told me that he'd spoken to her about having a new girlfriend. Apparently, Bonnie found out just before the meeting."

"So?" I snap. "They've been split up for months."

"It was poor timing on his part. He didn't think she'd take it so badly."

"You're telling me she's fucking up this opportunity because her ex is seeing someone new?" My jaw tightens. The morning after the wedding, she basically told me she cock-teased me to make Max jealous. Max, the fucking fool who gave her up.

"I get the sense it's not just about him seeing someone new. His new girlfriend works at Bradshaw, too, which is a dick move. They've been seeing each other for a few months. When were Max and Bonnie supposed to get married? Max has been pretty quiet about this new relationship, but you do the math."

"Since when did you become a fucking agony aunt," I reply flatly.

One of his brows arches. "Come on, mate. I know you don't do the relationship thing, but surely you can feel some sympathy for the girl. It's a hard situation. She had a bad day."

I pick up my gym bag and open the door. Then pause. "Did you talk to Bonnie about it?"

"About you kicking her out of the meeting? Very briefly. I said you'd calm down eventually. Which you will."

"Not the meeting."

"Oh, what then?" He's going to make me work for it.

"About whether she's upset that Max is dating," I grit out.

His eyes twinkle as if I've spilled some big secret. "Nope. I messaged my *wife* after Max told me." He smiles at me with fake innocence. "Why do you ask?"

"No reason," I snap, walking out the door. "Unless you're joining me to get trounced for the millionth time in your life, I'm out of here. Later."

My phone vibrates in my pocket as I head to the gym. I take it out, and my heart rate spikes when I see the name on the screen.

"McKenzie," I say, answering.

McKenzie was, and still is, the police officer assigned to Dad's case. Technically, the murder case is still open, but that means shit. After so many years, it's just a record in a police database.

Nothing stuck to Wicks. It was all circumstantial evidence. No DNA. No witnesses willing to go up against the Wicks clan. No weapons found. Nothing but a pile of bent coppers on the Wicks payroll.

When Dad was stabbed, I was twenty-nine, but the money was already rolling in. Against the Wicks' reputation, it was worthless. No one would talk.

The fact that Wicks is doing life for another crime is irrelevant. Two years after Dad's murder, the Wicks family became too arrogant. They started believing their East End myth that they were untouchable. But with arrogance comes sloppiness.

So much evidence was dropped into the hands of the police that they would have been a laughing stock not to nail Wicks, and a major operation finally took down the most senior bosses of the cartel in a media circus.

It's not enough. I won't rest until Dad's death is added to their criminal record.

It means fuck all to Donnie Wicks. He's not getting out, and he's got a good life in the clink. Another entry in the police database won't bother him.

But maybe I'll sleep a little easier at night.

In the early days following Dad's death, I hounded McKenzie and everyone in his unit. Obsessing over nailing Wicks was a good distraction from what was really breaking me—Dad was gone.

McKenzie clears his throat. "Wicks is dying."

That's why I like the guy; he cuts to the chase.

"I know. Cancer. I'm hoping it's the long-suffering type and he dies a slow, painful death." *I hope the guy is in so much pain he howls like I did when I found out Dad was dead. Fucking broken.* "Anything I don't know?"

He pauses. "He wants to see you."

Anger courses through my veins. "Why?"

"He won't say. He wants you to arrange a visit."

I let out a humourless laugh. "He wants to get all his sins out in the wash?"

"Don't hold your breath, son. Honest to God, I've no clue what he wants. He's not saying a word unless it's to you. The only way you'll know is if you see him."

I'm surprisingly calm, considering I've been waiting nearly a decade for this. Wicks has consistently refused to see me.

"Well, what's it to be, Jack? Am I arranging it?"

"Do it."

17

Bonnie

I'm in the Lexington office at eight a.m., ready to redeem myself.

New day, new outlook. Yesterday, Max told me to continue work as usual, so that's what I'll do. Jack kicking people out of meetings is just a normal day in the office, and the barbarian boss has forgotten all about it.

I don't feel good admitting I wasted a lot of time on Olivia's social media last night in between long, rambling conversations with Kate and Nisha dissecting every last detail on *why, why, just why?*

Kate tells me what I want to hear, and Nisha tells me like it is. Between both, hopefully, I'll meet in the middle and get through this.

Max has always been twenty steps ahead of me in this breakup. He'll be married with three kids, a dog, and a vasectomy before I've finished counselling.

I didn't take that much notice of Olivia before. We exchanged niceties in the office kitchen and smiled at each other in the hallway. She has an English rose look about her with dimples that people would pay to have surgically added.

She's been at Bradshaw for about six months and is in a pretty junior admin role. I've never even noticed her and Max flirting but clearly, I was blind. I didn't realise that she was exchanging bodily fluids as well as niceties with Max. I've been traded in for a younger model, and I'm only twenty-eight.

At least she's across the road in our Bradshaw office, and I'll rarely see her for the next few weeks.

I don't want to get back with Max. I said it to Kate last night and meant it. I'm finally at the point of no return. That's not what this is about.

The whole situation just stinks of disrespect. For me and for our relationship. I cannot fathom how a man who told me he loved me every day for years could put me in this horrendous situation and not seem that bothered about it.

He's missing a massive sensitivity chip if he thinks it's okay to go to our honeymoon destination with another woman *from the office.*

Now, I doubt he ever loved me.

Speak of the devil.

Max hurries up to me as I'm powering on my laptop. "Morning. I'm glad you're here early."

"Yesterday was an exception," I say sharply. "I'm usually early."

He eyes me warily. "Hopefully, you've calmed down now that you've slept on it."

"I'm void of all emotions." I smile brightly at him. "They're at the door downstairs."

His eyes narrow a fraction then he sighs. "Bonnie, I didn't mean for it to happen."

"Neither does someone who committed manslaughter. It doesn't make it okay."

His lips press into a fine line.

"Look, you could have waited, that's all. Let's leave it. How can I help you, Max?"

"Good." He nods curtly. "Listen, Bradshaw and Brown wanted to take you off the project. Bradshaw sent over an apology to Jack last night and said he would deal with it."

Damn.

I slump into my chair.

Short little cretins. Five years here and one minor mishap

later, I'm ripped out of a project that would advance my career. I may as well put my CV together because that's my promotion out the window.

"Wait." Max puts his palm up. "Jack responded at five this morning. He wants you to talk to him directly."

My pulse quickens. "Talk to him directly . . . is that good or bad?"

He flings his arms up. "I don't know. I tried. I emailed Jack before Bradshaw did, but he didn't respond to me."

"What does he want?" I feel a sliver of hope. "What should I do—email him? Call him? Isn't it too early? Should I wait until nine?"

I wish the instructions were clearer. The damn guy probably plans to re-enact the scene of firing Dad. Even though he can't technically fire me, he can cause a lot of damage to my reputation and career stagnation.

Max shakes his head. "He's obviously an early riser."

You already knew that. It's in his biography.

"Do you know if he'll be in the office today? He has to walk past here to get to his office."

"I don't know. He's a busy man." He thinks for a minute. "His PA sent around his work number in the email yesterday. She starts work at eight so she can let you know if he's free to accept your call. At least you'll have tried."

But I have his personal number.

"Be prepared to get on your knees and grovel. He's not known for second chances."

An image of being on my knees in front of Jack Knight flashes in my head.

Fuck.

"I will."

"Oh, and Bonnie?" He raps his knuckles on my desk. "Bradshaw doesn't know about your little outburst when you threw water over me. If he finds out about that, you'll definitely be taken off the project."

You're welcome, his face says as he walks away.

"Max?" I call after him.

He turns.

"Jack doesn't know about your little bedtime reading. How many times *have* you re-read *From Bricks to Billions*? If he finds out about that, he might feel uncomfortable knowing you've got a book about his life that's so overread, it's practically disintegrating."

I smile sweetly and turn my attention to my laptop.

Ten minutes later, I'm still stewing over strategy. I can't call Jack's personal number. It doesn't feel appropriate.

Definitely nothing of interest going on there. His words from the morning after the wedding burn into my brain and hurt much more than they should.

Nope. I'm *not* calling his personal phone.

There is already a surprising crowd in the office, considering it's eight a.m., but Canary Wharf never sleeps. All work, no play here. Jack's not in his office, though.

I open my emails, thinking about what I'm going to say, and then locate his office number. Maybe I could say I had women's problems, that always shuts men up.

A female voice answers straight away. "Jack Knight's office. Jess speaking."

"Morning, Jess. It's Bonnie from Bradshaw Brown. We've spoken before over email. You helped me get some pictures together for the mosaic for Sean's wedding."

"Ah, yes, Bonnie!" Her voice floods with warmth. "Thanks for sending me a picture of the final thing. It looked amazing! Kate and Sean must have been delighted."

"Umm, yeah, I think it went down well. Thanks so much for your help." I clear my throat. "Listen, Jess, I'm hoping to speak to Mr. Knight for five minutes today if that's possible? Could I schedule a meeting?"

There's a pause. "I hope you're okay after yesterday."

So, everyone knows.

I let out a sad little laugh. "I'm calling to redeem myself."

I can *feel* her sympathy down the phone. "He's back-to-back with meetings all day. Let me see what I can do, Bonnie. I'll call you back." She pauses. "Oh, and I shouldn't be saying this, but it sounds like you got unlucky yesterday. He's not usually that hot-headed."

I know she's trying to console me, but it somehow makes me feel worse. "Thanks."

At least I tried. A large part of me is relieved I wasn't put through.

My phone buzzes.

Fuck.

Double fuck.

Jack Knight flashes up on the screen. It's his personal number.

Gah.

"Good morning, Mr. Knight," I say in my most professional tone.

"Bonnie." His voice is low and hard, a growl rather than a greeting. In the background, there's a lot of noise, like he's walking fast.

See, *that's* what I'm talking about. The guy kicks me out of a meeting, fires people in front of me in a hot tub, gives my number to random guys, not to mention fires my dad, making him an all-round brute.

Yet my pulse goes from resting to racing just from hearing him say my goddamn name.

I make a mental note to go on a date with Christopher, the guy I'm messaging, ASAP.

"I'd like to personally apologise to you for yesterday." I'm proud that my voice is strong.

"Come and apologise in person."

"Of course," I say quickly. "Would you like me to schedule a meeting?"

"No," he says gruffly. "Come down to the basement. Last door on the left."

Thank God I had the good sense to get into the office early.

I take the lift.

With each floor, my stomach becomes more unsettled. He's not going to make this easy if he wants to see me in person at this hour.

Apologise and move on. In a week, it'll be forgotten. In a few months, you'll have your promotion, get on the register, and can jump ship.

My pep talk does nothing.

Why the hell am I meeting him in the basement? Besides the gym and access to the carpark, I can't remember what else is down here.

A morgue?

The lift doors open to the basement. I pass the entrance to the bike shed on the right and a cleaner supply room on the left, then arrive at the only door he can be talking about.

It's a door right beside the main gym.

I knock.

"Come in," a man shouts.

Inside is a boxing ring they didn't show us during the office tour.

And in the middle of the ring is a bare-chested, bare-footed sweaty Jack throwing savage punches at another bloke.

Holy. Fucking. Hell.

The muscles of his arms and chest flex with every punch he delivers to the other guy, who can clearly give as good as he can take.

The intensity on Jack's face could swallow me whole.

Damn.

Speechless. My head involuntarily tips to the side as I examine him, like a beautiful sculpture.

Loud primitive grunts come out of him, acting as my sexual alarm clock. His muscles contract every time he jabs.

Same as my vagina. My version of morning wood.

Jesus, woman. He's just a man.

Also a hulking, hot-as-fuck man, glistening in sweat.

Thwack.

Thwack.

Thwack.

The other guy lands a decent punch on Jack's chest. That must hurt. The muscles ripple but Jack ducks and comes back for more.

"Bonnie," a gruff breathless voice jerks me out of my daze. Why does it sound like a command every time he says my name? "Are you here to say something to me or stand there gawking?"

"I can come back later if now's not a good time."

He stops moving for a second and his dark eyes burn into mine. "No. We do it now."

"Uh, sure. I'd like to ask that you don't get me taken off the project."

Thwack. He resumes his punching.

"I know it didn't appear so, yesterday," I continue louder, "but I'm extremely dedicated to this project. Yesterday, I wasn't myself!"

I shout that last bit over the thumps and grunts.

"But I can guarantee that will never happen again. Being late is completely out of character for me. And I'm upset with myself for being late to something so important. It was extremely unprofessional."

I stop for air as he continues dancing and shadowboxing. Is the motherfucker even listening to me?

The nipple ring glistens with sweat. I hope the other guy gets him right on the ring.

"Can I start afresh and prove myself? Will you give me another chance?"

The punching continues. Now he has his back to me, giving me a perfect view of those defined back muscles and hard mounds of ass, but it's not helpful to my plight.

I fidget with my chain awkwardly. "Right, that's all, Mr.

Knight."

Is he going to address me at all? The guy is just damn rude.

Or . . . Jesus, he is planning on getting me in the ring to fight this out?

Maybe I should leave.

Just as I step backwards, he stops boxing and grunts something unintelligible. Is that directed at the guy he's sparring with or me?

He strides towards me with the intensity of a man who has been released from a maximum-security prison. His trunks hang distractingly low, so I have no choice but to flick my gaze down his ab muscles to the prominent crotch bulge.

I catch a whiff of fresh manly sweat.

As soon as our eyes lock, the burst of sexual energy is so palpable, a shiver runs up my spine.

This is insane.

He really isn't playing fair here.

I don't like the guy. I don't like the guy one bit. But I sure as hell *want* the guy.

I dare a nun to look at him and not lose her shit.

He stares down at me as his forearms dangle over the rope. "I asked you if you could work with Max." His breathing is still erratic from the workout. "You clearly can't."

Swallowing, I resume my grovelling, "Yesterday, I received some news that affected me, but I'm over it now. I can work with Max, no problem."

He leans farther over the rope until he's almost eye level with me. "Do you know how many architects bid on the factory project?"

"All of the London conservation firms. We are very privileged to win."

"Forty-two. I have firms all over the world trying to get ten minutes with me for a chance to work on a Lexington project." He glares at me so ferociously I must be missing the top layer of my skin now. "Many people would kill to be in your position."

"Of course—"

"And you?" he says, cutting me off. "I gave you thirty minutes of my time yesterday, and you threw it back in my face."

I'm going up against a vicious boxer and this isn't a fight I'm going to win. "I'm sorry it came across like that. To work with you and your team on the *Motor Works* factory is a dream for me."

I think he's looking for an ego boost.

"A project like this, on an iconic East End landmark I've grown up beside, and working with someone as . . . *visionary* as yourself . . . will be the most exciting highlight of my career."

The look in his eyes tells me he's not having any of it. "It doesn't seem that way to me. It seems you're stuck in the past, incapable of moving forward. You're too blindsided to see the opportunity right in front of you."

I don't know how to respond to that. Is he still talking about the project? "I see the opportunity and I want it," I say softly. "I can share work that I've done on previous projects to show you my experience. Max will vouch that I'm diligent."

My response displeases him. "I hold you to a higher standard than Max."

"*Why*?" I didn't mean for it to come out a hiss. But really, *why*?

He doesn't respond.

Unblinking, deep brown eyes bore into mine with startling intensity. Sweat trickles down his forehead but it doesn't seem to bother him. I resist the urge to wipe it away.

There's nothing worse than silence at a time like this, so I keep on talking for both of us. "I'll get on my knees and grovel," I joke, "if that's what it takes."

Just when I thought that stone jaw couldn't get any harder, he clenches his teeth and swallows hard. It seems I've pushed the man too far.

I change tactics. "Can we start afresh? Perhaps you could assess the situation after we present the first draft of the conceptual designs." I'm asking him to give me three weeks. That's fair.

I hold out my hand.

For an awkward beat, I think he's going to leave me hanging but then he takes off a glove and takes my hand in his sweaty calloused one.

There's no mistaking the current that passes between us.

I *know* he feels it, too.

Just as it is about to get weird, he drops my hand and nods. "To starting afresh."

I exhale a weak breath. His testosterone leaves little space for oxygen in the room. "Thank you, I really appreciate this, Mr. Knight."

Something flashes in his eyes at the title, but he doesn't correct me.

"I won't take up any more of your time."

He turns his back on me and swaggers to his sparring partner, waiting patiently in the middle of the ring.

I move towards the door, breathing freely now. That was close. To be taken off the project after the Max and Olivia revelation would be a kick in the teeth when I'm already sprawled on the ground.

"Bonnie," he says in his gravelly voice behind me.

I turn my head to see him gazing steadily at me. "The boots suit you. Better than your bridesmaid's shoes. Although you'd still take my fucking toes off with those boots."

Then he turns and goes straight into punching, leaving me staring at my black leather ankle boots, feeling more confused than ever.

One thing's for sure, never once has Max looked at me in the office the way *Mr. Knight* just did.

18

Jack

Being London's biggest property developer isn't as glamorous as it's made out to be, despite what the media would have the nation believe.

This evening, I got photographed coming out of a swanky restaurant with the Mayor of London after I was accosted by two females.

By midnight, another threesome will be added to my playboy persona along with the photographic "evidence." Fifty percent of the time, it's true and the other fifty, it's cock and bull.

In my case, my reputation definitely precedes me.

Life was simpler when I was a poor bricklayer.

The motion sensor lights illuminate the walkway of the fortieth floor as I walk to my office. The floor is in darkness except for one corner.

I pause in my tracks, frowning.

She's bent over her laptop and too engrossed in whatever she's doing to notice me. Her eyes fix on the screen as she absently brushes loose hair from her neck.

My chest tightens. Bonnie shouldn't be here alone at this time of night.

The light of the laptop screen bounces off her sculpted cheekbones and razor-sharp features. She must have Scandinavian blood in her with that bone structure. She wraps her lips around a pen, and it might be the sexiest thing I've ever seen.

Plump, pouty lips that women pay thousands to fake. Lips I'd like to taste.

I need a reality check here. I can't stop staring at her. That's all I've done since our little chat in the gym five days ago. Watch her from afar. Watch her laugh with others, charm my team and talk to everyone but me, the big bad wolf who kicked her out of a meeting. When she laughs, she lights up the room. When she scowls, she sets me on fire.

Then I go home and wrap my fist around my poor aching cock, which just wants to follow her around all day until she drops us a bone.

Pretending it's her. Pretending I'm pushing inside her beautiful soaking pussy as she bounces up and down on my cock, moaning my name like I'm the only man in the world.

Is that too much to ask?

She never comes near me, and there's been little reason for me to approach her. She keeps her head down, like the rest of the team, intent on not fucking up the opportunity of a lifetime. I forced the situation a few times, loitering around the area reserved for the Bradshaw team, asking questions I didn't need to know the answers to.

But I'm not the only one she doesn't go near. Except for work conversations, she doesn't seem to engage with Max. I think her comment about flirting with me to make him jealous was only to rile me up.

I just need to get to the root of *why*.

As if feeling the weight of my gaze, she looks up, and our eyes connect.

The pen drops from her mouth as I walk towards her.

I wish like hell I knew what's going on in her head. The woman is the most difficult person I've ever had to read. Most people, especially women, I can read. Viking could be plotting a slow and painful death for me, and I wouldn't know.

She stands up to greet me and that's when I notice what she's wearing. Tight white tank top sculpted around perfect breasts, stopping at just above the belly button and black running shorts high on the thigh accentuating her long toned legs.

Fuck.

With great effort, I drag my gaze back up to her face.

"It's ten thirty." I frown. "Why are you not at home?"

She shrugs. "I want to get something finished."

My chest tightens even further. I feel like an asshole that she's working these hours because of me. "I didn't mean for you to be this dedicated."

"It's just one night. I'll feel better when I've finished what I need to. Anyway, most nights I've been leaving before nine. Some of the team are usually here as well, so I'm not always alone."

I wince. Now I know I'm a major asshole. "I don't want you working this late alone in the office."

Her lips quirk. "Are you saying you don't trust your own security guards?"

"Of course, I do," I say dryly. "I'm worried about what happens when you leave the watch of my security." My eyes run over her body again. "Why are you dressed like that?"

She looks at me like I'm stupid. "I'm going to run home."

"To your flat in Brixton? That's ten miles."

Surprise crosses her face. "It's about seven. How did you even—" She stops. "No, not to Brixton. I'm going to my dad's tonight."

"Barking? No chance," I say firmly. "The route is dodgy as hell at this time of night. I'll take you home. You can run tomorrow morning when it's daylight."

"Barking is where my mum lives," she says in a tone that suggests I've pissed her off.

Yup, definitely can't read the damn woman.

"I'm staying at my dad's." The bite in her tone is unmistakable this time.

I frown, confused. "Phil's not your dad? The dentist?"

She inspects me through slanted eyes as I wonder what the fuck I've said wrong. "Phil's my stepdad. My mum married him when I was eighteen." Her teeth grind together. "You know my dad."

"I do?"

Her scowl deepens. "He worked for you for years."

My mind ticks over, trying to figure out who she's talking about. "What's his name?"

"Frank Casey."

It takes me a long minute for the name to register.

It can't be. How the hell did I not know that?

"Seriously?"

"*Seriously.*"

It all makes sense now.

She crosses her arms, staring at me, bewildered. "You really didn't know he's my dad?"

"No." I sigh. But now that I do, this complicates things. In these situations, it's best to take the bull by the horns. "You're annoyed at me because I fired him. Right, Bonnie?"

Her expression darkens. "I'm not exactly delighted about it, no."

"What did he tell you?"

"Are we off the record? I won't get in trouble for anything I say?"

"Completely off the record," I agree firmly. "Hit me with your worst."

She folds her arms across her chest. "You fired him out of the blue two days before Christmas for no reason. You didn't pay his last two weeks' wages. That's the mild version."

My jaw ticks.

"I'm sorry, Bonnie, I really am," I say softly, wondering how to manoeuvre my way through this. "I didn't know he's your dad."

"It's not really the point." Her breath stalls, and it's clear she's not comfortable talking about this with me. "What was your reasoning? It doesn't even sound legal."

"It was legal and above board."

Her eyes narrow. "You winked at me."

"I winked at you?" I repeat, confused.

"After you fired Dad, you *winked* at me. In The White Horse. You had a squad of women with you."

"A *squad*?" I smile. "I don't remember that specific wink, Bonnie."

My smile drops as her lips thin.

There's obviously a lot of emotion attached to this wink.

"I always tried to talk to you, Bonnie," I say gently. "If I winked at you, it was nothing to do with your dad. It was because I was trying to get your attention. You're hard not to focus on in *any* pub, but in The White Horse, well, I didn't stand a chance."

She's not having it. She just keeps staring at me.

I lean against the desk so that I come down to her eye level. "Are you going to hold a decade-long grudge against me? I'm truly sorry, Bonnie. Business decisions I make are never intended to hurt people, and I'm regretful that this one has impacted you." My eyes search hers. "Can we put this behind us?"

A disgruntled, noncommittal sound escapes her.

She thinks she hates me. Hell, she *wants* to hate me.

Deciding not to push it I revert to our original topic "Where does your dad live?" I ask.

"The Lewis estate."

The largest social housing estate in that area. He's in the catchment of the regeneration project. "We're rehousing him."

She nods.

"Right, well, you have three choices." I fold my arms over my chest, mirroring her. "One, you get a lift with my driver. Two, you get a lift with me on my motorcycle. Three, we run to your dad's house together."

"Or option four, I do what I want because I'm a grown woman, and I run home alone."

"No. Absolutely fucking not. Pick an option from the three." Options two or three only.

She skewers me with a glare. "You can't stop me from leaving this building by myself."

My jaw tightens. It's approaching eleven o'clock and I don't want to stand here arguing all night. "If you're in my building, I have a duty of care. Besides, I won't be able to sleep unless I know you're safe."

"You don't have a duty of care if I'm the one that decides to work out-of-office hours. I'll email you as soon as I get back."

I swear under my breath. Why does the woman have to be so stubborn?

She goes to walk around me, but I take her by the wrist and pull her towards me. "If I let go of your wrist and you run out that door, I'm going to run with you the whole way to your dad's place."

She tuts. "You're being ridiculous."

"Try me."

Her eyes flare, a war brewing behind the blue. "You've been drinking. You can't drive a motorcycle now."

I shake my head. "I had one beer at dinner. Hours ago. Besides, I break down alcohol quickly. I'm a big guy."

"That you are," she mutters. "So . . . was it a date?"

Her light tone doesn't fool me. I wonder for a second if I should fuck with her.

"Depends how hot you think the Mayor of London is. It was a business dinner. Come on, you've been in the office since eight this morning. You must be exhausted. Let me take you home."

"Fine," she huffs. "Option two. Motorcycle."

"Good choice." I wink.

That makes her even angrier.

"You're the boss, *Mr. Knight*."

"Maybe I overreacted slightly," I say, sheepishly. "Jack works too."

"Off the record, maybe you are giving me whiplash," she mutters. "Wait, why do you have the motorbike with you if you have a driver at your beck and call?"

"You're about to find out. Come on, grab your things."

She picks up her bag and follows me to the lifts.

I press the button for the lower ground floor, and the doors slide open. "Ladies first."

"I've never been on a motorcycle before." She steps ahead of me into the lift. "You won't go too fast, will you? I don't want to be in an accident because of a boy racer showing off his toy."

I chuckle as the elevator descends. "I got that out of my system a long time ago."

The doors slide open, and I hold my arm out for Bonnie to exit first. "The last bay to the left."

"Is that a—?"

"A Harley, yes." We stroll towards my beauty. I do feel like I'm showing my favourite toy to the girl I fancy in the playground. I'd better be careful not to show off on the bike . . . out of my system and all that.

She eyes it apprehensively. "I was hoping for a moped or one of those Batman and Robin ones with a sidecar."

My brows lift, amused. "You want to weave in and out of London traffic in a sidecar?"

She huffs her disagreement. "This thing looks vicious."

"Nonsense," I say as I open the locker on the wall. "She's not meant to look good. She's meant to *feel* good. Trust me."

"Why do men call their toys *she*?"

I shrug. "Only the ones we worship."

"That would be romantic if you weren't talking about a bike." Her hand runs down the side of the bike tentatively. "How fast does this thing go?"

"Nought to sixty in four to five seconds. Top speed is about 140 miles per hour."

Horror settles on her face.

"Relax. I'm not testing that out with you. Here." I hand her a size small helmet from my locker. "This one should fit you." I pull out the smallest protective trousers and jacket set I have. "And these."

She takes them from me. "You have a collection of leather outfits down here?"

I grin. "It helps to be prepared in case there's a damsel in distress. Go on, put them on. You'll thank me later."

She scowls but reluctantly kicks off her running shoes and pulls the trousers up over her toned legs. "How many distressed damsels have been on the back of this thing," she mutters. "I hope you wash these regularly. And by the way, this particular damsel is more distressed right now at the thought of being on the back of this beast rather than a nice safe run home."

"You've got nothing to worry about." I pull my own lightweight leather trousers up over my jeans, much quicker than Bonnie. "I'm a safe biker."

"I'm serious," she says sharply. "You need to go slow."

Her gaze trails down my leather-clad thighs.

I grab her by the waist and lift her onto the Harley. She gasps, and a flush rises on her neck. This is already an enjoyable ride, and we haven't left the parking lot.

"Bonnie," I say to her seriously, "I would *never* put you in danger. Come on, legs on either side."

She swings her right leg over so she's straddling the Harley. Lucky bike. "I'm quite high off the ground. I feel like I'm on a horse."

I take her helmet and pop it on her head, inching close to her face to adjust it.

She has no option but to stare back at me as I buckle her helmet. I could do it quicker but what's the rush?

God, she smells good.

She looks beautiful on my bike. My fingers tangle in a lock of blonde hair flowing from her helmet.

"Ready?" I ask softly.

She nods under the helmet. Her face looks heated. "Ready."

I hop on the bike in front of her. I wrap her arms around my chest. "Hold on tight, darlin'."

Her grip tightens around me as I turn on the ignition. I hold the clutch in and work the gears until the light comes on.

"Wait!" she calls out behind me. "You haven't told me the rules. I lean into the turn, right?"

This is going to be the wedding dance all over.

"You do nothing. The only rules you need to obey are to relax and hold on tight." I turn my head around until our faces are nearly touching. "Let me lead this time."

She nods solemnly. "I can do that."

"After this you'll be asking me to take you home every night."

"Don't flatter yourself, Mr. Knight," she counters breathily.

Grinning, I place my hand over hers on my stomach to try to reassure her then kick-start the engine into life.

She screams like I've just set the bike on fire.

"It sounds worse than it is."

"It sounds like a Boeing 747 taking off," she mutters into the nape of my neck.

The gate opens and I inch out, trying to get a space in the traffic to pull out.

I take a quick glance around again. "You okay back there?"

"Uh-huh." She nods feverishly with her eyes closed.

"*Fuck*," is breathed on my neck as I lean into the turn, taking us out into the main road. We're not even doing ten miles an hour. It wasn't easy resisting this opportunity to take the piss out of her.

I wonder if she'll notice if I take the long route home.

"I didn't think it would be this slow," she says in my ear as we cruise past the old flower market towards the factory.

More cars honk. If I don't speed up a tad, I'm going to get arrested.

It would be worth it.

"Still," I say, "best you hold on extremely tight. Keep a good grip on my chest."

I am acutely aware of her breasts pressed against my back. Thankfully the leather is restricting my cock from bobbing against my stomach in appreciation.

I wonder if I could convince her to get on my lap and straddle me.

Probably one for the second ride.

"The lady on the bicycle over there has kept up with us the whole way," she muses. "In fact, she keeps overtaking us."

"Oh yeah?" I turn my head slightly. "Never noticed." Because driving this slowly takes a lot of effort.

"I'm such a badass!" She laughs into the wind.

"The baddest."

As we turn the corner, a heaviness comes over me, like it always does. The memorial plaque on the brick wall with my dad's face on it comes into view. The face I inherited my arrogant grin from, apparently.

It looks like one of my sisters has added fresh flowers.

"Oh, Jack," she murmurs behind me. "This is where it happened."

"Yup." I slow the Harley to a stop, the engine chugging.

"I'm sorry," she says softly, resting her cheek in the crook of my neck. "No one deserves what you went through."

When I turn my head, our faces almost touch. If I believed in heaven, I'd say Dad is looking down at me and winking.

She looks at me tentatively. "Does grief get easier over time?"

I think about it. "I'm not sure if easier is the right word. Manageable, perhaps. There'll be days on end when I'm in great form, then bang, something will remind me of what happened. I'll see one of the Wicks family on the street or something."

"That's shocking he was never convicted for it. That must make it all the worse."

I smile sadly. "Yeah, I have this belief that I'll find closure if Dad's murder goes on Wicks' record. Some day." I frown. "I know work and life can get in the way and it seems like there is always tomorrow, but don't lose sight of what matters. I took my dad for granted. It's good you're visiting yours."

She nods and we are quiet for a moment.

Eventually, I clear my throat. "Come on, let's get my badass Robin home safe."

19

Bonnie

Six-foot-two recruitment manager Christopher is not the distraction I was hoping for.

I'm on my first non-Max date in *five* years. We're in a gorgeous Cuban bar in Knightsbridge with yummy cocktails and salsa dancers, and I'm grinding my teeth into stumps with frustration.

We've had a one-way conversation for sixty minutes. He hasn't asked me a single question.

Christopher describes himself as an entrepreneur. My view is it's a tad dicky to call yourself that unless you're confident you're nailing the title.

He works in recruitment and left his job to start his own company, but it sounds like he's trying to steal all his old company's leads.

We've been chatting daily over Bumble, but the online Christopher seems much less obnoxious than the offline version.

His lips move. They have been for twenty minutes.

He's talking about Jack. Why is he talking about Jack?

Oh no, he's still talking about the *gym,* not Jack.

Gah. I've got a problem.

"Takes a lot of dedication," Christopher drones on. "Especially now that I'm running my own business. I'm in the gym religiously six days a week, six a.m. on the dot. It's worth it, though. My body fat percentage is down to fourteen." He folds his arms over his chest to showcase his biceps. I'm not a fan. "Muscle mass hit forty percent last week. Pretty good, huh?"

Why's he telling me this? Does he think I'm a doctor?

I stifle a yawn. My architect partner Steve and I spent the entire day at the factory reviewing everything in detail. I'm so tired I have the social skills of a slug. "That's great that you're happy with your stats. I wouldn't want to keep you late this evening since you have to stick to your regime. Six tomorrow morning."

"Don't worry about me." He waves a hand dismissively. "Tomorrow is strength training rather than cardio. I can afford to be a little tired."

As he launches into details of his strength training regime, I realise that if I maintain eye contact and a slight smile, he thinks I'm listening.

When I narrow my eyes into slits, he looks vaguely like Jack. Jack.

I wonder what he's doing right now. Is he with Michelle Allard? The alpha-hole thing of making sure I got home safely last night was kind of sweet. I keep replaying our conversation in my head. Does it change anything that he apologised for what happened to my dad?

God, the way he looked at my lips last night . . .

I squeeze my thighs under the table.

Christopher looks mildly pissed off.

I blink. Did he ask me a question? "Can you repeat that?" I smile thinly.

"I asked if you go to the gym."

"Oh. The office I'm working from has a swanky gym. I might go." At this point, I couldn't be arsed talking about myself. The date is a dead end.

"What did you say you do?"

I didn't because he didn't ask. "I'm an architect at Bradshaw Brown." I sip my low-alcohol beer. I'm boring myself.

He nods. "I have a mate who worked on the Shard design."

His eyebrows rise in expectation. It's my turn to say something.

"That's nice. I'm doing a project for Lexington."

This hits the spot for him. His eyes light up. "Nice." He sucks through his teeth. "They've a lot of open roles on their website. Do you know the head of HR?"

Fuck me. Is he using dates to find leads for his recruitment business?

"I met her once."

He nods and flashes me a lopsided grin, which I think is intended to make me go weak at the knees. "Think you could swing me a meeting?"

"I don't think so," I say sharply. "Like I said, I met her once."

He's undeterred. The grin widens. "You could take me to your next work drinks for our second date."

Right, that's it. I'm not wasting any more time.

"Speaking of work, I have a big presentation tomorrow." It's not a lie. Having worked on this proposal for days, I thought taking a few hours off would help me relax. Instead, I feel tense. I should have stayed at home and masturbated. "Do you mind if we call it a night?"

It's obvious he minds that I'm the one to decide when the date is over, but he nods chastely.

I beckon the waiter over for the bill.

"I had a great time, Bonnie."

How? My first foray into the online dating scene has not been a roaring success. According to Nisha I'll have to do another ninety-nine or so to hit a good date.

"We'll do this again," he informs me.

I look at him, startled, and take the chicken route. "Sure, sounds good." Oh. I think this makes me one of those ghosters Nish and Becky talked about.

I've never left a restaurant so fast after paying the bill. Outside, Christopher confidently tries to finish the date with a kiss. He leans in and stares at me intently.

I move my head to the side just as lips touch mine, leaving a wet trail on my cheek from the corner of my lip.

Awkward.

I tell him I'm going to a different underground station, so I don't have to walk with him. It'll take me fifteen minutes out of my way but it's worth it.

I have more chemistry with the guy that delivers my *Spicy Slice* pizza.

At least now I have time to call Mum. I haven't been able to get back to her in days. Every night, as soon as I get home from work, I face-plant onto the sofa from exhaustion.

En route to the underground station, I send a message to Nisha and Kate saying that Bonnifer is not happening and send a video request to Mum.

It takes a few rings for her to pick up. When she does, I see an ear.

"Hello, love! I haven't heard from you in a few days. You have me worried!"

"Hi, Mum. Sorry, I know. I've been busy with work. This is a video call, by the way. I can see your ear."

"Oh. Oh, let me see." The screen fuzzes for thirty seconds as Mum works out how to turn the phone around. She comes into focus. "There we are. Where are you, love?"

"Just finished drinks with Kate. I'm walking to the tube." If I tell her I was on a date, I'll get interrogated.

She looks delighted and moves her head as if she's going to somehow see around the corner who's behind me. "Is she there? I wanted to tell her what a stunning bride she was."

"Sorry, Mum, she's gone home," I lie again.

"That's a pity. You'll have to bring her over for Sunday lunch soon."

I nod. "Sounds good. I'll sort it out in a few weeks when work isn't so busy. How are you, Mum?"

"I'm great, love, but missing you. I haven't seen you in ages." She pouts. "Aunt Leslie came over from dinner. She asked about you. I'm trying to convince her to join the bowling club. I really think she would love it."

The contrast between Mum's life and Dad's kills me. She has private health insurance, doesn't have to worry about working, and is in lots of different women's societies.

Mum met Phil, my stepdad, a few months after splitting from Dad. It was an East End rags-to-riches story. Phil was a dentist who owned his own practice in the city and fell in insta-lust with Mum. Having a dental practice near the Bank of England HQ means you're doing okay for yourself.

Six months after she split from Dad, Phil had already bought a detached family home in a leafy suburb with a brag-worthy postal code and moved Mum in.

I kind of resented her for that. Just like Max, I suspect she mentally left the relationship with my dad long before the official split.

I was eighteen so I went away to university and at least that way, it didn't feel as if I was picking sides.

A year later, Dad lost the house to the bank.

"I'm sure she would, Mum. I need to see Leslie. Sorry I haven't come over in a while. I've been working late every night. I promise I will soon."

A line forms between her brows. "Why are they making you work late? I don't like the idea of you going home in the dark by yourself to that little flat."

"It's fine, no one forced me to stay late," I say firmly. "I didn't go back to my flat. I stayed at Dad's last night."

Her expression pinches. "That's great you visited your father but don't forget about me."

"I won't forget about you, Mum." I sigh, mildly irritated. "But Dad's by himself most of the time. And that flat of his isn't the nicest. I need to check in on him."

"Your father's a grown man, Bonnie. You don't need to feel guilty. By all means, visit your father, but I'm not comfortable with you going alone late at night. Did you get a taxi?"

Now's my chance to get answers.

"Actually, I got a lift with Jack Knight."

Her face lights up as if I've informed her I've won the national lottery. "Jack Knight?" She squeals, her eyes gleaming. "How lovely! What a *catch*, darling. Oh, this really is fantastic—"

"Mum. He gave me a lift, that's all. In his own words, if I'm in his office, he has a duty of care."

"Uh-huh. He's such a handsome chap, isn't he?" she gushes. "Never mind how successful he is and *everything* he's done for the area."

"He's a client my company is doing work for. That's all."

"I always knew he would go for a down-to-earth East End girl. I saw his mother and twin sisters the other day when Phil and I went to lunch. Snooty bunch. They'd pretend not to know you. Don't ever think you're not good enough for him just because he has cash, love."

I exhale heavily. She's not even listening to me anymore. She's got me walking down the aisle and milking him for Knight grandbabies, all over a lift.

She's still talking about the Knight family when I say, "Mum, *stop*. And how on earth can you think Jack is such a wonderful person when he fired Dad?"

She frowns, my question throwing her off-kilter. "There was a bit of drama, love, but that was a long time ago. Why are you asking about it now?"

"I want to know the facts," I say lightly. "He went into a bit of a downward spiral after that. I'd like to understand all the details."

"It's nearly a decade ago, love. I'm not sure I remember everything. Maybe ask your father."

"Just tell me what happened, Mum."

She sighs but reluctantly starts to speak. "Your dad was always looking for ways to make more money. His wage wasn't huge, and he was competing with younger tradesmen."

I feel a stab of guilt. I couldn't afford my university fees on my own, so Phil offered to cover them outright. Dad, however, wouldn't have it and paid the rest of the fees himself. I was the reason he was looking for ways to earn more money.

"Sometimes he cut corners."

I slow to a halt on the pavement. My scalp prickles. Perhaps I don't want to know the details after all. But now I've started this train in motion.

She looks at me wearily. "He won't like me telling you this."

"Go on," I say, sharper than I intended.

"Your dad and a few others were," she pauses to find the words, "acting a bit *dodgy*. They figured they were owed a few extras, so they swiped some of the materials at the sites to sell on. It took the bosses at Lexington a while to notice because it wasn't enough to draw attention." Her lips curve slightly. "I think they saw themselves as East End Robin Hoods, stealing from the rich and giving to the poor."

I suck in through my teeth. This is a different story from what Dad told.

"I don't understand. Who did they give it to?"

"Themselves." She snorts. "Over time it seemed like small beans, but it added up."

The prickles on my scalp spread to my neck. "How much?"

She nibbles on her lips. "About half a million over a year."

Holy fucking hell.

I gawk at her through the phone. "Say that again."

"You heard me correctly. Half a million. Between the five of them."

I feel mildly nauseous. Do I know my dad at all?

And Jack.

My cheeks heat as I think about what I said to Jack last night. Bloody hell. What were my exact words? *You fired him for no reason. You didn't pay his last two weeks' wages.*

My throat bobs. "Are you sure? Did Dad tell you this himself?"

"No, your Uncle Pat told me." She smiles sadly. "I can't say I was that surprised. Your dad took a lot of risks, and they didn't always pay off. I knew something had gone down, I just didn't know what."

All this time, I didn't have the full facts.

I listened to Dad rant and rave about the injustice of being fired, the injustice of the good workers of the country not getting what they deserved, the injustice of the whole damn world.

Nothing was ever his fault.

I'm reminded of Christopher calling himself an entrepreneur when everything else he said made him sound delusional.

Why didn't Jack correct me last night?

"Did he pay the money back? Is that why he lost the house?" I ask.

She shakes her head on camera. "Bonnie, your dad was lucky Jack Knight didn't send him to jail. All things considered, he got off lightly. I think because they were East End guys, Jack went lenient on them. Your father put himself in enough debt to sink the Titanic. That's why he lost the house. I'm sorry, but you're old enough to realise the truth. He didn't want you to know. You know how proud he is."

I nod slowly. There's no doubt in my mind that Mum's telling the truth. I sometimes knew things fell off the back of a lorry and landed in Dad's lap, but Dad always had a joke and a story to go with it. He made it seem harmless.

"Does he know you know?"

She sighs. "No. I left it alone. It's better you do, too. He'll only get upset and drink himself into a state. No good will come from it now."

I let out a long breath. I'm not sure how Dad will react if I ruin the illusion that his daughter thinks he's the most successful man in East London. He holds onto these things a lot more now that he's not with Mum. These past few years, he hasn't seemed that stable.

I say my goodbyes and stand frozen on the spot, staring at nothing.

I spent ten years thinking Jack has wronged Dad. Ten years being awkward any time I've been in Jack Knight's presence.

Kate and I would come back from uni and meet Sean. Jack would sometimes be there and try to talk to me, despite being surrounded by an entourage of hangers-on.

Now, I don't know what to do with the truth.

I shudder, replaying the scene in my head. Jack should have put me in my place and told me what's what. I actually asked him if it was *legal* what he did to my dad.

Dad and his conspirators owe Jack *half a million pounds.* He should hold a grudge against me, not the other way around. Maybe he will now he knows my connection.

"Oh, God," I say out loud to the empty street.

Behind all the dominance, Jack was sweet last night. I'm not sure I know what to do with sweet Jack. The guy's a confused tap—one minute he's freezing cold, the next minute he's blistering hot.

Before I can overthink what I'm about to do, I take out my phone and locate Jack's number. And the one and only message he sent me at the wedding makes me laugh.

> Jack: Now you have my number you can send me all the nudes you want.

I begin to type: *Hopefully it's okay to text you off the record. Mum told me the truth about Dad leaving Lexington. I'm sorry for how I acted last night and for what Dad did. I'm mortified.*

The three dots tell me he is typing.

My breath stalls as I wait.

> Jack: Forget it. It's all in the past.

My breath gushes out. At least he doesn't hold grudges. Or demand his half a million back which he would have every right to do.

> Me: Why didn't you say something last night?

The dots appear then vanish. Just when I think he's not going to respond, they appear again.

Jack: Because he's your father.

Oh my God. My heart's about to break. Jack kept me in the dark so I would have a positive view of my father, but it meant a negative view of him.

What type of man does that make Jack?

A better one than my father.

A thousand thoughts rush through my head.

Jack: I hope you're not at the office?

Me: I'm in a bar in Knightsbridge. But leaving now.

I add the last part hastily in case he thinks I'm on the sauce, right before the presentation tomorrow.

Jack: Out with friends?

The reply is so quick I wonder if he's doing speech-to-text.

This makes me smile. At least Jack will think that there's a man out there somewhere interested in me, even if I'm not a Michelle-Allard-type gal.

Me: No, on a date.

I don't need to disclose that it was a disaster.

No response.

When I arrive at my flat in Brixton after thirty minutes

underground, there's still no response. After watching TV for an hour and taking a long bath, the phone remains silent.

When I realise my eyes are glued to my phone with the precision of a sniper on a target, I admit that maybe I'm a teeny tiny bit bummed Jack hasn't responded.

20

Bonnie

When I reach the chorus of the *Rocky* theme tune, I'm right there with Balboa on the steps, and my feet bang the treadmill so hard that people in the gym stare.

This morning we will present our first version of designs to the Lexington team and Nixon Lee, the architectural firm overseeing the entire regeneration project. Bradshaw is a cog in a much bigger wheel.

We will commit to having the final design and access statements and everything we need to apply for planning permission to the local authority within a few months. No small feat. I'll skip everything else in my life, some of which is shit anyway.

All I've done since the wedding is work on this proposal. So, the content is nailed, but I need to release some of this nervous energy.

The two cretins, Bradshaw and Brown, will both be at this morning's meeting, as will Jack.

I can't fail. My promotion is riding on it.

The treadmill says I've run ten kilometres.

I'm not one of those sexy runners. I'm sweating like a turkey at Christmas. My eyes sting from perspiration, and my hair sticks to my forehead.

I slow the treadmill to a halt, so I have time to clean it down.

I love running.

When my feet pound the pavement or treadmill I'm free of my worries and stress. Some of my best work ideas sprouted from a run.

After showering, I walk through the changing rooms to my locker, feeling marginally calmer.

Last night after the date, Jack emailed that he wanted to see me before the presentation, giving me no clue why.

But he says jump and we grab our poles.

There were no other email addresses from the team included so I can't tell if this is a one-on-one.

I didn't mention it to Max. He'll be furious that he's not invited, but the less I see of him right now, the better.

I want to apologise to Jack in person about Dad. It doesn't seem to bother him considering he took a while to even remember who Dad was. But it sure as hell bothers me.

It might not be professional bringing it up in this meeting. I'll play it by ear.

I'm not sure which I'm more nervous about: the chat with Jack or the presentation. Whatever Jack says to me could severely fuck up my mindset for the presentation.

Maybe that's his plan.

To mess with me.

Underwear.

My heart races as I root in my bag.

Where's my underwear?

All the good work that my run did flies out the window. I pack *two* laptop chargers and a mini overhead projector on the rare chance that the boardroom tech will fail, and I forget to pack a bloody change of *underwear*?

How is it that the simplest things are the ones that fuck you up?

I've brought a grey pencil skirt, so no-one will know but me, but still, the thought of presenting without underwear is a little disconcerting.

Goddamn it, no bra, either?

Wait, I set out my matching lacy power underwear set for luck before I went to bed last night. They were . . . on the chair beside the door to my flat. I groan. And I ran out with a coffee in one hand and my gym bag in the other. I can still see the underwear and bra neatly folded on the chair, right where I left them.

For luck.

Right.

I'm wearing a fucking white silk blouse.

As it stands, I have two choices. Bare breasts, or I wear my drenched tank top with the built-in bra under my blouse. Stinking the room out doesn't seem like a viable option.

I hope the air con isn't on in the room.

It's fine. I don't exactly have showstopping jugs. It won't be obvious at all.

When I change into my work outfit and stand in front of the mirror, my heart drops out of my fucking ass.

It's obvious.

My nipples show through the blouse—subtly—but enough to draw a second glance. With no bra to constrain them, there's a slight jiggle each time I take a step.

To me, they're as obvious as meeting a car with blinding headlights head-on. I'd feel more comfortable if a bunch of birds shit all over me.

He'll think I've done it deliberately.

The shops aren't open yet.

I text Nisha.

> Me: I need your bra!

> Nisha: ???

> Me: I need to borrow your bra for a meeting. I've got no bra! Hurry up, I'm in the gym.

I don't have time for this. It's eight forty-five, and I'm getting more flustered by the minute. I simply *cannot* present to a team of senior construction people with bouncing boobs.

> Nisha: Keep your knickers on. I'll be in the office at 9:15, see you then.

If only I could.

No, no, no, that's too late. I have ten minutes left before meeting Jack, then it's straight into the presentation. I feel sick.

Maybe if I can answer what Jack needs over a call, I'll have time to run to a shop.

Flustered, I pick up my phone and dial his number.

He answers on the first ring. "Bonnie." No indication to tell me whether it's sweet Jack or grumpy Jack today.

"Morning, Jack." My voice echoes around the bathroom. "Slight issue. I'm prepared for the presentation, you absolutely do not need to worry—"

"But?"

Grumpy Jack.

I draw in a breath. "Could we move our nine a.m. to nine thirty please? Or do it remotely? I'm so sorry, but I have a . . ."

A *what*? A crisis? Personal emergency? Catastrophe? "Something's come up that I need to sort out before the presentation."

My answer is a deep grunt down the phone.

Is that a yes? Apparently, when you become a billionaire, you stop responding in full sentences. "We can do it now over the phone if you're free?"

"Where are you?"

"Over the road at the Bradshaw Brown office," I lie.

"What's the problem?"

"Umm—"

"No, we can't do it remotely," he growls, ending the call.

Fuck. I stare at the phone in dismay.

It looks like I'm rocking the bra-less look for the most important presentation of my career.

৬

I leave the gym feeling naked. It's a skill to walk at pace with your arms crossed over your chest.

Is it considered unprofessional to not wear a bra? It sways more towards the casual side of business casual. Maybe I can cover my nipples with tape or Post-it notes.

I'm being ridiculous. It's probably like that spot on your chin that you think is taking over your entire face, but nobody else can see it.

The queue to the lifts is massive. Six rows deep and it's ten minutes to nine.

By the time I arrive at the fortieth floor, I'm sweating under my arms and my cheeks are crimson. I may as well not have taken a shower after my run.

Jess's smile fades when she sees me, and I know I'm in shit. "He's in his office expecting you. Be quick."

It's 9:01.

"Go quickly. Hurry. Knock first. Good luck," she calls after me, looking sympathetic.

My pulse races as I knock. It's the first time I'll have been in his private office.

"Come in," says the big bad wolf from behind the door.

When I enter, he is stalking back and forth like he's planning an attack.

Flustered, I close the door and take a few steps into the room, crossing my arms over my chest. "Sorry, I'm slightly late."

I'm trapped. The only contact with the outside world is through the floor-to-ceiling window.

His office smells of him.

Pictures of him on the wall catch my eye. Jack ice-climbing

on a glacier, Jack riding a motorbike in the desert. Basically, the wall is covered with Jack engaging in extreme sports in extreme environments.

When I meet his gaze, his eyes flare.

"Some advice," he starts in a hard tone. "When your largest client requests to meet you in person, you don't call them ten minutes before and ask to do it remotely."

I stiffen. He seems irrationally rattled. Two nights ago, I was wrapped around him on his motorcycle. I sense now's not the time to apologise about my shitty attitude to Dad's firing.

"I apologise. Would you like to see the presentation before ten? I'm not clear on what the agenda for this is."

He's about to answer when he stops short, nostrils flaring and jaw clenched.

Oh, fuck.

My breath stalls as his brown eyes burn holes through the silk to my breasts.

"Sean told me I was too hard on you in the last meeting. I'm making sure I have no reason to be this time." The muscle in his jaw jumps as his gaze moves between my face and chest.

It doesn't seem like the right time to point out that an entire team of ten is working on this, and two of us are presenting today. Does he assume I'm the only one capable of messing up?

"I understand," I squeak. I *feel* his gaze on me. My stupid nipples tingle, and to my horror, salute him.

So, this is how guys feel when they have unwanted semis.

"I shouldn't have bothered since you can't manage your time or priorities very well," he sneers. "Late one, last night, was it?"

My eyes widen. What the hell is he talking about? "Jack, that's not why I wanted to push this meeting. I had one drink last night and was in bed early." Alone. Not that it's any of his business.

His throat bobs. "Who's the guy?"

"My date last night?" I ask, confused. "Somebody I won't see again."

We enter a heated stare-off as I try to make sense of the

strange conversation.

Finally, he clears his throat. "My team will want to see exterior 3D visuals in detail. Do you have them?

I nod. "Yes. I've already gone over them with your team to get their approval before the meeting."

"What about the Affordable Housing statement?" he shoots back.

"Absolutely," I reply instantly. "The Environmental statement is also ready."

There's a tic in his jaw, and I wonder why the Environmental statement makes him angry. What the hell is wrong with him this morning?

"What are you doing, Bonnie?" he asks quietly.

My brow furrows. "With the Environmental statement? I can show it to you on my laptop if you would like?"

His strong jaw clenches harder. "Did you forget to put on all your clothes this morning?"

What?

He can't say that. Even if Dad did nick a load of building supplies from him.

Screw you, Jack Knight.

"Excuse me," I snap, incredulous. "I hardly think this is an appropriate question, *Mr. Knight.*"

"So, which is it?" He scowls. "Poor wardrobe planning after your date, or are you fucking with my head again?"

"*Wha-at*?" I stammer.

He can't talk to me like that. If I were a man, we wouldn't be having this conversation. "You have no right to comment on my dress code."

His eyes darken. "I do have a right when you're about to present to my construction leads, and all they'll focus on is the outline of your nipples."

"Your team shouldn't be looking at my breasts," I say haughtily, tilting my head up to maintain eye contact. "Will *they* all be wearing bras? This antiquated concept of gender should be banished from the workplace." It's worth a shot.

"How do you expect them to focus on anything else?" he snarls.

I pick my jaw up off the floor and answer coolly, "If they are that easily distracted, remind me never to enter one of your hotels for fear the thing will collapse."

He stares at me for a long beat, then lets out a frustrated breath. "Don't play me again, Bonnie. It's not fair."

"*Again*?" I blink rapidly. "When did I play you the first time?"

"The little act of seduction at the wedding to make your ex-fiancé jealous."

Maybe I did say that.

"*Me* playing *you*?" My voice rises. "That's a bit rich coming from you. I'm doing my damnedest here. You set a harsh deadline knowing we'll jump up and down to meet it, yet still, I can't do right by you. You think I'm trying to *seduce* you?" I laugh bitterly. "Get real. You aren't remotely interested in me, remember? I'm not your type. Why would I think that could possibly work?"

His eyes narrow. "What the hell are you on about? Not my type?"

"I *heard* you. I heard what you said the morning after the wedding."

He's clearly thinking hard. "What did I say?"

"I overheard you tell some guy you weren't interested in me before you dished out my number."

He stops short, staring at me as if I've lost my mind. Then his brows knit together. "You heard that."

"Yes."

"You heard me talking to Damon Manning."

He looks at me as if I've revealed some big secret. "Do you know who he is? Do you know what he does for a living?"

I shake my head. Why do I care?

"He writes for tabloids. I would never tell Damon a shred of truth, anything remotely near the truth. I can't stand the guy. I'm sorry you heard that. It was bullshit."

I roll my eyes. "Sure."

He takes a step towards me, closing the gap between us. "Do you really think you're not my type?"

"Yes, considering you gave my number to a guy you can't stand."

His lips twitch. "Did he call?"

"He did," I lie, annoyingly breathless as he looms over me. "But I turned him down."

He smiles arrogantly. "I gave him a wrong number."

I don't even notice myself backing against the wall. He's in my space caging me in with his arms.

"Must have got it elsewhere." My voice catches in my throat as he traces his fingers along my jawline, sending goosebumps down my skin.

Fuck.

This is unexpected.

A throb starts between my legs as his fingers slide slowly down my neck. It's the same erratic beat he must feel in my neck.

His lips quirk into a wicked smirk.

All I have to do is take a small step forward and my body will be pressing against his. My chest against his slab of muscles. My core against that growing bulge tenting in his jeans.

I can't breathe.

"You were always my type," he murmurs as he slides his hand behind my neck to push me flush against his chest. My nipples harden as they brush his shirt. "Even when you used to run around the White Horse with pink hair and a ring through your nose."

I try to swallow my nerves. "Someone was paying attention." I tilt my head up to meet his gaze.

He stares down, completely unfazed. There's no doubt who's in charge here. "The only reason I didn't pursue you is because I will never be a relationship wrecker. Don't think for a second that I don't think you're perfect. Believe me."

I do believe him.

I forgot what it's like for a man to look at me like this.

Undeniable want directed at me.

Right now, I couldn't care less if we were put in a viewing box for the entire financial district to watch, which we kind of are. I want this man, and I can't think past the carnal urge to straddle him with my bare aching pussy and give her what's she crying for.

My hands land on his chest to find he has the same swollen nipple problem I have.

"Is that why you said you flirted with me to make Max jealous? Because of what you heard me say to Damon?" He rests his hands on the wall on either side of my head, fully caging me in. "Answer me, Bonnie," he says hoarsely. "Tell me the fucking truth."

"I lied," I whisper. "I wasn't trying to make Max jealous. The truth is I wanted you, but I hated myself for it."

He lets out a low chuckle. "My poor ego. I'm choosing to take that as a compliment." He nods. "You hated yourself because you thought I wronged your dad."

I shake my head. "Not just that. I also thought you were arrogant," I confess. "You're too used to women falling at your feet."

His chuckle deepens. "Okay, darlin', you can quit while you're ahead. But your assumptions were spot on. I am arrogant. And women do fall at my feet." His smile tugs into a full-blown grin. "But it's not every woman's feet that I fall at."

I make a noise that is halfway between a whimper and a snort. "You're so sure you know what women want."

"So, test me," he replies, cocky smile in place. "You're attracted to me. Let's see if I know what you want."

I release an indignant puff of air. "See? You just proved how arrogant you are. I wouldn't kick you out of bed for eating crisps, but there are plenty of attractive men out there."

"I'm secure in myself. And I didn't get this body eating crisps in bed."

"Secure enough to offer yourself to *all* the bridesmaids."

"*All* the bridesmaids?" He grins. "How many are we talking here?"

My eyes narrow. "You gave Becky your number at the wedding as well as me. That's one hundred percent of the bridesmaids."

"Ah. I see." He nods, still with that infuriating grin. "Well, she asked for it. She wants an interview with my marketing team."

Does she fuck. Well played, Becky. Smooth.

"I gave her my office number. I gave you my personal number." His brows rise. "Are we done with excuses?"

"You kicked me out of a meeting. That's pretty obnoxious."

"You rolled in late to my first meeting and didn't listen. What did you expect? Praise?"

"It didn't quite happen like that. I didn't *roll* in. You make me sound gangsta."

"Bonnie." His hand presses my lower back, crushing me against a very hard cock.

"There's also the issue of the missing half a million pounds. I'm not in a position to pay you back . . . right now." In this lifetime.

"Take me for dinner and we'll call it even."

I nod but I'm not sure I can even afford to take Jack to the fancy restaurants he must go to.

"Any other complaints about me? Or are we done?"

"Yes," I rasp like someone who has been in the desert for a week with no water. "I think I got everything I needed out there."

His grin turns wicked as he takes my hair in his hand and pulls my head back to look at him.

"About fucking time."

21

Bonnie

Caught off guard is the understatement of the year. My reflexes are ten seconds behind Jack's. Before my legs can tell my brain, Jack has lifted me up by my thighs and I'm straddling his warm, hard torso.

Gasping, I wrap my arms around his neck for support, and I instinctively squeeze his waist with my thighs like the greedy lust-crazed animal I am.

My skirt strains at the seams.

We are eye to eye, heat bouncing between us. So much heat my skin feels like it's boiling.

I can't catch a breath, but I can feel his.

I can't talk. I'm completely incapacitated, floating mid-air on strong forearms as if I weigh nothing.

"I fucking love your face," he breathes out against me. "Those lips, those cheekbones. Goddamn it, those *eyes*. Even when you scowl at me like I'm the worst man on Earth."

"Speak for y-yourself," I stutter. "You have some seriously sexy eye energy going on."

He chuckles. One of his hands slides to my thigh from where he's holding me in an invisible chair. He brusquely pushes my skirt up until it bunches around my waist, exposing me to Jack and anyone with binoculars in Canary Wharf.

Spread open, naked, and squirming, I gasp louder this time. "You're a little primal, Jack," I say breathlessly.

"Just a little?" He smirks. "Maybe I'm behaving myself too much. I don't want to scare you off, darlin'."

His black T-shirt rides up his stomach.

Skin on skin.

My clit rubs against warm ab muscles.

Delicious. Wet. Friction.

The sensation sends shivers running down my body like a sexy taser. Holy fucking hell. Can you die of heart failure from being too turned on?

A deep moan escapes me from the depths of a place I never knew existed. I'm mildly embarrassed. The guy hasn't even touched me and I'm already spasming like a cow banging against an electric fence.

His stomach muscles jerk. "I knew you'd be drenched under that skirt. You're dying for me to touch you, aren't you, Bonnie?" My name has never sounded so sexy.

"*Yes,*" I whimper as my clit grazes his stomach. My hips buck but he holds me tight, pressing my body taut against his.

His biceps flex under the strain of holding me. He'll get used to it; I'm never climbing down.

His mouth takes possession of mine, pushing my lips open as his tongue thrusts against mine.

I'm caught in a wolf's jaw. Exactly how I imagined alpha wolf Caleb from *the Red Moon Canines*. I moan, digging my fingers into his back like a horny virgin mate.

Don't stop. Never stop.

A deep groan of approval vibrates from the back of his throat into my mouth.

I don't know who's making what sound. Grunts. Groans. Pants. Breathing like we've just broken through an ice lake. I try fruitlessly to clench down on his stomach.

I shouldn't be let loose on dating apps. I clearly have no restraint. Neither does the big bad wolf claiming me.

I'm seeing stars over a kiss.

Although I'm not sure if this qualifies as kissing. There's

nothing delicate about this, there's no gentle teasing or tongue skimming lips waiting for a response. No, this is being fucked in the mouth.

Moaning into each other's mouths like two Neanderthals, I grind myself to oblivion against his hard stomach.

We're both breathing too hard to continue the kiss.

His arm fatigues under my weight. He walks us backwards until we collapse on the black leather sofa in the corner.

My knees fall on either side of him as I land on top of a very hard swollen cock in just the right spot.

He's covered in way too much fabric. It all needs to come off.

I'm about to free him from his jeans but Jack has other plans. His hand slides around my inner thigh until he palms the slit between my legs.

"Soaking," he says in a ridiculously husky voice, his head tipping back onto the sofa. "You're absolutely fucking drenched."

His fingers graze up and down my opening with just enough pressure to tease me but not enough to tip me over the edge. It's delicious torture. His arrogant smirk tells me it's not by accident.

With my skirt bunched around my waist, I'm mooning all of the financial district straddling Jack but it's a price worth paying.

"Jack. *Please.*"

His thumb *finally* grazes my clit, and I'm so receptive I moan, grinding against his hand, begging him with my pussy.

"Yes," I whimper.

"So wet and perfect. You feel better than I ever imagined." He brushes my clit with his thumb in lazy controlled circles, grin solidly in place, telling me who's boss.

"Jack," I cry, grabbing handfuls of his hair. It must hurt.

"That's right, darlin'," he says roughly. "You're going to moan my name when I make you come."

He slips one finger deep inside me.

Oh. *Yes.*

A second follows, thrusting deeper this time. "First with my fingers. Then my mouth. I'm going to fucking devour you," he growls. "Then my cock. And you'll keep coming until I say stop."

I agree with his excellent plan. And poem. *"Yes!"*

My muscles squeeze and lock around him as he fucks me with his fingers. His thumb circles my sensitive clit faster and harder, and his fingers thrust in and out of my wet heat.

Tingling sensations shoot through my body. Delicious shock waves controlling my limbs make me buck and shudder around him. I've lost all ability to function.

Nothing else matters except my overwhelming carnal need to come hard on his hand.

"Jack. Yes. Jack. Jack." Random words blurt out of my mouth as he brings me so close . . . so close. "Make me come . . . I need to—"

There's a knock at the door.

I jump out of my skin, going rigid in his arms.

He shushes me.

Clearly not as alarmed as I am to know there's someone waiting outside his door, he continues to slide his fingers in and out of me.

Working me into a frenzy.

Repeatedly.

Relentlessly.

I need him to stop, but I want him to continue. I need him to make me orgasm so loudly that all of Canary Wharf hears me.

"Jack." Jess knocks again. "Bradshaw Brown is waiting for you in the boardroom with the senior team."

Fuck off, lovely Jess. Please fuck off for . . . thirty seconds.

I sink my mouth into his shoulder to stop from crying out.

"Yes, Jess," he growls into my hair.

"You also have a meeting with Newham council in forty minutes," she persists. "Shall I tell the Bradshaw team to reschedule?"

He curses loudly, and I hope to God Jess didn't hear. "Give me five minutes, Jess. I'll be with them."

I close my eyes, trying to block out the footsteps of Jess

walking away. My inner muscles quiver, and I *know* this will be the motherfucker of all orgasms. Vagina shattering. I might never recover.

Jack's hand disappears, and I'm planted back on my feet on shaky legs with my skirt still bunched up.

"What the bleeding hell?" I stammer, gaping at him as he stands to his full height.

"Not now," he says with a low chuckle. Bending, he takes the hem on my skirt and pushes it down over my hips and thighs. "I'm sorry, darlin'. Later. It'll give you time to fantasise about me."

I'm going to throttle him.

I glare at him until common sense slowly seeps back into my head. "You're right," I mutter. "None of the training videos on *how to present to clients* advised rubbing one out on your audience beforehand." I blow out a deep breath and smooth my cavewoman hair back into a work-appropriate ponytail.

He lets out a low laugh. "Yup, it's probably best you wait until after you've presented."

"After I present, you have a meeting with the council."

He raises his brows, amused. "Easy tiger. All good things come to those who wait. Are you okay to present?"

Oh, God. Am I?

"Is this your master plan so I say yes to everything your team asks and agree to do the work in half the time?"

"You got me." He straightens out his T-shirt which never looked like it was ironed in the first place. "I fluff all the design teams before my staff interrogates them. How else do you think I build forty-story buildings so quickly?" He checks his watch. "I've got something to do before meeting the council, so you'll need to knock ten minutes off now."

Interrogation? Knock ten minutes off?

Oh, Jesus.

He smiles, brimming with cockiness as he tugs on my ponytail. "Do the demo for me with your hair down." My hair falls around my shoulders. There's no *please*. He makes it sound like

I'm going to do a private dance for him rather than present the designs for a converted factory.

I'm too aroused to become indignant.

"Do you have anything to cover nipples?" I ask breathlessly, looking around the office for miracle band-aids.

His lips quirk. "Besides my mouth, no."

The man is impossible.

His smile slips. "But if I see any of my team leering at you, I'll throw them out the window."

"That's not helpful," I mutter, nerves bubbling in my belly. If I thought I was anxious before, now I have to do it in front of a man I just dry-humped.

"Hey," he says softly, lifting my chin. "Whatever happens between us is separate from the project. You don't need to worry about that. Do you trust me, Bonnie?"

I give a small shaky nod. "You're still an asshole though to leave a girl hanging."

"I am," he agrees cheerily as he adjusts the massive monster tenting his pants without a shred of shame.

"And someone needs to go at you with a lawnmower," I grumble. "I have first-degree beard burn now."

He grins at me. "I'll try to be gentler next time."

There's a next time.

I blow out a huge breath, placing my hand on my lower stomach to calm myself.

I've rehearsed this presentation a million times in the mirror. I even recorded an audio of myself doing it and added pauses to make it sound more authentic. I know what I'm going to say, how I will stand and what I'll do with my hands. Everything is one hundred percent prepped.

But none of those dress rehearsals were with an aroused clit.

This is not good. I'm not wearing underwear, our most important client has rubbed me into oblivion, and now I have to walk into a team of construction leads and talk about the plans for waste management of a factory.

I must look . . . *fucked.*

What the hell is wrong with me? Maybe it's a nearly-thirties crisis.

Jack walks to his desk and lifts his office phone. "Jess," he says, watching me. There's a pause. "Rearrange the Bradshaw meeting until after lunch."

She says something I can't make out and he grunts in response. "Yeah, I know it's last minute. Tell them I'm sorry."

"Thank you," I whisper as he puts down the phone. Now I can source the largest granny bra in Canary Wharf. "And thank you for trying to protect me against the truth of what happened with my dad. You should have put me in my place."

Those pesky butterflies are back in my stomach, stronger than ever this time, as we stare at each other.

"You're a sweet guy, Jack Knight."

Slowly, he smiles. "About time you realised."

Jack

Before I've closed the boardroom door, Bradshaw is on his feet and scuttling towards me, shaking my hand like we're old friends. His handshake is as limp as the rest of him.

I return the pleasantries as I scan the room. Jess has arranged it in a cinema style to focus on the big screen and the presenters.

They're all here, seated, waiting patiently—my senior team, the Bradshaw team, and the architecture firm overseeing all project phases, Nixon Lee.

My gaze connects with Bonnie's, and I smile. I've done fuck all work in the few hours since our meeting. At this rate, I'll have to put my dick in a straight jacket.

Her piercing blue eyes, normally ablaze with heat, are filled with uncertainty as she shifts her weight from one foot to the other.

Damn it. Would she be this nervous if I'd kept my hands to

myself?

God knows how I found the willpower to stop.

"You know the team, Jack?" Bradshaw asks. He beckons Bonnie over along with the other architect I've met once. Max comes over, too.

"Steve." The other architect assumes I'd forgotten his name. I had. He shakes my hand. "Good to see you again, sir."

Bonnie steps forward. "Good to see you again." A pause. "Sir."

Amused, I take her hand in mine, holding on to it for longer than necessary.

Dear God, she's breathtaking.

Now she has a bra on, thank fuck.

She pulls her hand from mine.

Max clears his throat. "Jack, I hear you needed to speak to Bonnie this morning about the brief. Is everything okay?"

"Perfect." I look at Bonnie. "Everything's perfect."

Her cheeks flush.

"I'm happy to be your point of contact going forward." Max steps forward. "Obviously, Bonnie is more than capable, but I have a holistic view of what the team's working on. I'll be able to direct any questions to the right person."

I force my eyes from Bonnie and turn to Max, who has a deep frown across his face.

I almost laugh. *You're an idiot, mate. You gave up the best thing that ever happened to you for a fling with an intern.*

I've got five years on him. I'm the one that should be hitting a midlife crisis.

"Sure, Max. Whatever is easiest for the team. Shall we get started?" I say cheerfully. It's their lucky day, presenting to deliriously happy Jack. "I have twenty minutes. My team will handle questions after that."

I take a seat beside the Lexington senior project managers and directly in front of Steve and Bonnie.

Steve introduces himself first and sets the scene, but my attention is on Bonnie.

As she introduces herself, her voice is strong, but it's clear she's trying hard to modulate her tone.

I need to calm her down. It's my fault she's unhinged.

"Bonnie has already gone through the designs and layout plans with me," I tell the room. A complete lie. "They're on track against our vision."

I give her a private smile and a nod.

She nods back.

"A key element of the style we propose is to mix the old with the new and to bring into focus the original features. The factory's most iconic features are, of course, its four slender three-hundred-foot chimneys. Each will be restored with viewing platforms added at the top." She clicks through a series of visual designs to bring home the concept. I'm impressed. It's a little rough but has a lot of potential.

She relaxes as she answers questions thrown at her by the team.

I sit quietly, taking in every one of her features, every curve, every line, every smile, banking it in my mind for later.

Fucking delicious.

"Okay, moving on. I've worked with the interiors team to provide an example interior 3D visual," she continues. "Right now, one of the walls is entirely covered with graffiti by the locals. The great debate is always whether graffiti is vandalism or art. But, like it or not, it plays a significant role in our East End culture. It was and still is, a key form of expression for youths of some of the poorest areas in London. Our proposed design fuses it in such a way that no one can ever doubt it is art."

Her delivery is stilted, but the quality and granularity of detail is evident in her designs.

I know my eyes eating her up is off-putting, but I can't help myself.

She pauses to take a deep breath. "With local street artists telling the story of the East End through the decades from when the factory was built, the art alone will make it a destination."

Christ, I wonder if she's still not wearing panties.

I place my laptop strategically over my lap.

"Moving onto the apartments themselves, they'll be located on the site of the original factory, positioned directly beside the Thames. We'll incorporate watery reflections, wild grasses, and marshland vistas inside, in natural colour palettes and woody, earthy textiles and fittings. As you can see here."

It's taking all my control to not kick everyone out of the room and finish the job I started.

As she answers a question from Sean, her eyes flit to the laptop balanced on my lap, then up to my face.

The flush flaming her cheeks tells me she knows *exactly* what I'm thinking. She gives me a warning look as her voice falters.

I read it loud and clear. *Fucking behave yourself, Knight.*

I wink. *Sorry, darlin', we've come too far for that now.*

She averts her gaze to Steve as he talks through the final part of the presentation.

Max stands up. "Are there any more questions?"

Everyone looks at me.

"He didn't ask any questions. Is that good or bad?" someone mutters behind me, followed by a panicked *shush*.

I clear my throat. "It's a start. Get ready to present the questions the guys asked by the end of the week. Jess, can you find another thirty-minute slot in my diary?"

Jess nods dutifully. "Sure, Jack." Unfortunately for her, she'll probably spend sixty minutes trying to find thirty minutes.

"Seriously, is that good or bad?"

I crane my neck to see the loud whisperer behind me. He stares back, horrified.

"If you're asking the question, perhaps you shouldn't be on the project. I'm not looking for good. I'm looking for extraordinary. Think you can manage that?"

"Uh." Loud Whisperer goes completely still. "*Yes?*"

"Jack," Jess cuts in, in the tone she uses to tell me I'm late.

"Yes, Jess." I wave my hand. "Let's wrap it up."

I stand, and everyone follows suit.

"We'll send over the conceptual designs by close of day," Max says. "The minor adjustments will be included, and the rest will follow by Friday."

"Great." I anchor my attention back on Bonnie, who looks one thousand times more relaxed now. "Let's do drinks tonight. I'll reserve an area in my hotel next door. It'll give the two teams a chance to get to know each other. Obviously, it's on Lexington."

I'm telling Bonnie. The rest can take it or leave it.

They'll all take it.

"In Maggie's," I add, and the energy in the room rises.

Not surprising. The name is deceiving. It's a nod to my amazing nan. Maggie's has been named the sexiest bar in the world for four years running. As it is also the most exclusive, most people don't get the chance to experience its sexiness.

"Wonderful idea. We'll all be there," Bradshaw says, puffing out his chest.

Max leans into me. "Jack, are we on track? Is this in line with what you are looking for?"

"Yes," I say, my gaze lingering on Bonnie. "Yes, we are definitely on track."

22

Jack

Everything about Maggie's is intimate, sexy, and as British as you can get, paying tribute to the 1950s when Nan was a wild child wreaking havoc in the East End.

City high rollers and parliamentarians rub shoulders with actors, athletes, and models without the fear of being judged or papped.

Mona, our hostess, opens the red velvet curtains for me. Staff and club members greet me with smiles, waves, and whatever else they can do to catch my attention.

In my twenties, the attention was priceless. I was a kid in a candy store. Blonde, redhead, brunette, shaved head. I was insatiable.

Now in my late thirties, it's mildly exhausting.

The Lexington and Bradshaw teams are in the area reserved at the back.

I scan the crowd for the reason I'm here. The reason that they are all here.

She stands out a million miles. Her cheeks are flushed again, likely from alcohol, as she talks animatedly to Nisha and Sean.

"Scotch, please, Mandy." I smile at the bartender as I take a position beside the bar in view of Bonnie.

"Right away, Mr. Knight. It's great to have you with us tonight."

Our overpriced signature cocktails are designed with the

perfect blend of alcohol and aphrodisiacs to keep the posh punters coming back to get their fix again and again. If they can afford the five grand annual membership fee, that is.

Apparently, the cocktails are to die for.

I wouldn't know. I stick to my neat Scotch.

I thank Mandy and leave a generous tip.

"Well, well, well, if it isn't Jack Knight," a woman drawls beside me. I turn towards the blonde nearly as tall as me. Anna. Ada. Something like that. Sexy as fuck. Kind of reminds me of Cruella de Vil.

I said I would help her charity and ended up sleeping with her in the process. "It's been too long," she says, eyeing me with the confidence of a woman who has never been turned down. "You're ignoring me."

"Not intentionally." I smile politely. It's not a lie.

"Have a drink with me."

I nod to the team in the corner. "Sorry, all work, no play tonight. My staff and suppliers are over there."

She's undeterred. Sexy Cruella de Vil comes right into my space. "Later. Just the two of us."

I throw back my Scotch. "It's not a good idea tonight."

"Why the hell not?"

That's a damn good question.

Anna or Ada's knee not so subtly manages to make its way between my thighs.

Is there a smooth way of turning a woman down that you've already slept with?

I glance back at the animated blonde in the corner. Bonnie spears me with a fierce glare that either means she wants to strip me naked so she can fuck me until she passes out, or do a *Dexter* on me, leaving me dead in a pool.

Hard one to read.

I tip my glass in her direction.

She ignores me and turns back to her mate, Nisha.

"Because I need to talk to Counsellor Adams," I say to Anna/

Ada, grabbing my opportunity. "Counsellor Adams."

Anna/Ada takes the hint and saunters off.

When Adams sees me, he freezes, then his face lights up like a guy who has just discovered how his genitals work.

Damn, this is going to be a long, boring conversation.

"Jack, my man!" And there starts the monologue.

Luckily, I don't need to concentrate too hard on what he's saying. A few nods on cue keep him going.

I lean against the bar, directly facing Bonnie. I probably shouldn't be so blatant, but I couldn't give a fuck.

She's sitting to the side, so she has to tilt her head to see me, but every time she does, my gaze is firmly fixed on her.

Nisha leans forward, whispering something to Bonnie that makes her blush even more.

Another guy on the team says something to her. She gives a wide open-mouthed laugh and flicks her hair over her shoulder before glancing over at me coyly.

This little show is all for me.

Nisha gets up and the lead architect from the company overseeing the entire regeneration quickly takes her seat. I hadn't noticed him waiting in the wings.

He says something to get Bonnie's full attention.

I clench my teeth as I watch her become more enamoured by whatever the hell they're talking about. She throws her head back and laughs. Her legs part slightly, and I hope to fuck she bought a pair of panties to go with that bra.

"Another Scotch, old chap?"

"Yes," I growl at Counsellor Adams. "Put them on my tab."

The lead architect, whose name I should know, says something else and Bonnie nods, smiling intently. Maybe free alcoholic aphrodisiacs weren't the best tactic.

The burning sensation in my chest grows and it's not Scotch.

She darts a glance around the table then slyly hands the guy her phone.

What the fuck?

No, darlin', I did not bring you out here to get off with another man.

As he passes back her phone, I snap up my own and type.

> **Me: Come here.**

She jerks her head around, shocked. "No," she mouths to me, then turns to the guy.

I curse between my teeth.

"Bad day, Jack? You seem a tad stressed."

"Most productive day I've had in a long time." I take the refill from Adams and type.

> **Me: Please.**

She smirks over at me, typing back.

> **Bonnie: See, that wasn't so hard?**

I sip my Scotch, watching her as she walks the long way around the bar. I'm not even pretending to listen to Adams anymore.

"Excuse me, Counsellor." I nod towards Bonnie approaching.

"I won't keep you from your lady friends, Jack." He winks approvingly at me as he turns back to the bar.

"I thought you weren't coming," she says as she reaches me.

"So, you did miss me." I sit on the bar stool so we're at eye level and gently pull her by the wrists between my legs. Close enough that I can smell her delicious scent but not close enough that the Bradshaw crowd will suspect. They're far enough away and drunk enough to be oblivious.

Her lips curve into a sassy grin. "Did you want me to miss you?"

"Very much so. For some reason, I've been distracted all day. Haven't been able to focus since a certain hot-headed mouthy cockney tried to come all over my stomach."

She visibly blanches. "Don't remind me. I'm so embarrassed. I'm out of practice. Do you know stomach-sitting is actually a fetish? On the bright side, at least you can't get pregnant from dry-humping a stomach."

"You can borrow my stomach anytime. Day or night." My hand trails down her hip confirming panties are intact. "I've been thinking about you all day."

"Oh." Her eyes widen. "Why?"

"Why?" I raise my brows. "What do you mean *why*?"

She sways slightly. She's a bit more drunk than I thought. "Ah, come on, Jack. All the women in the bar turned when you walked in. Literally, *every single woman* stopped what they were doing and stared." She hiccups. "Even the ones with guys."

"Really? The only woman I saw was you."

She rolls her eyes dramatically and laughs. "That's a great line."

I sigh. "Are you going to claim everything I say is a line?"

"I'll assess them on a case-by-case basis."

I nod to the Old Fashioned she's waving precariously in her hand. "How many of those cocktails have you had?"

"Just a few. I'm tipsy, that's all."

Says every drunk person.

She glances over at the Bradshaw table and tries to pull away from me slightly, but I hold her in place.

"What was the guy from Nixon Lee asking you?"

"Adrian?" Her cheeks heat as she takes another gulp of cocktail. "Oh, he was chatting about the factory designs."

She's lying.

"Questions that he needed your personal number for?"

"I don't have my work phone on me. It's at the office."

Uh-huh.

"So . . . about earlier on." Her flush deepens as she waits for me to take the bait.

"Ah, yes." With a grin, I intertwine my fingers in hers. "Earlier on."

She smiles coyly. "It was pretty hot."

"It was." I fight the urge to pull her flush against my chest. "If I had my way I'd pick you up in my arms, kiss every inch of your body, and give you a night so memorable that you'll never want to see another man again. But I suspect you'll be upset if I execute that plan in front of your co-workers."

She blows out her cheeks. "Holy hell that sounds like the best plan ever. But yes, I would be extremely pissed with you. Don't *you* care what the teams think?"

"About you and me? No." I lean forward. "I want to spend time with you, Bonnie."

"Damn." She groans. "Me too. I really want it."

"It?"

"You."

She looks up at me with such heat in her eyes my heart jerks in my chest.

Unnerved. That's how she makes me feel. It's both a blessing and a curse.

The forced proximity these last few weeks has allowed her to dominate my thoughts, which isn't helpful when you're in the process of erecting billion-pound buildings.

"I always thought I had more self-control," she says to herself as much as me. "That sex isn't worth the risk of all the office gossip. But I *totally* get it now. One-night stands with people you work with."

"Some things are more important than what your co-workers think." I shrug. "Learn to care less."

She eyes me sceptically. "Spoken like a boss who doesn't need to care about what anyone else thinks." She downs the last of the liquid in her glass. The danger with Old-Fashioneds is that they're so damn delicious you forget you're pretty much drinking whiskey neat. "Are we doing this then?"

I feel the pulse in her wrist quicken. "Elaborate, sweetheart."

"Fucking," she blurts out in a loud whisper. She doesn't wait for me to respond. "I mean I don't know if I've got the mentality for casual sex yet, but I'll damn well try. I can't even call it a rebound because it's been so long. But I think I'm ready. No emotional attachment. No strings."

I stare at her trying to keep up.

She breathes out heavily. "Just pure out-of-your-mind sex."

"God forbid you get emotionally attached."

"Nisha's done it. Jenny from Accounts slept with Bradshaw's son at the Christmas party. Why can't I?" She waves her empty glass in the air. "Is it too much to ask for some...just some show-stopping," she searches for words, "jaw-breaking dirty *sex*? *Mind-blowing* sex. Just vanilla though," she adds quickly.

I blink. "Is that a serious question you expect me to answer?"

She emits a giggle. "I promise I won't be weird," she babbles on. "As long as it's our secret. But why would you even tell anyone at Bradshaw? That's ridiculous. Sorry, I'm overthinking it. We can do this, and I'll be one hundred percent professional. I mean in work, not during the sex. I'm not a professional prostitute. But in work, professional. Yup. You don't need to worry about that. No, sir!"

"Breathe, Bonnie."

"Jack?" she asks when I don't say anything else. "Sorry. It's the free cocktails." She giggles nervously. "Drought. Hottest guy I've ever met. It's a bad combo. I'm a wee bit drunk and in unchartered territory. The last one-night stand I had was in uni with a guy who smoked weed in bed. One-night stands with billionaires probably have certain rules."

Another giggle.

"Bet you don't eat crisps or smoke weed in bed."

"You're right, Bonnie." I release her hand. "You're drunk. I'll get a driver to take you home."

"*What*? I'm not that drunk! I can walk in a straight line. I'll show you."

Her face scrunches in concentration as she takes a few heel-to-toe steps in front of me.

"No need."

"You haven't even let me do the turn test. The police wait until you do that before deciding the verdict."

"Bonnie." I sigh. "Come on, I'll have a driver for you in five."

The light in her eyes fades as she goes quiet for a moment. "This really isn't happening?"

"No, not like this," I say flatly.

She looks at me like I've just kicked a puppy. "I thought you'd be up for the job."

I chug my Scotch and grimace. "The job of being your rebound sex? That's not what I want from you."

Her face falls and she steps back, muttering under her breath.

"Boss man. Bonnie." I turn to see Adrian and Max. Max frowns slightly, looking between Bonnie and me.

I'm not in the mood for this. "Adrian. Max."

My jaw flexes as Adrian appreciatively scans Bonnie up and down and goes to hand her another Old Fashioned.

"I'll take that," I say, intercepting him. "Bonnie's getting a lift home with my driver. She's had enough."

Max frowns at her. "Everything okay?"

Her cheeks flush with annoyance, but she hides it quickly with a bright smile. "Everything's fine! I don't want anymore. Jack's right—those things are strong! Besides, I have to run ten miles tomorrow morning."

"Ten miles, Bonnie?" Adrian stretches out her name. "Impressive."

"I'm doing the London Marathon this year," she says. "So really, I shouldn't be drinking much, or it messes up my training."

Adrian, the prick, rakes his eyes down her bare legs with zero subtly. "That explains a *lot*."

I glare at him then turn to Bonnie. "I'll show you to my driver."

"It's fine." She smiles stiffly at me. "I can make my own way home. The tubes are still running."

"It wasn't a question."

She shakes her head like a stubborn child. "I'll get the tube."

My jaw tightens. "I have a duty of care to anyone from the team who is out late drinking with Lexington."

She mutters under her breath, "*his bloody duty of care again.*"

"Bonnie, take the driver," Max cuts in.

"Fine." She huffs. "I'm going to check if Nisha wants to go home too and pop to the ladies."

She walks off and I wonder why every conversation I have with this woman fires me up so much.

Bonnie

Who wants mirrored walls and doors in a toilet? The last thing I need to see is me sitting on the loo with my knickers around my ankles.

I wish I was on my own cheap plastic toilet at home instead of London's most glamorous loo—according to Toilets of Instagram.

I wish I'd never set foot in this obnoxious fancy bar.

That kiss.

I wish I'd never kissed Jack Knight like tomorrow was Armageddon and we were all going to die.

And I really wish I hadn't proposed "wham, bam, thank you ma'am" to Jack.

I wish I could rewind the whole damn day.

The low of the missing underwear, the high of humping a hot stomach, the second high of a successful presentation and now the plummeting low of offering myself up on a plate only to be rejected.

He was watching me from the bar the whole time. I might have had one too many Old Fashioneds, but I wasn't imagining that.

So, what the hell? What's the guy's deal? He clearly gets off on toying with me. Was his plan just to blue ball me or whatever the female equivalent is?

I'm a bloody fool.

Humiliated is not a strong enough word for how I feel.

Excited voices break the silence as the door of the bathroom opens.

"I couldn't tell you in front of the guys, I slept with him a few weeks ago. Right here in this hotel."

"No shit!" a second voice shrieks. "I knew it. I could tell by your face the minute he walked past. Lucky bitch. Ugh, I'm so damn jealous. He owns this place, doesn't he?"

My stomach plummets. For fuck's sake.

"He does." The first one giggles. "That's why the bar staff are treating me like a queen tonight."

I white-knuckle the toilet roll holder.

"Damn. How did it happen?"

"Same way it's happening tonight. I was here . . . he was here . . ." she says in a singsong voice. "The chemistry was off the charts. We talked and . . . one thing led to another."

I stop breathing in case they can hear me. They must think they're alone.

Get a grip, Bonnie. Why do you care? You are way too emotional over this.

I haven't even slept with the guy. This is what happens in the dating pool in London. Nisha's right, I need to harden up.

I care more than I'd like to admit.

"How was it?" the second asks.

Oh God, please shut up, woman.

"Ama-a-a-zing," the first says, drawing out the word. "I'll die if I don't get a repeat."

"Have you talked to him much tonight?"

"Enough."

"Is he interested?"

There's silence for a moment. Then she laughs. "I'm getting

some Knight tonight."

Her words slam into my chest. That's why he's trying to get rid of me. He has better options. I need to get the hell out of this bar.

"Do you think you could get him to introduce me to the tech tycoon he hangs out with, Danny Walker?"

More laughter. And lots of clicking from the camera sound of a phone.

"I think Walker is married. Or has a partner."

"Forty percent of marriages end in divorce," the second woman says smugly.

This woman is a bitch.

I pick myself off the toilet seat and breathe deeply through my nose. They're going to think I have bowel problems being in here the whole time.

When I open the door their eyes widen in surprise, but they continue snapping. I thought the duck-face selfie was dead.

"Excuse me," I mumble as I sidestep them to get to the sinks. Can't a woman use the bathroom in peace without people taking photos?

They ignore me. "Move more this way, there's better lighting."

It's the girl that was draped over him earlier, with a body to kill for.

She's not wearing a bra.

Maybe that's all it takes to get him interested. For a while.

Nisha looks to be in an intimate conversation with her arch nemesis Darren when I reappear from the toilets.

"Hey, Nisha?" I interrupt them.

She drags her eyes away from Darren.

"I'm going to head off. Do you want to come?"

Darren cocks a brow suggestively at her. "One more for the road?"

She shrugs, feigning indifference. "I'll stay for one more," she says, not looking at me.

For a fleeting second, I'm amused.

"Are you getting the tube home?" she asks.

"Yeah."

"Text me the minute you arrive home."

I lean in for a hug. "See you tomorrow."

I turn to leave and meet the intense stare of Jack blazing across the room. His glass pauses mid-air as he motions me over.

He's not alone. He never is. Redhead toilet selfie queen and her perky braless nipples look ready to eat him alive. She's quick.

I'll be damned if I'm going to get a lift from one of his drivers, like an annoying inconvenience he has to get rid of.

Averting my gaze, I stride towards the door with the pace of a professional race walker.

"Bonnie," a deep voice says behind me as that familiar masculine scent wafts up my nose.

Keep walking. Keep walking.

"Wait," he growls louder.

His hand slides around my wrist, stopping me in my tracks.

I turn and pin him with my fiercest glare.

"I told you I had a car waiting for you." Irritation laces his voice as he glares right back.

"And I told you I'm taking the tube," I snap, my heart pounding. "I don't need to do as I'm told. I'm not a child."

"You do need to do as you're told when I want you to be safe." He glowers at me. "You've had too much to drink to walk home from the tube on your own. I'd take you home myself, but I need to go back to the office."

Cursing under his breath, he takes my wrist and starts walking, leaving me with no choice but to trail after him unless I want to lose an arm.

Outside, Canary Wharf hums with bankers, oil traders, and tech people letting loose after a seventy-hour workweek. London's version of the city that never sleeps.

In silence, Jack leads me to a black Aston Martin. The driver greets us and opens the back door for me.

"Tommy will message me when you're home."

Are you going to fuck Redhead in the hotel again?

"You'll thank me in the morning when you wake up to run ten miles."

"You don't need to be concerned about me," I say, sulking. "You're right, this . . . us . . . was a ridiculous idea. Forget this morning. Forget tonight." I play the drunk card. "It was the Old Fashioneds talking. I just wanted to find out what all the hype was about." I flash him a plastic smile.

"What do you mean?" he asks, frowning.

"One night with playboy Jack Knight. Now I've realised what a terrible idea that is. It would complicate things. Forget I ever said anything."

He looks at me steadily for a moment before nodding his head towards the back seat. "Get in, Bonnie. It's late."

"I'm never putting myself out there ever again," I mutter to myself more than him.

"Putting yourself out there?" Hip lips curl in displeasure. "This isn't putting yourself out there."

I take one last fleeting look at him, swallow my pride, and get in the car.

23

Jack

The ball flies past the fifth hole, bounces, and disappears into the trees. It's Sunday afternoon golf with my two best mates, and besides their relentless piss-taking, it's my favourite part of the week.

As of late, I've been slack in attending, instead spending Sundays on construction sites.

Tristan lets out a low whistle. "In ten years of us playing golf, that's the worst yet. I hope you're suitably mortified."

"You're losing your touch, Knight." Danny laughs.

"It's my big blue balls," I grumble as Danny lines up to take his shot. "They're getting in the way of everything."

The ball lands just shy of the hole. He turns to me in satisfaction. "Looks like my balls are just fine."

"I must shake Bonnie's hand when I next see her." Tristan watches me with amusement. "Finally, a woman who doesn't want to jump in bed after Knight winks."

"She does want to sleep with me," I mutter dryly. "She practically begged me to on Friday night."

Tristan looks at me in confusion as he lines his feet up into position. "Then why do you have blue balls?" His club connects with the ball and our eyes follow it down the course where it lands just shy of the hole. Too bloody close.

I glare at them. "I'm trying to court the woman, and she's treating me like a sex toy—that's bloody well why. She's after a one-night stand."

They both laugh.

"It's not funny," I snap. "I'm being the perfect gentleman. Well, except for the lapse in judgement in my office, but that was her fault for poking her nipples at me." I sigh. "I can't win."

Danny chuckles. "Your reputation really does precede you."

"So, what does she want from me? How do I woo the damn woman?"

Tristan eyes me seriously. "She probably doesn't trust you. With everything she hears about you, she's got no reason to."

"And the lass got ditched by her fiancé," Danny adds. "She's been through a rough ride. Anyone would have trust issues after that."

I nod. "This week was supposed to be her wedding day. Wednesday. Sean warned me."

Danny frowns. "Only obnoxious people arrange a wedding on a Wednesday."

"Max wanted to keep the cost down. It was meant to be in Italy. I guess when you're on holiday it doesn't matter what day it is."

"Is she still hung up on Max?" Tristan asks.

"Why would she be?" I scoff. "I'm much more charming. I've got a massive dick and she knows it. Her eyes fell out of her head when she saw it."

"You have to be more to her than a massive dick." Danny smirks. "So does Max know you're trying to get with his ex?"

"I couldn't give a fuck what Max knows," I say flatly. "We're not mates. I just know him through Sean and the project. Besides, he ran off with some intern."

He cocks a brow. "I admire your restraint for not going after her before this."

I shrug. "I don't break up relationships. No matter how much I want to." It's the one thing Dad and I don't have in common. That, and the fact that I'm alive.

"You'll get there." He smiles. "I sensed she liked you at the wedding. Even if she doesn't want to. You two are a good match." He tosses me my golf bag to go to the next hole.

I catch a flash of red on his thumb. "What the hell is that? Are you wearing nail polish?"

He glances down at his thumb nail, painted red. "Yeah. The twins like to experiment on me."

I scrunch my nose up in disgust. "Why didn't you take it off before you came out?"

"Do I look like I give a fuck, mate?" He hits me with a glare. "I haven't slept in three years. I'll be their doll during the day if they let me sleep at night. Anyway, you think I know how to get this stuff off?"

Tristan and I exchange glances and laugh. Danny Walker, ruthless tech tycoon, has given all his power to three-year-old twin girls.

I study the thumb nail job. "They didn't do a very good job."

He frowns. "Not according to them." There's no mistaking the warmth under the layers of grumpiness.

Something surprising hits me right in the chest.

I'm jealous.

Eighteen holes and three beverages later, we're sitting in the club bar when I see someone's name flash on my phone that puts a bad taste in my mouth.

Fuck's sake.

"Are you going to stare at that or answer it?" Danny asks, looking up from his newspaper. "Who is it?"

"Damon Manning."

I learned the hard way it's better to know what the smarmy git wants because it usually means a story on me is going to press.

"Knight," Damon Manning booms cheerfully as I answer.

"Manning."

"How are you?"

"Busy," I reply. "You?"

"Can't complain. We should have drinks soon."

Like hell, we will. "I'm in the middle of something. What's up?"

"I heard Wicks had a change of heart."

I stiffen. Tristan and Danny eye me curiously. "What are you talking about?"

"He wants to see you about your old man."

How the fuck does he know?

"Come on, Knight. My sources never let me down. Work with me here. I can help you."

"I sincerely doubt that," I say dryly.

He continues, undeterred. "I'm used to getting info out of people. I can help you talk to Wicks."

"I don't think so, Manning," I snap. "You're not getting an exclusive out of me."

He chuckles. Insults wash over tabloid journalists like water. "You know it'll go to press, anyway, right? It's better if you have control."

"The news must be slow today if you're sniffing around a decade-old murder and a guy already in jail about to snuff it."

Manning chuckles down the phone again. "The Wicks family always makes headlines. As do you, Knight. It's a good combo when the news is quiet."

"I'm not your fucking entertainment, Manning." I snap my phone shut.

Tristan and Danny watch me in silence.

Danny clears his throat. "When are you visiting him in prison?"

I fire the phone on the table and clench my hand into a fist. "I'm in a queue. Turns out Donnie Wicks is a popular guy."

Tristan watches me for a few seconds. "Just be careful, mate. The press has got wind of this, and Donnie Wicks is the one person you see red over."

24

Bonnie

Today is my wedding day. And on your wedding day, you're supposed to look absolutely fabulous.

This morning, in the safety of my bedroom, I looked like a femme fatale. Heels that scream fuck-me-in-only-these-please. A tight blue shift dress that accentuates every curve. Dress hem closer to my hips than my knees. My long flowing hair teased into curls. Vaguely smoky eyes but not enough to look like I'm out on the town for the night.

Now, outside, I'm not quite as fatale as I'd hoped.

Big stinkin' raindrops slap the shit out of me, supported as they are by a filthy wind designed to piss you right off.

British weather at its finest.

The wind does its darnedest to pull my dress over my head, expose my good bits to the nation and leave me with a wind-burnt vagina.

When I finally make it into the Lexington building and onto the fortieth floor, I'm less put together than I had hoped, but heads still turn.

Heads actually turn.

Approving looks. Flirty looks. Lecherous looks.

Give it to me; I'll take it all.

Nisha is hammering away on her keyboard but stops when she sees me. "Nice," she says loudly, giving me an approving, almost sexual, once-over. "Max's jaw will hit the floor. Jack's too."

She smiles innocently. "If you're interested, but of course, *you're not.*"

"Not in the slightest." I sniff, plopping myself down at my desk beside her.

Nisha knows the whole story of the heavy petting incident followed by sharp rejection on Friday night.

"Sure." She rolls her eyes as she swivels her chair to face me. "Well, I'm glad you didn't hide away from Jack today because you shouldn't be alone. I really feel like you'll have fully moved on after today. What did the therapist say you should do today?"

"Have a helpful one-hundred pound therapy session. I broke up with her." I smile wryly. "Not only because I'm going bankrupt, but I feel ready to quit now. The sessions haven't been as useful these past few weeks."

She nods. "I still think you'd be better going out with Kate and me tonight. Nice meal, a few drinks to take your mind off things?"

"No. I'm going to sit in my PJs, eat my feelings, pour wine down my throat, and read smut. I might even wear my wedding dress and do a bit of drunk crying. Maybe I'll arrange a load of online dates. But tomorrow, I'll be over it."

Her lips press together. "I'm not happy about this."

I roll my eyes. "It's fine. I'm not going to go all *bitches-be-crazy.* All you have to do today is distract me." I lean towards her excitedly. "What the hell is happening between you and Darren?"

I couldn't believe it when she told me they went for dinner last night.

She groans. "Oh, God. I should know not to shit on my own doorstep, but he's damn good at sex. He should quit his job at Bradshaw and become a prostitute, he'd be much better at that."

I smile smugly. I knew this day would come. "But you went on an actual date with him last night. Do you want more?"

She blows out her cheeks. "*He* wants more. I just want a fling."

Why is it so hard for two people to get on the same level?

Take Jack Knight. The guy switches between hot and cold so

much I'm dizzy. Does he want me or not?

I glance at my phone clock. "Come on, we're going to be late. Better brave it and get this over and done with."

We have a meeting with the Lexington team at nine a.m. I haven't seen Jack since he pushed me into his car on Friday night.

I messaged to thank him for the ride, to be the bigger person, but that was it. His message back was simply, *Glad you got back safe.*

The meeting is in the largest boardroom in Lexington. Architecture firms supporting the other phases are there as well.

I walk in behind Nisha, feeling as if I am about to attend a United Nations summit.

Jack leans against the boardroom podium, talking to Sean and other Lexington seniors.

My skin prickles at the sight of him.

Everyone is in a suit but him. He looks sensational. Faded jeans, a white T-shirt complementing his Italian complexion, exposed tattooed arms folded lazily over his chest.

It's not often *he* is waiting for *us*.

I take a seat at the back, feeling my face grow hot as I replay the scene of serving myself up to him on a plate.

The rejection hurt.

There's a dull chatter as Jack talks to Sean, not in a hurry to greet us.

I turn from chatting to Nisha to find Jack's dark gaze fixed on my bare legs, where the hem has ridden up. I cross and uncross my legs and his hands tighten around the podium edge.

His gaze follows a path up my waist, burning into me like a red sniper dot. It lingers on my chest and collarbone before finally brazenly settling on my face.

Shit.

The dress worked.

I can't figure out whether he's angry or horny. Maybe the two are interchangeable with Jack.

There's a tic in his jaw as he gives me a nod.

I return my most confident smile and glance away to find Max also staring at me.

Damn, I feel like a total badass temptress. I may not be wearing fake-virginal white today, but blue-balls blue works well too.

An attractive blonde enters the room, smiling with dimples that won my ex-fiancé's heart and stole my honeymoon destination.

Olivia.

All the positive energy is sucked out of me. What the hell is Olivia doing here? She's not even on the project.

Nisha leans over and whispers, "She must be supporting while Teresa's on holiday this week."

When Olivia spots me staring, she looks sheepish but nods. I nod back, summoning what professionalism I can muster.

I suppose Max is fair game. She doesn't know me well. She doesn't owe me any loyalty.

A blue diamond around her neck catches my eye. My brain ticks over. I know that necklace. It takes me at least thirty seconds before I register from where.

It's not a coincidence it matches my dress perfectly.

I dig my hands into the side of the chair, trying to calm myself down.

No. Max wouldn't do that to me. It can't be the same necklace.

I found the necklace in his underwear drawer, hidden under Jack's biography. Max was terrible at hiding things. I was putting his clean socks away and found something hard in one of his socks.

It was beautiful, a blue topaz gemstone on an elegant silver chain. Unlike anything I would buy for myself because I usually wear my hand-made scruffy jewellery.

I thought it was a present. I was marginally disappointed but figured he must have returned it.

That was six months before we *de-coupled*.

A shiver runs down my spine as if someone has, not walked, but *stamped* over my grave.

Deep down, when Max told me about Olivia, I knew. I just

knew. I knew he was lying months before when a name flashed up on his phone, *Oll*. Who the hell has a nickname like that?

But my brain refused to acknowledge it and pushed it down.

Now, hit full whack in the face with it, I can't ignore it anymore.

Max requested the new admin position, and Olivia *happened* to fill it. But that's because he already knew her. It's so obvious now.

Max is a cheater.

I stare at his handsome face as he intently listens to Jack.

Fucking son of a bitch.

First my dad, now this. Does everyone lie to me?

Anxiety strikes my chest. A sudden, intense shot.

How many people in this room knew all along? Was everyone talking behind my back?

Does Sean know? Does Jack know? Sweet Jesus, does *Kate* know?

Keep focusing on your necklace. I white-knuckle the Amethyst crystal hanging from my neck. I knew today would be tough, so I wore a calming stone. I didn't think it would be this shit show.

If it works for holy men and monks, surely it'll work for me.

The crystal slides in my sweaty palms, hard and useless. The pain of the crystal's sharp edges digging into my palm are a mild distraction but not enough.

I'll die if I don't get out of this room. There's no oxygen.

Everyone else looks relaxed, listening intently. How? The more normal they look, the more my anxiety spikes.

Max. Olivia. Jack. I need to get out of this fucking room. That's the only thing that matters.

People turn curiously as I shuffle past them, trying to look as controlled as possible.

Jack continues talking as he watches me make my way to the top of the room.

"Excuse me, Jack," I mumble. "I'm not feeling well."

Without looking at him, I slip past him out the door, clutching my stomach to slow my breathing. I might be sick at this rate.

I know it's game over. Jack will take me off the project for disrupting another one of his meetings. Or if he doesn't, Max will.

Max. The C-word was invented for him. And I don't mean charmer.

The toilets are fully sealed. Practically soundproof, thank God. None of that bullshit where the bottom gap in the door is so big everyone knows your business.

I slump onto the toilet seat, my heart racing.

Was everything about our relationship a lie? Max might not have loved me in the end, but I thought he respected me. I trusted him so openly, it's scary.

He shat all over my trust.

He must have been seeing Olivia at least six months before we split to give her that necklace. And *Danielle*? What the fuck? Did he have a bit on the side of a bit on the side?

How many women did he really sleep with when we were together?

The door to the bathroom opens. I hear footsteps. The heavy footsteps of a man.

Please, God, don't let it be Max.

I can't deal with seeing him yet. I need to get my emotions under control, or there'll be a body pushed out the fortieth-floor window.

The knock on my cubicle door makes me jump.

"I'll be out in a second," I cry. Just fuck off.

"Bonnie." Jack's low voice comes from the other side of the door.

No. Anyone but Jack.

"I'm sorry," I whisper. "I need a minute."

I don't care if he takes me off the project.

"Let me in."

"I'm being sick," I lie. "Vomiting."

There's a heavy sigh outside the door. "Please."

I open the door a few inches to find his brown eyes peering

in.

"I have a stomach bug," I say, forcing a small smile.

He gently pushes the cubicle door farther open, forcing me to step back.

"You're trembling."

"Please just leave me." My voice cracks. I can't stand Jack seeing me right now.

He takes my hands and pulls me tight against him. My head barely reaches his chin. One arm wraps around my back and the other gently pushes my head down until it rests on a warm solid slab of chest muscle.

He's *hugging* me.

Jack's hugging me.

Stunned, my arms dangle at my sides. He takes my hands and wraps them around his waist, then his arms come back around my body, crushing me against him.

"Bonnie." I feel his warm breath against my forehead. "Do you feel my heartbeat?"

"Yes," I whisper. And I do.

"Good," he murmurs. "Close your eyes and listen to my heart and my breathing."

My head rises and falls slowly with the movement of his chest. He takes slow deep breaths. My body warms against his with every breath. We stay like this for minutes. I don't know how long. I don't know why he's here, but I need him.

With my face buried in his chest, I listen to his hypnotic breathing. Slowly, my breathing stabilises. I breathe in his scent. It surrounds me, consuming me, overpowering me. Protecting me.

"It's okay," he says quietly into my hair. "I think you had a panic attack. My sister used to have them after Dad died."

His fingers lift my chin so that our eyes meet. Our faces are inches apart. "Want to tell me what happened? What was it about?"

I inhale sharply and drop my hands from his waist. "I realised Max was cheating on me with Olivia. For months."

"Uh-huh." He doesn't look surprised. "How?"

"Max bought a blue necklace last year." I swallow the knot in my throat. "He didn't know I found it. He never gave it to me, and it was gone from the sock drawer, so I thought he'd returned it. Olivia was wearing it today."

He doesn't say anything. He just stares down at me, willing me to go on.

"I've never been cheated on before. I guess I always had the naive impression that my guy would never do that. Not Max. Realising it was all lies in the middle of the meeting with our co-workers, you and Olivia sitting there smiling, I...panicked."

"It was supposed to be your wedding day," Jack says softly.

How did he . . .?

I give a small nod, averting my gaze. "Shit day to find out."

His fingers nudge my chin forcing me to look up at him again. "Want me to beat the shit out of Max?"

I laugh and his hand drops. "Maybe. I don't know what I want to do about Max yet. I sure as hell don't want to confront him at work."

"That sounds wise."

"Wait." I frown. "Did the meeting end?"

"I told Sean to take over."

My eyes widen. "You walked out in the middle of the meeting?"

"Can't see anyone stopping me."

That makes me laugh. "That's double standards."

He smiles cockily back at me then his expression becomes serious. "Listen, you're a strong woman, Bonnie. You don't need anyone else to pick you up. You'll realise that. But if you want me, I'm here." His deep brown eyes hold mine. "I've got you."

My heart pounds all over again. "You're an amazing man, Jack."

"Glad you realise I'm not just a pretty face." A grin tugs at his lips. "Ask yourself this, do you wish that you were walking down the aisle right now, about to marry Max?

I think carefully. "No."

His smile widens. "Then today is a good day. You have exactly what you want." He studies me for a moment longer. "Do you feel better now?"

"Yes." I bite my lip. "I'm embarrassed but I feel better. Thank you."

"Good. Why were you going through a man's sock drawer?"

"I was washing his underwear! He has your biography hidden in there too."

The signature Jack smirk appears. "Oh, yeah? Did you read it?"

"I might have flipped through it," I admit. "It pales in comparison to the real thing."

His eyes hold mine as the air charges in the small cubicle. His eyes dart between my eyes and my lips. The butterflies are back in full flight in my stomach.

Kiss me.

"Everything will be fine, Bonnie. Betrayal is hard but you'll get over it. Don't even waste another minute thinking about him. There are better things for you out there." His steady gaze never leaves me. "Better people."

I nod, fighting back tears. "Thank you, Jack."

His fingers nudge my chin playfully. "See, I'm more than just an amazing sex toy. Now, I better go out and save Sean."

I bite back a giggle as he opens the cubicle door.

"Oh, and Bonnie?" He stops at the door, tilting his head to give me a slow, sexy smile. "For the record, I'm glad you're not walking down the aisle today either."

The afternoon is better. Surprisingly no one asks me why I left the meeting, and no one seems to connect that Jack left the meeting quickly after. At least not to my face, anyway.

I don't confront Max. I keep my head down and stay away from Max and Olivia. I remain calm. I go to lunch with Nisha. My afternoon workshop with the planners and interior design team keeps me focused.

Thankfully, Max stays away as well. I'm guessing he's not in my face asking what happened at the meeting since it's our doomed wedding day.

And when five thirty comes, I'm surprisingly relaxed.

I want to thank Jack properly.

I say goodbye to the guys in the workshop and then make my way down the hall to his office, hoping he won't be in a meeting.

"Jess." I smile at her over the divider. "Do you think I can have two minutes with Jack?"

She nods, smiling back. "He's just on his way out but it should be fine if you're quick."

I knock softly on his office door.

"Come in," he calls in his deep voice.

I push the door open.

Oh, shit.

Now I wish the floor would swallow me whole.

Michelle Allard and Jack turn to look at me from where they stand close together, facing each other. My jaw drops at her red, demure, sexy-as-hell evening gown.

The outfit I spent so long on this morning pales in comparison. Jack is in a tuxedo looking painfully handsome. The two hard mounds of ass fill the tuxedo pants perfectly.

His eyes find mine.

My stomach twists, the butterflies dying a slow painful death. The perfect couple on a fucking date. I'm so stupid.

I realise in horror that she has her hands on his chest. Oh God, were they about to kiss?

"I'm sorry for interrupting," I say, flustered.

"You're not interrupting," he says warmly. "Michelle's doing my tie. I hate doing the damn thing."

"I know you," Michelle says pleasantly as her hands rest on his tie. "The bridesmaid."

"That's me," I say with false cheeriness. I should probably be flattered she remembers me. "You look stunning."

"What did you want, Bonnie?" Jack asks. "Is everything okay?"

"It's nothing important." I wave my hand dismissively, taking a step back so I'm up against the door. "Sorry, I don't want to delay your date.

His brows draw together. "It's not a date. We're going to the Lexington hotel awards. It's a staff event. Go on, Bonnie. How can I help?"

"Jack, we need to go," Michelle says sharply, still with her hands on his tie. How long does it take a person to do a tie? I resist the urge to hiss at her like a territorial black mamba. "We're late and you're giving a speech."

"The speech can wait another minute," Jack says dryly. He nods at me. "Go on, Bonnie."

I'd prefer not to say this under the watch of a supermodel. "Thank you for earlier. Without you, the day would have been a lot harder. That's all. Thanks. You're a really great guy, Jack."

He stares at me with an unreadable expression for a long beat.

"I'm glad I could help," he finally says in a throaty voice.

"That's nice," Michelle snaps. "Can you resume this tomorrow? Jack, your staff are waiting on you. You're going to let them down."

I'm out the door before he can reply.

My stomach turns with the biggest revelation of the day, and it's not about Max, Olivia, or even Dad.

Michelle Allard is the luckiest woman in the world tonight.

25

Bonnie

Max is spending my wedding night with Olivia. Jack is spending my wedding night with Michelle Allard. I'm spending my wedding night with an Argentinian Malbec and four bearded men living in the Alaskan mountains who need a virgin to share.

> Kate: What are you up to now? X

There's been a steady stream of messages from Kate and Nisha since I left the office. Checking in, just in case I drown myself in Malbec.

It turns out Kate didn't know about Max cheating on me. I should never have doubted my best friend. She swears she won't tell Sean until I've confronted Max. I have to think about this because Max has the power to fuck up my promotion.

To calm the worriers, I'm providing them with blow-by-blow details on how the night is unfolding.

> Me: Getting a takeaway. Pizza. X

There's no need to add that I've polished off three-quarters of a bottle of wine as an aperitif.

It's the perfect night for takeout. In true stinking British-weather style, it's bucketed down all day with no relief. I feel much safer on the sofa in my vest, oversized fluffy terry cloth loungewear and large socks.

Not like Michelle Allard, forced to wear a backless shimmery evening gown. The poor woman must be freezing.

My chest tightens.

The doorbell buzzes. The delivery guy is here with my pizza.

"Just a minute," I call over the intercom, grabbing my cardigan so he doesn't get an eyeful of bra-less breasts. Although delivery guys are like nurses—they've seen it all before.

Wrapping the cardigan around me, I walk as fast as the large socks will allow me down the stairs. The rain is so loud, it sounds like it's inside the building.

I yank open the door. It's not a delivery guy with my caramelised onion and goat's cheese pizza.

Dark brown eyes burn into mine.

Jack is absolutely drenched. His tuxedo jacket is gone and he's only in his white shirt, stuck to his chest and biceps. His hands grip the door on either side, his large frame dwarfs the doorway.

I stare up at him, my heart in my throat. Too stunned to care that spits of rain are belting down on me.

He stares right back at me. "I half expected you to be in your wedding dress. Are you going to let me in or just let me drown?"

"Ja-ack?" I stutter as if he might be a hallucination from the Malbec. "What are you doing here?"

He leans in until his forehead nearly touches mine. Droplets of rain drip from his face onto me. "Making new memories. I couldn't let you remember today as your cancelled wedding day."

"No?" I ask breathlessly, blinking in shock. "What am I going to remember it as?"

He grins, a full-voltage grin stretching across his face. "Best night of your life."

A girly laugh erupts from my throat. I might be a little hysterical. "You're so full of yourself, Jack Knight. I don't understand. You're supposed to be at the awards ceremony. With

Michelle."

"I left after the speech. I had better places to be."

My heart jumps, and I laugh nervously again because it's all I'm capable of. "But you rejected me. I don't understand."

"I rejected your offer of a one-night stand." His eyes darken. "We're not doing a one-night stand, darlin'. You think you put yourself out there? That isn't putting yourself out there." Before I can react, he scoops me up off the ground in one easy hitch, balancing my ass on his arms.

I let out a surprised yelp. My communication abilities no longer extend to anything beyond "*Oh*."

His dilated pupils darken to almost black. "*This* is putting yourself out there."

Weeks of pent-up tension explode inside me, and I instinctively wrap my arms and legs around his drenched body, knowing I'll die if I don't feel every inch of him.

I don't care that I'm in my PJs in the street.

I don't care that it's hailing down from the heavens and I'm soaked.

I don't care if I look like a massive hoe straddling a hot guy as people walk past to the chicken shop.

I'm exactly where I need to be, doing exactly what I need to be doing.

His mouth crashes down on mine, and I go to fucking pieces.

One hand tightens around my waist while the other comes up to hold my head in place so he can claim my mouth. His tongue plunges into mine.

It's desperate and frantic and paralysing. It's a kiss that travels down my spine directly to my clit. Nothing has ever tasted as good as this man.

A growl rumbles from his chest as I grind my towelled loungewear against his hard cock straining in his wet trousers.

That's the spot.

Holy fucking hell.

I'm vaguely aware of my cardigan being open, exposing my

vest. I'm getting wetter by the second from the rain and the raging horn between my legs.

We sound like we've escaped from London Zoo. Small mewls escape me while he grunts like he doesn't give a fuck who's listening.

My hands are all over his body, his hair, his shoulders, his neck, the tattooed bicep holding me up. Sliding over every hard warm muscle I can find. I can't touch it all fast enough.

"Get a room!"

The yell breaks us apart and I come to, mortified and gasping for breath.

We're standing in an open doorway on the street, breathing hard. People are queueing for fried chicken just a metre away, for God's sake.

Jack exhales a heavy breath, walks us into the hallway and slams the door. Without putting me down, he starts to ascend the stairs.

"Put me down, I'm too heavy!" My protests are weak. The fact he can carry me effortlessly is insanely sexy. "We're going to fall."

He continues up the stairs. Perhaps it's for the best. That kiss made my limbs feel all flappy like one of those rubber dolls.

The doorbell buzzes, stopping Jack short. "Who's that? Do you have another suitor waiting to claim you?"

I giggle. "It's the pizza delivery guy."

Jack reverses down the stairs. "At least it's not the chicken shop. This pizza better be good. We'll be working up an appetite."

I giggle again into his neck. I've morphed into a flapping giggly mess since I opened the door to him. "Seriously, aren't you going to let me down? I have to see this man again."

Ignoring me, Jack opens the door.

The delivery guy is not expecting a grown man holding a woman in his arms like a small child. After the surprise wears off, he hands over the pizza box.

I thank him and take it quickly, my face boiling as Jack fumbles awkwardly with one hand to get something out of his pocket.

"Jack," I mutter, trying to avoid eye contact with the delighted delivery guy.

After painful seconds, Jack cheerfully hands the guy a generous tip. "Here you go, mate."

I sigh as Jack closes the door. "I'm never ordering from *Spicy Slice* ever again."

"Don't sweat it. I'm half Italian, remember? I'll find you a good pizza spot."

We hike back up the stairs, and I'm suddenly aware of how shabby my flat is. I can't actually let a billionaire in, can I?

"Why not?"

Shit, I said that out loud. Or can the guy read my mind?

"It's not what you're used to. It's temporary until I figure out where I want to live," I say in a rush. "I think the carpet was put down in the eighties. You can tell by the pattern. You're probably used to marble tiles. But it's the most modern thing in the flat. Everything else looks like it's from the Victorian era."

I'm babbling.

"Relax, Bonnie." He winks as he sets me down outside the door. "I grew up in a council estate, remember? I'm used to carpet from the eighties."

I push open the door that I left jarred open with a shoe. It's a risky strategy when you're living by yourself.

He scans the room, either intrigued or horrified.

I imagine the shabby interior through a billionaire's eyes. Oh, God. My underwear is drying on a clothes rack in the middle of the living room.

"Nice. It's cute."

Cute is what you say when you're being kind.

I discard the pizza on the kitchen counter. It's no longer the highlight of the night. It doesn't smell half as good as Jack. "I wasn't expecting visitors," I mutter, whipping the clothes rack out of sight. "You're drenched. I'll get you a towel."

"Sure. I don't want to flood your living room," he replies with a grin, strolling about the room, inspecting things in my living room too closely. I want to order him to stand on the spot.

Scuttling off to the bathroom, I contemplate my game plan. Neither the bedroom nor I am in any fit state to seduce anyone. My heart's bloody pounding here.

When I come back with the towel, he's in the kitchen and has taken the liberty of removing his shirt. Oh, Lord, I forgot about the tattoos.

There's definitely going to be a flood, man.

Jack Knight is the largest thing I've ever had in my flat.

"What are you doing?" I ask as I watch him inspect the boiler. It's one of those ancient ugly ones that takes up a huge chunk of wall.

He frowns as he looks on the bottom of the boiler. "When was the last time this was serviced?"

"I dunno." I shrug. I'm more concerned about the last time I was serviced.

He moves from the boiler to the stove, inspecting it with the same precision. "Do you have a gas certificate for this? This model is at least ten years old."

"I'm not sure. I just rent the place."

He turns to me, and his dark eyes sharpen as if that's the wrong answer. "Your landlord has responsibilities. I'll have someone come round this week and check everything out."

It's sweet how concerned he looks about my boiler. I feel it in my ovaries.

"Okay, Daddy." I fling the towel at him. "If there's going to be a gas explosion, hopefully it can wait until tomorrow. Now will you come and sit on the sofa, please." Taking him by the hands, I lead him away from the utilities and over to the sofa. "Give me a minute to freshen up. And don't touch or look at anything."

My request falls on deaf ears. I'm gone less than a minute and when I return, he's standing in the middle of the living room with a small pink object in his hand.

"What's this?" he asks with a teasing tone.

My face flushes with heat. The clit sucker. It shows how often I have visitors if I'm leaving my battery lovers lying around the living room. "Cooking utensil," I mutter trying to grab it off him, but he holds it out of my reach.

His eyes gleam as he turns the damn thing on, and it comes to life with the conspicuous buzz. "You're the worst liar I've ever come across, and I've come across a lot of liars in my business." He lets out a low chuckle. "It sounds like something you'd hear on a building site. A cement mixer. Looks like it's running low on battery, but you won't be needing that anymore."

"Is that so?" I croak, my eyes widening as his lips pull into a wicked grin. "It's got seven different settings. How many do you have?"

He licks his lips and stares at me with hooded eyes. My core clenches. "I have *all* the settings you need, Bonnie."

I squeal in surprise as he picks me up and tosses me onto the sofa.

"These need to come off." He tugs at my sweatpants, and I lift my hips so he can slide them down my legs, taking my panties down too.

A grunt falls from his lips as he gently pushes my legs apart and stares intensely for a long beat.

"Stop staring at me like that," I whisper, my heart beating wildly.

"Why, darlin'? You're so fucking beautiful," he murmurs, his eyes lifting to meet my gaze. "Everything about you drives me crazy,"

I bite my lip. God, this guy is intense.

I'm still not giving up the clit sucker though.

"Hands up," he says gruffly as his fingers find the hem of my top.

I obey and he pulls it over my hands and onto the floor.

"That's much better. You have no fucking idea how long I've wanted to see you naked."

"You're used to hot models." I squirm and try to close my legs, but his knee comes down between them. "I can't cope with this." I try to cover myself with my hands, but he pins them down above my head. "Don't look at the wobbly bits."

"The wobbly bits are going straight into the wank bank for later."

With one hand still holding me hostage, the other slides down over the curve of my breast. His thumbs circle my nipples until they are so hard, they hurt.

I moan, arching into his mouth. It's been so long. Apparently all it takes is a nipple flick and I'm putty.

My moans seem to open a floodgate for Jack. He dips his head down to take my nipple in his mouth and greedily sucks, letting out grunts of pleasure like someone has just let him off his leash.

I look down. His long eyelashes close over his eyes as he devours both my breasts like he's been given the gift of taste. Watching him is just as good as feeling it happen.

I never expected Jack to be this unhinged. I thought he would be more practised, reserved . . . in control.

It's startling and scary . . . and fucking wild.

I fist his hair as my moans grow frantic. I need more.

He looks up at me, a dangerous gleam in his eye. "I'm going to taste every inch of this body."

"Wait, Jack." I whimper, putting my hand out to stop him before he buries his face in my crotch. "I've heard you're really good at sex."

He stops and stares up at me in amusement. "Why do you look like that's not a good thing?"

"I've had one long-term partner in four years. Nothing since. I don't know any fancy tricks. You must know them all."

His lips twitch. "Fancy tricks?"

"You know what I mean," I grumble. "My moves are probably out of date."

"I've no doubt your moves are timeless." He grins. "And I have a few moves on my own. But this sofa is too small to showcase my best ones."

I eye him cautiously as he hovers above me. "What are you going to do?" I really don't like the gleam in his eye.

He winks and pulls me up from the sofa.

"Jack," I warn as he leads me towards the middle of the room.

"Relax, darlin'." Taking my shoulders in his hands he turns me around, so my back is flush to his chest.

Ignoring my stunned protests, he pushes me down so my butt is up against his crotch and my head hangs with my hair trailing on the carpet.

"What the hell—"

Damn, I should have vacuumed.

From behind, he grabs my hands between my legs with both his hands and launches me into the air, flipping me upside down until I land on his shoulders with his face buried in my naked crotch.

"Jack!" I scream.

What the fuck?

I'm screaming, and I can't stop screaming. Did he just flip me like a *stripper*?

"Put me down!" I gasp, half terrified, half euphoric. "I'm too heavy. And too clumsy! I'll fall."

"Relax." His facial hair tickles my thighs. "I've got you."

He has my ass in an iron grip.

Oh my God.

All I can do is clutch his hair for dear life as he navigates us into the bedroom. It's a good thing I have high ceilings.

"How's the view up there?" I can *feel* him grinning into my crotch.

"Dusty," I say breathlessly. "There's a spider on the ceiling I want you to get rid of. I hope you aren't afraid of them."

"Well, my view is un-fucking-believable down here." To prove his point, his tongue licks my clit as he stops at the bed.

My whole body clenches. "*Jesus.*"

In a swift motion, I'm tossed on my ass in the middle of the bed.

I gawk up at him. "What the hell was that?"

He towers over the bed, smirking wolfishly. "My version of carrying you over my shoulder like a caveman."

"Barbaric," I rasp.

"Oh, sweetheart, you have no idea." His dark eyes flash. "I'm going to fuck you with my tongue first because once that tight little pussy is clenching around my cock, I won't last. Not the first time."

Holy God, this man talks dirty.

"Do it," I say huskily, arching my back. "Please. And keep up the running commentary."

This makes him laugh. "That might be difficult if my mouth is on your clit."

He pushes my thighs wide in a deadlock. I can't move even if I wanted to.

My pussy clenches onto nothing, waiting desperately.

Then he sinks his head down between my thighs, and I feel his mouth latch greedily onto my clit.

Oh, my.

I feel *everything*. It's like my senses are heightened to supersonic levels. I feel his full lips, his facial hair, his square jaw, his tongue running circles over my swelling bud. This is like the full-throttle setting on the clit sucker.

"Bonnie." It's said in a slow, deep growl full of lust that makes my whole body shiver. "You taste so good, darlin'. You're so fucking perfect."

I let out a loud heady moan and squeeze my eyes shut. I feel each deep sweeping stroke of his tongue as he devours me. It's too intense. "Oh my God, Jack."

"Bonnie," he hums against my pussy. "Open your eyes."

I force them open and stare down at the beautiful man between my legs.

Jack's dark brown eyes hold mine. "Watch me." I feel the vibrations of his low rumble on my clit.

My legs try to close around his head, but he holds my thighs, spreading me as wide as I'll go in a steel grip.

I'm on fire. My body shakes and tingles as he sucks on my throbbing clit, never breaking eye contact.

The look in his eyes is so intense I don't know if I can hold his gaze. Watching him fuck me with his mouth feels a million times more intimate than anything I've ever done before.

"Jack," I pant, the trembling in my body growing more violent, "that feels so good. Keep going."

"Yes, darlin'," he growls from between my legs. "I love how you moan my name. Scream it when you come." It's an order.

"Don't stop. *Jack*, don't stop."

I can't hold it anymore. I don't know if it's the pressure building in my core or the look of pure pleasure on his face that tips me over the edge.

The orgasm blasts through me taking control of every cell. My legs try to buck out of his grip. I let out an almighty moan, pulling on his hair hard as the fluttering down below explodes into violent waves of pleasure.

Waves that go on for so long, I'm scared they won't stop.

"Oh." I stare dazed at him as I come down off the high and go limp.

"Oh, indeed," he says with a crooked grin, looking up at me from between my legs.

"The chicken shop probably heard that last scream."

"Darlin', all of England heard that."

I laugh giddily and stretch my hands above my head, almost *purring*. "That was amazing."

He comes up to my eye level, hovering above me and caging my head with his forearms.

His eyes darken into something primal. "Don't get too comfortable, sweetheart. Now it's my turn."

Oh, help me, God.

26

Jack

Mine. All mine and ready for the taking.

With her blue eyes wide, she stares up at me from the bed, more vulnerable than I've ever seen her.

I make quick work of discarding my trousers and boxers and stand above her at the edge of the bed.

Adrenaline pumps through my veins as I fist my painfully hard cock against my stomach.

Her eyes dart between my face and my hand moving up and down my length.

My expression must be unnerving her because her eyes grow to twice their size. "You okay, beautiful?"

"I'm not sure." She gnaws on her bottom lip. "It's fucking enormous."

I laugh huskily and climb onto the bed, caging her in with my legs and arms. It's not the first time I've had that reaction. "You want it, sweetheart?" I breathe against her mouth. "Take a good look at what's on offer. I know you're craving it. Fucking take it."

Her hands flatten over my chest and glide over my muscles. "Your body is amazing," she purrs as her thumb plays with my nipple ring. Something rumbles in my throat as she slowly makes her way down my stomach to my erect cock.

"Oh, my God," she whimpers, curling her fingers around me, a hint of fear in her eyes.

"See what you do to me? I've been obsessing about you since

the wedding. I'm dying to be inside of you."

Long before the wedding, if I'm honest, but I don't want to scare her off.

Her hand tightens around my cock in response. "Yes, Jack," she whimpers. "Please. I need it. Now."

I palm her slit and thrust two fingers into her. She's soaked.

Her ass lifts off the bed so her beautiful wet cunt can ride my fingers harder.

Removing my fingers, I sit up and grab my wallet from my trousers.

"No," she moans. "Don't stop."

"Impatient little thing, aren't you?" I chuckle, sheathing myself up. "Ready?" I growl. "As soon as I start, I can't be gentle. I'll make love to you all night but not this time. This time is going to be a hard and fast fuck."

"Please," she moans, spreading her legs wide for me as I come down on top of her, holding my weight with my arms. "I need you inside me right now."

Fuck, she's so ready. Her breathing comes in shallow bursts. Her mouth hangs open as she curls her back, dying for attention.

I line myself up at her opening and thrust hard inside her.

A deep rumble vibrates from my throat as nerve sensations spring to life up and down my cock.

Damn, she feels amazing.

She yelps, and I will myself to stay still for a second as she adjusts to my size.

When she lets out a breath, I pull out and slam into her with another deep thrust.

"Bonnie. *Fuck,*" I say as she clenches around me. "You. Feel. So. Good."

I suck in a harsh breath. I'm not going to last here.

I thrust in and out of her sweet tight wetness, grunting against her lips.

Feeling every quiver of her muscles clamping around my cock.

Owning my cock.

Owning me.

Each thrust makes those beautiful breasts jiggle. I can't get enough. It's wet and messy and carnal.

She's so needy too. Clamping around me with her heels digging into my butt and her fingers clawing my back, she moans every time I fill her to the hilt.

I could come listening to those soft feminine whimpers alone.

"Jack," she cries. "I'm close, Jack."

Everything about this woman is going to break me. How my name rolls off her tongue in desperate cries again and again. That look she gives me that tells me I'm the only man that can make her come like this. The feel of her pulse quickening when I touch her. Her scent, her touch, her breath. Everything is fucking intoxicating.

"Do you hear that, sweetheart?" I breathe against her as the slapping sound of our bodies joining intensifies. "You're so fucking wet for me."

I hitch her hip up so I can drive in deeper. Harder. Making sure I hit her clit with every thrust.

"Oh my God, Jack," she blurts out. "This feels so good. I want you inside me forever."

She gasps. "I didn't mean—"

"Shush," I growl. "Don't take it back."

"Jack." She arches her back and digs her nails into my shoulders as her body shudders in pleasure with the orgasm ripping through her. Her muscles clench around me, milking me for everything I have.

"Look at me when you come," I hiss, gripping her jaw so she's forced to look at me again. "I love your face when you come. I need to see it, Bonnie."

I can't hold it any longer.

Every muscle in my back and biceps tenses as I choke out her name, exploding inside her with a few final jerky thrusts.

Holy. Fucking. Shit.

"That was," she starts softly.

"Unbelievable," I finish, panting hard in her hair.

We lie there, my body covering hers until our breathing slows. She can't see the huge grin splitting my face.

There's no going back now.

"Jack." She laughs softly against my neck. "You're still inside of me."

I pull back to look at her and wink. "And that's where I intend to stay. I'm just getting started with you."

Bonnie

I wake up with the alarm clock of the London garbage collection. The lorry's loud automated message drills through my head, "This vehicle is reversing."

It means it's six a.m.

I'm absolutely wrecked but it's a good type of exhaustion. The kind I feel after I run a marathon or, in this case, a shagathon.

I haven't had a night like that in . . . well . . . ever.

I reach for Jack . . . and feel the bed cold.

My eyes snap open. He's not here.

Jack is too big and the flat is too small for him to be here making that little noise.

I sit up, suddenly apprehensive.

Did he leave without telling me?

I feel the pillow beside me. It's cold.

The last thing I remember was melting into his hot body and falling asleep naked in his arms.

After I made him a massive pot of potatoes, steak, and carrots because, in his words, the pizza wouldn't fill a bird, we fucked again—this time slower and lazier. And then again, and again until he finally dragged me into the shower and washed every inch of my body like he worshipped it.

Somehow, he managed to be romantic and fierce all at the same time.

I walk out into the living area pulling on a T-shirt. The living room is deathly quiet as if he was never there.

My heart sinks as I scan the flat. Yup, all his stuff is gone. All I have left of the evening is his scent on me.

Who leaves before six a.m.?

Does he regret it? Or is that how a night with Jack works?

He treats you like a queen, then disappears before you can assume it meant anything.

The cold hard reality of the morning sinks in with the drizzling grey London sky outside the window. I slept with our most important client. Maybe this wasn't such a good idea, even if it was the best sex of my life.

It was worth it, a little voice inside my head screams.

"Get a grip, Bonnie," I say out loud, sinking into the sofa. "Get some coffee and get ready for work."

The wine bottle from last night is still open on the coffee table, uncorked. Beside it there's a note I hadn't noticed before.

I had to go to the office early. You looked too peaceful to disturb. By the way, I deleted all your dating apps. You should put a pin on your phone.

PS. I know you'll look after it for me because I trust you.

Followed by a wink.

I grab my phone and my jaw hits the floor. My home screen is a lot less cluttered. He actually deleted my dating apps!

He better not have looked at my photos or messages.

I grin to myself. What a cheeky bastard. It's funny how if anyone else did this I would be raging, but with Jack, his arrogance turns me on.

This morning just got a whole lot better.

I know you'll look after it for me because I trust you. I read it out loud.

What is he talking about? Look after what?

Who knows.

Yawning, I trudge to the bathroom. There's no steam, meaning he didn't have a shower here this morning. I wouldn't use this shower either if I was a billionaire.

Something gold around my neck sparkles in the mirror.

What the hell?

It can't be.

With butter fingers, I fumble with the chain around my neck until the clasp releases and it falls into my hands.

I stare down at the solid gold chain with the distinguished Knight crest pendant, blinking rapidly.

Archie T Knight

It's engraved in small writing on the underside. His father's name. It's the chain that Jack always wears.

He must have put it around my neck when I was sleeping.

In the quiet of my small flat, all I can hear is my out-of-control heartbeat.

Max wouldn't even let me touch his gaming laptop.

I slap cold water on my face, drop some tissue into the toilet, flush and . . .

Holy crap, the toilet flushes properly, as if by magic.

I don't need to dump tons of water in the cistern like I've been doing since I moved in, because my landlord is the worst in London.

I laugh to myself because that's what you do when you live alone. I don't know if I'm more ecstatic about the chain or the working toilet.

I grab my phone from the living room and text him.

> Me: Did you fix my toilet?

Jack: I give you my dead father's chain and you ask about the toilet?

Another wink.
Oh shit.

Me: I've already put it on eBay. And sold my story to the papers that a billionaire property tycoon fucked me senseless then fixed my toilet.

I have to joke. The situation is too damn intense.

Me: I'll look after it for you. Thank you for everything.

Jack: Told you I knew a few tricks. I'm not one of those useless billionaires that has people tending to their every need. I'm a handyman. By the way, your bathroom sink needs unblocking.

I smile.

Me: That you are. A Jack of all trades. I don't know if I can afford your services, though.

Jack: Where do you think the term came from? We'll work out a payment plan in blow jobs.

Cheeky bugger. The dots appear again.

> Jack: Hope you are not too sore this morning.

My smile morphs into a face-splitting grin. I feel tender and stiff like I've had an electric drill between my legs all night, but I'll wear it like a badge of honour. It's a nice reminder.

> Me: It's okay, I knew what I was getting myself into. I knew you weren't a chocolate and foot rubs kind of guy.

> Jack: Try me. I can be that guy too. I'll give you whatever you want, Bonnie.

Goosebumps break out all over my skin. Those are strong words for a fling.

Is this a game to Jack?

I can't reconcile these two sides of him. If I'm to believe the press, Jack has a different woman in his bed every night, yet here he is being the sweetest man alive.

I'm not used to holding someone's gaze so intently during sex, but Jack wouldn't let me look away.

It was as if he were trying to reach into my soul.

Does Jack do this with everyone?

I'm in danger here of falling hard and after Max, I can't afford to leave myself open. My heart won't survive any more lies.

> Me: I don't understand. Why did you give me your father's chain?

I watch the dots, my heart beating wildly. The message

flashes up immediately.

Jack: Because I'm a construction guy.
I need to lay foundations.

I frown, not understanding.

Me: ??

Jack: Because I trust you. And I want
to prove to you that you can trust me.

Another message quickly follows.
I hold my breath reading it once, twice, three times.

Jack: And my nan always said trust is
the foundation to love.

27

Bonnie

I prepared myself for classic Knight—the swagger, the smirk, the orders growled with a half-grin.

I prepared myself for when he would treat me with the same casual arrogance he reserves for everyone because, despite the knock-you-off-your-feet-romantic messages, nothing got in the way of work for Jack.

I prepared myself for business mode Jack.

I hadn't prepared myself for *this*.

Every hair on my body stands as Jack storms down the aisle.

The guy talking intently in his ear and meeting him stride by stride isn't holding his attention.

No, that's all on me.

Feral is the only way I can describe the look.

His eyes blaze with such searing intensity that the entire floor must notice.

Oh, *fuck*.

I duck down behind my monitor like a frightened turtle.

Nisha laughs quietly beside me.

He said it wouldn't be weird at work. I meant by him ignoring me, not charging towards me like a horny bull.

"Jack," I squeak as he stops right at my desk.

"Later, bossman," the other guy says, walking off to leave me with a brooding hulky CEO staring down at me.

He leans over my desk divider with a slow lazy smile tugging at his lips and the subtlety of a brick.

I'm acutely aware of conversations teetering off around me.

"Morning, Bonnie." It's a low husky tone that should only be used in the bedroom.

"Good morning, Jack," I reply in a clipped tone, feeling prickly with all the eyes boring into me.

"Morning, Jack," Nisha chirps beside me.

"Morning, Nisha," he drawls, still looking at me. His brown eyes are half-lidded as his gaze drops to my mouth. "How are you?"

"Great!" I say brightly. "I'm just completing the CAD for the south tower." *Please don't look at me like that, it makes me want to have all your babies.* Out of the corner of my eye, Max watches us. "How are you today?"

"Never been better." He leans his forearms further over my desk divider until his fingers tickle my arm. Seemingly, he's in no hurry to do whatever billionaire property tycoons do at nine a.m. in the office.

I blink. "So, everyone's great." It sounds like I don't have a voice box. "How can I help you, Jack?"

This is surreal. The man was buried inside me last night. Most of the night. Everyone must be able to tell I was his lucky cock-warmer. I've even got a mild limp from sore thighs.

I can't cope.

He leans over and lifts my scarf gently. Talk about suggestive. A wave of heat rises up from my neck and consumes my entire head, scalp included.

When he finds what he wants under it, his mouth widens into a satisfied grin. "Nice scarf. I'm looking for one for my sister."

"Thank you." I smile politely. "It's from Zara."

I spent about thirty minutes this morning debating whether I should wear his chain. Did he want me to wear it in public? Did he *not* want me to wear it in public? Was I snubbing him if I didn't?

Who the hell knows.

People would notice an expensive manly chain in place of my home-made jewellery *especially* one with a Knight crest pendant.

In the end, I wore it but covered it with a scarf like a shameful hickey.

"How's your toilet?"

"Perfect," I bristle. "Thanks for asking."

He looks amused.

I narrow my eyes.

"I'll take you for lunch, darlin'," he says in my ear, leaning in closer. "Noon on the dot. If I can wait that long."

What the hell is he playing at?

"Jack," I say through a clenched smile, flinging daggers at him with my eyes. "Unless it's a project meeting, that's not advisable."

He chuckles. "She's mad at me again. She's always mad."

"Will you bloody behave?" I hiss in a lowered tone. "I don't want anyone to know about last night. People have grown ten ears since you came to my desk."

"I can't help it if you drive me crazy," he says in an equally lowered tone. Not low enough.

"You're going to get me in trouble."

His brows rise in amusement. "Last time I checked, I owned this place."

"That's not the point. No one can know."

"I don't care who knows, sweetheart. They're going to find out soon enough."

My nostrils flare. Of course, *he* doesn't care.

"I care," I bite out, feeling my professional smile slip. "I care a lot."

"Okay, okay." His voice drops. "I'll behave."

"You better bloody behave," I whisper-yell back at him.

"Everything okay?" Max interrupts as he comes to stand beside Jack. Max isn't a small guy but looks puny compared to Jack.

Jack slaps him on the back with just a little more pressure than would be considered matey.

Max coughs slightly at the jostle.

"Everything's perfect, Max. Exactly how it should be."

"Jack asked if he could see the designs of the chimney viewing platform," I say quickly. I smile sweetly at Max, the man I once loved and now hate to his very core.

Max's frown deepens as he turns his attention to Jack. "It's best to chat with me since I've a holistic view of the project."

"So you keep reminding me."

"I'll come with you now to your office if you'd like, Jack?"

"No need. Bonnie's an incredible architect. I don't need to talk to anyone else." Jack gives him a cocky grin, slaps him on the back one last time and walks off.

Completely at ease, the opposite of me.

The fucker.

It's only then that Max gives me his undivided focus. His glassy stare is a strange mix of confusion and annoyance.

My most professional smile returns.

How many secrets are we both hiding from each other? Did I ever truly know this man?

The anxiety and disappointment of yesterday has fizzled and morphed into something more slow-burning and controlled today.

Soon, I'll get my closure with Max's betrayal.

Today is not that day.

All day, I feel Jack's eyes on me, watching me with a slow-burning hunger like a wolf stalking prey. I'm on heightened alert that any minute he'll throw me over his shoulder, carry me into his office, and fuck the life out of me in front of the entire floor.

And all day I get angrier.

I refuse his offer of lunch.

I have deadlines. Deadlines imposed by *him* that I need to concentrate on, instead of being distracted by the broody cockney every time he makes his presence known.

At five on the dot, he saunters down the office as he always does on a Thursday. Nisha and I watch from our desks. I take a relaxed breath for the first time all day.

Nisha lets out a low whistle. "That's some Big Dick Energy he's directing at you."

I laugh meekly. "I'm exhausted. I feel like he's been prodding me with an electric rod all day."

"Yeah? Well, *savour* this. Every woman in London is gagging to be in your position right now. Even me a little." She looks sheepish. "You're not the only one who got lucky last night. Although it depends how you define lucky."

"Oh yeah?" I ask excitedly.

She swallows and lets out a strangled laugh. "I accidentally slept with Darren again."

"What?" I slap a hand over my mouth. "How?"

"A few of us went out for last minute drinks. Darren and I ended up being the stragglers when last orders rang. Then we went to another late-night bar, and one thing led to another. He's quite charming outside of work."

"I feel like you're in denial about how much you're interested in him."

"What can I say? Repeated exposure grinds a girl down." Nisha snort-laughs. "He's amazing in bed. *Terrible* project manager. He couldn't manage a child with two Lego blocks. Can I be attracted to someone who is great in bed but terrible at their job?" She looks at me seriously. "I've been torturing myself all day."

"He's a good-looking bloke," I say, mulling it over. "And it's not like you need a project manager."

She sighs. "Really handsome."

"What are we playing at?" I groan.

She rolls her eyes. "You're banging a billionaire hottie. I think you're playing a better game than me. Speaking of which, I'm hoping that means you don't care about what I'm about to tell you." She pauses. "Max was at the work drinks with Olivia last night."

I stiffen. "As a couple?"

"No, they kept their distance. Max was pretty coy about his

romantic getaway to the place you were supposed to go on your honeymoon. Maybe because he knows it makes him look like a total ass."

I sigh. "I don't even want to think about that."

"When are you going to confront him?"

I exhale heavily. "I'm not sure yet. He doesn't know I know. It's clear he has zero respect for me so if I confront him, he'll either deny it or take me off the project or both. I need to think about my options before I do anything."

"I agree. Play the long game. Revenge is a dish best served cold and all that. Although technically you already have revenge."

I look at her, confused. "What do you mean?"

She smiles. "You're fucking the love of Max's life. Jack Knight."

I can't stop the grin spreading across my face.

An hour later, I make my way down to the gym ready to tell Jack to rein in the Big Dick Energy at the office.

The boxing gym is empty but the sound of running water comes from the shower room.

Great, he's in the damn shower.

"Jack," I call out, making my way across the ring. "Are you decent?"

The water stops to a dribble then the door opens, letting out a gust of steam.

"For you, yes, very decent."

Holy God, give me strength.

He's naked.

He holds his arms up to rest on the top of the door frame, his wide bronzed tattooed torso dripping all over the floor.

When I say naked, I mean *completely* naked. In true caveman style, with zero shame. That damn thick, heavy cock is taunting me. It knows I'm about to melt into the puddle Jack's making on the floor.

His lips curl into that infuriating grin. "Too distracting, darlin'?"

"I have some self-control you know, Jack," I say haughtily, squeezing my thighs together. "I'm not going to fall at your feet every time you prance around naked. I'm here to tell you off."

What I mean is, *Please send me daily dick pics. I'll frame them on my wall.*

"Prance?" Mirth dances in his eyes. "She's angry again. Go ahead. Tell me off."

It takes every ounce of willpower to keep my eyes trained on his. "You're being too obvious, Jack. You're pissing me right off."

He licks his lips wolfishly. "You know, you're cute when you're angry. Your face scrunches up into an adorable scowl."

"I mean it, Jack." I give him my fiercest glare. "I'm serious."

"Okay." He leans in so his eyes are level with mine. "I'm listening."

"I don't want the project team to know what happened between us."

He considers it. "Would that be such a bad thing for you?"

"Yes!" I cry out. "The worst. I can't have anyone at work knowing about this."

His grin slides. "They knew about you and Max."

"That was different. Max and I were established. I don't know what this is."

"I do."

I blink. "What is it?"

"We're together." He says it simply, like it's a done deal.

My jaw drops slightly. "You don't do relationships."

"Is that a question or a statement?"

"You haven't had a girlfriend in years."

He holds my gaze. "I don't do things by half, so I didn't do it at all."

I eye him guardedly. Trusting another guy seems like an alien, impossible concept. Never mind trusting someone like Jack. Max has the temptation of what's on offer in the office. Jack has the temptation of what's on offer in the world. "Did you sleep with the girl who flirted with you in Maggie's the other night?"

He shrugs. "I don't know which one you're talking about, but I didn't sleep with anyone. I haven't slept with anyone since you gave me a glimmer of hope at the wedding."

Smooth.

"And now you've decided you want a girlfriend?" Just because he fancies a normal girlfriend today doesn't mean he'll feel the same tomorrow.

His brows shoot up. "I'm wounded. You make it sound like I'm picking random girlfriends off the street."

I swallow thickly. "What *are* you doing, Jack?" *Besides giving me long-awaited, Earth-shaking explosive orgasms.*

He smiles. "Courting you. You think I would fix any old woman's toilet?"

I can't help but giggle.

"And claiming you," he adds casually.

"*Claiming* me?"

He leans in to run his hand over my collarbone and winks. "Blokes won't come near you with the Knight coat of arms around your neck."

I try to look indignant. I'm not a piece of property but damn, that's the sexiest thing anyone's ever said to me.

Is Jack playing me or is this real?

"Jack, this isn't a game. You can't play with my feelings. Or my career! After Max..."

"I'm not Max," he says firmly, his eyes holding mine. "And I'm not playing with your feelings. If anything, you hold all the cards, Bonnie."

"Me?" I scoff. "You have women throwing themselves at you every minute of the day."

"You think I don't see guys eyeing you up? Having my girlfriend working amongst a load of construction guys." His lips curl upward. "Especially in that hard hat you wear on site."

"Girlfriend," I repeat in a high voice. *Can I do this?*

For a second, he looks almost vulnerable. "Are you okay with that?"

"Yes," I whisper, my heart thumping. "I'll be your girlfriend. But only if you behave at work and stop watching me."

He steps closer, towering over me, all trace of vulnerability gone. "You love me watching you in the office."

I purse my lips, trying to muster professionalism. "It's distracting." My eyes flicker down to his cock, now rock-hard against his stomach. "Very distracting." I swallow. "Does that thing ever go down?"

"Can't help it," he drawls huskily, his eyes hooded with desire. "I'm naked in front of his favourite person. Just looking at her drives him fucking wild." He steps closer until our chests are inches apart. "Take it. Take what you want, darlin'. You're wet just looking at me."

I'd love to prove the arrogant git wrong, but the truth is there's a flood down there that could rival the Atlantic.

I trace a slow delicious path down his wet shoulders, chest, and abs with my hands. When they settle just above his pubic line, his stomach muscles flex with anticipation.

"What are you waiting for, sweetheart?" he asks gruffly, keeping his almost black eyes trained on me.

I wrap my fist around his beautiful cock. It swells and pulses and strains against my touch. I'll never get enough of this.

He rests his hands on the doorframe above his head and breathes out heavily. "Good girl."

I take him in both my hands, stroking the entire length of him. I'm dying to hear those deep groans again.

His lips part and his head jerks forward slightly. The muscle in his jaw flexes as I increase my pace. His face strains with the first signs of climax and his breathing becomes more laboured. I love how he reacts to me. I love how he groans with pleasure at my touch. But most of all, I love his face when he loses control and comes undone.

"No," he groans, his voice raw with arousal. His body stiffens for a moment as he tries to keep control. "I want to come inside you." He pushes my hand away.

We have a frantic back and forth about birth control. He swears he's clean. Right now, I'm cleaner than the Virgin Mary.

His hands come around my waist, hitching up my dress so that it bunches on my hips. With one swift movement he rips the panties clean off me.

"Oi, mister!" I'm equally pissed off and aroused.

"Sorry." He doesn't look it in the slightest. "We'll go shopping for more."

His eyes lock on mine as his hand finds its way between my legs. Fingers teasingly slide up and down my opening, sweeping my clit at just the right pressure to make me feel turned on but starved.

My pussy clenches, craving friction. My nipples harden. My clit swells. My whole body aches with longing.

Oh God, I'm so ready.

A smile curves his lips as he feels how wet I am already. He knows exactly how easily affected I am by him. I should be embarrassed.

He hitches my left leg up, so it wraps around his waist, then impales me down on his thick cock in one swift movement.

"Ah!" I gasp. Too deep, too quickly.

"Sorry, sweetheart." He stiffens, still inside me. "You okay?"

I nod and tighten my leg around his waist.

"This is my favourite place."

"The gym?" I ask breathlessly. He's here every day.

"No," he replies huskily. "Your tight pussy."

My laugh quickly morphs into a moan as he holds my hips in place and begins to thrust. How does he know how to fuck me at exactly the right position to hit my clit? Every single time.

Hours of pent-up sexual tension at the proximity of Jack all day ripple through me. It feels so good to have him bare.

"You drive me crazy, you know that?" he says through clenched teeth as he thrusts his cock in and out of me.

I groan in response, assuming it's a rhetorical question. I cling to his biceps, feeling them flex each time he drives into me. We make sex standing up look easy, but he's doing all the work. My legs are like jelly around him.

My whole body tingles with pleasure from his thick, hard cock pumping inside me, again and again, bringing me closer each time. Hitting me in that spot right in my centre that makes me buck and shudder and scream.

"You belong to me now," he growls against my throat. "All mine. You're all fucking mine, Bonnie."

Maybe he *is* a werewolf.

"*Yes.*" It's a low prolonged moan from the depths of my stomach. "Yes, Jack."

"Come on me," he demands, hot against my forehead. "I need to feel your tight little pussy coming all over my cock."

I do as I'm told.

Our laboured breathing mixes as I ride him towards orgasm, moaning his name over and over again.

When he gives one final out-of-control groan and empties himself hard inside me, my hips buck with uncontrollable contractions. I spasm around him, clenching down on his cock, squeezing every last drop from him.

Holy hell.

I've never had that before. Perfectly timed orgasms. I thought it was a myth created by porn movies.

Breathing hard, he runs hot, open-mouthed kisses all over my neck. "I'll try not to leer at you too much, darlin', but only if you give me what I need."

"What do you need?" I croak, almost fearfully.

"You."

It's the sexiest thing I've ever heard.

He lifts his head from my neck to give me a wicked smirk. "Every fucking night."

28

Bonnie

I *really* hope this isn't the right house.

It's a massive white Victorian dream home high up on the hill, overlooking Greenwich Park, the home of GMT—Greenwich Mean Time—on one of the most prestigious roads in South East London.

It's a beautiful Saturday morning. The April sun is freakishly strong thanks to global warming, and I'm sweating like a pig after hiking up a hill that could rival San Francisco's Lombard Street.

There isn't a hope in hell I'm walking in through those gates.

With shaky hands, I dial Jack's number. He answers on the first ring.

"I thought you said you lived alone." I scowl, eyeing the massive black, boxy dog that could be Damien's protector dog in *The Omen*.

"I do. Why do you think," he cuts himself off. "*Oh*." I can feel him grinning down the phone.

The big white door opens, and out comes Jack, shirtless as usual.

"She's fine," he says, eyes on me. His voice comes through the phone and in person. "She just needs to smell you."

"Yeah, because that's what you do to food before you take a bite." The dog comes up to Jack's thighs and eyes me with a look that screams *he's mine*.

"She looks scary, but she's really sweet. She's excellently

233

trained." He grins. "Better house-trained than me."

"She looks like a thug. What type is she? A hellhound?"

"An Italian mastiff. Great guard dog. Her name's Lucy. My niece Poppy named her."

Poppy has more balls than me hanging out with that monster.

"She doesn't look like a Lucy," I mutter, staring at Lucy's massive jowls.

By some miracle, Jack coaxes me inside the gates. I stand stiffly as Lucy sniffs my crotch, praying she won't rip my panties to pieces like her owner. To my relief, she walks off bored.

Inside, his house is white and modern. Clearly, it's professionally designed and decorated, but I get the sense with Jack it's about getting the job done rather than an attempt to showcase his wealth.

It's also more tech-savvy than I ever imagined a house needed to be. The house can detect useless things such as the optimal time to open and close the blinds, so Jack doesn't need to.

In the space of a week, he's come to my tiny flat four times after driving me home on his motorcycle.

We've just hung out. For a billionaire, he's easy to please. I cook and he makes a half-assed attempt to help, then is relieved when I tell him to stop. His requests are always simple, hearty food. Meat. Potatoes. Pies. More meat. The guy eats simply but eats a lot. It's like trying to feed a racehorse in training.

And always, as soon as dinner is over, allowing me no time to digest, Jack strips our clothes off and humps me on every hard surface in the flat. That's why we don't go to fancy restaurants.

Jack gives me a tour starting with the roof terrace.

"Wow," I yell, running circles around it. "You can see everything from here! You can see Lexington HQ!"

It's a panoramic view of the city. Canary Wharf glass towers glisten over the Thames. Following the river down, St. Paul's cathedral and the Shard are in the distance.

He laughs, deep and husky, as he watches me.

"Here." He hands me binoculars sitting on the decking table

in the middle.

I take them excitedly. "Oh my God, I can see the pods of the London Eye!" I squeal. "This is so much fun."

I drag the binoculars further down the river. "I can see the Lexington Hotel at London Bridge! What does it feel like to see buildings you own from your house?"

"The view's much better from where I'm standing."

I tilt the binoculars towards his voice and Jack comes into view. He's watching me watch London.

"Charmer." I giggle pathetically. This man has turned me into a giddy moron.

"Come on." He juts his chin to the terrace entrance. "I'll show you the rest."

"I expected you to live in a penthouse apartment with tiger skin everywhere and mirrors on the ceilings," I say wryly.

"Christ, Bonnie." He rolls his eyes. "I'm not a porn star."

He should be.

He slaps me on the backside and leads me through each of the four floors by the hand, starting with the bedrooms. My mouth waters when I see the humongous bed in his minimalistic bedroom.

At the bottom floor, he shows me the wine cellar, the games room, the gym, and the sauna.

The gym seems to be the most used room. On the walls are pictures of a young Jack and his dad who looks exactly like him except without the Italian complexion. Most of them are taken in boxing rings, with Jack holding up medals.

"You look like him," I say as he wraps his arms around me, pushing my back flush against his naked torso. I touch the chain around my neck. "I'm so scared that I'll lose this."

"You won't lose it." His warm breath tickles my neck as he inhales my scent. "I trust you."

"You don't know that! I think you should take it back. I'll never forgive myself if I lose it."

I don't even know if he's listening. His hands come up to

palm my breast, and I feel the familiar thickness press against my lower back.

"There's nothing you could do that would make me mad at you."

"That sounds like a challenge," I grumble.

"Come on, I haven't shown you the best room yet." Taking me by the hand, he pushes open the door to the left of the gym to reveal a small *swimming pool* and a hot tub.

My jaw drops. "Remind me why we spent the last few nights in my crappy one-bed flat?"

He shrugs. "I wanted you to feel comfortable."

I snort. "And you didn't think I'd feel comfortable in a house with views of the city and a swimming pool? This is how you attract bunny-boilers. I'm never leaving this place. I'm moving in."

"Only if you follow the house rules."

"Oh yeah? What are the rules?"

He strips his shorts so he's fully naked. "No clothes in the pool area."

His cock is already swollen and hard.

No matter how often I see his thick masculine body covered in tattoos, I still shiver with intimidation.

I laugh to cover up how flustered I am.

His lips quirk as he takes his cock in his fist. "There are other house rules you'll have to abide by."

He's about to tell me when the phone in his other hand starts ringing. "*Fuck*," he says, his face darkening as he reads the caller ID. "Sorry, Bonnie, I'm expecting this. I need to take it."

I give him space and shimmy out of my summer dress revealing a very expensive red lingerie set purchased yesterday. I know Dad owes him part of half a million, but if Jack rips this set, he'll be buying me a replacement.

He licks his lips approvingly.

I catch snippets of the strained conversation. Wicks. Belmarsh prison. Unease swirls in my stomach as I watch his mood darken.

He blows out a breath through his teeth, shuts off the phone, and storms past me out into the boxing gym with such intensity my breath hitches.

I follow after him and watch him as he throws bare-fisted vicious punches at the boxing bag hanging from the ceiling in the middle of the room.

I've never seen him like this. The look in his eyes scares me.

"Jack." I wince as he smashes the bag with heavy grunts. "Wanna talk about it?" I ask tentatively from the corner of the gym, feeling self-conscious in my underwear.

He stops suddenly as if only realising I'm in the room. "Sorry, darlin'." His chest heaves as he tries to calm himself down. "That was the police constable that was on my dad's case. I'm seeing Donnie Wicks in two weeks. The date is finally set."

"Oh." I pause. "Why?"

His nostrils flare. "Sorry. Even hearing his fucking name sets me off. Fuck if I know. The cunt's dying and wants to talk to me. Maybe he's finally going to confess."

"Have you talked to him since . . ."

He shakes his head. "Nope. I demanded to talk to him for years. Threatened him with everything I could. Nothing worked."

He throws one final vicious punch at the bag then stalks towards me, taking my face in his hands. "I'm sorry, sweetheart. I didn't mean to scare you."

"It's okay," I say softly, placing my palms on his bare tattooed chest. His heart hammers. "I'm not scared."

His dark eyes lock onto mine saying something unspoken.

"You make everything better, you know that?"

I give him a small smile. "Do you want me to come as well? To the prison?"

"No, sweetheart, it's fine."

I bite my lip, not feeling comfortable. "Are you going by yourself? What if you do something you regret?"

He laughs softly. "The guy's in a high-security prison, Bonnie. I don't think I'll be able to get at him." He kisses my forehead. "You have nothing to worry about."

"Can I ask questions?" I ask tentatively.

"You can always ask whatever you want. Don't forget that."

I nod. "Do you know why he did it? I understand if you don't want to talk about it."

His eyes close for a moment as he exhales heavily. "Dad was a bit of a player. He fooled around behind Mum's back." His jaw tightens. "Wicks found out he was sleeping with his wife. It was a quick stupid meaningless fling. Dad thought he was invincible because he was a semi-pro boxer. But fists don't help you against a knife."

His lips press into an angry line as he struggles to continue. I have no words to take his pain away.

Then he looks me dead in the eye when he says, "I hired a hitman."

"What?" I whisper, staring at him in horror, waiting for him to tell me he's joking.

"I'm not proud of it."

"Did you call it off?"

"Wicks went to prison. It's harder to kill someone in a high-security prison if you don't have the right contacts."

"You would have killed him." I don't know whether it's a statement or a question.

"Maybe. Probably not. I don't know."

I blink, trying to understand. "Who knows? Sean?"

"Danny and Tristan. That's all. And now you, Bonnie."

"Why did you tell me?" I squeak.

A soft smile crosses his face. "Because I trust you."

My heart skips a beat. "Are you always this trusting?"

"No," he says gently, running a finger down my cheek. "But I've always gone by my instincts. They haven't let me down yet." He tilts my head so I'm forced to look him in the eyes. A frown creases his forehead. "I don't want any secrets between us, Bonnie. Do you still want to be my girlfriend, or have I scared you away?"

For the first time, I see the demons hiding behind Jack's cocky demeanour.

"Of course, I do," I say quickly, smoothing the worry lines from his forehead. "Your dad didn't deserve to go that way. I wish I could take away your hurt."

He pulls me close and sighs against my forehead. "It's okay, darlin'. You being here is all I need."

He kisses my head.

The funny thing is," he says quietly, "I'm called a player just like Dad. But the difference is I don't fool around with attached women even if they do throw themselves at me. Maybe if Dad hadn't had so many affairs when I was younger, I wouldn't have thought twice about going after you when you were with Max. God knows I wanted to."

"I wish you had. All along, I thought Max was the nice guy and you were . . . the dick who fired my dad."

"The dick?" His brows quirk. "You need to be punished for that."

"Oh yeah? What are you gonna do about it?"

He pushes against me so that I'm forced to walk backwards then cages me against the wall.

"On your knees, darlin'."

৯

I wake up, gasping for air, a heavy arm lying across my stomach.

Jack's black lashes flutter open. "Good morning, beautiful," he says in a deep groggy voice. Concern fills his eyes as they adjust to the sunlight. "Are you okay?"

"I just had a nightmare," I breathe. "I didn't mean to wake you."

He lifts his head. "What was it about? What's going on in your head?"

"I had a dream that I was getting married to Max. Everything was going wrong. Stupid things, my hair, the shoes. I couldn't walk in the dress."

Jack's face darkens.

"No, wait," I cry, lifting my head. "It was a nightmare not a dream. I was suffocating and screaming in my head. Then I woke up and saw you beside me, and the feeling of relief was enormous." I laugh, shakily. "I'm so glad Max called off the wedding."

He pulls me against his chest.

Exactly where I need to be.

"Spend the day with me."

"I can't." I groan. "I have to help my dad pack up his house. They're being rehoused. By you, remember?"

"I'll help."

"Don't be silly." I laugh. "You don't need to do that. He's a hoarder. It's going to take me all day ploughing through stuff he doesn't use trying to convince him to throw it out rather than taking it with him. It's fine," I say firmly. I visualise the state of my dad's house and feel embarrassed.

Then immediately guilty.

He shrugs. "I don't mind. I'll help. Why would I give up an opportunity to spend time with my girlfriend?"

Seriously? What a contrast to Max.

My heart is going to explode.

I stare back at him, wondering how the hell I'm so lucky to hit the jackpot.

29

Bonnie

"You do know that CDs are pretty much redundant now, right?" I look crossly at Dad. I've been boxing his things away for five hours and am getting nowhere. Now we have cleared most of the clutter into boxes, it's clear that the flat hasn't had a good clean in years. "These DVDs need to go, too. There must be *hundreds* here. Who do you think will actually buy these?"

"Nonsense, love." He rubs his hands together. "These beauties still sell strong down the market. Easy."

I roll my eyes. "Dad, the only way you'll sell these is if you get a time machine and go back to the nineties."

"Don't you worry." He gives me a knowing smile. "Your old dad knows a thing or two about business, love."

Except he doesn't.

I cringe and feel instantly guilty.

Thank God Jack didn't come.

That thought makes me feel even guiltier.

I used to die of embarrassment at some of the things Dad would say to Max. The nights when Dad would have a few too many pints and decide to give privately educated Max advice on how to be a successful businessman while Max sat in uncomfortable silence until he had enough and abruptly cut Dad off.

I grew up with it drilled into me that you should never be ashamed of your roots.

But sometimes walking down the street with Dad when his

trousers were shabby and hanging off him and he smelt a little squiffy, I hung my head in shame.

And hated myself for it.

It was one of my biggest worries about the wedding. That Dad would be too drunk and too embarrassing. Max's too, as he kept drilling into me.

"You used to love coming to the Saturday market with me." He smiles sadly at me, and I feel yet another pang of guilt. He seems to grow smaller every time I see him. And more fragile.

Every Saturday, Dad had a small stall in the local market. I helped him until I was about fifteen and it stopped being cool. Then Dad would go to the market alone after that.

Now he doesn't go at all.

"I've been at this for hours and you won't let me throw anything away. You do realise your new place isn't the size of Buckingham Palace, right?"

I sigh, as I find more knick-knacks at the bottom of the CD box. Things that wouldn't sell at a flea market. Dad has lived in the social housing flat since his house got repossessed ten years ago and has hoarded everything ever since.

I haven't told him that I've started seeing Jack. I don't want a drama. Is it weird that my boyfriend's company is rehousing my dad?

"What's this?" I ask, lifting up a sealed transparent packet.

He squints at it. "Nothing of value."

He tries to take it off me but something about it makes me freeze.

Inside the pocket is a gold signet ring that looks like it's designed to do damage to a face. It has a prominent, almost gaudy, crest on it.

A family crest that I'm familiar with.

"Where did you get this?" I ask curiously, turning it around. "You know this might actually be worth something."

"Nah. Here, I'll take it off you."

Something about how he tries to snap it away from me makes

me take a step back. I examine it closer, and my heart quickens.

"Dad." I gawk at him. "Do you realise this is Jack Knight's dad's ring?"

His throat bobs. "Archie Knight? Nah," he scoffs. "It's not his."

He looks like he has seen a ghost. Dad never had a good poker face.

"It's got his *name* engraved on it." *Exactly like Jack's chain.* "I know it's his. We have to give this to Jack."

"No," he snaps.

My brows shoot to my hairline. "Why on earth not?" I stare uncomprehendingly at Dad. "Is it about the money? Are you actually planning to sell this?"

"I'm not answerable to you, lass." His voice takes on a hard edge that I've heard before, but never directed at me. "Give me the fucking thing, Bonnie."

Dad never curses at me.

My hand tightens around the ring.

Dad's hands clench into fists at his sides, and I think he's considering physically overpowering me to get the ring.

"Can't you just leave well alone?" he asks quietly.

"No," I say in an unnaturally shrill voice. "If you don't tell me the truth, I'm calling Jack and telling him. He'll come and get it himself."

I've never been scared of Dad. Even when he came home blind drunk and fell around the house, breaking things.

But I seemed to trigger something dark in him. His jaw clenches and unclenches, and I feel the familiar tightness in my chest that I got the day I saw Olivia in the boardroom.

Finally, he exhales in an angry breath. "Call Jack Knight?" he barks. "You think he has time to answer the phone to you, lass?"

I don't respond. I don't want to lie to him.

When he speaks again, he is calm. "Look, the truth is I found it. The night his old man got stabbed. I thought he had just dropped it. At the time, I didn't realise he'd been stabbed."

I swallow hard. "Where did you find it?"

He pauses. "Near the alleyway."

Shit. This ring is evidence.

And if Jack finds out my dad has had it all this time, well, I don't know how he'll react.

"Dad, why the hell didn't you hand it in to the police?"

Silence. His face says everything.

"Is this about *money*? This ring could have DNA on it that would have convicted Wicks! It still could!"

He lets out a hard laugh. "Love, sometimes you're naive. You leave home, go off to that fancy college, and lose your wits. You think I'm going to hand in something that would convict Donnie Wicks? Do you know how it works around here?"

"You could've handed it in anonymously," I protest. "You still can."

"Nothing happens anonymously in these estates. Wicks has got police all over his payroll." His mouth twists into a grimace. "I'm not going against the Wicks family, love. They have people killed for less."

"But he's already doing life. It doesn't make a difference to him." *But it does to Jack.*

"Doesn't matter." He grunts. "It's a respect thing. You grass on a Wicks, and you won't live too long to talk about it."

"Why did you keep it for so long?" I ask, confused. "Why didn't you dump it?"

"I couldn't bring myself to. It's worth quite a few bob."

My mouth twists into a thin line. None of this makes sense. "So, it's about money. It's always about money."

"Don't be so harsh to judge, love," he snaps. "All my cash went on you growing up."

I wish I'd never found this bloody ring.

"I need to give this to Jack," I say quietly.

"Jack fucking *Knight*? Are you having a laugh, love? Are you trying to condemn your old dad to death?"

"What if it's evidence?" I shake my head. "I couldn't live with myself if I didn't hand this over."

His eyes narrow as he calmly replies, "And could you live with yourself if your dad gets his head kicked in one night?"

He stares at me steadily, knowing he's got me. I think he's being overly dramatic but he's right. I don't live here anymore, and I don't know what the Wicks family are capable of.

"Jack won't let that happen," I say faintly.

"Did Jack stop the sixteen other people from being murdered by the Wicks over these past ten years?"

"What about justice?" I ask in a small voice.

"Justice?" he echoes gruffly. "We have justice. Wicks is a lifer. He's paying for his crime, and now he's dying. Don't condemn me to an early death too, Bonnie."

His face crumples. Dad looks afraid. And old.

"I was in the wrong place at the wrong time. Are you going to crucify me for that?"

A wave of nausea rolls through me as I stare down at the signet ring, wishing it would disintegrate in my hand.

Would Donnie Wicks really kill Dad over handing in a ring that was at a murder scene *over a decade ago*?

But if I call Dad's bluff and he's right, I'll never be able to live with myself.

I need time to think.

Jack is visiting Wicks in two weeks' time. Wicks might confess and then everything will come out in the wash.

I nod. "Okay, Dad. I won't say anything for now. That doesn't mean I'm happy about this. Just make sure you keep it safe. For God's sake, make sure it doesn't go missing in the flat move."

He breathes a deep sigh of relief and takes me in for a hug.

I smile back wondering how I'll be able to look Jack in the eye ever again.

Then when he has turned his back on me, I put the ring in my pocket.

30

Jack

"Bradshaw messed up," Sean says in a harsh breath. "The conservation officers at the council have declined the planning application for *Motor Works*. It'll delay us by another three months now."

I look up at him from behind my desk. "How?"

Sean walks toward my desk and sets down papers. "Bradshaw didn't do proper due diligence on Newham council planning permission. It works slightly differently to the other London boroughs. They missed a form."

I scan the documents. It's a rookie mistake and one Bradshaw Brown should be embarrassed to make. "Call the leads in."

He nods and leaves.

When he returns, Max, Steve, Bonnie, and two others are behind him. All of them look nervous as they pile into my office.

I don't ask them to take a seat.

Max clears his throat, looking particularly twitchy. "Jack, I—"

"Three months," I cut him off. "Perhaps I should cut the Bradshaw contract and get professionals on it."

The room collectively inhales a breath.

I glance at Bonnie. Her shoulders slump like the final energy drains from her body. These past two weeks she's been acting strangely. Pulling back from me. She's spent most nights at my place, but her mind is elsewhere. She tries to distract me with lamb stews, bright smiles, and blow jobs, but I still see it.

She's hiding something from me.

I need to figure out why because it's fucking killing me. Somewhere between the bad dancing at the wedding and the nights spent fixing broken things in her flat I've fallen in love with her.

"Jack," Max braves again. "I understand that this is a slight setback. I'm working on expediting a resubmission with the local authority. It was an oversight by the architects, but—"

"Stop blaming your team, Max," I cut him off again. "You're the lead on this project. I hold you accountable." I run my tongue over my teeth. I don't have the patience for this shit, and I've no patience for the weasel who shit all over my girl's heart.

His throat bobs. "Yes, Jack."

"Make the three-month wait time disappear, Max, or I'll be looking at a different team."

His face pales. He has little chance of making that happen. I'll end up sorting it out, but I need to see them panic.

"That's everything," I say, dismissing them. "Bonnie, can you stay behind, please?"

She looks startled but nods her head.

Steve, the other architect, shoots her a sympathetic look.

Max frowns. "Jack, I can handle—"

"Close the door on your way out, Max."

Max is mortified. In my defence, the guy has upset my girl. I should tear him apart.

"Of course." He regains his composure and ushers Steve and Sean out of the room to try to claw back some control.

Bonnie and I don't speak until the others have left.

"I'm really sorry, Jack," she says in a soft voice. "I should have read the application properly. I missed that."

She's so pained looking. I stride towards her and bundle her up in a hug.

"You know this is just business, right?" I murmur against her forehead. "I won't take the contract off Bradshaw. I'm just giving

Max a kick up the ass. As I said, the buck stops with him. He wants the glory, he can take the guts with it."

"It's fine, Jack. I understand." She smiles up at me, but tears threaten in her eyes.

I sigh heavily as I lift her chin. "Something's bothering you, Bonnie. Sooner or later, you'll have to tell me."

She looks scared, as if I meant it as a threat. Did Max break her trust so badly she can't confide in me?

I planned to tell her that I've bought back her dad's old house that was repossessed, but I fear I'll freak her out even more. In a few months' time, he'll be able to move in.

I'll gain my girl's trust if it's the last thing I do.

Belmarsh is a prison south of the Thames and across the water from my regeneration project.

Once dubbed Britain's Guantanamo Bay because of the number of terrorists it held, it's one of three maximum security prisons in the UK.

If you make it to Belmarsh, chances are you're probably not getting out.

That didn't make me feel any better. Donnie Wicks has spent the past decade here. From what I heard, he's had a nice life, ruling from inside prison instead of the streets.

It's just an office change to him.

London's East Enders were still as fearful of him from the inside as the outside.

It takes me almost an hour to get through security. Everyone is watching—guards, cleaners, prisoners. I can think of better ways to spend a Friday afternoon.

Everyone knows who I am, and everyone knows who I'm visiting. We are two accidental celebrities meeting for a very fucked-up reason.

The press will be outside by the time I leave. It won't make the

News at Ten, but it's enough to get the local rags mildly excited.

It's clear Wicks gets special treatment. Like a V.I.P., he sits in a far corner away from the other prisoners with a prison guard entourage.

He extends his hand. Wicks expects me to rebuke him, but I take it with an iron grip, squeezing so tight I can feel the old man's veins squishing.

I tower over the bald, slightly overweight man, meeting his gaze for the first time in a decade.

I could do serious damage to this guy. I'm trained well enough to crush him before the guards have time to react.

He knows this but he meets my gaze head-on with a certain steel in his eyes that proves the mind makes the man more than the muscle.

Donnie Wicks never loses his temper or cool. He has people to do that for him.

"All right, lad." He smiles, a relaxed smile that could trick you into believing the guy hadn't been responsible for the death of at least twenty people. "Last time I saw you was the night you beat young Slater to a pulp. Great bloody fight that was."

It's a fucked-up opening but I expected no less. I remember that night. It was my last fight before Dad died.

I regard him coolly. I'm calm. Surprisingly calm for someone who has harboured a vendetta for ten years. But going on the attack with your enemy before they've shown their cards isn't wise. I didn't get to where I am today by doing that and neither did Wicks.

"Take a seat," he says with the relaxed ease of someone inviting me in for an afternoon tea at his house.

I clear my throat and sit in the plastic chair. Plastic because at a max security prison, a steel or even wooden chair is the perfect weapon.

"Well? What is it you wanted to say to me?"

Three prison guards watch me like hawks. No doubt our conversation will be recorded covertly.

I notice the crucifix around his neck. It's always the lifers that find God.

Donnie nods his head to one of the female prison guards. "Two teas, love." He looks at me. "You like tea?"

I clench and unclench my jaw, which is starting to ache. "I'm not thirsty."

"Suit yourself." He shrugs and leans back in his chair like we have all fucking day to chit-chat. "You've come a long way since that fight. Your old nan would be proud, God rest her soul."

"She's not dead."

He looks surprised. "Good on her."

I lean over and fight the urge to put my hand around his neck. "Wanna get straight to the point, Wicks? I didn't come here to have a nice chinwag."

It's only when he smiles that I notice how sick he is. Under the bravado is a weak sick man. Lung cancer, I was told.

The smile turns into a coughing fit to the point of choking. As his spittle lands on his chin, he takes out a handkerchief and gently wipes it away with a reserved calmness.

"Your nan's a lucky sod," he says, putting away the handkerchief. "She must have great health at her age."

I sigh a frustrated breath. "Get to the point, Wicks."

"All right, all right. I've got no place to be." He chuckles. "You've spent a lot of energy trying to nail me for your dad's death. I get it, lad. I would have done a lot worse if the tables were turned."

"And?" I snarl.

"I didn't kill your old man."

I actually laugh. A hateful laugh. "You drag me down here to say this shit?"

He puts his hands up. "It's true. It's a fucking paradox, right? The whole thing pointed to a revenge killing."

He gives me a lazy smile, taking out the handkerchief again to wipe sweat from his bald head. "Bloody meds give you the sweats. Truth is, I didn't give a shit that your old man was servicing my missus. Kept her gob shut from complaining about my girls. You think I was going to waste my libido on my washed-up missus? I had much better women bouncing on my cock."

"Bullshit. Are you trying to rile me into beating you to a pulp?" My hands white-knuckle the side of the table. "Because I don't mind joining you in here."

He waves his hands. "No bullshit," he says easily.

I study him carefully.

Fuck.

He's telling the truth.

Because cowards lie and Donnie Wicks is anything but a coward. All these years, he said nothing. He didn't outright claim or deny the killing. I thought his silence was his way of torturing Dad's next of kin.

I fight to control the sudden rush of adrenaline surging through me. "If what you say is true, who did it?" I ask in a level tone.

"You know I'm no grass, which is why you haven't gotten your answers before now. But since Gleeson choked it and I'm choking it, I figured I'd put you out of your misery."

"Gleeson?" I blink. "Who the hell is Gleeson?"

"Nobody, son. Absolutely fucking nobody." He lets out a raspy laugh. "Just an idiot who liked to get a few things off the back of a lorry now and then."

"You're saying this random guy, Gleeson, killed Dad?" I hiss.

"Now you're catching on. There was no big drama behind your dad's death. A sloppy robbery gone wrong, that's what it was. A guy in a balaclava making a quick buck."

I slam my fist on the table. Donnie doesn't flinch, but the guards inch closer.

He waves them away dismissively.

"How do you know this?"

"Come on, lad, don't ask silly questions. I know everything." The corner of his eyes crinkle. "You know why I want a closed casket, son?

"What?"

"Another paradox. Donnie Wicks dies at the hands of himself instead of all the men looking to put a bullet in his head. Have you seen a body riddled with lung cancer when it finally takes them? It ain't pretty. Now, your dad, he had an open casket, didn't he? Very unfortunate what happened."

It's his misplaced sympathy that finally does it for me.

I lift him up by the throat, feeling his weak pulse accelerate. And squeeze. He gargles as five heavy-footed guards pounce, knocking me to the floor. It takes all five to restrain me. They can beat me unconscious for all I care.

"It's all right, Bobby, let the young lad up," Donnie's strangled voice calls from above us followed by a coughing fit.

"Time's up, Knight," the head guard says gruffly.

I pick myself off the floor to see all five guards standing between a red-faced Donnie and me.

Donnie winks. "Good chat, lad."

He turns to walk off.

"Oh, Jack?" He calls after me casually. "There were others. They might not have put the blade in, but they were there. Next time you visit, bring me a beer."

31

Bonnie

Lies. Unless you're a pathological liar, they eat away at you from the inside out, like a parasite.

It's a dull unease bubbling permanently in my stomach, waiting to rise. I can never forget it's there.

Technically it's not a lie, it's an omission of the truth. It feels just as dangerous and destructive though.

It's just a ring, I keep telling myself. *Just a piece of expensive jewellery.*

Jack is, ironically, the perfect boyfriend, despite his lack of practice. Every night he takes me back home on his motorcycle. He doesn't care where we go, so long as he's with me.

And every night, I've let him fuck me hard and rough. Then I cuddle with my face buried into him so he can't see the lies.

He trusts me.

It's ironic. Jack is working so hard to gain my trust, he's not thinking about whether he should trust *me*.

But today, the constant dread will finally be lifted, thank fuck.

Jack visited Donnie Wicks in prison this afternoon. He messaged to say he has news. Donnie revealed the truth.

It's Friday night and we are back in Jack's bar, Maggie's. Impromptu drinks put on by Lexington as a thanks for all our hard work, even if we did mess up the planning permission application.

My Bradshaw Brown colleagues around me are ecstatic. My

jaw aches from the fake smile stuck on my face.

Max and Olivia are both here, dancing around each other coyly even though it's the worst kept secret in Bradshaw Brown.

I couldn't give a shit.

It's been nearly two weeks since I discovered the evidence buried in my dad's moving boxes. The innocent signet ring burning a hole in my conscience.

Thirteen days and nights of pretending that everything's fine.

When my boyfriend walks in, his presence instantly takes over Maggie's.

My belly flutters, as does the belly of every other woman in the bar, judging by the looks.

Sometimes I forget who he is—a guy with an unlimited supply of money, power, and women.

I forget because Jack lets me forget.

He flashes his signature panty-dropping grin at everyone in his path but there's an edge to it tonight and only I know why.

I'm buried in the Bradshaw & Brown crowd so he can't see me at first. He scans distractedly as people try to get his attention.

I down the Tequila shot that Darren has shoved in my face just as Jack spots me.

"Jack." Max slaps him on the back as the Bradshaw team parts to let him through.

He nods at Max but, still metres away, he's looking only at me. His dark eyes stay locked on mine, their heat threatening to burn every inch of my skin.

Before Jack, I've never had a man look at me like this.

Then he's in front of Nisha, Darren, and me.

"Hi," he says. "Can I talk to you." It's not a question.

Last night I couldn't talk to him. I was too anxious.

He leans over and lowers his voice. "Don't make me take you by the hand, Bonnie. You know I don't care who knows about us."

Nisha drags Darren away by the arm. Thankfully Darren is too drunk to pick up on the tension between our most important client and me.

I follow Jack to the bar as he ignores others' attempts to talk to him.

"At first I thought you were pregnant and too scared to tell me." His chest rises with a deep breath. "But the Tequila clearly knocks that theory out of the water."

"What? I'm not," I say quickly.

"For the record, I would be happy if you were carrying my baby. I don't give a shit if it's only been a few weeks."

My eyes bulge. "If I am pregnant, I wouldn't know yet." I laugh shakily. "That's not how it works."

He's not laughing. "Now I'm thinking it's cold feet. You don't want to jump into another relationship." His jaw clenches. "Or worse. You don't want to jump into another relationship with *me*."

"I do, Jack," I choke out. "I really do. These past few weeks have been amazing."

The creases along his forehead deepen. "So, what's wrong, Bonnie? I'm trying to work out what's going on with you, and it's killing me."

"I'm fine. I'm feeling a little under the weather this week, that's all."

He shakes his head. "No. You're off. The only time you're out of your head is when I'm banging you senseless. Answer me honestly, do you want to be with me?" Vulnerability flits over his hard, beautiful features, making him seem younger than his thirty-eight years.

"Yes," I whisper. "So badly."

"Because I want to be with you—you know that, right? I want to be the boyfriend that you deserve."

My heart breaks.

I nod, fighting the tears welling in my eyes. *You wouldn't if you knew what I'm keeping from you.*

"You can't hide what's wrong, Bonnie. I'll find out." The frown on his face dissolves. "Even Lucy noticed something was up when you were over."

I bristle. That damn dog sticks her nose into everything.

"Please, just leave it," I beg him. "Not here. Anyway...what did Wicks say?" I try to rein in the panic in my voice. "You never messaged me back."

"Sorry, darlin', I had to go straight to the police station."

My eyes widen. This is the miracle that I need. "Wicks confessed?"

He runs a hand through his tousled hair. "No. He gave me the fucking shocker of a lifetime." He smiles bitterly. "Turns out Wicks didn't do it. It was a guy called Gleeson. Stanley Gleeson."

I blink. "I don't understand."

"That makes two of us. Wicks wanted to get a few things off his chest before he snuffed it. He didn't do it. This guy Gleeson stabbed my old man in a fucking *robbery*. He stabbed him for bloody cash."

"And you believe him?"

He nods. "Yeah, actually I do."

I pause, trying to understand what this means. For the first time since I found the signet ring, the ball in my stomach unwinds slightly.

Dad's safe? Wicks won't come after him because he wasn't even involved. We can hand over the ring to Jack.

"Why did he kill him?" I ask.

"We'll never know the full story. Gleeson died a few months back. I got his record checked out. He was just a small-time thief. Dad must have fought back or ripped the balaclava off him or something. It sounds like the cunt just panicked in the heat of the moment." I can hear the pain in his voice. I wish I could take it away.

I've never heard of this guy Stanley Gleeson. "At least you have closure now, right?"

"Not yet." He grimaces. "Wicks said there were others involved."

"Others?" I whisper.

"I've got a private detective looking into all Gleeson's contacts during that time. It's only a matter of time before I find them."

"What did they take?"

"Wallet. Cash. Jewellery. Whatever he had on him." His tongue drags through his lips. "Which was a lot for a guy in that area."

"Maybe you should leave it, Jack," I say in a shaky voice. "This can't be good for you. You know what happened. The guy who did it is dead."

"You've never had anyone close to you die, have you sweetheart? I don't think I can explain . . ." He shakes his head. "I can't leave it."

"But you've got the guy who did it," I squeak.

"Let's just say I hope the others are dead. Because they're going to wish they were when I'm finished with them."

My mouth is too dry to speak.

I look at the anger etched in my beautiful boyfriend's face and start to feel very, very uneasy.

Ten missed calls from Jack. If I'm trying not to arouse suspicion, I'm royally fucking it up. Jack will wonder why I left the bar without telling him, go to my flat, and find I'm not there.

Instead, it's eleven on a Friday night, and I'm banging on Dad's door after the most claustrophobic underground ride of my life. Not only because it's sweltering heat and there's no ventilation, but because my nerves are so bad, I nearly puked every time the train lurched forward.

Dad will be on his own because that's his life. No one visits except Uncle Pat and me. A thought that I try to push to the back of my mind because knowing you are the sole child of a lonely parent is daunting.

I see the silhouette of his frame move towards the front door, and my heart pounds so hard I think I'm having an anxiety attack. I can still run away because I know after he opens that door *something* will change.

These past few weeks, I've been so fixated on Wicks confessing that there was no room for alternative scenarios.

Because that's why Dad was afraid of me telling Jack, right?

On the Central line, I told myself it was going to be okay. I concocted a plan. I would tell Dad I'm dropping in on him on my way home and casually bring the conversation around to what Wicks revealed to Jack. We would discuss it rationally, work through it together. Dad wasn't involved. He just happened to do something stupid after the event.

Jack would come around eventually. He would understand.

Everything would be out in the open instead of buried deep inside me, gnawing away at my stomach.

My rehearsed speech goes out the window the moment Dad opens the door.

"Wicks didn't kill Jack's dad," I blurt out.

Silence.

Fear looks back at me.

He recovers quickly, but I see it.

The dread resting in my stomach bubbles to the surface.

"Not this again, love." *Love* is said with no love. His mouth twists into an angry line.

"Wicks admitted it was a guy named Stanley Gleeson," explodes out of me.

He eyes me guardedly. "Where did you hear this rubbish?"

"Jack hired a private detective."

"Jack *Knight*? How the hell do you know that?"

"I'm dating him. He's my boyfriend."

His eyes widen. Now his face is as white as someone who has been dead for a few days.

"Tell me the truth, Dad." I'm trying hard to keep my voice steady, but I'm shaking. "Because from where I'm standing, I'm jumping to a lot of scary conclusions."

I don't know how long we stare at each other. It feels like a lifetime.

The silence is unbearable.

"Get in the bloody house," he growls through clenched teeth. "The neighbours will hear."

My pulse flatlines. I already have my answer.

I step into the kitchen.

"Sit down."

"No," I say, unable to hide the tremble in my voice. "You were there."

He reaches for the opened bottle of whiskey beside the sink. The smell of it makes the single Tequila I had rise in my throat. I force it back.

I gaze around the open-plan kitchen and living room trying to calm myself down. Everything is in boxes. The only things that remain are the pictures of me on my graduation day on the wall.

He's ready to move into a nicer flat and start a new life.

When he finally speaks his voice is so quiet, I strain to hear. "I was in the wrong place at the wrong time."

He stares into the glass as he pours as if it holds all the answers.

I take a seat at the table because my legs are too weak to stand. I decide if I transfix on a spot of chipped wood on the corner of the table, I'll be okay.

"I was struggling to get back on my feet," he continues quietly. "I was days away from losing the house. I remortgaged it to pay for . . ."

I squeeze my eyes shut.

To pay for my university fees.

"It doesn't matter why. It doesn't excuse anything." He swirls the glass in his hand and takes a large sip. It goes down without a hint that it's hard liquor. Still staring at the glass, he says, "We'd done it once before. Back then it wasn't this *cashless* society we have today. It happened so quickly, and the guy just handed over his wallet. Gleeson took the lead. All I had to do was stick on a balaclava and stand there beside Gleeson. It was a simple case of two against one. We hardly threatened the guy. He didn't even seem that bothered."

I sit very still watching his nostrils flare in and out as he takes deep breaths.

He drains the last of his glass. "I wasn't proud of it, but I figured we were choosing guys that had enough cash that it wouldn't matter to them. Guys around the East End that liked to show how well they were doing by draping themselves in gold and fucking expensive watches."

"Like rich dentists," I say faintly.

I remember that night. I was still living at home as I hadn't started university. Phil didn't even tell the police.

Maybe if he had, they would have caught Jack's father's killers.
Killers.

My chest tightens. Did I think that as plural?

Is that what I believe?

For the first time he looks me in the eye and when he speaks, this time his voice is firm. Confident. "He took something much worse from me, Bonnie. You. Your mother."

My gaze connects with the happy girl graduating on the wall. She had no clue what was happening around her. All she cared about was parties, getting laid, and making sure she got enough points to graduate with honours.

Ignorance really is bliss.

"You intentionally chose Phil," I say flatly.

"Do you blame me?"

I don't know. I always had a sneaking suspicion Mum met Phil before she split from Dad. Phil earned more money in a month than Dad did in a year.

If Olivia got robbed, would I be happy?

I answer him with another question. "Did Phil know it was you?"

"I think so. Maybe that's why he gave everything up without a fuss." He pours himself another measure. It smells cheap and foul, not like the stuff Jack drinks. "He had everything he wanted."

I watch him sink most of the glass in one swallow.

"So, the second time, everything seemed easier. Everyone

knew Knight sauntered around the pub flashing his son's cash. It meant nothing to him." He pauses. "Gleeson and I hadn't planned it that night, but Knight had a skinful in the White Horse and was firing twenties down as tips as if they were pennies."

I feel something rise in my chest. The dread again.

I can tell he wants to tell me everything, but I take it back. I don't want to know. I want him to stop talking.

"We felt like he was rubbing it in our faces."

He sighs. It's a horrible sound that I feel right in my gut. A low wheezy noise too big for his chest.

"All we wanted was the damn wallet and jewellery. He should have handed it over. Lord knows there was plenty more where it came from. But Knight thought he was invincible." His shoulders slump. "Knight goaded him. Gleeson. Before I knew what was happening, Gleeson had stabbed him."

"No, No, No," I hear myself saying. I repeat what Dad's telling me in my head, trying to rearrange his words so that they have a different meaning.

I stare at his frightened eyes and protruding bones creating unhealthy angles. Small blood vessels are broken across his face.

Dad was an attractive man in his day, back when I was Daddy's girl, helping my dad at the Saturday market. I thought that he was the smartest, most courageous man on earth.

Now I don't know this man.

I can barely breathe.

All I can do is stare at the stranger in front of me.

"You lied to me." I swallow. "You made me believe that you were scared of Wicks."

"I had to, love," he pleads. "Gleeson might not have the same leverage as Wicks, but I wasn't going to go up against him. I would have had a lit newspaper through my letterbox."

You're not courageous. You never were. You're a coward.

How have I not realised how cold the flat is until now? I shiver and rub my arms vigorously. What I wouldn't do to be in a steaming, excruciatingly hot bath.

"Does Mum know?" I ask, my teeth chattering. *Please God, don't say she's in on this.*

"Of course she doesn't."

I nod. It's the only redeemable moment of the night.

"You need to go to the police." I try for a calm and authoritative tone as if I'm telling him he needs to go to the dentist more than once every five years. It's way off the mark. I'm breathy and frantic. "Jack will find out."

He looks at me as if I've struck him across the face. "Do you want to see your old man go to jail for an accident that happened a long time ago? Is that it? Because the Knights won't go easy on me. Wicks isn't the only one with coppers on his payroll."

Mugging someone is not an accident.

He grips the glass. "Believe me, I've already paid in guilt. Not a day goes by where I don't think about what happened."

He's telling the truth. I hear it in his voice.

"I'll get arrested for assisting an offender, Bonnie. Maybe worse. Is that what you want?"

Tears form in my eyes.

"They'll let you off easy if you give yourself up," I say, blinking them back. "You were just a witness. You won't get prison time. You can say you were scared and that's why you didn't come forward before."

I don't know if I'm trying to convince Dad or me.

He was there.

He saw it happen.

He let it happen.

The wave of dread rises like a tsunami in my stomach.

Tonight was supposed to be different. I was going to sleep for the first time in two weeks. All the secrets were going to be out in the open, and Jack and I would move forward.

Now I'm trying to figure out if I'm a murderer's daughter.

Dad turns his back to me and stands at the sink. For a second I think he's ignoring me. Then I see his shoulders silently shake. I've only seen Dad cry twice before.

Everything is fucked.
No matter what happens, I've lost Jack.

32

Bonnie

I'm in the middle of a painfully hot shower when the door buzzes. The only people who visit me unannounced are Amazon delivery men, especially at eight a.m. on a Saturday.

But I know from the buzz it's not a delivery guy. I can *feel* the annoyance through the buzz.

With shampoo still in my hair, I wrap a towel around me and rush down the stairs.

When I open the door, he has a deep frown on his face.

I lay awake all night worrying about how I would face Jack, to the point I felt physically ill.

And now he's here.

For a moment, we just stare at each other.

My mind goes into survival mode. Nothing has to change. Jack knows who killed his father. He has his answers.

We can forget about this and move on.

We can go to Crystal Palace Park today. Jack said he hasn't been there since he was a kid and wants to go back. Jack wants to check if there's a cafe still there that his nan used to take him to.

We can do that today.

I'll do anything Jack wants. Today and every single day after.

A nerve throbs in his forehead. I recognise it now. It's the only giveaway when Jack doesn't feel in control. When my beautiful boyfriend feels vulnerable.

He clears his throat. "You left without telling me. You know I might not have much experience with relationships, but I'm pretty sure that's not what you do."

I take a breath. "I'm sorry."

"Where did you go, Bonnie?"

"Dad was ill." The lies are stacking up. "I was worried it was something worse, but he's fine."

A deep line forms between his brows as the wheels turn in his head. "You went to your dad's house at that time of night? I would have taken you."

"I didn't want to ruin your evening."

"If you think I'd prefer to drink in a bar surrounded by bankers and tossers than spend it with you, then you don't know me well enough."

My chin quivers. I do not deserve this man.

"I was worried sick, and your text messages were so damn vague." His jaw tightens then he sighs. "Look, it's fine. Is your dad okay?" He looks at me concerned. "What's wrong with him? I can go over with you today."

"He's fine," I say quickly, the thought of Jack coming into contact with Dad . . . "It was just a stomach bug."

He nods but stares at me, not convinced.

I'm a terrible liar.

And an even worse girlfriend.

His expression softens. "Well? Are you going to let me in?"

"Uh, yeah, of course." I open the door wider, and he follows me up the stairs.

"There's shampoo dripping down your face."

"Do you mind if I wash it out? There's fresh coffee in the percolator. I'll be ten minutes."

"Bonnie, wait." He grabs my arm, and my breath catches in my throat as his gaze remains fixed on me with an unspoken question.

He knows.

"Yes, Jack?"

"Where's my kiss?"

I force a smile, laughing shakily. "Sorry."

He grabs me around the waist and pulls me close, but he doesn't press his lips against mine. *Open up to me, Bonnie,* his dark eyes beg for a long beat.

I break the gaze by closing my eyes and pressing my lips to his.

His mouth is warm and comforting. Sweet but intense all at the same time. I feel his longing deep in the kiss. He needs me, and I'm hurting him.

Shampoo tickles my cheek. I use the excuse to dash to the bathroom. I can't continue like this.

The worst thing is that I can't talk to anyone. Telling Kate or Nisha would put them in an unreasonable situation. Also, Kate's just back from her honeymoon, so it wouldn't be fair.

And the one person who is calm and strong enough to help me will hate my guts when he finds out.

I close my eyes and stand still under the rainfall shower as the cold water runs down my body. It used to be a dribble, but Jack worked his magic. Now it's passable as a shower.

I turn the water fully to cold. I want it to hit my face so hard, it numbs my brain.

I could be rolling around naked in the snow at the Antarctic, and it wouldn't shock me enough.

The cold is as useless as the heat at wiping everything from my head.

Every time I close my eyes, I imagine it as if *I* were there. The questions eat me up. Morbid questions that I try to excommunicate from my head but can't.

Questions I don't want to know the answer to but haunt my every thought.

Did Dad watch or did he look away?

Did Jack's dad plead with them?

Did he die straight away?

Questions I will never, *ever* ask Dad.

I don't know if I'll convince Dad to go to the police. I don't even know if I want him to. He might not have stabbed Jack's dad, but he was guilty of perverting the course of justice. He might even get manslaughter or worse, murder.

From my obsessive internet searches last night, the police see things like this as a serious crime, and they always go to the Crown court.

Dad's not a bad man. He did a bad thing, but he's still my father.

Either way I'll lose Jack.

Thick arms envelop me pulling my back flush to a warm chest. I didn't hear the shower door open.

"Christ," he mutters behind me and turns the water to hot.

I feel his hardened cock against my butt cheeks as his hands come up to massage my scalp. His fingers knead my head in slow sensual strokes.

Damn, that feels good.

Tingles travel from the nerve endings on my head down my body.

I push my head back, sinking into his chest and moan softly.

Soon enough I will lose Jack but for now, I need him.

All of him.

I turn to face him, and my breath stops. I'll never get used to this view.

He's rock hard and his dark eyes blaze with desire. If he's not the most beautiful manly creature I've ever seen, shoot me down.

He slowly strokes himself. Long hard strokes as he keeps his longing gaze steady on me. There's nothing more arousing than watching this man touch himself. "I'm always thinking of you when I do this." He laughs softly. "I'm always thinking of you when I do anything these days. It's driving my trainer crazy."

The nerve in his forehead jumps again.

"I'm always thinking of you, Bonnie."

I swallow my tears. "I'm always thinking of you too, Jack."

"Good. So, we're both on the same level." He takes his hand off his cock. "I don't want any secrets between us."

Fuck.

"I have something to confess. That night at the castle I walked past your room, and I thought you were crying. I saw you," he clears his throat sheepishly, "touching yourself. I'm sorry, Bonnie. I'm an asshole. I couldn't look away."

His eyes stay trained on me.

Double fuck.

I wasn't expecting that.

"It's okay." I smile weakly. I should be embarrassed. I would be, under normal circumstances. Or maybe turned on. Angry? I don't know how I should feel these days.

He blows out a long breath and he physically relaxes. "You're not mad?"

"No, Jack," I say softly.

"In that case," he says, his throat bobbing, "who were you thinking about?" His brows draw together in anticipation and his expression tells me his mood hinges on my answer.

I pause.

"You."

"Damn." He breathes out heavily. A wide satisfied smile spreads across his face. "That makes me the luckiest man in London. You've just made my day."

I can't take this. The emotion is going to swallow me whole. If Jack says anything else sweet, I'll break down.

I wrap my fingers around his cock and the energy between us shifts again. He thickens in my hand as I slide up and down his length. Water trickles down his cock, lubricating my strokes.

A growl rumbles from his throat as he places his hands on either side of the shower wall and gives me full control.

"You're dying for my cock, aren't you?" he says in a husky voice, widening his legs. "On your knees, sweetheart."

I do as I'm told.

I take as much of his cock in my mouth as I can as he grabs a fistful of my hair. He's too big for me to take him all so I fist his base with my hand. I need to feel every inch of him.

"*Bonnie*," he says in a long hard groan that makes my thighs clench.

His hands tighten in my hair as I take him deep in my mouth. My hands slide over his buttocks to hold him in place as I suck up and down his entire length in a slow and steady motion that I know drives him crazy.

"Darlin', *fuck*, you're good at this."

My pace quickens as I slide him in and out of my mouth, sucking him from base to tip. Loving how he groans each time he hits my throat. Loving the feel of his dick swelling and pulsing in my mouth.

I'm going for Olympic gold at cock-sucking at this rate.

"Good girl," he breathes. "Suck it nice and deep." His hips thrust to hit my throat even harder, and I fight the gag reflex.

I stare up with wide eyes watching his chest heave up and down and his face contort. He's sweating. I love how much I can affect him.

I may no longer have control of anything else in my life, but I have control of this.

"Bonnie. So. Damn. Good. Fuck," he growls through his teeth. His thrusts grow more aggressive until my ass is backed up against the cold shower wall. "I'm gonna come, sweetheart," he warns in a ragged breath.

I need him to come harder than he ever has before. I've never needed it so badly. I suck faster and harder as his curses and groans echo around the bathroom.

His head falls forward, his eyes close and his whole body becomes rigid. His thighs tense and his ass cheeks clench. With a final strangled groan from him, I feel the jerky pulses of his dick emptying in my mouth, and I swallow down every last drop of him.

For a long moment, he stands with his eyes closed and his hands palming the shower wall above me, his cock still in my face. I see the Knight family coat of arms tattoo on his arm, and I quickly look away. After a beat, his fractured breathing calms.

"Bonnie." He opens his eyes to stare down at me, dazed. "*Damn.*"

In one swift motion, he has me lifted off the floor and my legs wrapped around his waist.

When he thrusts two fingers into me to find me wet, he groans and pushes them in deeper. "So wet, just from sucking my cock."

My pussy clenches around his fingers. I need him to literally fuck me out of my mind. To push down the guilt and dread.

"Fuck me," I demand, jutting my hips against him. "I need you inside me right now."

He chuckles softly and walks us both out of the shower and down the hall to my bedroom.

I think he's going to place me on the bed. Instead, he lies back on the bed, pulling me on top of him. He clasps his hands behind his head as if he's sunbathing but his jaw works, and I know he's fighting for control.

"Go ahead," he says with a lazy smile. "Sit on it. It's yours."

I slide my legs either side of him so that I'm straddling him. I lower myself down on his cock and let out a strangled moan.

He growls in approval but still he doesn't touch me. "Show me how you want to ride my cock, Bonnie."

Not a problem, happy to.

He watches through hooded eyes as I slide up and down on his cock, grinding at just the right angle to feel the familiar zings of pleasure stir and swell in my clit. Hot pressure builds at my core.

Oh. God. Yes. This is exactly what I need.

I feel each and every inch of him fill me to the hilt as I slide him in deep again and again.

His hand comes down to press gently against my stomach as his thumb caresses and works my clit. My stomach contracts at his touch and my head tips back. The pressure threatens to explode.

"So good, Jack," I whimper. My clit feels so sensitive, it's almost painful. "Oh God, I can't hold it any longer. I'm . . ." My head rolls back as my body spasms and wave upon wave of tingling pleasure washes over me.

Moaning, I squeeze tightly around him in intense heavenly contractions. I feel it in every nerve, every muscle, every cell.

"Oh, *fuck*." He groans as my movements become more frantic. "That's it. I need you riding me every morning. Exactly like this."

My pussy tightens and quivers around his dick as the orgasm explodes through me. It must send him over the edge, because in seconds, he shudders and grabs my hips holding me tight in place so that I've no choice but to take him deep as he empties into me with one final forceful jerk.

Still inside me and with his hands claiming my hips, he looks up at me with a raw vulnerability that I never thought Jack Knight capable of.

"You make me so happy, Bonnie Casey." His voice is thick with emotion. "I'm in love with you." He stares at me, giving me everything he has. The look makes my heartstrings snap. "I'm so in love with you. All I want is you."

Tears well in my eyes.

But not for the reasons he thinks.

I'm the luckiest girl in London, but my luck is on an egg-timer.

33

Jack

"Well, well, well, look who it is." Tristan's eyes gleam as I enter through the velvet curtain. Huxley Cocktail Club is Tristan's favourite private members' bar.

Apparently, they pump scents into the air to make you relaxed and horny.

Sometimes I'd prefer an old man's pub where the aroma is blue collar sweat and my choice of drink is lager or extra-strong lager.

"Leave it out, mate." I roll my eyes at him.

"Can I take your coat, Jack?" Alexia, the hostess, runs a hand down my arm. She's over six feet with a body perfect for modelling Victoria's Secret's underwear.

I should know, I've seen her in it.

"Thanks, Alexia." I smile back, trying to dodge the come-fuck-me looks she's sending me.

Her hand swipes over my nipple ring as she takes off my jacket.

I cock a brow at her, but she smiles innocently. I need to wear a badge saying I'm unavailable or something. Not that anyone would believe I have an actual girlfriend.

Danny and Tristan smirk knowingly at me as I sit down.

"Long time no see," Danny says dryly.

"Yeah, yeah." I wave my hand dismissively and take the Scotch Alexia places down in front of me. As she bends, I get an eyeful of cleavage. "How are you both?" I ask before they can take the piss out of my absence these past few weeks. This is the longest I've gone without seeing them, three weeks.

Ever since I told Bonnie I loved her, I can't get enough.

My Bonnie.

My girl.

I'm seriously in danger of becoming a pathetic wreck of a man. If she knew half the scenarios I'm concocting in my head, she'd run for the hills. Especially the one where enough young Knights are running about to form an East End version of *The Sound of Music*.

She's holding back. She hasn't told me she loves me yet, but I'll wait for as long as it takes.

"Tired as fuck," Danny growls. He looks wrecked. "I'm living with six females who all own my balls and I'm in the middle of opening two more offices in Asia."

Danny has three daughters under three. Counting Charlie, his fiancée, that's four females.

"So, Tristan's mother is still living with you, I take it. That's five though, not six."

Danny rakes a hand through his hair. "Callie's staying with us while she finds somewhere to live this year for uni. So, now I have both Kane sisters under my roof." His eyes throw daggers at Tristan. "Why she doesn't want to live with her big brother is beyond me. You have that massive house for just you and Elly."

"We'll fill it soon." Tristan laughs and takes a gulp of his drink. "Unfortunately for you, you live too close to the uni so she can get out of bed at nine a.m. and still be in time for class."

Danny sighs. "It's okay, I've found a solution."

I raise my brows, waiting.

"I've bought the house next door."

Tristan and I look at each other.

"For *you* to move into?" I ask, unable to conceal my amusement.

"Not me," Danny grumbles. "I'll put Charlie's mum and sister in there. With CCTV to watch Callie because I had to go down the station the other night. She got arrested for being drunk and disorderly on a bicycle."

"I'm not happy about that," Tristan mutters, running a line down his jaw. "That won't happen again."

Tristan and Charlie's younger sister is a bit of a live wire. "Damn. Bit extreme, isn't it? Buying the house next door."

"Don't you start. You've got no fucking clue, Knight. You live with a dog. Both of you can sit around farting, accountable to no one."

I laugh. "When you marry the girl, you marry her family. You knew that, Walker. Although, I might be married faster than you."

Danny and Charlie have been engaged for about three years.

"I've decided when we do get married, nobody is invited. Just me, Charlie, and the girls."

"So, no date for the wedding then?"

"At this rate, not until Mollie turns eighteen." He looks wrecked but his eyes twinkle, and I know he wouldn't change things for the world.

Mollie is his youngest and about six months old.

"You might be married faster, huh, Knight?" Tristan's lips quirk as he plays with his own wedding ring.

I can't hide my grin. "Bonnie is incredible. No other woman compares. I'm done."

Tristan studies me, smirking. "Sweet Jesus. A woman finally capable of taming Knight. How the hell did she do it?"

I shrug. "Just by being her. I'm a simple guy."

Danny looks at me thoughtfully. "Well, for what it's worth, I'm glad to see you happy, mate. Bonnie is a lovely lass." He pauses. "Any more updates on the case?"

I down my Scotch. "We're closing in. The barmaid from the White Horse was interviewed. She said she saw two guys running away roughly around the time of the incident. She didn't want to say anything when Wicks was thought to have done it."

"Does she remember after all this time?" Tristan asks.

"The police are doing a sketch of the two based on her description," I say. "Then they'll work their magic and age it. One of them will be the guy Wicks said, Gleeson." My hands tighten around the glass. "I almost feel sorry for the other poor fucker. I won't stop until he has the heaviest sentence there is. A fucking unreasonable sentence."

They exchange glances.

"Let the police do their job," Danny says in a measured tone.

"Yeah, yeah," I reply gruffly, downing the last of my drink. "Look, I have to shoot."

Danny's eyes narrow as I stand up. "Where the hell are you going?"

I wrestle a grin. "I have to unblock a sink."

"Fuck's sake, Knight. You do realise one of the perks of being a billionaire is that you can pay a plumber?"

"What can I say? I'm old-fashioned. I don't want another man touching my missus's plumbing. Later, chaps. See you for golf on Sunday."

"You bloody better," Tristan mutters as they both scowl.

"Where are you going, Jack?" Alexia purrs as I ask for my coat. "I'm planning to have a nightcap with you."

"Sorry," I say sheepishly. "I have a girlfriend."

She laughs in my face. "Sure, Jack."

Fuck's sake.

❦

Thirty minutes later, I'm in Bonnie's flat, grinning at her like a desperate dog with his owner.

"You didn't need to leave the guys early, Jack." She looks more exhausted than Danny.

Her pyjama T-shirt is looser than it should be. I worry she's training too hard for the marathon. All she seems to do is run, work, and fuck me...hard.

I sink into the couch, exactly where I'm supposed to be as

Bonnie curls up beside me. She tries to keep her eyes open but after minutes her head falls onto my chest.

I brush strands of hair away from her sharp cheekbones, careful not to wake her. With her mouth slightly ajar and face scrubbed of make-up, she looks younger than her twenty-eight years.

I could watch her sleep all night.

Her eyelids flutter, and I wonder what she's dreaming about.

I know I don't have her completely yet. Not the way she has me. There's something stopping her opening up.

Maybe it's because she was burnt so badly by Max. Maybe it's pictures of me with women.

Maybe it's seven billion pounds.

I don't know what it is yet, but I'll find out.

As gently as I can, I lift her into my arms and carry her to the bedroom. She stirs slightly, nuzzling into my neck, but her eyes don't open.

When I deposit her on the bed, I go to the bathroom and take everything from under the sink.

I was telling the truth to Danny and Tristan. Give me Bonnie's DIY projects any day over sitting in a members' bar with tits on tap.

Her sink is fucked, completely clogged up with whatever bloody products women use. This flat needs so many repairs, it's a joke. I want her living with me but if I ask her, I worry she'll freak out.

I might as well check the kitchen sink while I'm at it.

I rip off my top, sweating with the heat of Bonnie's tiny kitchen and start to move everything from under the sink. Who the hell keeps tampons under the sink?

A laundry soap box tips over onto the floor but thankfully it's empty.

Except it's not empty.

Buried at the bottom is something shiny in a cellophane bag. Something that looks like it shouldn't live in a laundry box. It's one of Bonnie's necklaces.

I'm not surprised she keeps losing her reading glasses.

I inspect the bag in confusion.

What the hell?

It's impossible.

The hairs on the back of my neck rise as I stare down at something I haven't seen in ten years.

Why the hell does my girlfriend have my dead dad's possessions under her sink?

34

Bonnie

Why do I have no shoes on? I can't run twenty-six miles with no shoes. Everyone is looking at me like I'm a moron.

I'm coming up to the mileage sign. I've been at it for hours. I should be at the twenty-mile mark.

I can't read it properly. Two miles? What the hell?

"Bonnie," Jack calls from the sidelines, "you have no shoes on."

I know that, Jack. I glare at him. Does he think I'm stupid?

I'm being shaken gently. Confused, I open my eyes and . . . it's still dark.

Relief floods me. It's just a dream.

All my dreams are unsettling these days.

I'm vaguely aware of a shadow hovering on the edge of the bed.

"Jack?" I bolt up.

He doesn't speak. In the dim light, the hard lines of his jaw work.

He flips on my bedside lamp, blinding me. He has a wrench in one hand and something else in the other.

My eyes adjust and I see his face twist in confusion and shock. His body is rigid.

He knows.

Dad has been found out. The police identified him.

He holds something up in front of my face and my eyes catch

up before my brain can.

No.

Fear explodes through me as I stare at the bag with his dad's ring.

I had moved it around the flat a million times looking for somewhere no one would ever look. Jack doesn't do laundry in his own house, why is he looking in my powder boxes?

Murphy's Law. This is karma for being a horrible lying girlfriend.

The bed dips as he sits on the edge of the mattress. He rests the wrench on his lap but holds up the bag, studying it as if it's nuclear waste.

"Why do you have this, Bonnie?" He fights to keep his voice low and controlled, but his dark brown eyes tell a different story.

I can't speak.

I can't breathe.

The only sound is the pounding of my heart.

Jack's waiting.

In the long, awful silence, Jack's waiting for me to give a rational explanation.

His eyes bore into mine, and I feel a panic attack threaten to rise.

I sit up straighter, gulp down a breath and try to speak. "My dad."

"Your dad," he repeats with a deliberate slowness. "What about your dad?"

"My dad," I choke as the words die on my tongue.

He audibly swallows, his large Adam's apple bobbing in his throat. "Bonnie, sweetheart. I'm trying to be patient. But you need to start explaining. Tell me where you got this."

My body trembles. "My dad was there that night." It's barely a whisper.

For a long moment he just stares at me. Did he hear what I said?

"What? What are you talking about?" The bed dips further as

he inches closer. His hands come down to rest either side of me on the mattress. I'm trapped.

A shiver throttles my spine.

I can't. I just can't tell him.

"Bonnie," he says, more desperately this time. He takes my shoulders and gives me a gentle shake. "What. Do. You. Mean."

I suck in a breath. "He was there," I say faintly. "My dad. He was one of the guys that robbed your dad."

"No." He shakes his head firmly as he stares at me for a long painful beat. "Are you fucking joking?" Jack has never shouted at me before. Not like this. "Do you think this is *funny*, Bonnie?"

I can't look at him.

Through tear-stained vision, I see the exact moment he realises the truth.

"How do you know this? Did he tell you?"

I nod. With the back of my hand, I wipe away the tears dripping from my chin.

"Fucking hell." The veins of his forearm flex as his hand forms a tight fist around the wrench. His eyes squeeze shut as he pinches the bridge of his nose with the other hand.

"Jack?" I whisper, hugging my knees.

"So, the second guy that ran away, the one the barmaid saw was your dad?"

I rest my chin on my knee to stop it quivering. "I guess so."

"You *guess* so?" he hisses, snapping his dark eyes open to glare at me. "Do you fucking know or not, Bonnie?"

I shrink back towards the wall, clutching my knees tighter.

"Talk," he snaps, nostrils flaring.

"He was in the wrong place at the wrong time." My voice shakes. "It was supposed to be a robbery to get your dad's wallet. He lost his job and was about to lose the house. But he didn't kill your dad. It was the other guy."

"Are you making excuses for him?"

Yes.

"No. I'm just trying to explain why it led to the horrible

tragedy."

"So, what the fuck was this?" he snarls. "You thought if I fell in love with you, what? You'd get inside info on the case? Throw me off the scent? What was this, Bonnie?"

"No!" I cry. "I only found out two weeks ago."

He looks at me like I walked over his grave.

"Why should I believe you?" he sneers. "You let me fall in love with you, and you're a fucking liar!" He fires the wrench resting on his knee across the room.

I scream as it hits the wall and chips of plasterboard fall.

"I'm trying to understand," he growls, his chest heaving. "Trying very fucking hard to understand why my girlfriend would lie to me over something as important as this." His voice rises. "I'm a damn idiot. You had me—hook, line, and fucking sinker. Who the hell are you?"

"Please, Jack," I cry, grabbing onto his bicep.

He jerks away.

I feel it like a slap across the face. "I planned to tell you. I was scared. I was scared for Dad. I hate myself for lying to you. I've been begging him to go to the police but . . . he's terrified of going to prison."

"I don't care how he feels," he roars, making me jolt. "I care about my lying girlfriend." He picks up the bag again and waves it inches from my face. "Why do you have this?"

I grip the pillow for support, bringing it to my chest. "I was worried Dad would throw it away. I took it from him. He doesn't know I have it."

He glares at me without blinking. "Have you had this since the murder?"

"No!" His question sucker-punches me. How can he think that? "I'm telling you the truth. I only found out a few weeks ago."

"Why would I believe a fucking word that comes out of your mouth?"

"I wanted to tell you. I just didn't want us to be over."

"You watched me torment myself. Did you know all along it

wasn't Wicks?"

I meet his unrelenting stare with wide eyes. Does he really believe I'm that much of a liar? "No Jack! I swear. You weren't supposed to find out like this. I was going to tell you."

"I wasn't supposed to find out at all you mean?"

"I was scared. I *am* scared. I didn't know what to do. I asked Dad to go to the police. I wanted Dad to go himself."

His eyes flare with fury I've never seen before. Fury directed at *me*. "How can I ever trust you after this?"

"But I love you," I croak. "You love me."

He stands to his full height, his dark eyes trained on me as his face contorts into a million different emotions.

"I don't even know you."

Taking the ring with him, he walks out.

"Wait!" I call after him, springing from the bed. "Please, Jack, wait!"

I follow him downstairs, tears streaming down my face.

"Please don't leave," I beg him as he shoves open the front door to the street. "Not like this. We can work through this."

"Are you for fucking real? You don't work through something like this."

He covers his eyes with his hands as he tries to control his breathing.

People on the street watch us.

When he looks at me again, the haunted look on his face makes me sob uncontrollably, and I don't give a shit who's watching the show, or the fact I've got no shoes on.

Not even the person flashing the camera in our faces.

35

Bonnie

It's a crisp Sunday morning. At eight, London hasn't fully woken up yet, but I haven't slept.

I thought running from my flat in Brixton to his house in Greenwich would calm me down and help me find a solution to this. That on my run I would find the words to make him forgive me.

But instead, I lost focus and ended up falling on my face, scraping my hands and knees. I shouldn't be surprised since functioning as a human is difficult. I haven't eaten or slept since Friday night when Jack stormed off. It's been two days but feels like an eternity.

I would prefer to feel empty instead of full to the brim with this heart ache.

Yesterday, I told Dad that Jack will go to the police. Dad's in denial. Like I've been for weeks. He said they'll never be able to pin it on him because a barmaid from ten years ago isn't a reliable witness. I could hear the fear and anger in his voice though. So, now the only two people that know about this shit show aren't talking to me.

I've never felt so alone. I wish I could tell Mum, but I don't know how she will react.

I ring the doorbell because I know he won't answer his phone. He ignored all my texts and calls yesterday.

Today will be no different.

Lucy barks immediately in the back garden, and the panic I tried to suppress during my run rises in my stomach.

Jack appears at the door, topless and drenched in sweat. He looks like he's been boxing all night.

He stands rigid in the doorway, staring at me.

Maybe coming here wasn't a good idea. If looks could kill, I would be meat for Lucy.

I swallow the massive lump in my throat. "Can I come in?"

"There's nothing more to say."

He's different today.

He's cold and detached. The anger that burned through him on Friday is gone.

Somehow this woodenness is much, much scarier.

My eyes fill with tears. "I can't stand us not talking."

"I was brought up that if you don't have something nice to say to a lady, then don't say anything. But I'll make myself clearer," he grits his teeth, "I'm not interested in anything else you have to say."

I feel a sharp sting of pain from his words. *He can't mean them.*

"So, what, it's over?" My voice breaks.

"I thought I made that clear on Friday night," he says in a detached tone. His eyes skim over my body. "What did you do to your knees?"

I smile sadly and shrug. Does he think I give a shit about my knees? "I fell. It's just a little scrape."

"Fuck's sake," he mutters, widening the door. "Come in. I'll get a cloth."

I follow him in because right now, I'll take whatever he's willing to throw at me.

He strides into the kitchen in silence. I walk behind him, so nervous I try to quieten my footsteps.

I'm glad Lucy's out the back. She's probably as angry as her owner.

With his back to me, he runs a cloth under hot water, then

rummages to find the first aid kit in the cupboard.

The tension in the air is unbearable.

"I made a mistake, Jack," I say quietly to his back. "I didn't know what to do."

He turns, his eyes cold. "You covered for your killer Dad."

"He's not a killer."

"You know my father was alive for thirty minutes on that pavement?" His knuckles tighten around the cloth and every muscle in his body appears to tighten. "He could have saved him, but he didn't. He ran away and let him bleed out."

"I didn't know that," I whisper, feeling nauseous. "I'm sorry."

"I don't blame you for that, Bonnie. I blame you for lying to me."

"I was going to tell you," I repeat, knowing how empty that sounds.

"When?" He stares at me flatly. "When, Bonnie? When I proposed? When you got pregnant? On our tenth wedding anniversary?"

"No! I-I don't know," I stammer, leaning against the table for support. "Soon."

He steps forward with the cloth and antiseptic and gets on his knees before me. In silence he washes each knee without any of the warmth I usually feel when he touches me.

I blink back tears.

He's not doing it out of love or affection. He's doing it out of obligation.

My arms hang awkwardly by my side. I want to reach out so badly and wrap my arms around his shoulders just to feel his warm skin, but I don't.

"I need you," I say softly. "Don't reject me."

His hand comes to an abrupt halt on my knee, and he stares at my leg.

When he finally looks up, his eyes are void of any warmth. "What do you need?"

I need him to look at me the way he used to, like I'm the most important person in his world.

Because the way he is looking at me right now is breaking my fucking heart.

"You." Tentatively, I run my hands through his hair. "Please, Jack."

He winces as if I struck him and rises from the ground to tower over me so that I'm eye level with his broad chest, glistening with sweat from boxing.

"You want it?" he snarls. "Fucking take it."

My eyes grow like saucers. Is he serious?

He rips his gym shorts down and steps out of them, spreading his legs wide. He fists his cock in his hands, and it rises against his stomach.

I search his eyes, begging for him to grin at me and tell me how much he loves me. Tell me that everything is going to be okay.

Nothing.

Swallowing my nerves, I place my palms on his chest. His heart is beating fast, surely that must mean he cares?

My fingers trail down his pecs and lower stomach to his perfect V. His muscles tense but he doesn't stop me. I take that as a good sign because I'm desperate. Not for sex. For him. Just to touch him. To be held by him. To have all of him again.

His dark eyes dilate as I wrap my fingers around his thick length, feeling him pulse against my hand.

He might not forgive me, but he wants me. At least I still have that.

This is *mine*. I can't lose it. I can't read in the papers that he's been with other women.

I can't lose *him*.

He doesn't touch me back. A muscle in his jaw flexes as I tighten possessively around his cock and as his eyes blaze down on mine, I've no clue what's going on behind that fire.

I tilt my head up to kiss him but instead he grabs me by the hips and flips me around until I'm tight to his chest, his hardened cock pressing against my running shorts.

"Take' em off."

His gruff voice sends shivers down my spine. This isn't how I wanted him, but it's the only way I can have him. So I bend down and pull my shorts and pants down past my legs, gingerly stepping out of them.

He doesn't bother to wait for me to take off my top.

Giving me no time to warm up, he lifts my hips and thrusts hard inside me, grunting.

I cry out and fall forward as he stretches me.

"Open wider."

His legs nudge my thighs impatiently so he can force his cock deeper.

I suck in a breath and do as I'm told.

"Is this what you wanted?" he growls from behind me, holding my hips in place as he drives himself deep over and over again. "My cock buried inside you?"

Not like this.

It's raw, primal fucking without love.

But I take it.

I take it all because I miss him.

I vaguely hear Jack cursing breathlessly behind me.

His hand slides around my stomach and his fingers circle my clit. A choked cry escapes me because it's the only sign of affection I get.

His breathing grows laboured behind me as the thrusts become faster. He hits a place that only he can hit, and I don't believe anyone else ever will be able to.

Holding me in place, he grunts his way to release. A deep growl rumbles in the back of his throat as he comes hard inside me with a final jerk.

His fingers immediately leave my clit. His way of punishing me, I guess.

My body collapses against his, covered in his sweat. I want to turn to see his face, but he holds me in place with one hand caging my stomach.

I feel the other hand come around my neck, brushing my hair off my back. Everything's going to be okay. He's going to bury his face in my neck and kiss me.

He doesn't.

It takes me a minute to understand what he's doing.

The chain.

He's taking back the chain.

A sob leaves my throat.

When it slips off my neck, I feel him disappear from behind me.

I can't move.

"Have a shower," he says in a low rough voice, breaking the silence behind me. "Then let yourself out. I'll be in the gym."

I don't need to turn around to know he's gone.

I was wrong.

Hate sex is the worst type of sex.

Four hours later

I can't ignore Kate forever. She's called three times already today.

When you live by yourself and don't answer your phone the first time, your friends jump to the worst conclusion.

I try to sound breezy. "Hey, Kate."

"Bonnie!" She, on the other hand, does not. "Why are you not answering your phone! Have you seen it?"

My stomach lurches.

Dad.

Jack's gone to the police.

"What?"

"Seriously?" She shrieks. "You haven't seen it? Oh, my God. Wait, I'll send it to you now."

"Great." Talk about getting me all worked up.

Moments later a message flashes on my screen.

I click on the link, hyperventilating. Will it show a picture of Dad?

Except . . . the link isn't about Dad. It's a picture of Jack and me. I zoom in on the article.

"What is this?" I say more to myself than to Kate.

"Are you in the middle of a fight?" she asks. "I can't believe you got bloody papped! Actually, not *papped*—it was just a random girl with a camera. But everyone's paparazzi these days. Still look how many likes and comments it has!"

It's from Friday night. It shows Jack and me outside my flat in Brixton. I look like I'm trying to plead with him, and Jack looks irate.

Oh, fuck. That's all I need.

"It's a pity they caught you like that," Kate muses. "It's not the most romantic of shots."

No, it's most certainly not.

My cheeks burn. I'm screwed. On one hand, it's not Dad being exposed, which is a good thing, but on the other hand, it's me being exposed.

What a mess.

I sigh loudly into the phone. "Bradshaw and Brown are going to have a fit."

"I wouldn't worry," Kate says reassuringly. "I doubt your old bosses are on social media. Besides, it's not ground-breaking news. The only reason I came across it is because I was hungover and spent hours on Instagram."

She has a point.

A message from Max flashes up.

> Max: Care to tell me why you are in a fight in the street with Jack Knight?

Kill me now.

36

Jack

"I'm busy." I glare at Danny and Tristan in the hallway.

Unfortunately, Lucy, the traitor, has other ideas. She leaps all over the two of them, begging them to come inside. I feel slightly appeased that their custom-made designer suits are being slobbered over.

Danny pets Lucy. "Your security is rubbish. A welcoming guard dog and an unlocked front door."

"And?" I shrug. "If anyone decides to rob the place, they'll find me here. I'd be happy for the boxing practice."

He strolls past me into the lounge area. Tristan follows.

"Didn't you hear I'm busy?" I mutter.

"Fuck off." Tristan snorts. "What are you doing then?"

"I'm babysitting."

He narrows his eyes on me.

"Poppy's in the garden."

Tristan looks out the window to see my seven-year-old niece.

"She's the only company I can tolerate right now," I say wryly.

They follow me into the kitchen.

"Were you working today?" Tristan's lips quirk. "You can never tell with you since you dress like a fitness instructor rather than a CEO."

I wave off his words. "What's the point of being a CEO if you can't wear what you like? Anyway, I worked from home today."

Danny eyes me. "Since when do you work from home? You

look rough. Very buff but rough. Is that all you're doing now—punching the shit out of a boxing bag?"

"And my trainer. There are worse things I could be doing for stress relief."

"True." He shrugs. "I'm glad you're hiding here rather than out banging women like you usually do when something goes wrong."

"I'd rather have my dick slammed in a door than pick up a woman." There would always be women. Plenty of women. But I had no interest in another pointless night with a woman I had no connection to.

He pauses and glances at Tristan before turning his attention to me. "So, are you going to keep us hanging? Your messages were a little cryptic. Have the police taken him in for questioning yet?"

"No." I open the fridge and rummage through the mountains of meat to find three beers.

"Why not?" Danny asks.

I lean against the open fridge. "I haven't told them about Bonnie's dad yet."

"Why not?" Tristan prompts.

"I don't fucking know, mate," I snap, slamming the fridge door closed. Ignoring them, I flip the lids off the beers with an opener.

Danny leans over the kitchen counter to take a beer. "I think you do know." He pauses, studying me. "When did you see her last?"

"Four days ago." An uneasiness fills my gut. I didn't plan for us to have rough sex. Hell, I didn't even plan for her to come to my house. "It's over. I've nipped it in the bud."

"You've *nipped it in the bud*?" Danny barks, folding his arms over his chest.

"Do you hear yourself?" Tristan chips in, inspecting me through slanted eyes. I'm not in the mood for their little tag team pep talk. "So, what, that's it? You're not going to try to work through this?"

"I don't tolerate liars," I say through clenched teeth.

Danny sighs. "I don't know the girl well, but I'm sure she was just scared, Jack."

"She lied to me for weeks. Maybe years." I let out an angry laugh. "Who the fuck knows?"

Danny shakes his head, frowning. "People make mistakes. That's how relationships work."

I glare back at him. "Since when are you the morality police?"

He swears under his breath. "Hasn't she been punished enough? You're not the only one who has lost a parent here. Bonnie might never be able to have the same relationship with her dad."

"That's not my problem anymore," I bite back. "I don't trust her. If she'd told me, we would have worked through it." I rub my neck, agitated. "I don't blame her for her dad's actions, I blame her for lying to me. I disclosed everything to her—what Wicks said, what was happening with the barmaid, and she still lied to my face. She might never have told me if I hadn't found the ring."

"Okay." Tristan nods. "I get that. But you can be a little intimidating sometimes, Jack. Especially about this. She was probably scared to lose you."

"Bollocks," I sneer, taking an angry swig of beer. "Now, are you done with the intervention? Because you two aren't very good at it."

Danny smiles. "No, we're not done. People don't always react how you want them to, Jack. She's not a puppet." He shoots a look at Tristan. "Remember how volatile Charlie and I were when we first started dating? But I love her, so I didn't give up."

"You and Charlie didn't have to work through a murder, Walker."

His brows lift. "You're not the only one having to deal with this. Don't you think she needs you too right now? This is a terrible situation for her to be in."

My jaw tightens. "She should have thought about that before lying to me."

"Fuck's sake, mate, you sound like a broken record," Tristan says. "You saw the news article of you two, right? You were caught fighting in the street."

"And? I'm in the news all the time."

"Bonnie's not. She's not used to the media circus that surrounds you. You deliberately tried to protect her from it. Now you're gonna feed her to the sharks?"

"It was just a random person who saw an opportunity," I grumble. "The story has already died."

Tristan frowns, cocking his head at me. "You've already lost one of the most important people in your life. Are you really willing to lose Bonnie as well?"

I look away. They don't get it. She's not the woman I thought she was. All the times she made me believe I was the most important guy in the world to her, with those big blue eyes and that soft voice, she was keeping something massive from me.

She made me believe that we were serious. That she loved me. I confided in her. I would have told her anything. I would have given her everything.

But you don't lie this big to someone you love.

And no matter how much her tears are haunting me, my nan was right. If I can't trust Bonnie, I can't lay a foundation with her.

They exchange glances then Danny sighs and shakes his head. "You're a stubborn shit, Knight. You and Lucy can sit here farting. You'll regret this sooner than you think."

Bonnie

"Are you ready, love?" Mum wraps her arm around me.

No. I'll never be ready for this. We stand on the steps in front of the Hackney police station in East London.

I told Dad we were going to the police today if he didn't do it. I know he thinks I'm bluffing, that his little girl would never do this to him. My dad always said that I was the person that kept him going.

Would I still be after this?

Perhaps, I'll be able to sleep a little easier.

At least Mum knows. I've never needed Mum so badly.

"We're doing the right thing." She looks at me supportively. "Your father will realise that."

My stepdad Phil doesn't think he'll do time. It would likely be a suspended prison sentence if anything.

But he's neglecting the fact that Dad's opposition is the Knight family, and they have connections.

I smile sadly at her. Regardless of what sentence Dad does or doesn't get, he won't forgive me for this.

I take her hand and climb the rest of the steps to the station.

37

Jack

"What's my favourite girl doing?" I run my fingers through Poppy's hair. She's the spitting image of my twin sisters when they were kids. Long glossy brown hair and dark brown eyes.

Sometimes I think my heart will burst when I look at Poppy. She's the first of the grandkids as Mum constantly reminds me. According to her, I should have knocked out at least three Knight babies by now.

I thought I was moving in the right direction.

Poppy's feet dangle on the edge of the chair and her brow is set in deep concentration as she leans over a large piece of paper with a marker in hand.

"Uncle Jack, you know you're not allowed to touch my hair," she says crossly. "Mummy rang when you were upstairs. I told her you were in the toilet. For ages and *ages*."

I chuckle, leaning over her small frame at the table. "Thanks, Poppy. What's that?"

"It's a letter to Santa to say sorry. Mummy says if I don't, I won't get all my presents." She pouts. "And Mummy says I won't even get any presents from you."

"Is that so?" I quirk my lips. "What am I getting you?"

"A pony," she says firmly, with a confident smile.

"A toy pony?"

"No, a *pony*," she repeats indignantly, like I'm a moron. Who the hell taught her to roll her eyes like that?

Shit.

"I'm not sure you're ready for livestock yet," I negotiate. "Maybe we could start you off with a, uh, goldfish?"

"Fine." She rolls her eyes again. "I'll put it on the list for Santa."

I smile. "He might not be able to deliver a pony either. Logistics of the sleigh. What's this letter about? Why do you need to say sorry?"

She bites her lip tentatively. "Okay, I'll tell you. I told a lie, and Mummy is really mad at me. And Mrs. Magee says that liars go to the place for the naughty people."

Her little face turns grim.

"Uh-huh." I nod, seriously. "And where is this place? The naughty corner?"

"No, silly." She tuts. *"Hell."*

"I think you're probably safe, Poppy." I chuckle. "Why did you lie?"

Her lips quiver. "Because I tried on Mummy's dress and ripped it, and I was scared that Mummy wouldn't love me anymore if I told the truth. So, I said Minnie did it."

I try not to grin. "The cat? You didn't stand a chance with that lie, love." I pick her up and prop her on my knee. "Your mummy will always love you unconditionally. No matter what you do. Your Uncle Jack, too."

She shakes her head and pouts again. "But your bunny lied, and you don't love her anymore."

I stiffen. "What are you talking about?"

She shrugs as she writes large wonky letters with the marker. "Mr. Danny said so. I think I'll marry Mr. Danny instead of you."

I grimace. Poppy heard us talking from the garden. How much did she hear? Jesus, how much did we say about Dad's murder?

I can't remember if any of us cursed. My sister is paying a small fortune to send Poppy to some bullshit "etiquette after-school class" and will kill me if I teach her bad language.

My phone buzzes on the table.

"Is it Mummy?" she asks.

I glance at the name flashing. "No."

"Hi," I say, answering the phone.

"Jack," McKenzie, the copper on my dad's case replies. "I have news."

I change the phone to my other ear, away from Poppy. "Go on."

"We've got a pretty safe tip on the second guy."

Fuck.

He pauses. "But you already knew that, didn't you?"

No point denying it. "Yeah, I found out a few days ago."

He clears his throat. "Bit of a tricky situation for you."

"Did Frank Casey contact the station?

"No. Your girlfriend and her mum came in."

I swallow thickly. "Thanks. I'll call you later."

I hang up and stare in silence as Poppy adds invisible dog under pony.

"That's not true, love," I whisper into her hair. "What you said about Bunny. I still love her, no matter what she's done."

38

Bonnie

Bad things come in threes, they say.

Well, I've lost my boyfriend, my dad, and probably the role on the *Motor Works* project, so hopefully, that's me done for a while.

And wearing healing crystals around my neck?

Bullshit. I hate wearing jewellery now. Having something around my neck is too much of a reminder of what I've lost.

Funny how the three things used to be a) my ex-fiancé breaking up with me, b) my ex-fiancé is still my boss and c) finding out my ex-fiancé was cheating on me.

Now those pale in comparison.

But what do all six have in common? Men.

I'm sick of it.

Dad hasn't been arrested but the police have asked him to come in for questioning. I only know this through Uncle Pat because Dad's upset and refuses to speak to me.

Of course, I've had no contact with Jack.

No matter how many times I turn my Wi-Fi off and on and restart my phone, there's no *stuck* message from him waiting to get through.

The only messages are mindfulness memes from Kate and Nisha and other messages that you send your friend when you've got absolutely no clue what to say. *You're braver than you believe. There's light at the end of the tunnel.* That sort of thing.

At least they both know so I can actually talk about it.

Nisha says Jack hasn't been in the office all week but it's all right for him, he's the CEO. I've been working from home saying that I'm feeling poorly.

It's not a complete lie because I'm sick with dread.

It's been two days since Mum and I went to the police station and yesterday, the revelation in the case made the local news.

Thankfully all the report says is that there is a second man in for questioning. No names given. There's not much coverage because it's a ten-year-old crime—people get stabbed all the time in London. But this *is* Jack Knight's dad we're talking about.

Anything about Jack makes the news.

Including the apparent fling he had last Friday night that went wrong, i.e. *me*.

It's always the woman that the media makes out to be desperate, crazy, and running after the guy, especially if he's a billionaire and she's a nobody.

So, if my dad's crime doesn't rob me of the design role then having a ruckus on the street with the client CEO will.

My phone lights up. Max. I told him about Dad yesterday. To be fair to him, he was pretty supportive.

"Hi, Max."

"How are you today?" he asks.

It's the most excruciating time of my life, thanks for asking.

"Fine," I say because that's what he wants to hear.

"Bonnie," he starts hesitantly, "there's no easy way to say this. I had to tell the partners."

"I'm off the project," I finish for him. "It's fine, I can't work on it anymore anyway. Not after . . . everything." I let out a small laugh because there isn't much else to do. "Bit of a conflict of interest."

I hear a heavy exhale. "Just a little."

"Does everyone in the office know?"

"Bradshaw and Brown don't want a scandal so only HR knows about what's happening with your dad. The last thing they want is for that to get out."

Nice to see that they care so dearly for their employees after years of service.

There's a long stretch of silence until he finally clears his throat. "But everyone has seen the social media story. Are you going to explain it to me? Did Jack harass you because of your dad? That's not on, Bonnie."

"And if he did, what would you do about it, Max? As my mentor and my boss?"

Silence.

Empty words, Max. Now I realise that all the words you ever said to me were just gas.

"No," I say firmly. "Jack's a good man. That's not why we were arguing. We ..."

"Bonnie." His voice turns cold. "*Please* tell me you didn't sleep with Jack."

I don't reply. This is the last conversation I want to have with Max.

"Jesus, Bonnie!" he snaps. "You actually had sex with *Jack Knight*?"

He sounds so disgusted, I wonder if it's because I'm his ex-fiancée rather than his subordinate.

"I thought you had more self-respect than to become his one-night stand! What the hell?"

"It wasn't a one-night stand," I say, my voice cracking.

"Come on, Bonnie!" he says down the phone. "I didn't realise you were this naive. This makes things even more complicated. No wonder Jack wants you off the project."

For some stupid reason, this hurts the most, and my eyes fill with tears. *Again.*

Why am I surprised? Of course, Jack wants me off his project.

"Have you seen him?" I ask in a small voice, hating that I need to ask Max.

"Who, *Jack*?" he barks in a tone that says I shouldn't be asking. "No, he hasn't been in all week. He's taking calls from home." I hear another harsh sigh. "You'll need to return your Lexington laptop."

The thought of going to the Lexington office makes me recoil in horror. "Can't I give it to Nisha?"

"No," he snaps. "You need to give it back personally as part of the off-boarding. You know this."

I close my eyes. "Fine, I'll bring it in."

"Today, Bonnie."

Fuck.

I guess the sooner I get this over and done with the better, especially if Jack isn't in.

"My promotion . . ."

"Is unlikely," he finishes. "Just for this round."

"That's bullshit," I say, stunned. "I deserve that promotion."

He lets out a long breath like he's talking to an unreasonable child. "We need to let the dust settle. With the situation with your dad, the partners can't be seen to be promoting you in front of Jack."

I was wrong. Olivia wasn't the biggest threat to my relationship with Max. The two little dicks, Bradshaw and Brown, are the ones he's in bed with.

My blue shift dress hangs off me with a little more space around the hips than it did last week. My heart hammers in my chest as I step out of the lift onto the fortieth floor.

Nisha greets me at the lifts for moral support. "Hi, love."

The office is packed. Everyone else looks too normal, tapping away on their laptops. Their lives haven't been royally fucked up this past week.

My boyfriend hates me.

My dad hates me.

Now my bosses hate me.

"Hey." I smile sadly. "Let's get this over and done with. I just need to hand in the laptop at the tech bar."

She tuts. "This is shit that you have to leave the project. You've worked so hard, and you haven't actually done anything wrong. It doesn't seem fair."

"It's fine," I say with a small shrug. "So, the truth . . . is everyone gossiping about the picture of me and Jack?"

She nibbles on her lip as we start to walk down the aisle. Unfortunately for me, the support guys sit at the far end of the floor.

"The truth, Nisha," I press in a low voice, ignoring the turning heads.

"Yes." She sighs. "Some of the admins found the link and have been showing everyone."

I swallow nervously. "What do they think?"

"You had a one-night stand," she says through a false smile.

All eyeballs are on me. Those colleagues who aren't looking at me are nudged by their neighbours of my incoming presence.

"I mean it looks like a lover's tiff a mile off because it is. All the women are obviously jealous. None of them know about your dad though."

My eyes widen. "I'm a laughingstock. They'll think that's why I've been taken off the project."

"People do it all the time."

I grunt a laugh. "Yeah, not with the CEO of Lexington though."

"Speaking of one-night stands," she says through gritted teeth as Darren approaches us.

"Bonnie!" Darren booms too loudly. Anyone that hadn't noticed my arrival before does now. "So, you and bossman, huh?"

"Keep your voice down," I hiss. I half consider battering him with the laptop then flinging myself out the window.

"Shut up, Darren," Nisha spits out, shoving him in the arm.

He grins. "What's the matter, Nish?"

He turns back to me and leans in. "Listen, do you think you could get the deadline extended? And ideally, get the budget increased to bring in a few deputy project managers to help with workload. I'm swamped."

I stare at him blankly. "How the hell would I be able to do that?"

"You could mention it to Jack next time you're—" He winks. "You know."

"No, I don't think I'm in a position to swing that."

"What's the point of romping with the boss then?"

I suck in a breath. I do not need this shit right now.

"Darren," Nisha grates, narrowing her eyes. "I won't tell you again."

"Bonnie." Max appears behind me, casting an appraising glance my way.

My face prickles with embarrassment. People aren't even pretending not to watch anymore.

"You need to do a twenty minute debrief with one of the Lexington security officers," Max says in his most professional tone. "To keep us above board." He pauses. "We can discuss new projects for you in the next few days."

I exhale a ragged breath and follow him down the aisle. Everyone stops talking as I pass them. Those that know me well give me sympathetic looks.

I've blown it. Bradshaw and Brown will have me cleaning up muck after this. I'll be lucky if I get to design toilets.

Nisha stays at my side like a guard as we stop at the security officer who is surrounded by so many screens, he looks like he's single-handedly operating an air traffic control tower.

"Hi," I say to the guy who doesn't look up. Any minute now, please.

Nisha inhales sharply. "Oh, *shit*."

Huh?

"He isn't supposed to be in today," Max murmurs, looking over my shoulder.

Nisha's eyes meet mine in horror.

Please, God, no.

My pulse goes from resting to racing in a nanosecond.

I don't turn around.

I don't need to, to feel his presence.

39

Bonnie

Heart pounding, I stand still and stare at Nisha.

I can't do this. I can't see him here in the office. I want to flee down the aisle or hide under a desk.

What's he going to do?

Ask me to leave or ignore me?

Either will break me. If there is anything left to be broken.

"Just keep your head down," she warns through gritted teeth.

Even Max looks uneasy.

I haven't seen Jack since Sunday when I turned up at his house begging for forgiveness then he fucked me and basically told me to get out. Five days ago.

I can hear him approach . . . and with every footstep my anxiety rises.

He's right behind me.

I can smell him.

I freeze, the hairs lifting on the back of my neck.

"Jack," Max says in a low voice. "Bonnie is just handing in her laptop and doing the security debrief."

I turn slowly, trying to calm myself down. I'm handing in a laptop for God's sake. The world isn't ending.

Except it feels like that with the way one hundred sets of eyes are watching me. You could hear a pin drop.

The moment I lift my gaze, his eyes are already locked on mine with such startling intensity that I have to look away.

I can't do this here. I'm so humiliated I might as well be naked in front of the whole team. I'm the stupid girl who slept with the CEO.

"I'm leaving," I say weakly, looking at Nisha. I can't look at Jack.

His large masculine hand captures mine.

"No. You're not."

Stunned, I look up at him then down to where our hands join.

His grip tightens.

"I don't understand," my voice wobbles as I gape at where our bodies join.

Jack tilts my chin up to look at him with his other hand. "I should never have abandoned you when you needed me. I'm sorry, Bonnie." His voice and eyes are thick with emotion that makes my heart knock against my chest like it's trying to escape.

He turns very calmly to Max, still clasping my hand.

"Regardless of what happens between Bonnie and me, I wouldn't take her off the project. I don't know if that's you or the partners saying that, but it's bullshit."

Max's eyes bulge as he looks between Jack and me. His mouth opens and closes, but no sound comes out.

"I spoke to your partners an hour ago. Bonnie stays on the project. She's worked harder than anyone, Max. Including you."

Max swallows hard. I can see the lie all over the fucker's face.

Jack turns his attention to Nisha whose mouth is hanging open. "I take it everyone is talking about the pictures online?"

"Yes, Jack." Her expression hardens. "Everyone thinks Bonnie had a one-night stand with you that went wrong."

He nods, sighing, and looks around the room. "Then it's probably better I address the rumours head-on."

Head-on?

What the hell is he going to do?

His dark eyes blaze as he stares at me for a long beat.

Clearing his throat, he addresses the floor. "Since I already have everyone's attention," he says dryly, "I want to clear up a few rumours so you can all get back to work." He pauses. "A week ago, I made a mistake. A very public mistake that ended up splashed over social media. It was my fault."

Jack doesn't look in the least nervous about his public announcement. I, on the other hand, am about to empty my bladder in the middle of the aisle.

"The paps claimed it was a one-night stand. It's not. Bonnie and I are in a serious relationship. Unfortunately, when you're in the public eye, sometimes things you do get distorted. Exaggerated," he adds. "Those pictures were of a couple's discussion. That's it. No drama. There's nothing to know."

He shrugs.

"Bradshaw and Brown know about us, and nothing is against any work policy of either of the companies." His jaw tightens. "Not that it fucking matters what they think," he mutters to himself glancing at me.

"So," he continues casually with a hint of his signature smirk, "any questions?"

He's opening the floor to *questions*?

My palm clasped in Jack's sweats as curious eyes inspect me. For a second, I panic that the floodgates will open and people will ask intimate questions such as *is Jack's dick as big as his kiss-and-tells claim?*

Jack leans in to me. "It's fine, Bonnie. You'll see."

My face floods with heat. I look at Nisha helplessly and she smiles, eyes wide.

There's an unbearably long pause. Then slowly, everyone gets back to work. Row by row, they go back to tapping on their laptops.

"No questions," Jack murmurs in my ear. "Sounds like there's nothing left to gossip about."

"I have a question," Darren pipes up beside me.

Nisha shoves her elbow into his ribs.

Jack's brows lift.

"Nothing," Darren mumbles sheepishly. "Bonnie can ask you

later."

"Great." Jack nods to me. "Bonnie, let's go."

He beckons for me to follow him back to the lifts. This is so surreal.

What just happened?

He slows down his stride so I can match his as we walk down the office. I throw glances up at him but don't dare speak.

The entire walk mustn't last more than a minute but feels like a slow marathon.

He presses the lift button and pulls me inside in silence.

When the doors close, his eyes lock on mine, and the Jack Knight confidence that owned the office floor disappears.

"Bonnie, I'm sorry."

He's nervous.

I've never seen Jack nervous. Angry and agitated, yes, but never nervous.

"I should never have left your side. I love you. I love you so much it kills me not to be with you."

Tears rim my eyes. I never thought I'd hear those words again. It's only been a week without his love, but it feels like a lifetime.

The lift dings open on the fifth floor.

"It's full," Jack growls at the poor unsuspecting employee in the wrong place at the wrong time. Jack's gaze never leaves mine.

"S-sorry, Mr. Knight," the guy stammers, scuttling backwards. Something drops from his hands as the doors close again.

Jack slams his hand against the lower ground floor button, and we start to descend.

"Forgive me."

"What? What for?" I croak. "I'm the one who kept a massive secret from you."

"For pushing you away," he says slowly. "For seeing everything black and white. I'm too used to everyone acting like I want them to. But things aren't as clear cut as I make them out to be."

I fight to hold back the tears.

"I'm so sorry, my love. If you'll let me, I'll never leave again.

Whatever happens with the case, with your dad, with the project, whatever shit is in the media, we're in this together." His voice thickens as he pulls me into his arms.

"Jack," I say hoarsely, melting into him.

His mouth crashes down on mine.

His tongue slides into my mouth possessively, igniting pulses of pleasure in every cell in my body.

A whimper leaves me as I fling my arms around his shoulders. I need this so badly. I need him.

His chest heaves, and he growls into my mouth in response, like he has ached for this for a lifetime. For me.

We're not kissing.

We're *claiming* each other.

Our bodies are flush. I can barely breathe. The warmth of his body radiates into mine, his hard chest delicious against my breasts.

Our hearts hammer wildly together, like one.

We'll have to stay like this forever. I'm never letting this man go again.

Just when I think I'm going to become a puddle on the lift floor, Jack pulls away and cups my face in his hands to look at me.

"I've got you, Bonnie."

Three little words way sexier than *I love you*. The gravelly sound of them gliding from his throat makes my spine tingle.

That's the thing. These past few months have taught me that I don't need a boyfriend or a fiancé or a flatmate or even a boss.

I can take care of myself.

Besides the plumbing. I'll get a plumber for that.

I've got me.

But despite seven billion pounds, more property than the Crown, and a dick that should have its own church and followers, Jack Knight sees me as much as I see him.

"I've got you too, Jack."

40

Bonnie

One week later

The sun shines through the slits in the electric blinds.

My body clock has synced with Jack's, and now I can't sleep past five. Or perhaps it's something to do with the massive bulge pushing against my ass every morning.

I can tell by his laboured breathing that he's still sleeping.

I writhe my ass against him, and he groans in his sleep, his cock pulsing against my lower back. A muscular forearm tightens around my stomach.

A giggle escapes me. The guy has Big Dick Energy even when he's sleeping.

He stirs behind me, his chest heaving into my back.

"Morning, darlin'," he says against my neck.

I feel his teeth against my skin and know there's a cocky grin spreading across his face.

"Morning," I say breathlessly.

Will I ever get used to waking up with Jack spooning me? I hope not.

I clear my throat, trying to sound awake. "Are you getting up to go to the gym?"

"No need," he murmurs against my ear. "I can work out right here." The hand that is settled on my lower stomach slides down into my thong.

"Jack—" I gasp as he strokes slow tortuous circles on my clit, still sensitive from last night. "We've literally just woken up."

"Yeah, but I've been dreaming about you all night," he rumbles grumpily behind me.

I feel his hands move my thong to the side as his cock presses impatiently against my slit.

"Open, darlin'. Let me in."

My thighs part to let him in. I close my eyes and squeeze the pillow as the tip of his cock nudges my entrance. No matter how many times we do this, I'm always as nervous as I am excited.

With his freakishly long dick and the number of werewolf books I'm reading, I'm half expecting Jack to shapeshift with the next growl.

"Relax, Bonnie." He chuckles, interrupting my crazed mind. "Stop holding your breath."

I release the breath I was holding as he nudges my legs wider with his knee and slides his cock inside me.

I'm wide awake now, adrenaline pumping through me.

His fingers continue to stroke my clit with just the right pressure as he slides in and out of me.

It's a slow, lazy fuck as we haven't properly woken up yet.

"This angle," he grunts into my hair. "So deep." Cursing, he thrusts into the deepest spot in my core again and again.

I could come just listening to Jack's groans.

The man is an excellent multitasker, yet all I'm capable of is moaning into the pillow.

I'll never get used to this.

My core quivers and tingles with pleasure as his thrusts become more urgent.

His fingers lose their rhythm on my clit as he comes apart.

"Bonnie," he groans into my hair as he comes hard inside me.

That voice. His cockney accent gets gruffer and thicker when he's turned on.

I'm done for. I shatter seconds later, squeezing his cock.

My back arches with the force of my orgasm and my legs

shake like a freaking woman possessed.

I collapse face-first into the pillow.

"Turn around," Jack says gruffly. "I need to see your beautiful face."

Blissfully, I turn to face him.

"I'm the luckiest man alive." He grins lazily at me, his face inches from mine. "I get to see you first thing in the morning, last thing at night, and when I'm sitting in the middle of a fucking ridiculous board meeting."

"Uh, actually." I prop myself up on his chest and smile sheepishly down at him. "In a few weeks you won't see me when you're in the boardroom." I swallow thickly, suddenly nervous. "I'm quitting today. I'm telling you first before Max and Bradshaw Brown."

"Don't be silly," he says gruffly. He widens his legs to let mine rest in between them. "Everything's fine in the office. Nobody passes any remarks on us." He winces. "Besides the threesome story with us and Michelle Allard."

I roll my eyes. "It's not that. I've learnt not to give a shit about rumours. And for the record, if we were to have a threesome it would be a reverse harem for me."

He slaps my ass, annoyed. "I don't share."

"I mean it, Jack," I say, steering him back to the original conversation. "I'm handing in my notice today."

He studies me with a frown. "I thought you were happy."

"I *am* happy. But it's not about the factory or you." I sigh. "For years I've been hanging off Max's coattails. It took what happened to open my eyes to see that Bradshaw Brown isn't the best place for me. The partners don't give a shit, and I'm sick of coming second in a boys' club. They actually started talking to me this week." I snort. "You know why? Because of you."

I don't mention that Max is being so passive aggressive after the relationship reveal that I can't stand coming into work.

"They are two jackasses." His jaw flexes. "I'll sort it."

"No, Jack," I cut in quickly, running a finger down to his jaw to relax him. "I've been offered an opportunity. You remember the architect I talked to when we went for drinks? Adrian? You probably don't."

"Yes, I do." I feel his chest tighten under me. "He was flirting with you. You gave him your number."

"He wasn't. He got me in contact with a design company." I pause, biting my lips to hide my grin. "Do you know Lauren Torres?"

"Of course, I do." He looks at me confused then his brows rise.

I smile. Lauren Torres is one of the most prolific architects in Europe. She's also one of the world's leading female architects. "I've been offered a job at her company. They have offices in London and Paris."

And it's a package that left me salivating. Not because of the cash, as good as it is, but because I feel like I can go places there. They're taking over my sponsorship for the conservation training *and* a hell of a lot more.

His expression softens. "Then I'm happy for you, darlin'. I like having you close to me at work. I'm a selfish bastard." He pulls me in for a kiss. "But I want you to be happy and follow your dreams."

"I'm glad you said that."

Fuck, how am I'm going to say this?

I have to do this. I'll look back with regret if I don't. If it's meant to be between Jack and me, then it's meant to be.

"My first assignment is in Astana," I blurt out.

His frown is back. "Astana," he repeats. "Astana, *Kazakhstan*?"

"Yup." I smile weakly.

He nods slowly. "For how long?"

"Six months."

"The fuck?" He jerks his head up, nearly headbutting me. He pulls back to stare at me.

"Kazakhstan is leading the way in cutting-edge architecture," I ramble nervously. "The perfect storm of soviet, medieval, and modernism. And, uh . . ." I fade off, wilting under his gaze. He doesn't want to discuss Astana's architecture.

"It's only a ten-hour flight and one stopover," I squeak.

"*Fuck.*" His head flops back onto the pillow in defeat. With his eyes closed, he pinches the bridge of his nose.

"Jack?" I whisper, not blinking. I prod his chin willing him to look at me.

Silence.

When he opens his eyes again, he's shaking his head with a small smile. "I guess I'll be doing a lot of trekking in the next few months. We'll get you some good hiking boots."

I breathe out tentatively. "So, we'll be okay? You can do the distance for a while?"

This time his smile reaches his eyes. Under the covers, his arms tighten around my waist. "We'll be *more* than okay, Bonnie. It's six months. We'll make it work."

Relief floods me.

"I'll put a picture of you up in my office," he says with a hint of a scowl. "Since I won't get to see you. Maybe you can do a mosaic for me. Preferably made up of naked pictures of you."

I laugh.

"And I've got a private plane, so I'll get the journey down to seven hours."

The perks of being a billionaire.

I smile brightly down at him, my hand mindlessly circling his nipple ring. "Maybe I'm pushing my luck here but there's one more thing."

He groans. "Jesus Christ, don't say the next assignment is in Australia or somewhere."

"No." I laugh. "It'll be back to London. I'm going on my honeymoon."

He shakes his head, not understanding.

"Max and I were supposed to go to Svalbard," I explain. "You know the island in the Arctic, part of Norway? Max went with Olivia." I pause. "So, I'm taking myself. When it's hot enough to go again."

"I'll take you," he says grumpily. "You don't even have to ask."

"I know," I say delicately. "But I feel like I need to do this alone."

His eyes are stormy as he processes that.

I get it. A large part of me is screaming not to do this. To stay in London and be with Jack every night.

But every decision I've made the past few years was influenced by a bloke—my dad, Max, the bloody partners—and I need to do this.

My body rises as he lets out a long breath from under me.

"Okay. But you know my promise extends across time zones. Wherever you are in the world, I've got you." He smirks. "I only have one condition."

"Oh yeah?"

"Whenever you fly home from Astana, you come directly here to my house in Greenwich. Give up the flat lease in Brixton. You know that place has put me off chicken altogether?"

I barely restrain an eye roll.

My legs spread wide as I star fish on top of him in the luxury super king-size bed.

"Sold."

EPILOGUE

Jack

Two weeks later

"Ready?" I squeeze Bonnie's hand tightly.

She smiles, failing to hide the worry etched in her beautiful face.

The London Marathon is tomorrow. She needs to do this first, so she can concentrate on the race.

He opens the door before I can ring the bell. He must have been listening on the other side.

"Dad," Bonnie says breathlessly beside me.

"Mr. Casey." I stare at the man I've been obsessing about for weeks. He looks older than his seventy years. Maybe a guilty conscience does that.

He's a free man until his court case. With no other criminal record, he'll get a suspended sentence. Likely community service.

Months ago, I would have fought the verdict tooth and nail.

Now, I'm relieved.

"Frank," he says nervously, refusing to look me in the eye. "Call me Frank. Please come in."

I can tell by his tone he doesn't mean it. My company built this flat, but I'm not welcome here.

Bonnie warned me he likely wouldn't apologise. Her mum said he doesn't want to see me.

Well, that's bloody tough. I want Bonnie to repair her

relationship with this man. He'll just have to tolerate me.

We walk in behind him to the kitchen. I'm gripping Bonnie's hand.

I take a moment to inspect the interior as I always do in one of my flats. It's one of the social housing flats. It's not as shiny as the luxury high tech ones, but it's a damn sight nicer than the old grey council blocks.

"Tea," he mumbles. "Whiskey?"

"Tea." I clear my throat. "We're on my bike tonight."

"Tea!" Bonnie cries in a high pitch.

"I have biscuits." Frank shuffles around the kitchen, ignoring the elephant in the room.

"Dad," Bonnie croaks, on the verge of tears. "I've missed you. Can I have a hug?"

He rummages for bloody biscuits, and for a second, I think the fucker is going to ignore her.

I'm about to say something when he stops and turns, staring at the floor.

Her soft hand tightens in mine then she releases me and tentatively moves towards her dad.

Don't break her heart, you shit, I warn him with my eyes.

Perhaps he's not the soulless sap I thought, because tears brim his eyes when he gives his daughter a quick, awkward hug.

My heart constricts.

I'll do anything for her. Including forgive this man. Forgive a man who's too proud to say sorry. That, and let him off with half a million pounds. And buy back his house.

This man is my father's killer and my lover's father. It sounds like a sick poem.

Okay, so he didn't twist the knife directly . . . but he let my father die.

I can be the bigger man.

"Frank, I'd like to put the past behind us."

For the first time, he meets my gaze head-on, suspicion evident in his eyes. "There's a court case coming up. If coming here is your way of intimidating me, son, well I—"

"It's not," I cut in firmly. "Eventually I'll ask you for your daughter's hand in marriage, and I'll need your blessing."

Bonnie splutters beside me. "W-What?"

I shrug and give her a wink. "I'm a traditional guy."

"Oh my God, Jack." She laughs nervously.

I squeeze her hand. We can talk about our future later.

I haven't told Bonnie yet about buying her father's house. She's still continually apologising, and I don't want her to feel as if she owes me. And I especially don't want her to feel like I'm buying her love. I'll wait until the dust settles.

"So, Frank, how about that tea?"

He nods and turns his back to open the cupboard.

But not before I see something flash between father and daughter.

Hope.

Bonnie

One day later

Although I've done everything right, I feel sick with nerves.

I lubed my nipples—and Jack's, too. I'm stuffed with protein. *And* I've found the perfect ass to pound the pavement behind.

The London Marathon starts off conveniently close to Jack's house in Greenwich. Thousands of us shuffle from leg to leg, waiting for our signal.

What an atmosphere.

The owner of the perfect ass turns to wink at me.

The horn blasts for our section.

The two lovely mounds of muscle flex as their owner falls into a rhythm and I follow in quick succession.

My strategy must have been published in *Runners Weekly*. All eyes are on the target.

I chose his running shorts. After declining my first request for mankini bottoms, he conceded to tight-fitting Lycra shorts, which probably means Jack's dick will make front page news during marathon coverage.

That delectable derrière will be mine tonight.

I'm the luckiest girl in the world.

So, 26.2 miles of this . . . easy.

Bonnie

Two weeks later

It's funny how even the biggest things die down and become yesterday's chip paper.

Besides Darren constantly nagging me to ask Jack about upping the budget before I orgasm, nobody seems to be that bothered about us anymore.

Nisha said she did me a favour by sleeping with Darren because there's more gossip about *that* than Jack and me.

There's only one person in the company it bothers. Max *hates* that Jack and I are a couple. But what's good for the goose is good for the gander. He started it. He'll never say it of course, but his passive aggressive comments are moving more towards the aggressive end of the scale.

Which is why what I'm about to do feels all the sweeter.

I step in line with Max as we walk out of the Monday morning meeting.

His cold gaze meets mine. "I have one minute, Bonnie. Is this urgent?"

"That's fine," I say casually, keeping up with him. "Shall I pop in an invite in your calendar about handover?"

"What?" he snaps. "Handover for what?"

"Handover for me *leaving*, Max." I look at him innocently.

He stops in his tracks. Finally, I have his full attention. "What *are* you going on about?"

I feign confusion. "Did the partners not tell you?"

His eyes sharpen. "Tell me what?"

My mouth forms an "O," and my hand comes up to my throat. "Oh dear! I'm leaving in three days. I handed in my notice *weeks* ago. I can't believe the partners didn't tell you."

Actually, I can. I bet on it.

He freezes. Not breathing. Not blinking.

His face turns a deathly white. His mouth gapes, and I resist the urge to pop something in it, like my pen.

"*What the fuck*, Bonnie?" he hisses and some spit lands on my cheek. "Are you serious? This is ridiculous. No." He shakes his head violently. "You're under an obligation to tell me. You can't just up and leave without notice. This is negligence!"

"Max." I smile sweetly. "Didn't you hear me? I *did* give notice. I told the two most senior people in the company. It's their responsibility to disseminate important information and put in place contingency plans. It's not my problem if I'm not important enough to talk about in the boys' club."

I curse myself for the unprofessional slip. *Boys' club* slid off my tongue before I could stop it. Still, the look on his face is worth it.

"I'm not surprised Bradshaw and Brown didn't inform you," I continue, tipping my chin up. "Not because they're trying to screw you over but because they don't value my worth. I was always hidden under you. But that," I say simply, "is not my problem."

Max looks like he might vomit. "But the presentation," he whispers hoarsely.

I didn't realise how much Max needed me until I handed in my notice. He's only figured it out right this minute.

I do the majority of the work, and Max takes the credit. He has a presentation for our second milestone in a few days' time, and he's royally screwed.

Not my problem.

As Jack said, this is business.

If Bradshaw Brown loses the account because I leave, then it's their fault for being short-sighted.

I've done knowledge transfer for Nisha and Steve. I wasn't going to leave them in the lurch.

"What the fuck, Bonnie?" Max rarely curses at work. He puffs air into his reddening cheeks. It pleases me that it's an unattractive look on him. "You bang a billionaire and think you can skip off into the sunset? How could you not tell me this?"

I smile apologetically. "Well, this is quite the oversight, do forgive me. Especially since you've always been upfront with me throughout our relationship."

He narrows his eyes suspiciously.

I don't feel the need to tell him I know about his cheating on me. It'll drive him crazier trying to figure out if I do.

Revenge really is best served cold.

No tantrums. No drama. Just getting back at Max in the most passive-aggressive way I can find.

"Don't worry, Max," I say gently, adopting my most concerned expression. "Jack knows you're his biggest fan. I'm sure you'll convince him to extend the deadline. I can ask him to sign his biography for you if you like?"

His nostrils flare to full capacity as he pulls in so much breath I'm surprised if there's any oxygen left for the rest of us.

I try not to grin as I turn and saunter away.

You can definitely read a man by his nostrils.

Bonnie

Three months later

Jack slows to a halt outside the Archie Knight Boxing Centre.

He might own half the London skyline, but this small community centre tucked away beside the *Motor Works* factory is his dream.

Sometimes he coaches here himself.

I'm only home from Astana for three days.

We've managed to make it work. If you asked me at Kate's wedding whether I would trust Jack Knight to do a long-distance relationship, I would have laughed my face off.

Now I trust Jack more than anyone else in the world. And I'll do everything in my power to make sure he trusts me.

We see each other in person once every three weeks but I always feel like he's with me. He's my biggest champion.

I miss him shitloads though. I miss my clit sucker too, but I can't tell Jack. I didn't have the guts to take it to Astana in case airport security searched my bag.

He's right, he does have a lot of settings but *come on*, Jack's lips don't vibrate.

It's worth sacrificing the clit sucker for a few months because working with Lauren Torres has been more than I could imagine.

I've never felt so alive.

For so long I let my dream be stifled into something smaller. Something mediocre. I was blind to how cynical I'd become working under Max.

All I wanted was to be the best architect I could . . . under Max.

But that's not my dream. That's Max's dream, with him standing at the top of the hierarchy.

One day, I want to be a Lauren Torres.

"Ready to visit your dad, darlin'?" Jack asks.

I nod. Dad got a suspended sentence for two years with community service.

Dad lives only a few streets over in the new social housing as part of Jack's regeneration project. I still love to hear from Jack and Nisha about what's happening on the project.

Dad greets us with a smile. It's more genuine than the last

visit.

"Frank," Jack jumps off the motorcycle to shake his hand.

Someday soon Jack will get his apology.

But for now, we'll just accept . . . progress.

Jack

Roughly one and a half years later

"Happy thirtieth, darlin'."

We are dancing in the garden of our Greenwich home with fifty of our closest friends.

"Thank you, Jack." She smiles up at me, eyes shining and emotion wells in my chest.

My girlfriend is making a name for herself. She's working her way up in Lauren Torres's company. Now, she adorns more heritage architecture articles than gossip rags exposing so-called threesomes between us and Michelle Allard.

Next week we are attending the UNESCO Cultural Heritage Conservation Awards, and Bonnie and her team have been nominated.

The body-hugging brown leather dress compliments her slender athletic figure perfectly. Her blond hair is swept up in a French braid. Wisps of hair escape, framing her jawline. My dad's chain adorned with crystals clings to her collarbone.

My sexy Viking.

Her hips thrust in a steady sensual rhythm against mine and she has a gleam in her eye.

Blood flows south.

Fuck. Now's not the time for my dick to pay homage to his favourite person.

I shoot her a warning look.

I have something much more important to do.

"You haven't got your present from Lucy yet."

"No." She groans. "I don't want any more dead birds."

I chuckle. "I hope you'll like this more than a dead bird."

I nod over to the DJ.

The music lowers, and my stomach squeezes tight.

Everyone goes quiet. Most of our close friends know what I'm about to do.

Poppy walks in with Lucy beside her, both delighted at being the centre of attention.

I eyeball Lucy. *Don't fuck this up for me.*

Bonnie looks at me in confusion.

She scans the garden then turns back to me and asks in a lowered tone, "What's going on, Jack? Is there something wrong with the sound system?"

There's nothing wrong with the sound system, but my fucking heart might give in. This is definitely one of the most nerve-wracking things a bloke has to do. Or a gal.

"No, Bonnie, everything's fine."

With clammy hands, I untie the ribbon around Lucy's neck as she gives me a lick. Attached is a small box.

Danny's wife, Charlie, smiles at me encouragingly. They finally got married a few months ago.

Bonnie's hands go to her mouth when I drop to one knee. She looks like she is about to scream but no sound comes out.

For the first time in my life, I don't know if I'll be able to get my words out. It's a risk doing it in front of everyone.

I look over at her dad and he nods. I've already asked him.

"Bonnie, I've waited forty years for this. There's a lot I've been blessed with in my life. I was obsessed with building the most prestigious hotels, the tallest office blocks, the most luxurious apartments." I pause to take a breath. "The truth is all I need is you. So long as you're with me, I'd happily leave it all and work on a construction site. You are, and always will be, the love of my life. Will you marry me?"

She stares at me with wide eyes. Her lips part but she remains quiet.

Bonnie? Don't leave me hanging.

"Yes!" she squeals, flinging her arms around me. "Of course, I will."

Bonnie

The day after the proposal

The lounge room door bangs open so loudly I scream.

"Ja-ack?" I stammer, his name barely off my lips as a naked Jack barrels through the lounge pushing me backwards until he has my back pressed against the wall.

Everything about him is erect. He towers over me standing to his full height with his cock pushed against my stomach.

His piercing brown eyes blaze down at me as his jaw works. His hair is dishevelled, and his bare chest is glistening with sweat.

He looks unhinged. What the hell is wrong with him?

"Are you okay, Jack?"

He doesn't answer. He grabs my wrists and forces my arms against the wall.

"There's my little mate," he growls. His teeth come down to graze the delicate skin on my neck.

His little *mate*?

Doesn't he mean fiancée?

His teeth continue to pull at my neck as his hands hold mine above my head. It's like he's swallowed a gallon of testosterone, and Jack's levels were already through the roof.

I yelp a little.

"I can smell your arousal a mile off."

Oh, my God.

"You've been reading my books," I gasp. "Which one?"

"Did I give you permission to speak?" His eyes darken in a

predatory smirk. "The one hiding under your side of the bed."

Oh.

A little shiver escapes down my spine.

I'll never survive that epilogue.

MORE BY ROSA LUCAS

The London Mister Series
Taming Mr. Walker
Resisting Mr. Kane
Fighting Mr. Knight

Billionaires in Charge Series
Fifth Avenue Fling
Manhattan State of Mind
Empire State Enemies

Billionaire Brits
Love to Loathe Him
Dare to Love Me

ABOUT THE AUTHOR

Rosa Lucas is a contemporary romance author based in the UK. She writes stories featuring strong, sassy heroines who speak their minds and emotionally guarded alpha heroes with rugged charm. When she's not lost in her fictional worlds, Rosa can be found roaming the countryside with her own Happily-Ever-After guy— who refuses to read her books, likely out of fear he'll see himself in them... or worse, not see himself at all—always on the hunt for a scenic hike that ends at a cozy pub.

Learn more at: rosalucasauthor.com

STORIES WITH IMPACT

WWW.PAGEANDVINE.COM